Tales of the Zombie

CREDITS

Tales of the Zombie

Edited by
BILL OLVER

Big Pulp Publications

Black Chaos: Tales of the Zombie

ISBN 978-0-9896812-1-6

Visit us online:
www.bigpulp.com
Facebook (Facebook.com/bigpulp)
Twitter (twitter.com/BigPulp)

Distributed by Ingram Periodicals.

Ebook versions available from Amazon
and other online venues

Big Pulp Publications
BILL OLVER Editor/Publisher
BILL BOSLEGO Associate Editor (Editorial)

Cover illustration by Ken Knudtsen

Also from Big Pulp Publications
The Kennedy Curse (2013)
APES HIT (2013)
Clones, Fairies & Monsters in the Closet (2013)

Periodicals
Child of Words (SF&F)
M (horror and mystery)
Thirst (Passion and obsession)

Table of Contents

1   **Wild With Hunger** by Lee Clark Zumpe

11   **The Southron Wind** by J. Adrian Cook

24   **As You Were** by K.J. Newman

29   **Pool #4** by Cecelia Chapman

31   **Like the Jellyfish** by Katherine Sanger

37   **Fathoms** by Rich Hawkins

44   **The Staggering Boy** by Douglas Ford

47   **Graveyard Slot** by Christopher Keelty

58   **Ferals Like You** by Cheryl Elaine Williams

71   **Survival of the Fittest** by Milo James Fowler

74   **Dust** by Noah Bogdonoff

84   **Last Rites** by George Cotronis

87   **Snoring Wakes Them** by Harri B. Cradoc

98   **Nothing Else Matters** by J. Rohr

109   **Run for the Roses** by Gerri Leen

112   **Only the Lonely** by Conor Powers-Smith

118   **Instinct** by John Dodd

121   **Preservation** by Rebecca Boyle

134   **Carrion Luggage** by Shane Simmons

145   **Mama Noodle** by KJ Hannah Greenberg

153   **Zombie Chic** by Peter Andrews

155   **The Risen** by Steven Axelrod

173   **Expediency** by Paul Lorello

179   **The Chosen** by Thomas Logan

189   **Alice, in Decline** by E. Manning-Pogé

For he being dead, with him is beauty slain,
And, beauty dead, black chaos comes again.

VENUS AND ADONIS
William Shakespeare

WILD WITH HUNGER

by Lee Clark Zumpe

"You'd not think it possible," said Noah Brownlow, one of three men elected to the Board of Guardians of Basingstoke and appointed by the Central Poor Law Commission to investigate claims of neglect and abuse at the workhouse in neighboring Ravenwood. The eerie serenity that met them in the village amazed them all, though the hoards of people skulking along the highway leaving town had provided adequate evidence to support reports of the mass migration underway. "Not a single soul about the place." Shutters covered every cottage window on the outskirts of the village, confining the shadows to silent chambers and still corridors. Flower boxes, once brimming with brightly-colored, radiant blossoms, spilled over with brown, shriveled flora. As they proceeded, they encountered only cold autumn winds traversing vacant roads. "What has become of them all?"

They had questioned many of those they met fleeing the village. Some muttered indistinct warnings while others simply wept. Most had nothing to say at all, their spirits seemingly overpowered by some awful burden.

Their carriage led them through the narrow streets of impoverished Ravenwood, the noise of its measured passage ricocheting down dead-end alleyways. The three gentlemen scanned the ramshackle tenements crowding the village. Within the squalid lodgings dwelled generations of paupers—virtual slaves of the ironworks at the edge of town. Some buildings featured once prosperous store fronts, their doors now boarded and their hearts festering away with neglect.

"It's midday, and the streets are barren." James Naughton stroked the ivory grip of his cane, his apprehension manifesting itself in uncontrollable, uncharacteristic restlessness. Since hearing tales of the abandoned township, fears of plague had unsettled the noted physician. It had been little more than a decade since he had watched cholera ravage London. "Either they are all dead, or they hide from death."

"I'd prefer not to dig their graves just yet, Dr. Naughton." Sampson Digby patted his nervous companion's shoulder. "We may find that everyone is engaged in some local festival, or occupied by some other community affair."

Their carriage came to a standstill outside the notorious workhouse. Silence promptly filled the void, pouring in from every quarter. Overhead, terminally gray skies drifted over the marred landscape. The Hampshire countryside had been deforested and partitioned, allocated and apportioned over centuries of constant habitation and exploitation. After all, land—like people—had to be meticulously managed and manipulated.

Built to accommodate no more than 100 inmates, the population of the Ravenwood workhouse had exceeded 300 at last count. Its design lacked both imagination and grace, and its slipshod construction left its residents lacking basic facilities and any sense of well-being or security. Its shortcomings were by no means unique: Similar institutions across the country suffered from epidemic overcrowding and scandalous mismanagement. The purported severity of conditions at Ravenwood, however, accentuated its extensive deficiencies and magnified its disgrace.

"Let us see if we can find someone to answer all of our questions," Brownlow said, stepping out of the carriage. A glance toward the driver revealed a terrified youth prone to disturbing delusions and apt to be influenced by superstitions. "The administration block should be just through the gate. Perhaps the Master and Matron will greet us."

"Your optimism cannot curtail my trepidation, Brownlow." Naughton's gaze followed a solitary rat as it cautiously skirted the workhouse's perimeter wall searching for its next meal. Unimaginable filth had accumulated in the streets adjacent to the complex. Heaps of foul-smelling waste and debris attracted great black clouds of flies. "I am accustomed to sensing the presence of death, hovering like an unwanted shadow over a patient's bedside as I labor to keep blood coursing through his arteries." Naughton lowered his head as he set foot in the street, the weight of the oppressive sky pressing down on him. "Death is no guest in this place—he has dominion over it."

Peter Hawley peered out the window of the shop belonging to the village coffin-maker. Across the boulevard, three somber fellows marched right through the gates of the Ravenwood Workhouse—formerly a residence of all those unable to support themselves through more traditional means. The townsfolk once looked upon it as a blessing, since it removed from plain view all those unfortunate wretches whose unmistakable undernourishment and infirmity made those more privileged feel acutely uncomfortable. Hawley's own father, in fact, had habitually praised the limitless benevolence of English law for providing sanctuary to those whose blood and sweat greased the wheels of the empire.

The surviving villagers—those who had not fled or fallen victim to the predatory creatures inhabiting the workhouse—now considered the place a malignant pest house. Their commendations became condemnations when word of the first mutilated corpses spread through the parish. Young Peter had seen them, his father's former employer coughing up vomit as they packed the tattered mortal remains in shoddy caskets. Their flesh had been slashed and shredded. their entrails yanked through gaping breaches and their skulls split and emptied.

The workhouse custodians claimed wild dogs had gained access to the men's block, blamed the viciousness of the attacks on famine or madness, and distanced themselves from the initial victims by seeing to their swift and supposedly secret disposal. Neither the coffin-maker nor the undertaker could keep from recounting the scene when swayed by gin-and-water, and the tale quickly circulated around Ravenwood.

"Who's that lot, then?" Peter's friend Dudley Potter joined him at the window. Dudley, a few years older and wiser than 15-year-old Peter, had been out foraging for food all morning. The closure of the marketplace just before the exodus had left the boys few culinary options. "You'd think they'd know better than to go right into the bloody nest."

"They're outsiders, I think," Peter said, watching the last man slip into the menacing darkness that had engulfed the workhouse. "They must not know what's happened." Peter hesitated, yearning for a return to normalcy but unable to dismiss the fear of venturing out into the open streets. Though the things generally slept during the day, their voracious appetites sometimes sent them into the shadowy alleyways before dusk. "We should warn them."

"Bah," Dudley answered, turning his back on the workhouse. "Let 'em go. At least two of them are rather plump," he said, thrusting out his midsection and patting his stomach. "They should make an ample feast—enough to keep the gorgers off the streets tonight, I'd wager."

"And tomorrow?" Peter looked to Dudley for guidance since no one else could offer it. His parents had both disappeared weeks earlier, most likely dragged off to the workhouse in the middle of the night by the gorgers. The coffin-maker had packed up his belongings earlier than that, predicting the suffering to come. "What will we do for food, for lodging? What will we do when they come for us? What will we do tomorrow?"

"We'll worry about tomorrow later." Dudley plucked a few wormy apples and a handful of moldy berries from his pockets. "Let's get something in our bellies right now."

"The stench is overwhelming." Brownlow held a kerchief to his face, covering his nose and mouth. "No one should live like this."

The architects of the Ravenwood Workhouse devised the main segment of the facility in a cruciform pattern, with administrative offices in the base and the kitchen directly behind. The infirmary and lunatic cells lay at the opposite end of the section. At the intersection of the two wings, in the segregated dining hall, inmates would be fed paltry meals without the luxury of utensils or the comfort of conversation. The overlords demanded silence, even among family members.

The men's comments echoed through the vacant corridors as they approached the hub of the workhouse.

"Abandoned, just like the rest of the village," Digby said, cold indifference shading his tone. "Just like the poor to take flight at the first hint of hardship." Unlike his companions, Digby did not necessarily take issue with the accusations leveled at Ravenwood. He believed the worst scenarios would prove to be the result of undue overstatements of less inflammatory pieces of evidence. Authorities deliberately kept conditions at workhouses inhospitable to persuade as many people as possible to find employment elsewhere and to circumvent the inherent weakness of an overly generous welfare regime. "Sure to end up in London begging along the turnpike near Fortune Green or picking pockets in Saffron Hill."

"If so," Naughton said, turning an anxious eye toward the others, "they'll carry with them whatever ailment besieged this town."

"Digby, I believe," said Brownlow, "would have much preferred the poor await inevitable death here, by pestilence or starvation."

"It seems the only noble recourse, does it not?" Digby's aristocratic background effectively stripped him of all compassion and goodwill. "Out of sheer gratitude, one would assume they favor death amidst their peers to the shame of afflicting disease and distress upon their superiors."

As the men entered the heart of the facility through a heavy door on groaning hinges, the fate of at least some of the villagers became painfully evident. Bones lay scattered across the floor, meat and muscle indiscriminately stripped from them. Collected in vast mounds in the unlit corners, more substantial mortal remnants drew rodents and insects alike. Hundreds of disfigured and decapitated corpses congregated in that place, their limbs detached, their innards hollowed out and strewn across the long tables where inmates once dined on moldy bread and fetid soup and loathsome gruel.

Behind them, the door thundered as it closed. The tell-tale latch of the lock perished beneath the clamor.

"For the love of God," Digby said, covering his mouth as he choked on his own vomit. His eyes fell reflexively to the floor which he found damp with gummy blood and viscera. Arms and legs, half devoured, revealed gluttonous bite marks. "What manner of nightmare have we been fated to endure?"

"Plague is not the author of this slaughter, Naughton." Brownlow recognized his colleague's concurrence, though he expected no verbal reply from the physician. "Yet, such depravity and debauchery cannot be the work of rational men."

"Not of men, at all," Naughton said, less affected by the grisly scene than the others. He knelt, inspected a half-eaten arm which had been ripped from its socket. He examined, too, a nearby skull—its cap smashed and removed. The recurring petite, crescent-shaped wounds left him with little doubt. "Cannibalism is an aberration of nature and demonstrates degeneration of the soul. What makes this occurrence particularly unspeakable is the age of those involved. Children caused this carnage."

All the blood in Brownlow's heart dried up in that instant, and the faceless, nameless dead surrounding him ceased to exist as individuals. They became provender, forage, feed for famished cattle. Naughton's revelation sickened him, yet simultaneously he found himself validating the nightmare as necessity.

"So finally it has come to this," Brownlow whispered, his observations not intended for his colleagues. "Like animals driven to the brink of extinction, survival suppresses civility. We provoked this atrocity."

None of them noticed the shifting shadows displaced by a pack of lean, lithe predators stealthily gauging their prey. Little more than sinewy, swarthy silhouettes set against the immeasurable darkness of a somber, windowless institution, they moved with uncanny dexterity and speed. Coal-black and sprite-like entities, had the shade not thoroughly cloaked their advance, not one of the men would have mistaken these things for the children they once were.

"Stop! Stop!" Digby's panicked cries no sooner escaped his lips than he found himself engulfed in impenetrable darkness. Sharp-clawed, tiny hands carried him along cramped passageways so confining his struggles proved futile. "They have me," he screamed, the first moist mouth nuzzling his flesh. In an instant, their fingers tugged at his vestments and their teeth ripped at his skin. "Oh God, please help!"

Naughton thrust his open palm against Brownlow's chest, stopping him dead in his tracks.

"Surely, you don't intend to pursue them?" The doctor showed neither fear nor agitation. He remained cold and detached, drawing on his scientific background to help him maintain his composure. "Anything that can take down a man of Digby's girth that quickly and quietly would certainly have the two of us for dessert." Retracing their steps, they each muttered unintelligible curses when the found the door through which they had entered the chamber locked and impassable. As Digby's fading cries reverberated through the darkened hallways, Naughton scanned the room searching for another route of escape. He spotted a pass-through window that led outside into a courtyard. "Follow me—and be quick about it."

Brownlow helped the doctor through the tight aperture. Outside, the sun still shown though the gray skies stifled much of its brilliance. Eager to join his colleague, Brownlow pushed his upper body through the swinging door.

"No!" He felt the nails tear into his lower leg, pulling him back inside. "Naughton—help me!"

"Here," Naughton said, handing him his cane. "In the head—strike it in the head, Brownlow."

Having tasted the light of late afternoon, the chamber seemed that much more inundated by darkness as he let himself fall to the floor. He rolled over quickly, saw the thing that had frustrated his retreat. Its jagged teeth, discolored by blood, protruded over its scabby lips. Its saucer-like white eyes housed a narrow, vertical sliver of black. It kept its filthy hands near its chin, fingers fidgeting incessantly as it studied its intended victim.

The hunger in its expression reminded him of the rat he had seen outside the compound searching for sustenance. Though physically repellent, its wretchedly emaciated frame and its feigned frailty temporarily beguiled him, entrancing him with the same deadly proficiency a cobra employs to paralyze its prey.

When it lunged toward his face, Brownlow shrugged off his momentary stupor and swung the cane, burying the ivory grip deep in the thing's skull. A rush of frothy black blood spurted from the gaping wound.

They had killed one.

Peter Hawley watched wordlessly through a breach in the curtain wall surrounding the workhouse. Two of the strangers had somehow eluded the voracious gorgers—descended right into their den and escaped back out into the light of day using the very aperture the monsters used when they set about prowling the town for victims after dusk.

And they had killed one.

They hauled the twitching corpse away from the building, deeper into the light of the declining day. Peter recognized its gaunt and wiry frame, its sunken cheeks, its unsettling blue-black pallor and its elongated limbs terminating in razor-sharp claws. Though want and untimely death had transformed it into this hideous creature, Peter knew it had once been a small boy of perhaps 5 or 6 years of age.

"D'ye see it, Dudley?" Peter squatted in a dark recess hugging his knees tightly against his chest. His companion rested an arm on his shoulder, watching the unfolding scene with negligible interest. "D'ye see what they've done?"

"Hush, pray," Dudley Potter said, smothering any further commentary for the moment. "That's a good lad." One of the strangers knelt over the body, inspecting it methodically, poking at its extremities and prodding its torso. Clearly a learned man, Dudley expected him to reach the same conclusion the workhouse nurses had come to before they had fled the facility. In the children's ward in Ravenwood, the dead had developed a habit of not staying dead for very long. "Never said you couldn't kill one," Dudley admitted, though he had certainly inferred it when he spoke of the horrors he had seen before meeting Peter. "Problem's getting one on its own, away from the pack. Like wolves, they is."

"What should we do, then?"

"What's there to do?" Dudley answered quickly in a hushed tone. "I let you drag me here to show you that they're like all the others." Dudley, an orphan who had spent ample time in workhouses across the English countryside over the short but exhausting span of his lifetime, felt no attachment to the strangers. Unlike Peter, he regarded most adults with disdain and distrust. "If they're smart, they'll leave; if not, they'll die when night falls. Either way, they'll be neither a help nor hindrance to us."

"We could go with them…"

"Go if you want, I don't care," Dudley said, but his grip on Peter's shoulder suggested his apathy lacked substance. "I rather like having the run of the town to myself. And I prefer being hunted by animals to being ill-treated by masters and matrons and beadles and chaplains."

By now, Naughton had made his shocking discovery and recoiled in revulsion. He stood back from the disabled corpse, jabbing it repeatedly with his cane, ensuring that the semblance of life would not again return to it. Brownlow, visibly disturbed by his companion's revelations, reflexively scanned his appendages searching for open wounds.

"The hour is late, Dudley. If they go back inside, the gorgers will have them." Peter saw the men searching their surroundings for an alternate route of escape. A mound of firewood entangled with leafy, creeping vines concealed the narrow fissure in the wall where the two boys hid. "They've no hope unless we act." The men had stumbled on the facility's self-contained bone yard. A great basin rested at the center of the weedy lawn. Nearby, the rammer—used to pummel the animal bones into gritty dust for fertilizer—lay dormant in unchecked vegetation. "Let me show them the way."

"Why? So they can deliver us to a workhouse in some other town? You're like me now, Peter," Dudley said, pinching the younger child's ear. "No home, no family—a sad little orphan. Do you want to end up like those things in there?"

"No…" Peter scowled. "But, if we help them, they might take us in…"

"Listen to me," Dudley said, pointing toward the strangers. "They're not to be trusted. They'd sooner see us rot in some workhouse than welcome us into their own homes." Dudley had never known the love of a parent or the generosity of a stranger. He had, however, experienced all of the most deplorable traits of guardianship, including derision, neglect, and the depravities of exploitation and abuse. "Stay with me, Peter," Dudley said, almost pleading. "I'll take care of you. Promise."

"That firewood," Naughton said, gesturing toward the perimeter wall. "We need to haul it across the yard. We can build a fire beneath the pass-through window. If we can keep it going all night, it may keep them from our throats." His companion, Brownlow, stood idly, his gaze fixed upon the corpse sprawled across the ground. Its uncanny eyes stared vacantly skyward. "Do you hear, man—we must act promptly to save our own hides!"

"What is it?" Brownlow nudged it with the tip of his black shoes, noticing for the first time the bloodstains spattered over the bottle-green of his redingote and light gray trousers. "Beast or boy?"

"Both," Naughton said brusquely, minding the advance of eventide. "In life, it had been a child; in death, it becomes an animal driven wild with insatiable hunger. It is an uncommon phenomenon, but one that has precedence in the annals of medicine."

"Gratuitous neglect," Brownlow muttered, repelled by its protruding ribs and pelvis, its sunken eyes and skeletal limbs. "An overriding attitude of apathy affected their mortal degeneration, left them lacking the nourishment and affection any child deserves."

"After death liberated their underprivileged souls," Naughton added, somewhat less disposed to ascribe blame, "their unchecked hunger reanimated them and incited them to acts of cannibalism and cruelty." Naughton wiped blood off the ivory handle of his cane on a kerchief and tossed aside the soiled linen. "Tonight, Brownlow, unless we act now, we will join Digby and the countless others who have become victims of these bestial predators."

"We must survive," Brownlow said, finding strength in his resolve to not let the Ravenwood atrocities go unpunished. "We must expose the source of this incident, warn others that the path our society has chosen can only lead to more suffering, more malice and more death."

"If thoughts of retribution will fuel your instinct to survive, so be it."

Quietly, but with a hurriedness generated by equal parts fear and disgust, Naughton and Brownlow began to stack firewood beneath the pass-through window. When they had conveyed a sizable amount, Naughton broke off and began collecting dead vegetation to use as kindling.

When darkness threatened to smother Ravenwood, the doctor knew the time had come.

"I think I hear movement in there, Dr. Naughton," Brownlow said, heaving one last bundle of wood onto the pile. "I hope you have devised some method of lighting our bonfire or this night may be quite short for the two of us."

Naughton dug through the pockets of his cassimere coat, finally retrieving a small cylindrical tin.

"Fortunately, I picked these up on my last trip to London," he said, a mildly conceited smile stretching across his face. "Surely you have seen them in apothecary shops," he continued, plucking a small bit of wood and coarse paper from the container. "They call them 'friction lights,' or 'lucifers' depending on who you ask. It's a wood splinter tipped with a mixture of antimony sulphide and potassium chloride. Gently rub it across the surface of the sandpaper, and…"

A wavering flame danced on the end of the splinter, its assertive defiance of endemic darkness symbolic of the inherent arrogance of science and its crusade against the unknown.

An hour later, an inferno raged in the bone yard sending fiery tentacles across the brick face of the workhouse. Once the flames were established but before the blaze became unapproachable, Naughton managed to open the pass-through window with his cane so that smoke and flames spilled inside the edifice.

"This fire will do more than keep the things from making a midnight feast of us," Naughton said boastfully. "It will rid the town of them once and for all."

Some time after midnight, a handful of creatures tried to escape—or perhaps they simply could not bear the suffering any longer and opted for a more abrupt end. They scuttled out through the passage, engulfed in flames, and shambled into the courtyard where they finally collapsed.

Naughton, not fully satisfied with the finality of their termination, beckoned Brownlow to follow him.

"Take up the rammer and follow me," he said, pointing toward the basin where bones once were crushed by workhouse inmates.

Brownlow strained as he lifted the heavy iron rammer. He turned to his colleague for further instruction, but found none necessary. Naughton was engaged in the grisly business of crushing the skulls of the smoldering things—and Brownlow soon followed suit.

Dozens more spilled out over the ensuing hours—shuffling, crawling and writhing. Most appeared singly, through a few seemed to approach destiny hand-in-hand or in small groups. Naughton and Brownlow tended to each in the order of its departure, permanently relieving the pangs of unappeasable hunger that had constituted a preternatural semblance of life.

"May God forgive me," Brownlow whispered. He alternately fumed and wept as he participated in the extermination. "May God forgive us all."

Being a man of science, Naughton initially remained detached and unaffected by the gory scene. Either fatigue or the burden of involvement gradually tainted his perception, and—much to his astonishment—he began to take certain pleasure in dispatching the creatures.

When two figures of slight build and slender frame scurried from the darkness along the fringe of the courtyard, it was therefore unfortunate that Naughton was the first to react. Instinctively, he raised his cane and struck with animalistic speed and ferocity. The first boy fell at his feet, a crimson fountain spewing from his fractured skull.

The second boy vented a chilling scream that drew Brownlow's gaze.

"Naughton—no!" Brownlow could see clearly by the morning's light that neither child had been transformed; Naughton, though, saw only monsters. "They are not like the others," Brownlow cried, but Naughton's eyes revealed his madness. "Leave him be!"

Peter Hawley had convinced poor Dudley Potter to trust the strangers, to leave their hiding place and seek refuge. Now Dudley had a hole in his head, and a wild-eyed man towered over Peter ready to strike a deadly blow.

Peter ran toward the second stranger who seemed to understand that something terrible had just happened. The boy hoped he would make the other man understand, too; but, as he approached, he saw a wealth of anger and frustration and distrust in Brownlow's eyes.

Brownlow lifted the heavy rammer high above his head as Peter tried to arrest his momentum. It came down with crushing force, catching Naughton in the forehead as he affected one last, ineffective swipe at the boy with his cane.

"It's over," Brownlow said, holding out an open hand to Peter. The dawn illuminated Ravenwood, exposed the pillar of smoke still rising from the burning workhouse. Other survivors, if there were any, would see it as a sign of hope. Brownlow rejected hope, considered it a precursor of complacency and apathy. Hope, without action, was an empty promise.

"Don't worry," Brownlow said, patting Peter's head. "We'll find you something for breakfast. I'll see to it. I'll take care of you."

THE SOUTHRON WIND

by J. Adrian Cook

"For the last time, we could never sign that," hisses Meade. The word "sign" is pronounced "eh-zign". It is the last trace of the general's Spanish accent and Curtiss loathes it. He hates even more that nobody else seems to notice. He decides not to render the word phonetically in Pitman shorthand as he scrawls, just in case somebody else reads this record.

Stanton raises a hand to silence the angry Meade. He growls from behind a tremendous beard, "What the General means, sir, is that your settlement would destroy the Republican party and probably these United States." These last words are exhaled at great speed. He places his handkerchief before his mouth. Struggling to write at pace, Curtiss observes that even the boat's gentle rocking on the Potomac is causing the Secretary of War seasickness.

"Well now, that would be a shame," says the wrinkled mouse of a man across the table: Stephens. He leans back in his chair, letting it creak to fill the tense silence that follows his bon mot. He looks to Lee for approval, but the old General stares with sad eyes out the porthole as though not listening. Lee's uniform is immaculate, but the face above is haggard. Only Lee's aide smirks as he writes.

The angry lull gives Curtiss a chance to catch up and wipe his sweating brow with his sleeve.

"You are mocking us, sir," says Stanton, glaring behind the handkerchief.

"I apologize, I could not resist," says Stephens, leaning forward "I trust you have another suggestion?"

"Never Washington. You shall never have her," says Meade.

Stanton coughs, waving off Meade once again. "Kentucky, Missouri, Tennessee, West Virginia. That is all you can expect."

Stephens laughs. "Sir, those states are not yours to offer."

"Nor is it your place to insult us!" roars Stanton, standing.

Curtiss accidentally drops his pen. Even Lee wakes from his daydream.

Stanton steadies himself on the table, then continues unabashed: "Your citizens starve. Your soldiers desert. It is no secret here that your currency is worthless and your merchants trade with U.S. dollars. Your treasury is dry. You cannot afford to besiege us, sir, your…blasphemous army be damned!"

Lee leans toward Stephens and murmurs something. Curtiss does not catch all the syllables, but guesses the rest. He writes, "Lee: We are wasting our time here."

The stairs leading to the upper deck creak. A pair of long legs, clad in black, descend into the heat of the lower deck. Their owner ducks to avoid banging his bearded face on the ceiling. That careworn face peers around the room, looking tired, lean and pale.

Stanton whirls about, shocked. Meade, Curtiss and the boy with the coffee pot leap to their feet. Only the Southerners remain seated.

"Pardon the intrusion," says the man.

"Mister President, you should be in Philadelphia!" exclaims Stanton.

"Mister Pinkerton slipped me into Washington six years ago. I'm sure he can slip me out again if need be," says Lincoln. "General…" he says, shaking hands with the scowling Meade. He then crosses to the other side of the table to shake hands with Stephens, who rises in friendship.

"Why, Mister Lincoln, it is always a pleasure," says Stephens.

"Last time we met, it was on another boat two short years ago. We were discussing your surrender, if I recall," says Lincoln.

"How circumstances change," says Stephens.

Lincoln releases Stephens and turns to Lee, offering his hand. "You're well, General?"

Lee takes the hand, rising. "Somebody has planted a cemetery in my estate, sir," he says.

"Indeed," says Lincoln. "This war has planted dead in all our backyards."

"Except the ones walking around," growls Meade to Curtiss, quiet enough that the Southerners cannot hear. "You should be writing this down."

Curtiss scrabbles for his dropped pen on the floor and snaps it back to the paper. "Yes sir, General."

Lincoln backs toward one of the wooden chairs at the end of the room. "I am here as an observer only, gentlemen. I have every confidence in Mister Stanton."

"Actually, General Lee and I were just leaving," says Stephens.

"Oh?" says Lincoln, disappointed.

"Yes, we've been at it many hours now and tempers are flaring," says Stephens.

"They want all the border states. California. Kansas. New Mexico and the District of Columbia," says Stanton into his handkerchief.

"Except Delaware. You may do with Delaware as you wish," says Stephens.

"Well now, that does sound a little harsh," says Lincoln. "Surely that is not your final word, Mister Stephens."

"Perhaps not. However, I think it's better if we meet again tomorrow. It's very hot down here. It'll give you and your staff some time to mull our offer."

"Agreed," sighs Lincoln. "Tomorrow at nine?"

"Certainly," says Stephens, turning toward the stairs on his side of the room. "Oh, yes, just so's you know, General Moore crossed the Potomac at Harper's Ferry three days ago. He should be along shortly, if that influences your decision."

Meade and Curtiss watch the rowboat carrying Lee and Stephens pull away from the Pennant's side and cut across the uncannily still waters of the Potomac. The Confederate soldiers on board gasp and sweat in the heat. Even these hand-picked bodyguards look spindly and threadbare. If these scrawny men laid siege to Washington, they would surely starve before the defenders. But then, Curtiss reminds himself, Moore's army does not need food.

Meade glances back at Lincoln, who is trying to calm a blustery Stanton. "I seem to recall you handing out pamphlets to the boys for McClellan two years ago. Are you still a good Democrat, Lieutenant?"

Curtiss considers his answer. He is not very proud of the party of his father and grandfather these days. "I suppose so, sir."

"Good," says Meade. "I'm appointing you as Lincoln's escort while he's in Washington. Keep an eye on him and report to me tonight."

Curtiss thinks again. Meade is not looking at him, so that means he's plotting something. "Report what exactly, sir?"

"There are many people in Washington and within reach of a telegraph who would like to know if the President intends to surrender, for example," replies Meade.

Curtiss nods, hiding his disgust. Even during this crisis, the vipers are still playing politics. The Democrats want to know what the President is thinking even before his cabinet does.

On the other hand, spending a day with the President of the United States opens doors, perhaps one leading away from Meade. A life in civil service is stable and prosperous. Charity has always wanted to live in Philadelphia. Curtiss suppresses the excitement of these possibilities and replies, "Yes, sir."

"Let me save you some consternation," says Meade, still averting his gaze. "His ignorant bumpkin persona is an act. He plays it so you will underestimate him. And he has a reputation for venturing into dangerous places lately. If he is hurt, you will answer."

The new earthworks at the edge of Georgetown crawl like a termite nest. Among the blue-uniformed soldiers working spades, piling sandbags and cobbling hasty watchtowers on the frontline facing the woods, knots of civilians in bright clothing sullied with mud infest the trenches. Mixed with the men in soiled top hats are women in their Sunday dresses. The women unused to work rest in the shade or stand about uncertainly while those filled with religious zeal overexert themselves on the spades.

Standing on the new concrete ramparts of Fort Scott, the sight withdraws a gasp from Lincoln. At his side, Curtiss notes that at last a merciful northwestern breeze is dragging the sweltering heat from the city.

"You ought not to stand so close to the edge, Mr. President," warns Pinkerton, Lincoln's chief spy, in his Scotch accent. He takes a break from scanning the crowd below to glare at Curtiss, long jacket folded under his arm. "My sources say that there are many foreigners working down there. There could be agents." Not much ambiguity there: he suspects Meade has sent Curtiss to spy. Let him, thinks Curtiss.

"Is that so? Tell me more," says Lincoln, not moving.

Pinkerton huffs. "Our plight has brought many people from Europe to help the defense. Lord Beauchamp himself is here with his household."

Curtiss catches something unpleasant in the air. He sniffs his sweat-drenched uniform. But the smell is in the breeze, not his clothing.

"Well, if there are Englishmen helping us here, I'd say that's cause for celebration. Oh, look! There's Julia Ward Howe with Senator Sumner!" Lincoln waves.

Several people on the ground see the wave and gesture to their comrades, pointing to the tall figure leaning over the battlements. Somebody hollers something indistinct and soon the whole earthwork is applauding and cheering. A platoon sings "Battle Cry of Freedom" while somebody else starts the "Battle Hymn of the Republic" within the trenches. The two songs swell and compete in cacophony for a minute, but the Battle Hymn triumphs and drowns its opposition. Lincoln removes his hat and wipes tears from his eyes as hundreds of human voices bawl to him.

Turning from the earthworks, Curtiss inhales the northwestern wind. He leaves Lincoln and peers toward the distant wooded hills and the turnpike to Harper's Ferry. The leaves shiver in the wind.

Lincoln steps from the battlement, beaming. "There now, Allan, that wasn't so bad, was it? I can scarcely believe we're contemplating surrender. My God, what is that smell?"

"The Southron Wind," says Curtiss, watching the road. There is movement. Not cavalry scouts on horseback, but a column of soldiers. The shades of the forest hide the color of their uniforms, but Curtiss knows they are Confederate grey. He knows also that the men who wear them are already slain. Their bodies were dragged from a hundred battlefields along the Mississippi, the Rappahannock and the Potomac or pillaged from hellish Confederate army prison camps. Rotting flesh and offal foul their uniforms. Amongst them march the necromancers who command, devilish men who hide their faces behind black neckerchiefs soaked in lavender oil to block the smell. Above their ranks flutters a flag bearing the symbol of a jackal-headed man bearing a cross, the standard of the Initiates of Anubis, flying beside the Confederate battle flag.

Below, the men who have fought the dead before need not be told that Moore is here. As their nostrils catch the stench of the Black Column, they quietly leave their work and man the fortifications. Word spreads among the people in the trenches: the Southron wind blows from the northwest. Jubilation sours to terror. Scores of the faint-hearted kiss their loved-ones goodbye or scurry away without a word, leaving entrenching tools scattered in the filth, heedless of the chides of women like Julia Ward Howe. They swarm from the trenches toward the canal road leading back to Washington.

Lincoln joins Curtiss at the battlements, no longer smiling. In the distance, the Black Column wheels into the forest, vanishing from view only to be replaced by another.

"This is a fine time to leave, Mister Lincoln," says Pinkerton.

"Soon, Allan," says Lincoln. "May I borrow your telescope?"

"Sir, the roads out of the city are already choked with traffic. If you don't leave now, you won't escape before the enemy lays siege," says Pinkerton.

"Oh, for God's sake, Allan," cries Lincoln, losing his temper. "Siege or not, I'm not leaving Washington again! It was an error the first time and I should not have listened to you! Now will you please hand me your telescope?"

Pinkerton's eyes widen. This kind of outburst is clearly uncommon from the President. Pinkerton's shock is momentary, for his bushy brows furrow again and he withdraws a brass telescope from inside his jacket. He hands it to Lincoln wordlessly.

Lincoln unfurls it and points it toward the Black Column, scanning. "Have you ever fought the dead, Curtiss?" he asks.

"I was at Second Winchester, sir," says Curtiss. "But I did not fire my gun on that occasion."

Lincoln sighs. "They're hideous," he says, folding the telescope and handing it back to Pinkerton. "Hideous. Let us continue our inspection." He steps from the battlement, shoulders slumped.

Lincoln opens his mouth but withdraws his fork at the last second. A tinned oyster dangles from the end. "How can you eat with this stench in the air, Lieutenant?"

Curtiss takes another bite of canned beans. "Breathe through your mouth and hold your breath while you're chewing," he replies.

Lincoln gazes at the oyster, then at Pinkerton, who sits away from the fire pit, staring into the dark, also not eating. He takes another huff of the death on the wind. Grimacing, he scrapes the oyster off the fork back into the tin, then leans back against a pile of sandbags.

Murmuring men lounge everywhere in the trench, but allow the President's fire room for privacy. Nearby, somebody plays something lonely and Irish on a fiddle.

"Are you married, Curtiss?" asks Lincoln.

Curtiss tosses his empty can on the fire. "Yes. Charity. Bossiest woman I ever met," he says. "Except for Meade."

Lincoln chuckles. "You're fond of her, though. I see it. I'm very fond of my wife, also. She didn't want me to come here again. She's certain I'm going to die."

Curtiss stares into the fire. He would have thought getting to know a President would be stilted and awkward, but Lincoln's manner eases him. Lincoln is different than the other politicians he's met. Where others use public personae to mask their ambition, Lincoln's jaunty hayseed act masks other things. Cleverness, certainly. But as the President's face relaxes in contemplation of the fire, sadness leaks through. While Lincoln's appearance on the battlements had stirred nothing in Curtiss' soul, somehow this sad frown swells him with pride. Maybe with this intelligent, compassionate man in charge, this sorry nation has a chance for redemption.

Lincoln's frown disappears in a mischievous smile when he sees Curtiss studying him. This would be an excellent time to test what the President is thinking. Curtiss mulls Meade's orders, searching for wording. Finally, he says, "My wife wrote me today. She believes that the government will surrender."

Lincoln says nothing, watching the flames.

"Is it true?" asks Curtiss.

Pinkerton casts a suspicious frown at Curtiss, but hunches his back against the firelight once more. He is listening carefully, too.

"My boy…Lieutenant…" says Lincoln. "I've seen this Union shatter and unite again. I've seen us become a nation. I've seen freedom for the negroes, first in the liberated South, then the border states. We were so close to victory, weren't we?"

"Yes," says Curtiss.

"To give up now would be so very hard. Perhaps harder than fighting. We shall have to see."

The foul Southron wind now blows from the north. Curtiss stirs the campfire's embers with a discarded ramrod, imagining troops of silent dead encircling the city.

Lincoln will not go to a hotel with Pinkerton. Now he lies in an exhausted slumber near his pile of sandbags. His face is still pale and lean in the firelight.

Were it not for Lincoln's soft snoring, Curtiss would swear the President was dead.

Curtiss quietly steps from the fire, brushing sand from his jacket.

"Where are you going, then?" growls Pinkerton, still hunched in the darkness.

"My assignment ended at midnight, sir," says Curtiss. "Unlike the President, I have quarters I'm willing to sleep in."

Pinkerton grunts and resumes his vigil. Curtiss steps among soldiers in the trench, some huddled and sleeping, some wide-eyed and unable to rest. As he ascends the trench's wooden stairs, an unseen sentry challenges him in some sort of nasal New York accent. "Who goes there?"

"Lieutenant Curtiss, 33rd Pennsylvania," answers Curtiss.

The sentry enters the lamplight, rifle at his hip. He scrutinizes Curtiss, then drops his gun to order and salutes. As Curtiss tramps past, he suddenly blurts, "So what does Father Abe say, Lieutenant? Are we going to surrender?"

Curtiss turns to regard the man. The sentry's hand trembles on the rifle, repressing emotion, but what emotion Curtiss cannot tell. It could be fear of upcoming battle or fear that he will not get to pull his trigger and avenge a fallen comrade, maybe a comrade who marches with the Black Columns.

"As you were, soldier," says Curtiss. He trudges toward the canal road, preparing for a weary walk and an angry Meade.

† † † † †

Meade is still awake, ignoring a large stack of papers on his bureau. Instead, he stares at a map of Washington spread on the table, one tired arm supporting his bald head, the other hand picking his beard. He raises red eyes as Curtiss enters and salutes. He glares until it becomes clear that he is waiting for a report.

"I regret to say I cannot judge the President's inclinations," says Curtiss.

Meade straightens and paces back and forth. "Damn, damn, damn."

Curtiss watches the General in his peripheral vision, knowing that making eye contact may spark an outburst of temper.

"You've heard that certain Democrats are trying to amend the constitution to remove the Natural-born citizen clause from the presidency, haven't you?" says Meade, angry. "And I suppose you've heard they're trying to get me to run in the primary next year? I suppose you think I'm just going to use a surrender for my own political advantage? Watch the Republicans die and then sail into the Presidency?"

Curtiss knows better than to answer. But it's true, the thought occurred to him.

"Well, damn you, then," he spits. "If I get elected President, it won't be because of Lincoln's shame. It will be because I fought and won!"

Curtiss stares at the floor.

"Now, I know you can read people, Curtiss. I know you can tell what they're thinking. So if that man is going to surrender to those Southern sons-of-bitches, I have to know."

"I can't read him, General."

Meade scratches his bald head, then points to the door. "Get out," he says.

When Curtiss descends the narrow staircase into the Pennant's hold, he sees a Southern Army Captain sitting at the table used for negotiations, writing a letter. The coffee boy places cups on the table. There is no sign of Stephens, Lee or his aide. Curtiss scrapes his chair along the floor and takes his seat at the desk behind the table. Stanton and Lincoln duck into the hold, still chatting about the weather at this time of year in Steubenville. Meade follows them. They all look tired and ragged, Meade from spending the night pacing, Stanton nauseated from the Southron wind, and Lincoln looking his usual self.

The three men take their seats at the table, glancing at the Captain. Lincoln and Stanton continue murmuring until Meade finally clears his throat and growls, "Where are your superiors, Captain?"

"General, actually," says the man in an Irish brogue. He finishes writing a line and then places the letter aside to dry. "Mister Stephens thought it best to send me ahead to chat with you." He rises, extending a hand to Meade and grinning. "I'm General Sullivan Moore."

The room goes silent as the three men draw their breaths and recoil from the man. Nobody stands or takes Moore's hand. The hand wavers, then falls to Moore's side.

"Suit yourselves," Moore says. "You know, contrary to popular belief, we necromancers are very clean. It prevents the spread of disease."

Lincoln bumbles to his feet and extends his hand uncertainly. Moore takes it and shakes. Stanton and Meade remain seated, glowering.

"Thank you, Mister Lincoln," says Moore, taking his seat. "Now then, let's begin."

"I have no interest in negotiating with a sorcerer of damn nigger voodoo," says Meade. "Did Stephens mean to insult us?"

"That was not his intent," says Moore. "He merely asked me to give you a demonstration, by your leave."

The Northerners do not answer.

Curtiss speaks: "Excuse me, General. Should I be recording this?"

"No," says Meade, then glares at Moore.

"I'll take that as consent," says Moore. "Now, the last two years have marked some wonderful advances in the creation of servants. I have three new soldiers waiting outside which I would like to show you."

Stanton's swallow is audible.

"Oh, fear not. These aren't those poor devils rotting away on the front lines. These are pristine specimens and I assure you they are unarmed. No harm is intended. You have my word as a gentleman."

Stanton and Meade turn their gaze to Lincoln. Lincoln nods his assent.

Moore about-faces, clicks his tongue and shouts, "Squad, enter!"

The door opens and three figures march in. Their movement is precise and crisp, their steps vigorous. Their uniforms are new and unsullied. It is only their eyes that are dead and dispassionate.

Moore barks commands. "Wheel right! Left face! Ten-shun!" The men follow orders like mechanical contraptions, their eyes unfocused and unblinking. It is after the creatures stand to attention that Curtiss notices that one of the soldiers is a black man, his frizzy hair matted and sticking from his forage cap.

Stanton stands, stuffing a handkerchief to his mouth. He shoves his chair aside, wheezing, and flees the hold, feet slipping on the stairs. Silence follows his departure.

Perhaps the other men don't see it, but Curtiss observes Moore's tiny smile. The man is enjoying this.

Moore clears his throat. "Mister Stanton is not alone in his...reaction. Some are...unprepared for the emotions stirred by our science."

Meade and Lincoln say nothing. There again on Moore's face is that tiny smile, secretly relishing the northerners' discomfort. He continues: "When our art was first practiced, we had yet to incorporate the science of embalming. You may find it hard to believe, but those rotting hordes out there are actually somewhat embarrassing now. The army of tomorrow will not emit the Southron wind, as you call it. Nor will they be limited to simply 'Aim' and 'Fire.'"

Moore faces the dead men, clicks his tongue again and shouts, "Aim for my chest! Aim for my legs! Aim for my head!" The three dead soldiers pantomime Moore's commands with absent rifles. Curtiss imagines the rifles, their aim unflinching, steady and unforgiving. "Ten-shun!", click-click, and the soldiers are again passive.

"Impervious to pain, immune to the terrors of battle," continues Moore, punching the black man in the gut, who neither bends or shrinks. "As you Yankees have discovered, they can be killed by destruction of the brain or the severing of the spinal column at the neck." Moore steps in front of one of the white soldiers. "But they go to their deaths without fear." He withdraws a ramrod from his belt and gingerly sticks it into the dead soldier's eye socket, maneuvering it past the eyeball. He leaves it there and clicks his tongue. "One-oh-eight, drive that ramrod into your head."

The soldier's fist swings upward from its side and strikes the ramrod. There is a tiny click as the ramrod penetrates the skull and sinks into the brain. Then the soldier simply drops into an unnatural heap. No blood flows.

Lincoln gasps.

"Monstrous," mutters Meade.

"Is it now?" says Moore, turning on the General. "The souls have long departed from these lumps of flesh. Is it monstrous to send these unfeeling creatures into battle or to slaughter thousands more young men?

"This is the future, sir. It need not be one in which we are enemies," continues Moore, smiling broadly. "Think of the possibilities! Here you see the Saxon standing side-by-side with the Negro, no disagreement, no feuding. Neither sees the other as unequal. White and black work together in perfect harmony. Faith, these servants work twice as hard as any negro cotton-picker. The slave-holders can never compete and will be driven out of business. You must believe me, this is what my order and our founder Mister Welles wished all along. You see before you the end of the evil of slavery!"

His declaration is met with silence. Lincoln, leaning on the table, stirs. "I sense your…presentation is over. Can you leave us alone to discuss, sir?"

"T'would be my pleasure, sir. Take as much time as you need. Mister Stephens should be here within the hour." Moore clicks his tongue to command the soldiers.

"If you wouldn't mind," says Lincoln quietly, "could you leave your servants? I wish to examine them."

Moore's predatory smile widens into one of genuine delight. "Sir, it would be my honor. I'll leave you to it. Good day." Moore grabs his letter, backs out of the room and shuts the door.

Lincoln crosses the hold. He stops before the black soldier and stares into the man's dead eyes. The soldier does not react. "What does it mean, General?" he asks. "Why do you think Stephens wanted us to see this?"

Meade snorts. "Intimidation. They know they don't have the resources to besiege Washington and they hope to scare us into surrender."

Lincoln holds his hand to the black man's cheek. "He's so cold," he says.

Meade continues. "They want more territory and they think if we are frightened we'll sign away Washington."

Lincoln moves past the dead heap on the deck to the remaining soldier. "And what is the meaning of this?" he asks. He removes the soldier's grey forage cap and strands of long, blonde hair fall to the uniform's shoulders. The face which Curtiss had formerly considered merely youthful is actually feminine. This soldier is a dead woman. In life, she would have been a stark, powerful beauty, but now her unnatural pale stare is terrifying.

Meade gasps and sputters, speechless in horror and outrage. Lincoln turns to him, waiting for an answer. When none comes, he turns to Curtiss. "And what do you think, Lieutenant? Why would the Vice-President of the Confederacy order his most notorious general to parade a dead girl in uniform for us?"

Shocked, Meade swivels to gape at Curtiss. Curtiss drops his pen, which he realizes he is clutching painfully. Lincoln is waiting.

He closes his eyes and thinks. "I would say, Mister President…that he wants you to imagine what Moore will do to our citizens after Washington is besieged."

Lincoln nods, approving. "So what would you do in my shoes, Lieutenant?"

"Truthfully, I wouldn't want to be in your shoes, sir," says Curtiss.

"Indulge me. If we fight, we may lose and thousands more will die. If I surrender, the nation will cry in outrage. My party will be utterly destroyed."

Curtiss shakes his head, unable to believe the President is asking him this question. He clears his mind again. "I imagine they'll be just as outraged if Washington falls. And then they will hear Julia Ward Howe is dead and marching on Philadelphia wearing rebel grey."

"So?" says Lincoln.

"So…" stammers Curtiss. "So, I would surrender, sir."

Meade spins away, his hands trembling, attempting to hide his fury. Lincoln turns back to the woman and searches her empty eyes. Perhaps he searches the eyes for a solution, some missing answer that will solve his woes. But there is nothing. The woman merely stares back with unfocused eyes, waiting for the order to kill. Lincoln's exhausted frame emits a long, shuddering exhalation. He slumps to the table and takes his seat.

After Stephens and Lee board the Pennant an hour later, the Government of the United States of America surrenders.

"Where will you go now?" asks Lincoln.

Curtiss turns his head to gaze out the coach house window, watching crows wheeling and playing in the buckwheat field. He sloshes the brandy in his mouth and swallows it. "I'll go back to Lancaster," he says. "The wife wants more children and I expect she'll have them whether I'm around or not."

Lincoln chuckles. "What do you do in Lancaster?"

"I farm corn," says Curtiss.

Lincoln's tired eyes widen. "You're a…farmer? Why, I'd have thought you a newspaperman or a mayoral candidate at the very least."

"Nothing so heinous, sir," says Curtiss, taking another sip of his brandy.

Lincoln laughs again, then turns to admire the play of crows and sunlight in the buckwheat. He frowns. "You have a wit, Lieutenant. Which is why I've asked you here before you head home. I hear Meade has tired of your services."

"Yes," says Curtiss. Meade relieved him of his duties without explanation after the surrender.

"Then you may have heard my secretary, Mister Nicolay, was murdered two nights ago."

"I'm sorry to hear that, sir," says Curtiss, although he is not that sorry. He has heard of so many strangers dying that it no longer matters. "How did it happen?"

"Road agents on the way to Philadelphia," says Lincoln, pouring more brandy into his tin cup. "So I have need of a secretary. The post is yours if you want it."

Curtiss studies Lincoln's face. The surrender on the Pennant has not brought him relief. He is more pale and creased than ever. He is an old man. An old man with two years left in his presidency unless an unfriendly Congress finds an excuse to impeach him. Already the Democratic buzzards are circling. Already the Republicans are disintegrating: Charles Sumner has returned to Boston and has called for the creation of a new party. Until this painful farce of a Presidential term ends, Lincoln is no different than one of Moore's servants, dead on his feet, unable to find peace.

"No, thank you, sir. I'd best be getting back home," says Curtiss.

A loud pop silences the conversation. Lincoln swivels in his chair. Curtiss takes his feet and draws his revolver. It came from outside.

The terrified owner scans the deserted coach house from his perch behind the bar. "Was ist los? Was ist das?" he babbles at Curtiss, not realizing he is speaking German.

A flurry of gunfire just outside the door answers him. A bullet lodges in the wood, spraying splinters into the room. The owner flops behind the bar. Curtiss darts in front of Lincoln, blocking the line of fire between the door and the President.

The door swings open. Black powder smoke drifts inside. Curtiss aims his revolver.

"Are you alright in there, Mister President, sir?" asks a voice. It is Allan Pinkerton's Scottish.

"I'm unhurt, Allan," says Lincoln.

Pinkerton shuffles into the coach house, his smoking revolver drawn. Curtiss lowers his weapon.

"We're leaving, Mister President," says Pinkerton.

"What's happened?" asks Lincoln.

Without answering, Pinkerton bustles Lincoln out the door toward his carriage and waiting cavalry escort, Curtiss covering the rear. Lying behind a bush near the door is a ragged man in Union blue, blood pumping from a hole in his chest. He gasps quietly, a dirty Colt revolver lying beyond his reach in the dust. The flies have already found him, swarming onto his face and tasting his bloody lips.

The face is familiar. Curtiss has seen him recently. Was it one of the soldiers that rowed him from the Pennant? The sentry at the edge of the trench at Fort Scott? Or one of the countless defeated and sullen faces of the men retreating from Washington?

Pinkerton manhandles the President into the carriage and shuts the door.

"Enjoy your home and your rest, Curtiss," says Lincoln, leaning out.

Pinkerton climbs the coach to ride shotgun and urges the driver forward. Reins crack and the coach rattles away, the four Illinois cavalrymen keeping their horses in tight formation with their Spencers trained on all horizons.

After they have gone, the coach house owner shuts the door. The Philadelphia pike is silent. No wind blows. Curtiss closes his eyes. Somewhere over the hills to the west waits his quiet farm. He knows tiny corn ears will be growing golden tassels. The stable roof needs mending. Charity sweeps the verandah, watching the road for him. Peace is less than a week away but he cannot imagine it. All is drowned by the soft gasps of the assassin dying at the door.

AS YOU WERE

by K.J. Newman

Francisco Medina had loved beautiful things ever since he was a boy. He remembered his grandfather taking him to the National Museum of Art so he could see high culture, the old man walking along with his hands behind his back like a general inspecting his troops. Every now and then, his grandfather would stop and announce the name of a painter, how he died, and what he'd meant to Mexico. Grandfather never spoke about the paintings themselves, but Francisco was enchanted by their colour and possibility, by the curved lines and soft dabbles of light. When he was sixteen, he decided that he would paint.

At once, other artists hated him. He was a prodigy. A fully formed talent that had the enviable, almost unbelievable gift of being able to transfer his exact vision to the canvas. Whatever he saw in his mind's eye came gracefully from his brush. There was no trick to it, no illusion, and no trial and error phase where he learned to sketch or hold a brush, or took out library books about drawing figures and colour theory. Francisco Medina was *talented*. Like it was a gift from a pagan goddess who'd fallen in love with him. As the years went by and his successes grew, critics never faulted his techniques, though their opinions on his subject matter began to cool.

"Why don't they like me anymore?" Francisco threw a newspaper down onto a café table. He was twenty-three, growing a goatee, and afraid that the end of his career was looming. It took half the time to tear an idol down as it did to build them up.

The paper had nearly landed in the coffee of Ricardo Barth, a blue-eyed modernist who had grown up in Chihuahua with a German father. He was a few years older than Francisco, and had entered into the art scene at around the same time. Barth was cursed with potential the way Francisco was blessed with talent. As a result, he'd become very good at not resenting people. According to Barth's thinking, Francisco's success had eclipsed everyone else's—not just his own—so there was no point in taking it personally.

Barth glanced at the newspaper. It was, as he suspected, the *Sun* article about the decline of political art in favour of commercialism. He'd read it that morning, and noticed that it cast Francisco in a villainous role.

"People like her never liked you," Barth shrugged. "Art critics are ridiculous creatures anyway. They want everything to be a secret, they want to champion the underdog and be proven right fifty years from now, so they can jump up and say: 'Look at my articles from the early days! I always knew that Van Gogh was better than all that mainstream trash! I was a Cassandra!' It's stupid."

"They love you."

"Exactly. That's exactly how you know they're all talking out of their asses." He moved the paper aside and signaled for the waitress as Francisco sat down across from him. "Who else loves my work? Nobody. I don't even like it myself most of the time, but it's what I'm good at so I'm stuck with it. You sell paintings to nice, normal people. Who in the art world can understand that?"

"It's the third time I've been called saccharine, and she says I'm a trite sentimentalist who paints a Mexico that doesn't exist."

Most of Francisco's pieces were landscapes. Sometimes he would paint an iguana, and one of his most famous paintings was of four pigeons, but it was the land that he wanted to bring to life. Barth had gone with him a few times on missions to find significantly interesting and beautiful places, making his own sketches of any carnivalesque figures they might come upon. He'd noticed that Francisco was very particular about the places he'd set up his easel, and that being painted seemed to change a place. As the work went on, sometimes two or three weeks in a row, the colours of the world deepened or softened to match the colour of the painting. The rust on a cemetery gate might seem more elegant, more lovely simply for having been painted.

Then there was the green streak. It had obviously been an accident, and as much of a surprise to Francisco as it was to Barth. They were in the country, and had come across a colonial church in some disrepair, but not without charm. Four days into the painting, with his easel set up in the graveyard and the majority of the piece already finished, a rifle shot in the distance had startled Francisco and his hand had slipped. Looking back, Barth could never be certain what he'd realized first—that there was a shocking green streak across the church in Francisco's painting, or that a green streak had suddenly appeared on the side of the church standing before him in reality. Neither of them had spoken as Francisco hurriedly covered up the mistake. Once the painting was complete, the church was more charming than ever.

"I'm glad you don't paint doom and gloom," Barth nodded as the waitress dropped off an extra menu.

A few months later, the two of them went out to a resort town on the coast. It was the off-season, but there were still plenty of tourists. They set up a couple of canvases on the beach, and Francisco looked around for something beautiful. Barth looked around for something grotesque.

"I quite like the little starfish," Francisco smiled, getting his palette ready.

It took Barth a moment to spot it. A pink-orange creature clinging to the rocks with some bright seaweed. He had to agree, it did look quite romantic in a nautical sort of way. It took him awhile to settle on his own subject, but eventually a loud and gluttonous American couple made their way into his line of sight, and the problem was solved.

"My model sits nicely." Francisco chuckled, once they'd been painting almost half an hour.

"I don't think I've ever seen one move. How do they move? Like spiders?"

"I imagine they use the suction cups on the bottom of their legs and inch around."

A pale little boy seemed to pop out of the sand near to Francisco's rocks. His hair was bleached almost white by the sun, and his neck and shoulders were an angry bright red. The same red as a toy devil. He was wearing trunks covered in some cartoon character, and he went straight over to the starfish and picked it up.

"What's he doing?" Barth narrowed his eyes.

"Just looking, probably. He'll put it down in a second or two. Children are always curious about animals. Maybe they don't have starfish where he's from."

The little boy held the starfish up to the sun, watching for a few seconds as the creature's legs pulled in closer to its center. It didn't seem to like drying out. The little boy smiled. He lowered it down to his chest and pulled on one of the legs. First gently, then as hard as he could. The leg snapped from the center of the body like it was made of rubber, and a spray of orange intestines stained the sand around the boy's feet.

"Hey!" Barth stormed over to the boy, scolding and shouting. He took the starfish out of the child's hands and laid it back on the rock. Then he grabbed the boy's arm and demanded to be taken to see his parents, presumably to tell them that they had a budding serial killer on their hands.

Calmly, Francisco kept painting. He painted the starfish in one piece. Unharmed. Happy. Lovely. When he was finished, he went over to the sand, where the creature curled in a shadow, all its legs in place. He picked it up and tossed it into the sea before Barth could come back and see what he'd done.

When Francisco did his first portrait, things changed. By then, he was twenty-six and married. His career was stable thanks to his continued popularity with the average consumer, and a lucrative licensing contract with an American company. His paintings were being printed on everything from wall calendars to alarm clocks. It was on a Thursday, during a quiet dinner at home, when his wife—a beautiful law student named Silvia—told him they were going to have a baby.

"Wonderful," Francisco smiled.

The next day at breakfast, he was distant and dreamy. He dropped his coffee and burned his wrist. He shut himself up in his studio and didn't come out for lunch, or for dinner.

Barth was in New Zealand for most of that year. A woman in Auckland wanted a real Mexican fresco painted by a real Mexican artist, so he went. He liked the country, but was extremely relieved when he got home. Almost straight from the airport, he was ordered to attend a welcoming party and to see the new addition to the Medina family.

"Oh!" Barth cooed as Silvia put the baby in his arms. "A little princess! We'll have to buy you presents."

"Don't start spoiling her already!" Silvia laughed.

The baby's name was Febe, and she watched Barth with a pair of stunning and strange eyes. The colour of warm coffee and filled with an old soul's knowledge. Barth gave a low, fond whistle.

"She's going to be smart. Too smart for Francisco to handle."

Silvia smiled warmly and took her daughter back.

"He's in the studio. Again. Go and bother him. Remind him that you're the guest of honour and he was the one who insisted you come right over."

Francisco was painting, of course. A seascape being done from reference photographs. On the wall behind him was the portrait. It was a beautiful young woman with twin braids and a strangely familiar set of features. Barth recognized the deep brown eyes instantly.

He tilted his chin at the canvas.

"Do you think that was right?"

Francisco didn't answer.

After that, they didn't see much of each other. Francisco told himself that it wasn't anything to do with the portrait. They had always been on different paths. Was it such a surprise that time would push those paths further apart?

Francisco stood in shock watching the evening news. A car collision had taken the life of promising young painter Ricardo Barth, age forty. In his hand, his cell phone was ringing with an unusual urgency. He knew that it was Silvia, without even looking at the caller ID, and that she had heard the news. There were images of firefighters and two cars, crumpled into one another like they were made of paper. A woman with perfect hair was droning on in the foreground, and every now and then, they'd show that picture of Barth he used for gallery catalogues. It was a black and white photo, and he looked very serious in it. Not how Francisco remembered him at all.

He went into the studio and picked out a canvas. With a bottle of tequila in one hand and the brush in the other, he spent days on end painting, painting, painting. Working at an exhaustive pace, with no thought other than perfection. When he emerged from the studio, he looked like he'd been fighting in a war. His beard was grown, he'd lost five or six pounds, and his eyes were glassy and feverish. Without saying anything to Silvia or Febe, he went into the back garden and sat on the bench.

It was almost sundown when he heard the doorbell, then the scream and clatter.

Febe came out to find him.

"Mama has fainted," she said. "Uncle Ricardo is here."

by Cecelia Chapman

Those who remain walk the broken streets in the dark of the moon. We search for our lives drenched in tears of sadness and the blood of our open sores. We hide from our countrymen. They think they want to save us. But aren't they the same ones who built the plant?

Imagine the silence of an empty town. A dead town, a destroyed town. Walls, roofs, furniture splintered, shelves fallen, floors upended. Everything you possess, your past and all your dreams are in rubble. You only hear the sounds of loose things falling, water dripping, animals searching for food, or maybe they claw the dirt dying in agony.

Close your eyes. See the looters going through the rooms of your home moving very quickly in their haste. They are pawing through your possessions by cell phone light as it ticks off radiation levels. You know you will never return to your town, your old life, it is over forever. Your children will not be able to go outside. You will not sleep well for the rest of your life. In fact your life may now be very short with a brutal end. You will watch your family suffer around you in an evacuation shelter. You will watch everyone you ever knew, grew up with, and loved your whole life, get sick, suffer and die.

If you can, close your eyes again. See us. We stand before you in the darkest of the dark nights because you do not want to see what we have become. Our ugliness makes us strong, we choose to mutate. We are united with one purpose, focused. We stand together in our anger and desperation. Did we have a choice? They told us no accidents would ever happen at the plant. But they betrayed us, our trust, and they continue to lie to everyone. And still they do not listen to those whose lives they destroyed.

Now they want to build more plants. Yes. Do they think of those who lost everything they owned and still live without decent food and shelter? They do not even answer the questions of the people and still they want to build more plants.

How many more accidents like this can the earth take? How long before the radiation levels rise in the currents of the sea and reach you, the food you eat, the water you drink, the rain that falls on your face when you are in love? It is not just us now. It is all of you that will become like us.

We will never see the light of day. We will never see our families again because they will be frightened by what we have become. But we will take care of them because their own government ignores them. We will stay. We will hide and watch. We will stalk the heads of corporations and big business who refuse to hear what the people need and do not want. We will hunt down those who poison the land, the water, the air in their greed. We wait.

LIKE THE JELLYFISH

by Katherine Sanger

I was thirteen and Crystal was three when we went to the beach. I watched as she gathered up all the pieces of jellyfish the surf had washed up and put them together, melding them like they were Play-Doh. Once they were assembled, the jelly started wiggling and flexing, and she dropped it on the sand and clapped and giggled. I just stared. Crystal had been unhurt by the venom of the jellyfish. I had seen Crystal try to nurse wounded birds back to life before, but this was different. This wasn't wounded; this was dead. And now it was alive.

Mom hadn't seen; she thought the jellyfish had somehow washed ashore in one piece and was suddenly threatening her unwanted baby girl. She shrieked and pushed me out of the way, screaming threats of punishment and ruining the sand-castle I'd been building all afternoon while she conducted her "business" on her cell phone. Luckily, there were no tourists near us, so no one could overhear for free what she normally charged $5.99 a minute for.

"That's it," Mom declared, now that she'd been distracted from her phone. "We're going home."

I packed up the towels and shovels and pails, then dragged them and Crystal to the car. Mom had bought it in better days, and the once trendy sports car had now been turned into a family car. Sort of. Crystal sat in my lap in the front seat, and I put the seat belt over both of us. There wasn't enough of a back seat in the car for either of us, and my mother said that she had grown up just fine without all those safety things. She expected we could do the same. I wasn't convinced, but she'd made it clear that while I was plenty good enough to take care of my sister when she was working, I wasn't up to the task of "actual parenting."

When we got home, Mom went straight to her bedroom.

"Amber Lynn," she called to me. "You make your sister a good dinner. I have a date tonight, and I won't be home until late. Tomorrow we can go grocery shopping."

"Okay, mom."

"And don't use that tone with me! My dates are what keep you in shoes!"

"Okay, mom." I didn't think I'd had a tone at all, but she always heard one.

I wasn't sure what I could make for dinner. The refrigerator looked kind of bare. I thought we still had a box of macaroni and cheese, but there might not be any milk and butter to go with it. I could always just use water instead of milk if I had to. Again.

I knew I shouldn't complain. We had a house—it had been grandma's, and it was all we had left, but at least we had it. Mom earned enough to pay the taxes, when she was working the phone lines, anyway. And Crystal and I had a room to share, two beds, clean sheets when I could find enough change at the Laundromat. And we had Mom. Most of the time. Some of the time.

I was mixing the water and butter with the powdered cheese sauce and macaroni when she left. She had changed into something just slightly more revealing than what she'd been wearing at the beach. I thought I was probably the only girl at school who was more disapproving of her mother's clothes than my mother was of mine.

"I'll be back after bedtime," she said. "Don't wait up." She faked some kisses in our direction. Crystal, sitting at the table waiting for dinner, nodded seriously. I didn't bother. Mom didn't care what I had to say. She didn't look back as she walked out the front door.

I served Crystal her food and wandered to the door and locked it. I knew the routine—put Crystal to bed around seven, sit down in front of the TV, and watch stupid sitcoms until about 10, worrying about where Mom was and what she was doing, and trying not to worry about where she was and what she was doing. Mom would come home, yell at me for still being awake, then stumble off to bed, complaining about how "expensive" her dates were. I knew it was just code for the fact that she'd spent the money she'd earned picking up a rock or a dimebag on the way home. Maybe we'd really get groceries in the morning. Maybe not. But at least she was consistent. Sort of.

I watched all the re-runs, waited past the news, and then watched infomercials until the light came in through the bars on the windows. It was morning. I hadn't slept; Mom hadn't come home. Our weird unspoken pact had been broken. Where was she? I picked at the hangnail on my thumb, staring at the door, waiting for it to open.

I don't know when the annoyance turned to fear. Maybe it was when Crystal stumbled out to the living room in her threadbare footie pajamas, rubbing her eyes.

"Mom?" she asked me.

I shook my head.

She stared at me, serious as always.

"We'll go get her," I said. "Promise."

"Breakfast?"

"Sure."

There wasn't enough cereal for one, but there was some bread that hadn't gone completely stale, so I toasted it and gave her that with some grape jelly to go with it. I didn't eat anything. My stomach had started to hurt.

Crystal ate quickly. "Mom."

"C'mon." I took her hand, and we headed out.

I wasn't supposed to know where Mom worked. She had tried to keep us away from it. I wasn't sure why. I think she would have sold me if she'd been just a bit further down on her luck at any point, but that had never been put to the test.

But I knew she used the motel about half a mile away. I'd found one of the room cards in her pockets one time when I was doing laundry, and when I showed it to her, she snatched it away, telling me that I had just saved her $5 and she loved me. I wouldn't have minded if she had said she'd loved me any other times, when money wasn't involved, but I took what I could get.

The motel charged hourly rates and didn't look that bad from the outside. I wasn't too sure what the inside looked like. I didn't really want to know, but thought maybe we'd have to find out. The pit in my stomach sank further, and the pain had started to build behind my eyes. Something felt wrong. Even more wrong than usual.

We went to the front office.

"Hi, my mom is staying here."

The guy behind the counter had a lot of hair on his chest, but not too much on his head. He wore a shirt that looked like it had once fit, probably when it was in style, but now it hugged his beer belly a bit too tight.

"Your mom, huh?" he asked.

"Yeah, she, um, didn't feel good last night, so she stayed here."

"Sick, huh?"

"Yeah. I don't know her room number, though, but we wanted to see if she felt…well enough to come home," I said.

He looked me up and down. I felt myself blush and wondered if he would refuse to help me. At the same time, though, I was glad that I was wearing loose clothes that concealed what my mom had referred to as my "budding business partners." I tried to cave my chest in a bit more, the opposite of the straight posture the teachers at school always encouraged.

"Mom," Crystal said, and the guy's demeanor changed. He leaned over the counter to glare at her.

"She's just a kid."

"Yeah, so am I," I said.

"Not so much," he said, and I felt a shiver. He smiled at it.

"Only one room still got someone. Room 202. Second floor." He grabbed a key card and pushed it into a little slot, then pressed some buttons on top. He pulled it back out and held it over the counter to me. "I normally charge $5 for these extras. But I think I can let it go for a little kiss."

I stared at him. He couldn't be serious. He didn't flinch or blink, just looked back at me.

I couldn't move. My brain had stopped thinking and my body didn't know what to do without it.

Then Crystal tugged on my hand. I leaned forward. So did he. But I moved faster and snatched the key card out of his hand, then turned and ran from the office, dragging Crystal. He laughed as I ran, the sound cutting off as the office door slammed behind me. Maybe he hadn't really wanted the kiss. Maybe...it didn't matter. I didn't start breathing again until we were at the stairs. Crystal had kept up, but she put her arms up to me when we stopped. "Up! Ammer-in. Up!"

I lifted her up onto my hip. The once-plastic soles of her pajamas were mostly rubbed through. "I'm sorry, Crystal. C'mon, let's find Mom."

"Mom." Still serious. Sometimes I thought she was purposely serious, keeping her smiles from me, trying to convince me to be a better sister to her. But I was already trying my best.

We counted down the rooms. I hadn't been paying attention to the numbers as we walked, so we'd come up the stairs at the wrong end. Mom's was the next to last room.

I put Crystal down and knocked on the door.

No answer.

"Mom?" I asked.

"Mom," Crystal said.

Still nothing. No sound at all.

I knocked again.

We waited. I felt the fear churn in my stomach again. It had gotten quiet while I dealt with the guy behind the counter, but now as we stood in front of the door, the fear flared again, and I thought I would double over with the pain. I slid the key card in while I was still upright and saw the light blip green. I pushed the handle and the door opened.

My first impression was that the room was red.

Weird color choice, I thought.

Then I realized that it hadn't originally been red.

It had been beige, with almost puke-like green mixed with it.

But the red was overlaid on it, a sticky, filthy sheen of red.

I choked, my fear bursting and coming up and out of me. I threw up all over the threshold, Crystal still stood behind me, shielded by the fact that the door hadn't opened all the way.

"Mom," she said again. I looked down at her through blurry eyes. Then I pushed the door the rest of the way open.

Crystal took it in, her eyes curious but not scared. She just looked...serious.

Like normal. Like nothing had changed for her.

We entered the room.

I don't know why we did. It was like we had gone so far already, and my stomach had stopped roiling, and there was nothing that could get worse. We had to follow it to the end.

There was a suitcase, closed, on the floor in front of the bed, and next to it… next to it was Mom. Well, parts of Mom.

I could only guess that the rest of her was in the suitcase. Had her date run out of room? Were these the leftovers? Had he gone to get another bag?

I stared at the pile: a hand, a leg, a chunk of hair. I couldn't see the whole, just the parts, and I had to focus on each one individually. It looked like she had been ripped apart by a shark, then all her parts had washed up on a bloody, carpeted shore.

Her head sat next to the pile, eyes open.

Like the jellyfish on the beach, but bloody.

Crystal stood there, and I couldn't tell what she was thinking or what she wanted to do. She just looked satisfied, somehow. Like we had figured out the mystery and everything would be all right now.

But it won't be all right, I wanted to shout at her. Mom's dead!

Like the jellyfish.

I stared at Crystal, her blond hair, her freckles, her purple and pink pajamas. Her hidden talents.

"Crystal, I need you to do something. Remember the jellyfish?"

She turned to me, serious, and nodded.

"I need you to do that again. Fix this like you fixed the jellyfish. Make her… make her Mom again. Like the jellyfish."

Crystal looked into my eyes. I couldn't see anything in hers but blue. I didn't know what she could see in mine.

"Okay."

She opened the suitcase, and then began assembling the body parts.

Putting them together.

Humming.

They fit together, almost seamless where she made them attach to each other. The skin was too pale, but the severed edges healed, grew together, made a person. Made Mom.

When Crystal was done, she stood up. Her pajamas were stained red, the pink and purple more garish then before. "Mom," she said.

Before her, lying on the floor, was Mom.

Mom wasn't breathing.

Her chest wasn't rising and falling.

But her nostrils contracted, then flared like when she was all kinds of mad.

Her eyes opened, pale, like her skin, and cloudy.

I took a step back, pulling Crystal with me.

Mom blinked a few times, oriented on us, and stretched her mouth open wordlessly. Then she stood up and stumbled towards us. I took another step back, tugging Crystal again.

Behind me, I heard a noise—the door. I turned and saw the door swinging in, being pushed by a suitcase on wheels. Behind it was a tall, thin man, remarkable only for the fact that there were red splatters on his shirt and jeans.

"You—" He pointed past us, at mom.

I barely even saw Mom move, just a quick blur. Suddenly she was past us and on him, dragging him to the ground, her face in his hair, his screams loud and desperate. There was a crunching noise, a horrible cracking sound, and then this... wetness. Chewing. Gurgling.

And the guy—the guy who had just had a piece of his head bitten off by my mother—started twitching and moving again. He raised an arm, then put it back down and tried to stand up.

I turned away from the door, pulling Crystal with me, running to the closed bathroom door. I crashed into it, fumbled it open, and rushed in. I pushed Crystal into the bathtub and slammed the door as hard as I could. I clicked the lock, not sure that it would actually work, but there was nothing else I could do. There were two people out there who had been dead and now they weren't.

The bathroom was messy, towels and soap thrown around, dripping red. I ignored it, or tried to anyway, pushing away the thought of what had caused this blood and tried not to think about what I had just seen. We had to get out. We had to...

There was a knife, a big one, sitting in the sink. I got it and held it, the handle slick, the blade bent in places. But still sharp. It cut my finger when I tested it. I sucked air but kept quiet. Maybe they would forget we were in here.

I climbed into the bathtub with Crystal, pulling the curtain down around us.

Seconds dragged into minutes, and I heard nothing.

Finally I heard the man from the motel office in the bedroom.

"What the hell—" followed by a shrill scream.

Then nothing again.

I looked over at Crystal. She was smiling.

by Rich Hawkins

Here was the edge of the world, where the detritus of civilisations washed up on the ragged shore. Harry pulled up his collar against the cold as he faced eastwards, the sea to his front, the ragged cliffs to his back. He shivered. The wind had teeth and liked to find the soft parts of him.

There was a storm out to sea, where the sky met the water and the waves rose and fell like grey knuckled hills. The beach was deserted save for his own withered form scuffling across the sand. The coast was a place of grey and rain and quiet desperation. The shore stretched to the south, swallowed by the pale mist. Gulls glided above the sea, scanning the water for fish darting under the rolling surface.

It was midwinter, and the world was heavy and slow, a lumbering beast waiting for the sun to warm its blood. Harry walked the beach every day. The sea gave things to him. A car number plate. A Darth Vader action figure. Food packaging from Japan. A dog collar with the name Snowdrop inscribed on the metal tag. A small plastic box rattling with milk teeth.

Harry limped across the water's edge. The sea was broiling, full of rage. He wondered what it would be like to walk into the surf and let the waves take him down to where the light couldn't reach.

He halted, squinted his eyes. His vision was not what it used to be. A reminder that his body was failing by degrees.

The sea had returned something.

He broke into an awkward stumble, his feet slapping on the sand. His legs throbbed and his spine felt hot and rigid. His body hated being old.

A man was washed up on the beach. A crumpled form lying where the sea had spilled it. Harry was breathing hard by the time he reached the man. He wiped his mouth.

The man's body was starkly white against the dark sand.

Harry crouched next to him. His eyes were staring and blank. Black hair. Alabaster skin mottled with bruises. Splayed, gangly limbs. Clothes torn to rags. Bare feet. Something had nibbled at the tips of his fingers. Harry's hand hesitated over the man's neck. He placed his middle and index fingers in the hollow between the windpipe and the large muscle in the neck. The man's skin was too cold.

No pulse.

Harry's heart patted wetly against his ribcage. His breath swelled within his throat.

Maybe he was mistaken. He tried again.

Nothing.

Harry moved the man's head to one side and water spilled from his mouth.

The sea roared beyond him. Thunder cracked and boomed, the anger of fickle gods.

Up the steep pathway winding across the cliffs, every step hindered by the crumbling ground, every breath stolen by the wind. Harry's house was a ragged shape against the sky, looking out over the sea. It was hunched, bowed and battered. Scarred, pitted walls. Metal rusted quickly here, as if time was not the same as in other places. He wondered if the aging process was somehow accelerated here, an anomaly, a fold in time and space. But everything fell eventually. The sea would consume the beach then the cliffs and his house with them. But he'd be long gone by then. There was some comfort in that.

Once he was inside he called the police.

"Where's the body, Mr. Cripps?" The female constable was lumpy and damp-mouthed, a body made out of odd parts. Her fellow constable, a tall, awkward man with a clipped moustache, coughed into one hand and stared at Harry.

"I don't know," said Harry. "It was right here. He was right here. A man."

"Maybe he got up and walked away," the male constable said. No inflection in his voice. Dull as dirt.

"He was dead," Harry said. "I checked his pulse. He'd drowned, I think."

"You think?" the woman said.

"Yes."

"But you're not sure?"

"No."

The constables shared a look.

"So where has this mysterious man gone?"

Harry shrugged.

The man looked at the sand around them. "The only footprints I see are ours, Mr. Cripps. If he walked away we'd be able to see his footprints, don't you think?"

"Yes," said the woman. "That's very true."

"I can see why you're both in the police," said Harry.

"No need for sarcasm, Mr. Cripps."

"Sorry. Maybe the body was washed back out to sea…"

"Maybe," the man said, glaring at him. "Are you sure there was a body, Mr. Cripps?"

"Yes, of course."

"Wasting police time is not a laughing matter," said the woman.

"I'm not laughing."

"I'm not laughing," the man parroted back at him.

"I'm not wasting police time, I swear."

The constables exchanged a loaded glance. The woman's face was creased in all the wrong places when she looked at Harry, and her lips formed a thin, cruel smile.

"We'll be the judge of that."

Night fell with the sound of the surf beating in his ears. Harry couldn't sleep. Thoughts of the dead man on the beach crowded his mind.

He sat up in bed. Rubbed his chest. Heart burn. He switched on the bedside lamp and perched on the edge of the bed. Sagging limbs in the yellow light. Hairy arms. Pot belly.

Alice smiled from the framed photo on the bedside table. He looked at her for a long time, at her small mouth and soft chin, her dark eyes the colour of earth and mulch. She had been his anchor, rooting him to this world.

He sometimes forgot her face and he hated himself for it.

Almost a full moon. Dying stars and afterglow. The only sound was the waves pushing towards the shore. There was no wind. Harry walked the beach in his long coat, boots and woollen hat. He stood at the spot where he'd found the man's body and looked out to sea. He closed his eyes, listened to the water rushing and heaving. The sea was muscular and brutal, finding its beat, its dark heart. When he opened his eyes he almost expected to see the dead man at his feet, washed up again.

Rain began to fall. Typical but predictable. He fancied a mug of soup and a soak in the bath while listening to some Bach on the portable radio.

Footfalls nearby, discernable in the rain. Almost upon him. Harry turned towards the sound. A pallid, bloated figure lurched towards him. He opened his mouth to say something but the words stuck in his throat. He raised one hand weakly as the figure collapsed into him and knocked him to the sand. Harry let out a small cry. Confused and startled, he lost his bearings. Rain on his face. His fingers touched naked shivering flesh that wasn't his own.

The bloated figure scrambled on top of him, a gurgling chuckle in its throat. Its skin was clammy and cold. Dripping wet. Long white hair and a putrid face. Eyes like soft eggs. Stinking of the sea. Fish-rot on its breath. It was barely a man.

Harry tried to push the man away but he was too slick and blubbery to gain any purchase upon, writhing and buckling, an awful parody of lust and desire.

Harry cried for help.

The man gripped the sides of Harry's mouth with spongy fingers. Harry screamed, his tongue horribly exposed. The man forced his hand into Harry's mouth and it tasted of seawater and brine. He gagged as the hand wriggled past his teeth, his squirming tongue. Harry put all his strength into his legs and pushed the man away from him.

The man fell onto the sand and let out a low grunt.

Harry stumbled to his feet as the man rose on sagging legs. He staggered away, not looking back and not stopping, until he was inside his house. Once there, he locked all the doors and windows, and turned off the lights. He hid in the kitchen holding a brass poker. The taste of rot was in his mouth.

Soon enough, there was a scratching at the windows that was too desperate to be the rain.

Morning came with a dour light and a lull in the rain. Harry found footprints outside the house and smudges on the downstairs windows.

It rained again.

Harry decided to stay inside the house all day. The doors were kept locked. He took a long bath and drank whiskey to remove the briny taste from his mouth. There was a faint tremor in his arms.

He decided not to call the police; they had no interest in him. He looked at old photo albums and went through Alice's old things stored in the spare room. His chest ached with her absence. Four years now. Time did not heal. Nothing healed.

The storm lashed the house. The walls creaked and groaned. Harry watched the sea from an upstairs window. In the failing light he saw a child walking up the cliff path from the beach. A little girl in a white cotton dress, soaking wet, picking her way past patches of scrubland and dark rock. She was willowy and bedraggled, head bowed, long hair flattened to her face. A wraith in the rain. Harry shrugged on his jacket and went outside, down to the cliff top and winding path. The storm took his breath away. Rain in his eyes.

The girl was gone.

He searched for her. She had vanished. The wind screamed at him.

The next day, after a night of fitful sleep, Harry went down to the beach. A light drizzle dampened his shoulders. He stood and watched the sea foam and shiver. He watched waves as tall as houses swell and rise and fall.

There were footprints in the sand. Adults' and children's. Big and small. There were even handprints, as if left by a child besotted with the splayed shape of its small fingers.

His own footprints were trapped among them.

Something was floating on the inch-thick film of water before the shallows. A white square of plastic, which he recovered before it was washed out to deeper water. He shook drips from it and turned it over in his hand. He closed his eyes. Opened them. His mouth made shapes. Something unraveled inside him.

A younger Harry and Alice stared at him from the photo. Blackpool, 1973. On the North Pier. Their honeymoon.

The last time he had seen the photo was the day before Alice left him. They had been reminiscing about the first years of their marriage and their desire for a baby. Their marriage had lasted, but their hope for children had not.

Alice had called herself barren.

A part of Harry, despite his love for Alice, had never forgiven her.

The sound of waves hitting rocks. The fury.

There were figures crouched in the shallows. Ragged, thin things bunched together watching him. Dull eyes and blank faces. Torn holes for mouths. Deformed by their time in the sea. Ravaged by saltwater and strong tides. Skin missing from bodies. An eel thrashed in the hollow of a man's chest cavity. Worms and crimson cilia squirmed and scraped in a young boy's eye socket. A red-haired woman's face had been sucked from her skull.

Harry dropped the photo and stepped away from the churning sea, his eyes hot with tears. He turned away, tripped over his feet and fell down. Sand in his mouth and between his fingers, under his nails.

The figures began to move out of the water.

Harry climbed to his feet and spat sand.

Thunder out to sea.

Harry ran.

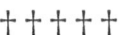

He slammed the door shut. The click of the lock was too loud. He closed the curtains at the downstairs windows and took the brass poker from the fireplace and the feel of it in his clenched hand was not a comfort.

Trembling limbs. Cold sweat on his face.

Harry called the police.

Not long until dusk. He'd been waiting over an hour for the police. He was going upstairs to use the toilet when he saw the police car from the same window he'd seen the girl yesterday, parked on the gravel road leading to his house.

He downed several shots of whiskey, mustered some courage, and stepped outside. The area was deserted. No skeletal figures or little girls. When he reached the police car he realised it hadn't been parked, but abandoned. The headlights were on. Key in the ignition. Dashboard lights. The driver's and front passenger's doors were open. Fresh blood on the windows and the ground around the car. No sign of the officers. The radio shouted punches of static and panicked, faraway voices.

Harry fled back along the road and over the cliff tops. The sea was writhing. Figures were rising from the shallows and emerging onto the beach. Clothes that were dripping rags. Naval uniforms from the First World War and beyond. Old dresses that were in fashion a century ago. A withered man in a dinner jacket. An emaciated woman in a Victorian bathing suit. Some of them were without arms. Some were naked. Sagging bodies and spindly limbs. Stomachs bloated with rot. Sucking wounds. Skeletal rotted things that thrashed and groaned as they pushed through the water.

Hundreds of bodies.

Some of them looked up at him and they were grinning.

Harry parted the net curtains. His hands were shaking. Shuffling figures roamed around the house. Gaunt faces peered in through windows. Fingers scraped upon glass.

The sea was giving up its dead.

They moved away just before dusk and walked inland. Harry flipped the light switches but the power was out. No TV or radio. He dialed the number for his cousin's house in Ipswich, but the line was dead.

He sat in the dark. The moon was full. Even the sea, usually so tempestuous, was silent.

Harry cried for a while, looked at a photo of Alice sitting in the small wooden boat.

The search parties had only found a handful of splinters and a torn jacket.

He held the photo against his face. Tears ran into his mouth. They tasted of the sea.

There was a slow, clumsy knock on the front door.

He wiped his eyes.

He lit a candle and went to the door.

A human shape was dark and ragged through the frosted glass, backlit by moonlight.

Harry opened the door.

She said nothing. Her face was lost to shadow. Crawling things laboured under epidermal folds. Wet mandibles clicked, bone against bone.

She held out her hand for him.

"You came back for me."

He took her hand. The cool scrape of her wedding ring against his.

The roar of the sea was all he could hear now. Waves breaking on rocks. Ships lost to ocean trenches. A million lives taken, but now returned.

Those deep fathoms.

THE STAGGERING BOY

by Douglas Ford

Belinda noticed the staggering boy first, and the sight of him worried her enough to make her come over and nudge me away from my book. "I think he's *re-tarded*," she whispered to me, taking care to enunciate those last syllables so I would hear. She knew to respect the power of certain words, to give them their due, but also not to say them too loudly.

I looked up from my book and squinted to where she pointed—beyond the swing-set and rock wall to the outskirts of the playground, and I could see why she would think so. The boy showed signs of some crippling defects—one arm bent at the elbow with an upraised wrist ending in a twisted claw of a hand. The fingers did not look right, some probably missing or only partially formed, and he dragged his left leg, the ankle bent in such a way that it looked broken, if not outright deformed. His mouth hung open, and I knew that I would only need to get closer to see long strands of drool running down his lips.

We watched him together. I could feel Belinda's hand on my lower back, the perspiration from my shirt soaking through to my skin. At first, I thought she did so to feel my presence, but now I suspect she wanted to reassure me somehow. I thought, *yes, probably retarded* but had enough fatherly wits to caution her from making judgments. "Maybe his brain works fine. It could just be his body." And before I could stop myself, I added, "He must be a cripple."

"We don't say *that*," Belinda said.

I regarded her gleaming blond curls. "No," I said, "you're right."

"I should go over to him," she said. "Maybe he doesn't have anyone to play with."

Across the playground, children squealed and screamed, the sound of a fall weekend in Vissaria County, and the staggering boy remained alone. I gave a gentle squeeze to my daughter's arm. She preferred this form of approval to hugs. "I think that would be great," I said.

From my bench, my book in my lap, I watched as Belinda crossed the playground, purposefully ignoring the calls of the others to join her in tag or war, approaching the far point of the playground where the staggering boy had stopped and dropped, painfully it looked, to the knee of his good leg. He seemed to dig at something in the dirt. With his hand he scooped forth something clumped and writhing. Belinda approached him and stood with her back to me, watching. I imagined her lip turning up as the staggering boy put the writhing clump into his mouth.

When she came back, I pretended not to have seen what she reported. "Worms," she said, confirming my suspicions.

"He's eating worms? You know what they say about boys. They all do."

She shook her head. "He's covered in worms. Tiny, wiggly, white worms."

We both watched the boy reach down and pull forth another clump.

"He's sick," I said. "You should probably stay away."

"Who brought him here?" she said.

We scanned the playground. We looked for someone who could take charge of the staggering boy. Because it would not be me.

The wind had picked up. It carried a strange, dank smell.

"Where's his mom?" Belinda said.

A part of me flinched at that. She lived with *father*, not *mother*. Did she imagine that others asked the same question about her? *Where's her mom?* The playground had started to thin because of the rising wind, or the staggering boy, or perhaps both. Few parents remained, only kids, the kind I imagined with alcoholic parents at home, oblivious to their whereabouts. The kind who scrawled profanity on climbing surfaces and exposed themselves to each other under the slide. Why did I bring Belinda here?

Belinda said, "Maybe he's got a brother here—someone who's supposed to look out for him. He shouldn't have all those worms."

"He's probably alone," I said.

We heard laughter come from behind the rock tower. "Are they hiding?" I said.

"From you," Belinda said. "They were talking about it before. They're pretending you're a terrorist. They're plotting."

"Why me?"

She shrugged. "I want to ask if they know where the boy lives." And she walked toward the rock tower.

I almost stopped her, but instead I looked back in the direction of the staggering boy.

But he no longer scooped writhing masses of dirt. He wasn't doing anything I could see. He'd done what I'd hoped he'd do all along: gone away, hobbled back to whatever institution he called home, probably some underfunded hospital that granted him a modicum of freedom. Don't just sit here and wait to die, they'd said to him. Go get some sun. Play with some other children. Would he try to join the others behind the rock wall, stagger over while leaving puddles of drool and maggots behind him? Could he be the source of the laughter I heard, the miscreants behind the rock wall picking the maggots off of his body and forcing him to eat them for their entertainment?

But it had gone quiet. When Belinda returned, she had blood on her shirt, her hand curled into a fist under it. I thought I saw tears, but I realized she was holding those back with fury. Before I could ask about the blood, she said through grinding teeth, "They bit me."

I looked at her hand, saw the teeth marks.

"Who bit you? The retarded boy?"

I followed her eyes to the rock wall.

"I never want to go here again," she said.

"Neither do I," I said.

"I showed him though."

"What do you mean?"

But she stopped talking, and the laughter behind the rock wall had stopped, giving way to a silence that kept me from going there. Instead, I took her back home, washed the wounds on her hand before I began looking for the others. I found those and cleaned them too. I felt her skin begin to become cold, impossibly cold, so I helped her undress, and only then did I find what she had in her pocket.

The curl of flesh that looked like a misshapen finger, torn or rotted off. Most likely, I knew, bitten.

I opened the door and threw it outside, pausing to feel the wind as it continued to pick up. That strange, dank smell had followed us home. Inside, I listened to it howl as I drew her the hot bath she would stagger to without my help, and I would use it to keep the cold away, even though I knew I could not.

GRAVEYARD SLOT

by Christopher Keelty

Richie's TV was on the fritz, and Mom was parked in the living room watching her *American Idol* or *The Apprentice* or *So You Think You Can Castrate a Dachshund* or some other bullshit. He had to pull the old Magnavox from the back closet of the basement, its plastic belly bulging with tubes and capacitors. It was hidden behind three dusty boxes of old magazines that Richie relocated, swearing under his breath. When he wrapped his arms around the Magnavox, strands of sticky spider web clung to his hands like a mummy's wrappings. They tore free with a sound like Velcro, and Richie swore he felt hairy legs scramble across the backs of his fingers.

Carrying the beast up the basement stairs was out of the question, so Richie set it on a plastic milk crate and cleared off the basement sofa. The thing smelled like an old sneaker full of potting soil. At some point Mom had hopes for the basement, which she referred to as the "rec room," but the fourth time it flooded, it became a repository for the dreams Mom had given up on: boxes of skinny jeans that would never fit again, toys left from Richie's childhood, reserved for the day he produced a grandchild, and a museum-quality archive of twenty-first century fad exercise products.

After attempting at least seven different configurations, Richie gave up connecting his DVD player to the Magnavox. There was no cable or antenna, either. Over-the-air broadcast had gone digital, in accordance with federal regulations, rendering the Magnavox as useful for watching television as a microwave. Richie could hear Mom upstairs, rocking with laughter at something on the HD screen. Digging through the shelves where the Magnavox was interred, he exhumed his Panasonic VCR and three shoe boxes of VHS cassettes.

These were the tapes he couldn't bring himself to throw out when he mothballed the player. Among them were movies, or alternate versions of movies, too obscure or unpopular to get a DVD release, like the pre-rerelease *Star Wars* where Han shot first, or stuff he'd taped off television, like the original *The Stand* miniseries or the TV edit of *Blade Runner* with extra footage and an alternate ending. There were bootlegs, their images blurry and dull from copying and recopying: the four-hour rough cut of *Brain Candy*, the subtitled and uncensored edition of *Battle Royale*, and the copy of *Meet the Feebles* he'd worked to obtain back when the movie wasn't available in the US. These were treasures, or had been once, and while they may have lost their currency, Richie held to them like gold doubloons.

On one tape he found five classic episodes of *The Simpsons*, and two of *The X-Files*, taped off the air with the commercials paused out. Back in high school, he and his friends would trade tapes they'd recorded, trying to show each other up by finding the most obscure, sought-after material, but most of his friends had lost interest in underground movies when they discovered booze and sex and money. Only Richie and Phil—who worked the late shift at the Video X-Press—kept the dream alive.

As the night crept into the wee hours, the time TV networks referred to as "the graveyard slot" and filled with infomercials and public-interest programming, Mom moved from her assprint on the sofa to her assprint on the bed. Richie was too tired to move upstairs. He lay on the sofa, an open two-liter of Pepsi and a half-eaten package of Keebler cookies within arm's reach, while John Carpenter's remake of *The Thing* unspooled across the Magnavox. It was, in Richie's estimation, one of the finest horror films ever made, but the slow-thrum bass score and early-80s pace were better than a sleeping pill at that hour.

Richie slept through the end of the movie, and the whir of the automatic re-wind, but he snapped awake around 3:15, his mouth parched and sticky from the soda and the basement air. It was the moaning that woke him. The moaning, and the plaintive soft shuffling of slow feet.

On screen, a crowd of slow zombies dressed in tattered funeral rags slumped their way down a small-town Main Street. The image was black and white, fuzzy and darkened around the edges like a kinescope recording. It popped and fuzzed with broadcast static, and Richie took it for *Night of the Living Dead*, a Midnight Movie staple, until he remembered there was no more Midnight Movie, at least not that the Magnavox could pick up. Was there something else on the videotape? No, the black plastic tongue of *The Thing* protruded from the VCR's mouth, automatically ejected after being rewound. This was something else.

Richie blinked and squeezed his eyes to clear away his grogginess. The image was strange—there was no camera movement and no editing, just one steady shot, elevated as if from a crane, of the undead mob. The production values were totally wrong for the black and white era. Romero's *Living Dead* had been light on the grue. Those first seminal zombies were basically ordinary people with pale make-up and a few wounds and scabs. These were state-of-the-art. Their skin sloughed off in greasy slabs, exposing stubs of bone that dripped putrefying black slime. Their eyes were bright and harsh, eyelids drawn and crumpled, the way their lips peeled back from brown teeth and jaws.

Richie knew every zombie movie ever made. There were a few he hadn't seen, sure, but at least he knew *of* them. This was no 80's Italian flick, no Fulci or Argento. It wasn't a J-Horror, which rarely made use of the Western zombie. It wasn't Tom Savini, Dan O'Bannon, or any of the recent zombie masters, Danny Boyle or Zack Snyder or Edgar Wright. Perhaps it was something new, some retro homage to Romero's classic, but that couldn't have flown under Richie's radar. Not with production values like this. Not when Phil still read *Fangoria* cover to cover and frequented every horror message board on the web.

Richie thought about calling Phil, but Phil still lived at home and didn't have a cell phone. His parents wouldn't take kindly to Richie phoning at quarter to four in the morning. It dawned on Richie that he had the VCR connected. He shuffled through his tapes for a minute, settled on taping over *The Simpsons*, which was after all available on DVD, and popped the tape in. The moment the heads settled into place, however, the image went dead. It left behind a blank black screen that buzzed almost inaudibly with the electric charge of cathode rays. After a moment the static kicked in.

Richie was dying to call Phil, but he wanted to speak in person, so he forced himself to wait, chewing his fingernails as if he were the one hungering for human flesh, until 7 PM when Phil's shift began. This meant several hours at home with Mom, who spent the time in her spot on the sofa dressed in pink sweatpants and a Mickey Mouse sweatshirt, watching TV and eating. There was one uncomfortable exchange, when they both happened to visit the kitchen at the same time, during which Mom asked, as she always did, whether Richie was looking for a job.

Finally, 7 PM arrived and Richie raced to the Video X-Press. Bianca was there with Phil, leaning on the counter and sticking out her ass in her ripped-up jeans. How Phil, twenty-nine years old with the pimpled complexion of a fourteen-year-old and still living with his parents and a collection of Star Wars action figures, managed to keep a girlfriend like Bianca, Richie would never know. He must have a cock that needed to be strapped down, Richie thought. Bianca was no bimbo, either. She knew movies, she knew comics, and she knew gaming. Richie would never admit it, but he avoided discussions of Manga when Bianca was around, afraid she might make him look stupid.

Video X-Press was the last real video store in town, holding out even after the Blockbuster was replaced with a blue-and-gold kiosk near the grocery store checkout. The X survived thanks to its elderly customers, who hadn't adopted the new technology, and to its extensive collection of VHS pornography. The back room of the X was at least as large as the rest of the store, its shelves jammed with white plastic cases that would probably light up like a dance club if someone ever brought in one of those CSI jizz black-lights.

To accommodate the customers who kept it in business, the X was open until 2 AM, except Sundays, when they closed at 11. Phil closed most nights, and since money was tight, he was left alone with the security cameras. The store got quiet after eight, and often served as a late night hang-out for Phil, Richie, and Bianca. The only customers were single men who moved straight to the back room with no chit-chat.

"I love how they don't even make eye contact," Bianca said. Making fun of the masturbators was a frequent pastime, but it never got old.

"Sometimes I make it a game," said Phil. "I stare hard, the whole time they're at the counter, and see if they even look up once. Most don't."

"We should get a stopwatch and time how long it takes them to return their videos," Bianca suggested with a smile.

"One guy came back ten minutes later," Richie said. "I swear. He rented like three videos, too."

"Christ, I hope he washed his hands!" Bianca kicked her feet as she laughed.

"That's not the worst, though," Richie told her. "What about when they're back there for like an hour, and then leave without renting anything?"

Bianca shrieked and clapped both hands to her mouth. "Ohmygod, no!"

"It's not funny," said Phil. "I've had to clean up after a few guys. I shit you not. Why do you think I always restock when some teenager slips back there alone?"

"I always figured you were hoping to see his boner," said Richie.

Richie had waited all day to tell Phil about the previous night, but now found himself sheepish. Maybe it was Bianca's presence, but he'd also begun to realize how crazy it sounded. He'd found a secret channel broadcasting underground zombie movies in the middle of the night. They'd say he'd dreamt it. That's exactly what Phil did say, when Richie finally forced the story out.

"I wasn't dreaming," Richie said. "I stayed awake for like an hour afterward, flipping channels and trying to find that station again, but it was just static."

"Of course it was just static," Phil said. "There's no more analog broadcast. Nothing that TV could pick up. Either you were dreaming, or it was something on the end of that tape that you forgot you had."

Bianca was sitting on the counter, sipping a Diet Cherry Coke through one of the twisty-straws from the bin next to the popcorn and kiddie movies. "What about a pirate signal?" she said. "I've heard of pirate radio, why not TV?"

"Do you have any idea what kind of equipment you'd need?" Phil asked.

"Besides," Richie added, "this wasn't some low-budg homebrew flick. These were top-rate effects, and with the number of people in the shot you're talking serious production cost. Hell, just getting that big a cast together would have gotten noticed. They'd have to close down a street, set up a crane. No, this was serious, not some college filmmaker."

"Could it be a network thing?" Bianca asked. "Maybe they were calibrating equipment in the wee hours? Or somebody at a local affiliate having a little fun, turning the old equipment back on?"

Richie shook his head. "I'd have recognized the movie."

"There's ten million zombie movies," said Bianca. "How do you know it wasn't some old one?"

Phil and Richie just stared at her, as if they didn't understand the question. After a beat, Phil raised his arms in gesture to their surroundings. "What do you think we do all day?" the gesture asked.

"It wouldn't hurt to ask around," Richie said. "I suppose it's not crazy to think we could overlook one zombie flick. Someone will recognize it. Old school film, black and white, but top-notch effects, and somewhere in it is one long shot of a zombie mob crowding a suburban street."

"I can't think of anything," Phil said. "But there's plenty of people shooting vintage stuff these days, using eight millimeter and stuff. I'll run it up the message boards and see if anyone bites. If you see it again, try pressing record instead of sitting there being dumb."

Richie tried just that. He spent the next night in the basement, flipping channels in a vain attempt to find the signal. It was mind-numbing, spending hours watching static, so he brought his laptop downstairs and tried a few message boards and search engines. There were dozens of fan sites dedicated to reviewing old vintage movies, even the terrible type that wound up on MST3K, but none of the summaries or still images matched what he'd seen, not even close. He found a few online casting notices for amateur zombie flicks, but they were strictly no-budget affairs. "MUST PROVIDE OWN MAKEUP/OWN WARDROBE," they all said. There was no way any production relying on actors for their own makeup and wardrobe was getting the kinds of results he'd seen.

He searched the next night, and the night after that, pushing himself to stay up later in hope that he might find something, but it was all just static and snow. Phil started playing the store's zombie movies on the closed circuit system, in alphabetical order, keeping an eye out for even a single scene that matched Richie's description. He called around to other video stores to ask about their inventory, wondering if some elusive movie had escaped their notice. He confessed to Richie that he'd set up an old TV and antenna and stayed up flipping through channels.

"Tried every UHF frequency," he said. "Bupkis."

Bianca was getting annoyed with both of them. She'd never been a fan of zombie movies, and she was bored to anger with Phil's unofficial Video X-Press film festival. When Richie came to the store she left soon after, muttering about his and Phil's new obsession.

Richie gave up watching hours of static. He began to spend his nights watching VHS movies, spinning around the dial as each tape rewound. He got used to sleeping on the musty couch. Mom complained that he smelled pretty mildewed himself, but he told her he was considerate enough not to mention what she smelled like. She asked when he was getting a job.

One night, after he'd fallen asleep to *Scanners* for the third time, Richie awakened to a familiar sound of moaning. Before he'd shaken off sleep, he was stumbling to the VCR to switch the tape and press record. His heart leapt at the sound of the reels turning, the magnetic heads engaging. Finally he could show Phil and Bianca that he wasn't crazy! Then the sleep wore off enough that he noticed what he was taping.

It was the same angle, the same crowd of zombies, but they'd changed. For one thing, the quality was much better. This didn't look like some 1950s kinescope. It looked like TV from the 70s or 80s, like an episode of *MacGyver* or *Sledgehammer*, clearer and crisper and in color. He could see the exact shades of zombified flesh, green and gray and yellow like a blister about to burst, and the purplish black of the ichor that oozed from nostrils and beneath fingernails. Worst of all, he could see the vivid blues and greens of their sunken eyes which, despite their state of decay, were very much alive.

The broadcast quality wasn't all that had changed. Last time, the zombies had done little more than shuffle down the street. Now, they'd found prey, and descended into mass chaos. There were living people among the crowd, their limbs flailing as the zombies surrounded them like wild dogs. Grabbing with rotten limbs, the undead tore the living into scraps, stretching their torsos taut before perforating the flesh with grime-encrusted claws, spilling hot entrails onto the pavement. Blood was everywhere. They smeared themselves with it like oil wrestlers. They crammed tattered flesh and slippery organs into their mouths, tilting back their heads and swallowing in jerking gulps like waterfowl. This went on, the supply of victims seeming endless, until the creatures began to swell, and then to burst, their putrefied bodies too fragile to contain their gluttony. Whole body parts spilled from their ruptured guts, sticky and slick with blackened undead humours.

Richie made sure the VCR was recording. This was incredible—one long shot, with no cutaways or visible special effects. The butchery on screen couldn't be achieved with trick floors, fake limbs on amputees, latex dummies with air bladders, animatronics, or any other trick he knew. CGI had come a long way, but if this was CGI, it was the CGI *War and Peace*. Richie felt nauseous. He couldn't conceive how any filmmaker could achieve this in a single shot. He couldn't wait to show Phil.

Then he noticed him, in the middle distance, easily recognizable by his black-framed glasses, greasy hair, and pale pimply complexion. Phil was in the movie. He was being eaten.

Richie sniffed in betrayal. So Phil had known all along. He was so full of shit. He'd figured out where the signal originated, and kept it to himself so he could go be part of the action. Gnarled, blood-stained hands reached into Phil's abdomen and tugged, fighting against the rope-like strands of his guts. At least now there would be an explanation, Richie thought. Tomorrow Phil wouldn't be able to keep the shit-eating grin off his face.

Except there was something strange about the way Phil stared into the camera, and the way his mouth moved, the same pattern over and over again. There was no sound—the moaning had died away at some point, and the video gone silent—but Richie cocked his head as he studied Phil's face. That horrified grimace kept spreading the same way, forming one short vowel, and one long

Richie felt a chill when he realized what it was. Phil was staring straight down the barrel at the face of the friend he hoped was watching, and he was screaming Richie's name.

The signal cut to static.

Richie didn't sleep. He considered calling Phil's house, even if it was two hours before sunrise, but there was still a good chance Phil had staged an elaborate prank, and Richie would only look worse if he made a panicked late-night call. He rewound the tape and watched it twice to be sure of what he'd seen. Phil appeared on screen a few moments before Richie first noticed him. He emerged into the zombie mob from some indeterminate point, looking around confused for a moment before the hands and teeth found him. At that point his eyes searched until they found the camera, and he commenced his desperate screams for help. It looked incredibly real.

It wasn't real, Richie told himself. It couldn't be. Phil was just an incredible asshole.

He phoned Bianca at eight. Unlike Richie and Phil, she had a day job—a long-term temp gig in the office of a an old folks' home—and had to be up during normal human hours. It went to voicemail. Richie tried her twice more before noon, at which point his own phone rang, and Bianca's irritated voice greeted him.

"You've been blowing up my phone all morning," she said. "I didn't think you ever got up before one."

Richie told her what he'd seen. In hindsight, his tone was probably more dire than he intended. Going sleepless for twenty-four hours, six of them spent alone watching and re-watching his friend being devoured, had that effect The longer he sat awake, isolated in those hours between night-owl and early bird when no one was awake but the insomniacs, the more his brain convinced him that what he'd seen was real.

"You're being fucking ridiculous," Bianca said. "I saw Richie last night before I went to bed, and for once he didn't say anything about any zombie movie. Call him yourself, and stop being such a pussy about his parents."

"You're right, he's probably just messing with me," Richie said. "I'm sure it's nothing."

"He's not messing with you, he's not anything." Bianca said. "You sound completely exhausted, and your mind is playing tricks on you. Think about it. There's no sound, and you said yourself it's not an HD screen. You probably saw some actor who looked like Phil, and your brain took it from there."

"You're right," Richie said. "Thanks."

"Don't call me again," Bianca said. "I already have one nerd boyfriend, I'm not looking for another one."

Richie took her advice and called Phil's house. While he did that, he played back the tape and paused it when Phil—or the actor who looked a lot like Phil—came into view. Recorded on an old VHS tape and paused, the image did suffer, but the Magnavox had a big enough screen, and damned if that didn't look exactly like Phil.

Phil's mother answered. She had her own special tone of voice for when Richie called, something between "Of course you would be calling in the middle of the afternoon," and "You're the reason my son is still living at home and working nights at a video store." She told Richie she hadn't seen Phil. She didn't think he'd come home after work last night, and he wasn't at home now. She suggested he call Bianca.

Richie did, leaving three more voicemails. He thought it would be best, he said, if they spoke in person when she got off work. Maybe they could meet at the X.

On the glassy screen of the Magnavox, Phil's mouth was frozen on the long second syllable of Richie's name. Upstairs, Mom shouted at the TV.

It was dangerous to keep a VHS cassette paused too long. It put tension on the tape itself, and if the tape ripped there was no easy way to fix it. Richie had to make sure that tape survived, at least long enough to play it for Bianca. Except when she met him that night outside the X, she had no interest in the tape.

"You look horrible," she said. Richie was slumped against the brick of the X's strip mall exterior when she pulled up in her Honda.

"You look nice," he said, quite honestly. She'd come straight from work and for once, Richie thought, she wasn't dressed like a comic book fanboy's wet dream. She looked like a grown up, or at least like an actress in one of those office-romance pornos. The X stocked a bunch of those, though they weren't especially popular with the masturbators.

"I mean it, Richie. Have you slept at all?"

"Not in about 36 hours, and not much for the past few weeks. I finally got the tape I wanted—but it's not what I was expecting." He held out the videocassette, but she drew back like he was offering a hot dog bun stuffed with hot coals.

"I'm not watching that," she said.

"But Phil—"

"It isn't Phil." Bianca wore a sneer of irritation, but something in Richie's expression softened her expression. He realized, witnessing that change, how pathetic he must seem. "Phil's mom told me you called. I know what you're thinking, and you've got to get a grip. Maybe he is fucking with you. Maybe he's fucking with both of us. Or maybe he just got a whim to take a drive somewhere. I'm not sure. The one thing I am sure of? He wasn't fucking eaten by zombies."

Richie offered the tape again, begging silently with his posture. Bianca smiled slightly as she shook her head.

"Go home and watch something else, Richie." She picked up a pack of cigarettes and tucked one between her lips, squinting at him as she started up her engine again. "Put on some cartoons. *My Little Pony* or *She-Ra* or something. Sit with your mom and watch *American Idol*. Just no zombies. You need to chill out—and get some sleep."

As Bianca pulled away, Richie held up a hand to stop her. He meant to ask her, if she talked to Phil, to have him give Richie a call. But she drove away.

When he got home, Mom was watching *Maury*. It was the wrong time of day, but she kept a backlog of episodes on DVR in case the only thing on was the news. Mom hated the news, which she only ever called "the Bad News." Richie considered Bianca's advice. There was room on the couch next to Mom, and they were just getting to the part where Maury announced the results of the paternity test, and either way a fight would break out. Mom's fingers squeezed the remote control in white-knuckled anticipation. Richie frowned and headed for the basement.

He set the video of Phil—or Phil's doppelganger—on top of the Magnavox and rooted through the boxes of tapes for something cheery. There were more *Simpsons* episodes, but he'd already watched them three times each during his hours searching the static. There was some *Aqua Teen Hunger Force*, but that reminded him of nights watching Cartoon Network with Phil, and a stone of worry settled in his belly. He settled on *Bad Taste*, which wasn't exactly cheerful, but at least it made him laugh. Forty minutes in, he had to switch it. Yes, it was aliens instead of zombies, but a movie with cannibal themes was still a bad idea.

Richie tried *The Big Lebowski*. Like most of his friends, Richie could quote a good portion of the movie verbatim, and it was one of the few he owned both on DVD and on VHS. He just hadn't been able to bear throwing the VHS out. A few of them had talked about a road trip to Lebowskifest, but that was back in the good days before everybody got girlfriends and jobs and apartments and was suddenly too busy to stay up watching B movies.

Lebowski turned out to be the perfect choice. Just when the Dude was explaining to Walter and Donny how his peed-upon rug had really tied the room together, Richie fell into an easy, undisturbed slumber.

He woke up to the click-thunk of the auto-eject. The TV showed static. Richie turned over on the sofa to go back to sleep, but the long shadows thrown by the light of the tube nagged at him. His mother used to call that static "ant races," because it looked like a million black ants on a white background. Digital TVs didn't show ant races. When they weren't getting a strong enough signal, they just went dark, or showed a flat blue screen. When Richie was around fourteen, he and Phil stayed up with the volume down low, flipping through channel after channel of static because they heard sometimes the scrambling on the pay-per-view porn channels wasn't so good and maybe you could see a set of tits, or even a pussy. He and Phil never saw anything, but Richie had jerked it once or twice, home alone, to ant races that he'd convinced himself were really naked porno babes.

The same way he convinced himself some actor was his friend Phil, Richie thought. He looked at the tape, resting atop the Magnavox. Richie stood absently and went to the TV, then started flipping through channels on the VCR. Static. Static. Static. Click, click, click. He frowned and looked at the box of cassettes on the floor beside him, and that's when he heard it.

The moaning started quiet, so quiet he could hear the dragging wet feet, and the soft sound of rotten flesh in motion, like someone squeezing a sandwich bag full of jelly. When Richie looked up, it got louder fast.

They were back, the whole horde of them, and they were clearer and more vivid than ever. Richie would have sworn he was looking at an HD screen. There seemed to be hundreds, pressed together on that familiar street. The sidewalks and gutters were red now, as red and clotted as the runnels of a decades-old abattoir. Within the burgundy muck were amorphous black blobs, some of them clumps of hair, some hunks of chewed bone or organ gristle. Others he had no hope of identifying. The zombies picked up objects from the gutters, worrying at them with loose teeth before tossing them away. One, near the edge of the screen, found a live rat in the storm gutter and tore into it, spilling wet pink entrails down its gray chin. The rat squealed in frenzied agony and tried to squirm away, twisting and biting at the gray face of its attacker even as it was being eaten alive. The zombie took an intestine in its teeth and yanked the rat away, drawing those guts out like a strand of elastic pink bubble gum. The other zombies fell upon their companion as if it were another victim.

Richie felt his gorge rise, but he studied the screen with intensity, looking for some sign of Phil. Would he resume his grand performance from the night before? Perhaps tonight he'd be in zombie makeup himself. Richie leaned in so close he felt electricity tickle the fine hairs on his face.

It was one of the zombies near the back who moved first, raising his eyes as if noticing the camera for the first time. His mouth fell open in a groan, and he raised a skeletal finger. He was pointing straight at Richie.

This is new, Richie thought. *Breaking the fourth wall. Overdone, but creepy.*

The others took notice, too. One by one they raised their gazes, until every one of them was staring at him. Richie first felt a chill, and then a sense of panic. Their moaning grew still more, until it seemed no longer to originate from the television, but from all around. Richie scanned the basement, expecting to find living corpses advancing on him, but he was alone. Still the moaning grew. He killed the power on the TV. The image vanished, but the moaning continued. Richie yanked the power cord. As he expected, it did nothing.

They were outside. He heard the drag of feet outside the hopper windows. Their putridity slithered through every crack in the foundation. Richie ran upstairs, where Mom was parked on the sofa, dreaming in front of the late-night infomercial that had replaced whatever program she fell asleep on. Richie shook her. She swatted at him like he was a dream. Couldn't she hear the moaning? It was deafening, Richie thought, so loud it might have been inside his skull. Loud enough to wake the dead.

Richie grabbed his keys. The car, he thought. He had to make it to the car. He could drive away, drive until the horrible moaning was behind him. He could go to a place where they had no TV, and no VCRs. He'd live with the Eskimos if he had to—and if he had to, if it was necessary to make a life where there were no zombies on late-night TV, he would get a job.

Richie threw open the front door, ready to make a dash to the car, but they were on him immediately. Their gaunt hands, flesh falling away from the fingers like snow melting from branches, were astoundingly strong. Finger bones sunk into the flesh of his shoulders like hooks, pulling him through the open door even as he resisted. The smell of them was an assault, unimaginable in its offensiveness.

They dragged him off his feet and tore at him, ripping his clothes and his flesh with equal ease. Richie saw his own stomach laid open, his intestines vomiting forth like a cluster of slimy, fat earthworms. The pain was incredible, but he was too shocked, too lightheaded, to scream. As they pulled out his insides and began to eat him, Richie was dimly aware of his mother, in her spot on the sofa, cackling at something on the TV.

FERALS LIKE YOU

by Cheryl Elaine Williams

Okay, I had our IDs, my keys, my purse and five hundred dollars in bribe money in case we got stopped on the road. We had safety in numbers since all three of us were going out together. I was driver, my son would ride shotgun beside me in the four wheel drive, and my daughter would sit in the back, ready to pull out the tire iron from under the seat if we needed to bash a jumper.

All this for the weekly trip to the Big Box Store. What a time we live in, right?

I paused at the doorway to our garage and took stock of my team. "You all look scruffier than usual," I complimented them. "This is good."

"Tryin' to." Logan slipped into his leather duster with the knife slashes in the front. He looked every inch the rugged seventeen-year-old I'd raised to kick zombie ass. I watched with approval as he retrieved his semi-automatic pistol from the hat box in our hall closet. Then he checked to see that it was loaded.

"Got my banger, ready to go," he said, caressing the piece with pride. His Dad would've been proud of him, the thought hit me. The way he'd stepped into being a steady protector of his sister and me without being pushed to do so. I was positively touched.

"Uh, Mom," he said as an afterthought. "We're low on ammo. Can you handle that or should I go in with you all?"

"Best you stay with our wheels. Write down what you need." I handed him my shopping list and a pen. "Make it clear so I can show it to the clerk. You know I don't know guns and all." He scribbled the info down while Rena, my youngest child, checked herself out in the hall mirror. The sixteen-year-old posed in profile, then swirled to see how her butt looked. She growled in frustration as she pulled her blouson out of her jeans, then tucked it back in again.

"These clothes make me look fat," she grumbled to no one in particular.

"Don't blame the clothes," Logan taunted her. "You can't stay away from sticky buns."

"Shut up. You're mean." She flounced the shoulder pads so the material set-tled in a manner that accentuated her boobs. "Mom, these clothes don't fall right. Why do we have to wear rags, anyway?"

"So no one thinks we have money," I answered her as I zipped up my cheap hoodie. "So no one jumps us on the road. We don't want them breaking into the house while we're gone because they think we have stuff they don't."

Rena's snort told me what she thought of my logic, but I knew I was right. These days, everybody dressed down so they wouldn't make themselves a target. You had to. People in our area were living on the poverty line because the zombie crisis tanked our economy. It just wasn't safe to look prosperous. Or to appear anything but ordinary.

And so I led my very ordinary family into the garage to climb into our old SUV. Damn, I reflected, but it was hard these days to raise my kids anything close to normal. It was sad to think they'd never enjoy the same kind of life I knew growing up. Not when zombie spawn roamed the area. Just today, the morning news had reported a roamer this side of the city, in our southern suburbs. The location was three miles distant, but that was still too close to let our guard down. Those loner ones, the stragglers, reminded me of hungry deer and raccoons that sometimes hit our garbage cans.

All wild things knew where food could be found.

"Come on, beauty queen," I said, holding the car door open for Rena to slide into the back seat. She balked at this and shot a disgusted look at her brother.

"Why can't I ride shotgun like him?" Rena pouted as Logan took the front passenger seat. "Why is *he* the only one to be protector?"

"Because your brother's had training." I kept my voice steady but firm. "And he's caretaker of Daddy's gun. We all agreed on that. He has the permit."

Rena's eyes flashed defiance. "But I know how to shoot. Ugly let me try it once. When we visited Grandpa's farm."

"Shut up about that," her brother snapped back. "You'll get me in trouble."

"I'm not hearing nice things," I reminded them both, slipping behind the wheel. "Words can be as cruel as bullets."

"You could let me be protector for one day," Rena growled. "What's the big whoop anyway?"

"If you don't get in now, I'll leave you behind." I tapped my fingers on the wheel, waiting. Rena stuck her tongue out, hopefully not at me but at the world, and slid into the back. I hit the garage door opener and the door behind us slid upwards, bathing us in midmorning light.

"Reenie, honey," I reminded her, "You're as much my protector as your broth-er is. You have the tire iron back there. That's a skill in itself. You're watching our back."

"Not the same thing as firing lead," Rena insisted, but I shushed her.

"Your time will come, honey." I turned the engine over and backed down our driveway into the street. Logan beside me stayed alert, looking left and right for any jumpers who might smash into our windows. That happened to my neighbor six months ago, so we always stayed alert for a reoccurrence. When all seemed calm, Logan settled his semi-automatic pistol in its secure holding space on the dash. Ready for use if needed.

"Reenie," I said, "Monday at school, you can ask them to get you a learning permit. So you can take weapons training."

"You gotta write her a note, Mom," Logan mumbled from the seat beside me. "They won't do nothin' without a note."

"A note? I didn't write you a note."

Logan gave me a pained look before answering. "Dad wrote it."

"Oh. Guess he did." I brushed over that real quick. "We'll talk about it when we get home. You can tell me what to write."

"I can do that," Logan offered. Sometimes he was just the sweetest young man. And he had a bright future ahead of him, too. Having that weapons proficiency certificate would give real meaning to the high school diploma he was going to get next June. My son was well on his way to graduating into a profitable security muscle job, that is if he continued his physical conditioning at the same level the school had him doing now.

Rena's future I saw as more sedentary. I was trying to interest her in working from home via computer like I did. She chafed at that idea, but I was secretly hoping she'd want to follow my example and work online, instead of heading out into the big world with all its dangers.

But the three of us had time to make all those decisions later. Right now our major concern was a shopping trip to get food on the table.

"Reenie," I said as we drove through our housing plan, "there's nobody I'd rather have with me in the store than you, girl. I feel safe with you there."

"Yeah, you need me to push the shopping cart." Rena's tone dripped boredom.

"The cart's a weapon. Our first line of defense if someone lunges." My voice sounded testy to my ears so I forced myself to be pleasant. "You have strong arms on you. One push, you can do a lot of damage with that cart. Honestly, I'm depending on you, Reen. I can't watch everything all around me, all the time."

Logan twisted in his seat to look back at her. "Ram 'em in the knees. Go for the legs, that drops 'em fast."

"Listen to your brother." I grinned sideways at my boy. "Tell her, Loge."

"Yeah, all that metal, you can do some good bashing." Logan demonstrated with his hands. "Run those wheels over their ankles. You break a bone and they're staggering."

"Yuck." Rena make a choking sound from the back seat.

"There's lots of tender bones in the top of your feet," Logan went on, his voice bubbling with enthusiasm. "They'll be screaming if you catch 'em there. You luck out if all they got is walking shoes on. Good place to stomp, too."

"Stop, already." Rena slapped her hands over her ears, I could see in the overhead mirror. "I don't wanna stomp nobody."

"What, you'd rather shoot them?" Logan asked.

"Well, I wouldn't have to get close to them that way."

"What if they get close to you? You do what you have to," Logan reminded her. "Y'know, you don't have it in you to be a shooter."

"You're a loser," Rena shot back. Logan ignored this and leaned forward to play with the radio. A bulletin came on, reporting more eyewitness accounts about that morning's zombie sighting in the neighboring township.

"The loner zombs are the worst," Rena said over the running commentary, and that got me to thinking about her Daddy and what happened to George not even two years ago. Fortunately for me, the guard shack on the hill came into view.

"Look sharp, everybody," I said. "Checkpoint's coming up."

Logan switched off the dial and settled back in his seat as quiet descended upon our vehicle. The road turned upward and we drove past a no man's land of junk cars and old stoves and refrigerators piled high as a barrier to outsiders. The checkpoint sat where our access road intersected the main drag. Homeowners in my plan paid monthly dues to maintain a 24/7 watch. I recognized the two women standing guard and smiled wide as I hit the window button.

"Hiya, Liane," the taller woman said to me. "Y'all have your ID's?"

"Hi, Mary. Sure do." I passed three cards through the window and my neighborhood friend noted all our names on her clipboard. Guard Two, who was an outsider sent by the cartel, leaned in to check my gas gauge.

"Mrs. Collins," she told me, "you're down to a quarter tank. You don't want to run low when you're out on the street."

"Thanks for reminding me," I said, according to the accepted formula of trade between us and our protectors. "Can you help me out with that?"

"Sure can." Guard Two strode off to the nearby shed and returned with a gas can. I passed the required fee out the window and waited for the fill-up. Guard One handed me back my ID cards and a security pass to show I had cartel approval to exit and later re-enter. Easy as anything, we were soon on our way.

"They don't do all that when the school bus comes," Rena commented. I had to laugh at that.

"The school district is a cartel all its own," I reminded my kids. "They get their cut through taxes." I drove through surprisingly crowded streets to Washington Plaza and the Big Box Store. It was tough finding a parking spot until a parking lot monitor waved me towards an empty space in the back.

As we got closer, I could see why it was empty. Two cops stood in that bare spot on a sea of broken glass, interviewing a van driver who gestured at her busted windows.

"They took everything," the woman wailed. "I was only gone ten minutes."

Logan turned in his seat to address Rena. "You see why I'm stayin' behind while you get to shop? I can handle the assholes."

"What, you think I'm wimpy dimpy?" Rena muttered insults under her breath while running a quick comb through her hair. Meanwhile we circled the lot looking for an open space.

"Bingo. There's one next to those vans," I crowed as we crossed into the far back lot behind the loading dock. "See them, those two monster vans?"

"I see. New stock must've come in." Rena unbuckled and hung over the divider between the front seats to get a better look. "The stores lie when they say they can't get new stuff in."

"They did today. It won't be unloaded yet, of course," I said. "But we can ask at the desk what came in." I recalled the extra bills I'd stuffed in my purse and in my clothes. Maybe I could slip someone a twenty to put aside a really hot item for us.

I threw Logan my keys and the daughter and I headed inside to shop. We were at the firearms and ammo counter when the wall alarms began buzzing and the overhead lights flashed on and off.

"Fuck almighty," Rena moaned.

"Lockdown," our clerk explained apologetically. "It happens sometimes. That means I gotta shut down here." She grabbed back the box of ammo she was showing us and locked it under the counter. "Sorry, Ma'am, Miss, you have to go to the wall."

Go to the wall? Another clerk rushed past us calling out the same instructions. "We're not done yet," I said, disappointed. "We need bread and milk."

"Ma'am, follow everyone else. It's regulations."

Okay, the daughter and I and our trusty cart merged into the flow of customers. Clerks wearing the store's official green jacket hustled us along. One shouted rather too close to my ear, "Walk along the walls and wait for further notice. They'll announce what to do from the speakers. Main thing, keep the aisles clear. Stay out of the center of the store. Go to the walls, everyone. Go to the walls."

Alright, we were walking along the wall and were about to get trampled. Too many people. Someone crunched my foot by accident. The person said, "Sorry," but I didn't turn around. Couldn't, in fact. My daughter's face had turned sickly pale so I touched her wrist to reassure her.

"Mom, I don't like this," she whimpered.

I didn't like this myself but we had to put a brave face on things. "Let's hang back," I whispered. I planted my hands on the cart beside her hands and together we slowed our pace. Others pushed past us, which was just what I wanted.

Someone shouted from that crowd surging along the wall, "They saw a zomb outside. A zomb!" The crowd had no way of knowing if that was true or not, but soon clerks in the familiar bright green smock of the store were standing at every aisle, shouting for us to go to the back of the store. "There's police at the back of the store waiting to help you."

Rena called out, "Are they gonna walk us to our cars?" Nobody could answer her, and so we allowed ourselves to be pushed onward and ever forward until the familiar 'Restrooms' sign became visible, the one that flashed orange lighting in the far back area of the facility. We could see that security guards were waving people into that long hallway that led past the restrooms. What lay beyond that I had no clue, but a woman ahead of me assured her companions, "They got the dock doors back there. That's where they do the loading and unloading."

I said to Rena, "We know that area from the outside. We parked near there today." My daughter gave a strained smile, mouth tight.

"It's like we're cattle," Rena complained, and I brought my finger to my lips, warning her to lower her voice.

"Don't start anything," I cautioned. "Don't add to all this mess."

"But, Mom. This is crazy." My daughter stopped walking at that point. I stopped too, and the frantic people around us pushed past our little bubble and around the shopping cart we both clung to for dear life. After a minute the rush had passed us by and we stood blinking at each other, confused.

I glanced over my shoulder. No store clerk in sight. "I have to sit down," I said. We were by the shoe aisles and there were little benches where you could sit down and try on shoes. I wheeled the cart down to the very end of that aisle and Rena kept pace with me. I pushed a shoebox off that bench and plopped myself down. My daughter sat by me and it occurred to me that we were more or less shielded there by the cart. Somebody was probably looking down at us from the ceiling, but it would take them time to get to us. For now, we were out of the line of vision for people on the floor.

After a minute, several store clerks did a sweep down the main aisle that intersected our aisle but they never looked our way.

Shielded by the angels, I thought. *I wish.* How long would this pocket of safety last?

A male voice boomed from the back of the store. The man's voice carried out with reasonable clarity to where we sat. No one bothered us because everyone apparently had congregated by then in that long hallway running past the restrooms to the dock doors.

"Citizens, my name is Sergeant Wilcox of your community police department," the man intoned over what I assumed was a loudspeaker of some kind. "I have asked you all to join me on this spot because of a safety issue. You can help me, and I can help you." A roar of questions went up and the man halted his talk. When he began speaking again, I caught only snatches due to the cacophony of voices.

"Because of the threat of infestation of rampaging elements, we are here to take you to safety."

Rena and I exchanged concerned glances. She whispered, "Is this about zombies?"

"I didn't hear zombies." I wasn't going to move until I heard the term zombie. Because if the rampaging infestation was human, I knew I could handle that myself. So could Logan sitting in our SUV with a banger and tire iron.

"We live and work together in this community," the police sergeant continued, "so you know your police department has your best interests at heart. As part of this effort, we have opened the dock doors where you can see two large vans we have trucked in to take you to safety. Two travel vans. We ask you to begin loading now."

Rena stared at me, wide-eyed. "Auschwitz."

"What?" I shook my head. "No, they wouldn't. This is just stupid stuff. Somebody's covering their asses."

"Mom, we studied this. They didn't always use trains. They used vans, too."

This was new to me. "Vans for what?"

"Gas vans. They packed them in vans and gassed them."

No way. My mind couldn't accept this. "Honey, those are just delivery vans. We're lucky they had them there. We're parked back there, you know. That's where we left Logan."

Rena leaned forward and grasped her knees. "We're gonna die and he'll get away. No fair."

My mind raced like crazy. "No, Reen, we're not going to die. There's an explanation for this."

One they didn't want us to know, a little voice in the back of my mind told me. That was when I began to get scared.

The police sergeant boomed out more instructions. "My friends, it's for your convenience. You're not safe here. We can't just let you walk out of here into danger. Not with zombies out there in the parking lot."

Rena mumbled, "There we go. They're blaming it on zombies."

Doubt tugged at my innards. My trust level went to zilch. I listened as the officer's voice interrupted all protests.

"Citizens, you see police presence here to provide for your safety. I ask you now to begin an orderly evacuation of the store. We want you to exit in a straight line and enter into van number one. Then we'll fill van number two. We plan to transport you to the Municipal Building auditorium. From there, we'll provide taxi rides home. As you know, the municipal building is attached to the police station and we can better provide for your safety in such a central location. Until the safety situation is stabilized."

He paused to let the protests die down, then added, "I myself will ride with you in this van. That is my promise to you. Now, who will take my arm and allow me to lead them in?"

All that faded away as I looked through the criss-cross silver bars of the cart to see a beefy fellow in a store jacket tromping down the aisle. Straight towards us.

"Reenie, they see us. Be brave." I jumped up and grasped the handle of the cart. "Follow my lead." I began to push the cart in the guy's direction, trying in all desperation to look like I belonged there.

"What're you doin' here?" he demanded, staring us both up and down.

I kept my manner cool like I was the store employee and he was just a drone. "We're the mystery shoppers. We're on the payroll. We answer to the head manager."

"ID?" the man demanded. I merely smiled like his question was such an annoyance.

"You know we have to be anonymous on the floor. Our ID's are on file in the office." He wasn't buying that, so I added, "Let's go see the head manager."

"Lady, you don't even know the lingo." He reached for his cell phone but I stopped him with my hand, giving him a knowing look.

"Wait," I said. "There's something in it for you." Then I opened the clasp of my purse. I showed him the twenty pressed behind a plastic strip.

"Overhead cameras," I said with a smile. "I don't want to be obvious. I'll give it to you in the office."

He smirked and said only, "You'll give me more than that." Then he went all formal on me. Beckoned for me and Rena to follow him, which we did. He led us to the front of the store, behind the Information Desk, opened a door to a private office and we followed him inside. A female supervisor dressed in suit jacket and skirt, obvious managerial type, looked up from a bank of security cameras.

"You did right, Eddie," she told the employee as she rose to her feet to take his report.

"Ms. Cummings, they say they're mystery shoppers," the fellow told his boss. She raised a grey eyebrow at that.

"Mystery to me." The sixty-something woman walked over to me and confiscated my purse. Thank goodness I'd retained my personal ID in a pocket on the outside and my fingers closed over that now, hiding it from her.

She asked, "You were going to give my man something?" Then she went straight for the twenty dollar bill which she had obviously surmised was there from the activity she'd viewed on the screens.

I kept my cool as she rummaged for more cash. She found an extra hundred but missed the other big bills. This take seemed to satisfy her since she handed over the twenty to her man and took the big bill for herself. Then she shoved my bag back at me.

"Eddie," she told her associate, "we can afford to be flexible about these two. We'll mention this to no one."

"Yes, ma'am," Eddie responded, a grin highlighting his face.

"Get these two jackets to put on. They'll walk out of here as store employees."

Eddie jumped on her command. He retrieved two green employee jackets from a storage closet and brought them back to Rena and me to slip on. I must say, even with our very casual clothing, the jackets made us look official, like genuine store employees.

"These two will walk out with us," the manager instructed Eddie, "when we evacuate the building."

"Ma'am?" Eddie asked for clarification. Clearly he wasn't with the program.

"Edward, we don't want anyone to know we gave them a break. No one will question me if I accompany them outside."

"Yes, Ma'am." Eddie snapped to attention. His boss went on with a comment clearly meant for my ears.

"We expect they may have additional money concealed in their vehicle. You of course have your security weapon to protect us as we check that out."

"They owe us, Ma'am." The man's response showed him to be in complete agreement with his supervisor's quest to rob us blind.

I fussed over Rena's jacket, trying not to make it obvious that their conversation was affecting me in any fashion. When my daughter's eyes strayed their way, I mouthed a silent warning. Rena, bless her, played the game along with me.

I figured we had a good chance of getting out of all this alive—if our luck continued to hold and nobody stumbled.

The manager's heels clicked across the floor as she returned to view the security screens. "Look, they have the first van fully loaded. They're starting to load Number Two."

I couldn't help glancing over at those screens, which faced outward towards the general room and thus were visible to anyone within its confines. One screen showed the parking lot behind the dock. My eye focused on the row of parked vehicles just behind those two vans.

There was my own SUV still in its parking spot. "Loge," I gasped in spite of my previous vow to remain low key. To my ears, the word sounded like a strangled cry.

The manager lady turned on me. "Yes? You see something?" Her eyes were steel, traveling from my face back to the screen. "You have a loved one in the parking lot?"

"My son," I admitted. "He's a good boy. What—what are they doing out there? There's people running around. Are they going to the cars?" An officer on the screen had begun to go down the row of parked vehicles. My eyes were drawn to a small sedan where the officer ordered the occupants to get out, then conducted a man and woman toward the second van.

"Why are they taking the people from outside?" My hand was at my throat in shock. I found myself experiencing trouble drawing air deep into my lungs. "Those people are safe out there. All they have to do is drive away from any zombs. The police don't need to take them into custody."

"Yes, they do. They'll talk." The manager lady walked back to me and I cringed at her overbearing presence. The woman towered over me by half a foot. I felt diminished by her power, but at the same time I tasted true anger in my throat, bubbling up onto my tongue. I became wholly invigorated by my rage.

Don't move against her, I warned myself. *She can kill us both right here. Or order us killed.*

"The police don't want them to drive off," the woman explained to me. "Don't you understand? No witnesses. No customer in this store or in that parking lot will ever see the light of day. They're being culled."

Mass disposition. Rena was right. But why? Why?

The woman somehow read the question in my eyes. "This is all a manufactured crisis, this zombie business. There's no zombies. Maybe there was once, but no more."

No. No. My husband had died in a zombie fight. George died a hero. He was a hero, wasn't he?

"There's no zombies today," she said, clearly enjoying my distress. "The cops work as partners with the corporations. Out bosses at this corporation, this store, we're all part of it." She looked at me with pity. "There's too many people out there for us to service. We have to cull some of you."

Some of us?

"A certain percentage of you have to die," she said simply, "so the rest of us can survive. Or society will collapse. The earth can't sustain us all. You came here on the wrong day, is all."

I found my voice and kept it level, even. "I don't want to be on the outs. I want to be with the ins. The insiders, like you. Is there a place for us?" I begged. "Can we serve?"

She blinked, considering this, but her eyes appeared dead. She looked tired and old. "Do you know somebody? A person in power, in the hierarchy?"

Not me. "My neighbor works with the cartel," I remembered.

"Those weasels. Small change." She waved her hand in the air.

"Please," I cried, "I'm only asking to save my son. He's out there and they're going to pull him in."

Her mouth twisted like my plea gave her a sour taste on her tongue. "I can't save everybody. I can't do that."

Eddie broke up our parlay. "Lady, we're saving you and the girl. We haven't heard a thank you."

Before I could speak, the woman pointed at the screens. "Look, they're shutting the doors of both vans. That's our clue to vacate." It hurt me to my soul to hear Eddie ask, "When is it they start the gas?"

"Not our concern." Boss Lady pointed at Rena and me. "Come on if you're coming."

Rena slipped her arm around my waist and I held her as we both started forward after those two. I kept my eyes on the security screen as long as I could, the one that showed the back parking lot. I tried to find my SUV but it wasn't in the spot I remembered it being in. All I saw was an empty space.

My heart went to my throat. I thought my knees would buckle and it was Rena who kept me upright. "Look," she gasped out, and at that moment my heart told my eyes where to look. There was my SUV racing past a line of cars two lanes over. The driver had his head tucked down, but I recognized the black duster over his shoulders. Logan had learned to drive that way in defensive driving at school. Damn, but they'd taught him well. Nobody in that lot tried to stop him now. The police were still working that front line of cars.

I didn't know the details, maybe I'd never know, but my son now barreled out the back gate of the Big Box Store and out of their control. Like a robot, the cop up front kept walking down the line. Going to the unsuspecting persons in the vehicles that remained.

Rena whispered at my ear, "Did you see that?" I could only nod, unable to speak. Such a load off my shoulders. None of us was truly safe in this world, but my boy would live to fight another day.

True to her word, the manager lady and Eddie walked us out the exit door as our escorts. The security guards gave her a deferential nod. Because we were with her, we were invisible. The outside security people let us pass. Anyone with a green store jacket on their backs got passed through to their wheels. I saw them allowing such drivers to depart the lot with no problems.

Boss Lady turned to me. "I'm betting you have a few things in your glove compartment. Or under the floor mat."

The bitch was in for a surprise.

"Your vehicle's just sitting there, of course," she reminded me. "After they took your son."

I wanted to laugh out loud. "They didn't take him. My son got away." I held my head high as I said with triumph, "He split before they got to him. In our SUV. I saw it all on your screens, just as we walked out."

The woman's lip turned downward, betraying a disappointment she couldn't hide. "Can't win them all. What about your pockets?" She snaked her fingers under the green store jacket I wore and rummaged in the pocket of my hoodie. "Ferals like you hide your shit. You got something pinned in that lining?"

"It's all yours." I ripped off the store's jacket, then unzipped my hoodie and flung it at her. A small price to pay to get away from this maggot. She searched one half of the hoodie, her flunky searched the other half while Rena and I kept walking. I slung my store jacket over my shoulder so the guards at the end of the lot could see its bright green color. It felt almost unclean to put the stupid thing back on.

Fortunately, the cop seated in the squad car at the exit sign waved us out, no problem.

"Careful walking out there," the officer cautioned us. "Traffic's heavy."

"Thank you, officer," I said. Killer. We stopped at the curb and waited for the light to change. Home free! I almost danced while crossing that busy intersection. Such a different world. Out here, no one was aware that a culling had just occurred up at the Big Box Store. I wondered if the news media would even follow up on reports that certain citizens of our township went missing today.

Probably it would all get buried, because the broadcast and print media, the ruling classes, and big business were all in cahoots—to further their agenda that some of us were expendable.

A honking of a car horn caused me to jump. Rena squealed when she saw it was Logan driving past in our four wheel drive. He pulled to the side of the road and I jumped in the back. Rena climbed into the passenger side next to her brother and grabbed him in a bear hug.

"Let's keep moving," was all I could say as I collapsed against the seat. Logan stepped on the gas and sped down the road.

"Mom, Reen," he announced, "I'm taking us all to Grandpa's. We're not even going home."

"To the farm?" That seemed wise. Without even hearing our story, my son seemed to know it was beneficial to get out of this area.

Rena slapped the dashboard in front of her. "It's not here. Daddy's gun." I could see from my seat in the back that Logan had removed his weapon from its place on the dash.

Rena glared sideways at him. "Are you hiding it?"

"I traded it," Logan said, voice taut. "Had to." He turned down a side street and we veered into a long stretch of back road that was little traveled. This made me feel very comfortable and I sensed we were on the right path, headed towards a more quiet place and personal freedom. If you could find such a thing in our world.

"How could you give away Daddy's gun?" Rena demanded.

"I told you, I had to. I gave it to some store employee in the parking lot," Logan went on. "His girlfriend was in the car parked next to me. She pulled in after you guys left. We started talking and then he came out." Logan gave a long sigh. "Then it got weird."

Rena and I stayed silent while he collected his thoughts. I knew what my son was dealing with. Another moment when his world turned upside down forever.

"The girlfriend was waiting for him to come out on break. So the guy comes out and tells her to get the hell out of there. Said something was going down inside and it was gonna be bad news. I'm hearing this 'cause my window's down, and I asked him, what the eff. He goes, you better get out, too. Cops are rounding everybody up and will make 'em disappear."

Logan's swiped the back of one hand over his forehead as he told the story. "Then he looks at the banger on the dash and says, how much you want for that? I said, not for sale. He goes, not even if I saved your life? I said, if things are as bad as you say, I'm gonna need that piece."

"We could use it now," Rena broke in.

"The guy was shitting himself. Look what he gave me." Logan reached into the arm rest and pulled out a money clip fat with bills. I saw '100' on the outside bill. "This much will get us to farm country," he said. "There's no going home because the lot cameras have our license plate. If they wanted to check up on this set of wheels, they could track us to the house easy."

"Or send out an APB," my daughter said.

I shook my head. "It might not get to that point," I suggested, but my boy disagreed.

"The guy I traded with heard a cop say, no witnesses. He thinks they'll let all employees outa the lot and then track them all at home. Get 'em there."

If so, greedy Boss Lady and the flunky wouldn't get to enjoy the money they pulled out of my hoodie. "It's too big for me," I said. "Grandpa will help us. We're family." And so we drove straight along the path of the sun's rays that marked a golden path in the high hills that led toward freedom. Rena started to cry as the full force of the day's terror settled upon her. I myself was too numb to weep.

"I thought you both were dead," Logan admitted as we took the final stretch of road to the family farm. "I circled around 'cause I thought I might see your ghosts floating upward." He barked out an embarrassed laugh. "Rat ass crazy, huh. Then you both came walking by. I couldn't believe it."

"I can believe anything," I said, "now that I have my protectors with me. That's you two." I leaned forward and massaged the shoulders of both of my fine kids. "Loge, can you find a gun for Reenie?"

"I'll have to," he said. "if she's gonna ride shotgun with me. You will, won't ya, Reen?" He grinned at his sister and she beamed. It definitely looked like things would be better between those two from now on. Another load off my mind.

A shadow on the top hill caught everyone's attention. Somehow it didn't fit in with the terrain.

"Some fool person's out by themselves," I observed. "It's either drunk—or a zomb."

We all started to giggle at that point. Yet two weeks later on that same hill above Grandpa's spread, we truly did find evidence of zombie infestation. Proof that the undead were still out there. Truth to tell, our clan felt safer battling them one by one in the high grounds, rather than fighting monster human beings in the wastes of civilization.

SURVIVAL OF THE FITTEST

by Milo James Fowler

You don't expect to step out on your balcony and get yourself shot. But that's exactly what happened to Jason Peters' wife when she went to hang up their laundry on the clothesline. She hadn't been outside for more than a split-second before Jason saw the splash of crimson on their sliding glass door and heard the report of Sanders' rifle across the parking lot. She stumbled inside in wide-eyed dismay with a blood-spattered lump of wet underwear in her hands.

"Not hungry?" Sanders barely glanced up from his meal.

Jason sat across from him over a couple bowls of refried beans—nasty enough stuff when there had been electricity, and now cold, straight from the can, it was downright disgusting. But not nearly as bad as having your wife shot by a neighbor. Grey stubble jutted from Sanders' jowls and silver hair spilled over the neckline of his undershirt. The hunting rifle, his prized possession, sat cradled under one arm.

"Did you get tired of shooting the dead?" Jason couldn't touch the beans. He sat with his fists clenched under Sanders' oak dinner table.

"Not too many of them around anymore. I'd say the plague's over. Those zombies are all but exterminated. But it's not like we're getting out of here anytime soon. The blow horn on that military chopper last week made it sound like—"

"Why'd you do it?"

Sanders stopped chewing—or moving the bean mush around in his mouth. He fixed red-rimmed eyes on Jason. "She'll live." It was a statement of fact.

"That's not the point. You—"

"I'd do it again." He jabbed his spoon into the bowl. "Until you get it in your heads that times have changed. One woman to one man? That won't cut it anymore. Not when she's the only female in this complex."

Jason stared at the rifle—as far as he knew, also the only one of its kind in the quarantined apartments. "You can't be serious." His voice sounded hoarse.

"You two doing the deed, day and night? Every hour on the hour?"

Jason's jaw worked, but no words emerged.

"You'd better be. That's what it's gonna take to get our species up and running again." Sanders gestured out the sliding door of his third-floor apartment at the sun shining on silent, litter-strewn asphalt and the gutted remains of a few scorched automobiles. "How many guys do we have left here? Maybe half a dozen? Out of something like a couple hundred tenants. Think of this as a microcosm." He paused, narrowing his gaze. "You know what that is? A *microcosm?*"

"We don't know the larger situation. They might not all have been infected. There was a mass exodus—"

"Bet you're wishing now you'd gone with 'em." Sanders chuckled.

Jason and Maria thought they'd be fine. Plenty of emergency earthquake supplies were stockpiled in the spare bedroom, and they'd done well enough rationing them. A veteran from the Afghan War, Jason had always been prepared for anything.

"Go talk to him," Maria had said with a wince as Jason cleaned her shoulder wound.

"Bastard's out of his mind," he'd muttered. The bloody bullet and forceps lay on a china plate from a set they'd registered for just a few months prior.

"Reason with him," she'd said. "Show him we're not his enemies."

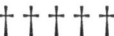

"But you're not going anywhere." Sanders dropped his spoon into the bowl and swung the muzzle of his rifle around to stare Jason right in the eye.

"Hey, hold on—" He kept his trembling hands under the table.

"You saved me a lot of trouble and ammo coming here like this." Sanders chuckled again. "What is it, Dr. Peters? You look scared."

"You need me." Jason fought to keep his voice even. "You'll need a medic—"

"Like you've helped anybody but yourself these past months. You with all your provisions and your *woman.* While the rest of us have fought tooth and nail just to *survive!*"

Jason should have known it would come back to bite him in the ass. At the epidemic's peak when the undead ran rampant in the streets, tearing out the throats of anyone they crossed, fists had pounded against the door of the Peters' third-floor apartment. Jason had barricaded the door and Maria had reinforced the windows, and they'd stuffed pillows over their ears to muffle the strangled cries for help.

Sanders lowered the muzzle just an inch. "I want you to know, Peters, that there's nothing psychosexual about this. Survival of the fittest, that's all. We've got to make sure our species survives. And it means getting that wife of yours pregnant as soon as possible. With as many sperm donors as possible."

As if on cue, Sanders' front door creaked open, and in strode the other surviving tenants of the Palm View apartment complex, filthy men easily twice Maria's age who grinned as they swaggered toward the dinner table, winking at Jason under the gun.

"We'll put a bun in that oven real quick." One from the back of the pack started pelvic-thrusting and groaning. The other men guffawed.

Jason didn't know their names; he barely recognized them.

"I'll probably need to move into your place," Sanders said. "A shot at this range, your head will fly apart in a million scraps. God knows it's near impossible to get that much blood out of anything." He brought the muzzle up. "Last words, Doc?"

One of Jason's hands under the table unclenched, holding a ring. Every muscle in his body quivered like a sea slug out of water, but his voice somehow remained calm. "Not that it's any of your business, but my wife is already pregnant."

"We don't mind!" laughed the pelvic-thruster.

Jason brought both of his hands above the table. "The best thing about this? She'll be able to raise my baby without neighbors like you."

He released the grenade in his grasp, and a blast of brilliant white tore through the room.

by Noah Bogdonoff

13.

I wiped my left hand on my pants and kept my right grip firm on the *yad*, Hebrew for "hand," a metal pointer devised by ancient rabbis to keep my sweaty palms away from their holiest of books. A synagogue full of old Jews, holocaust survivors, mumbled and chanted while I tried not to let my voice crack. I squeaked out the final syllables of my reading and closed my eyes as I heard the chorus: *"Ah-meh-ehn."* I opened them and scanned the crowd for my family. I prided in my mother's big, brown, wet eyes, her gawky black hat pulled down to shield her from embarrassment. My father seemed to be falling asleep. My sister's seat was empty; she had started crying during the *amidah*.

The old Jews forced me to drink something called slivovitz. I didn't know why. It was a tradition.

"You're a man, now," my uncle said to me. "Have a drink."

I tried to think of something witty to say. My wool suit itched.

"Have two!" said a cousin, shoving more of the drink into my hand. I took a sip from one glass. It tasted vile.

The audience of relatives laughed. I set the glasses down on a table and wandered away, dimly aware of heat building in my cheeks.

14.

Mom stood behind my father, reading the newspaper over his shoulder. The smell of omelets filled the room. "What *don't* people smoke these days?"

"Turkey," said my father.

"Oregano," I said. "They've figured out that it isn't pot."

The omelets sizzled in their pan. Mom's face flushed and she raised an eyebrow at me as if to say, *"And how would you know?"* but I returned it with a skinny smile and a shrug—*"I wouldn't."* Dad ruffled his newspaper to fill the void in conversation. It folded over, a corner landing in Emily's drink.

"Ew," she said. "You have to make me another."

"How do we ask, Emily?" said Mom.

"Can you please have to make me another drink!" she said.

Dad seized Emily's cup and brought it to the sink. He dumped it out. "One Orangutan's Rosy Bottom, coming up!" he said. I watched as he poured the orange juice first and then the grenadine, which settled at the bottom He pulled a bottle of seltzer from the refrigerator and shook it lightly. "Honey, could you open this? It's stuck."

"Go outside and open it yourself," said Mom.

Dad shrugged. I watched him exit and then seized the newspaper, searching the headlines for the one that had turned my mother testy. A sense of urgency picked at me as I pulled the newsprint closer to my nose, catching wind of its inky scent, its factory-fresh odor. The smells must have been as much a part of my father's Sunday mornings as the Orangutan's Rosy Bottom was to Emily's. I read more closely—war, elections, sports...The tiny print irritated my eyes. Finally: "Synthetic drugs may be responsible for surge in violence."

"What's pot?" said Emily.

"Shut up," I said.

Dad strode back into the room, seltzer in hand. His shirt was soaked. "Don't worry," he said. "The Orangutan's Rosy Bottom lives again."

15.

We huddled together underneath Angela's porch, five of us. Three cigarettes, two cans of beer. The acrid stench of Angela's compost pile clogged our throats. We washed it down with smoke and alcohol. James had brought the beer, Ellie the cigarettes. All of it was stolen from their parents. I wondered what it would be like to have parents who smoked and drank. I sipped the beer, feeling the corners of my mouth pinch as it hit my taste buds. I imagined drinking a stale loaf of bread. Angie blew smoke in my face. All of our eyes had long since turned red.

Outside, the lawn was perfectly landscaped. The crickets chirped. Citronella candles and store-brand bug zappers kept the mosquitoes away.

We traded items of contraband and a cigarette felt its way into my hand. The burning end pushed a warm, seductive wave of shadows across Angie's face. Her lipstick lingered on the butt of the cigarette. When had Angela started wearing lipstick? When had we all started doing this? Inside, our younger siblings slept on the couch, old cartoons casting an eerie light onto the porch above us. I listened to the crickets. I closed my eyes. Angela's lipstick touched my mouth as I kissed the cigarette.

Eric spoke up. "When do our parents get home?"

"Eleven thirty," said Ellie.

"Eleven," said James. He looked at Ellie. Ellie looked at Angie. Angie looked at Eric. Eric looked at me.

I looked back at Angie and then to the others. Above us, the night broke open with the roar of conversation, stiletto heels on hardwood floor, laughter, drunken laughter, stifled laughter as we heard one of our parents say, "Where are the kids?"

"Inside here."

"Watching TV? No, that's the little ones."

"I swear, if they've gone to some party—"

"Come on, now, they're fif*teen*. What could they possibly *do?*"

Laughter. And then a pause. "It smells like smoke. Do any of you smoke?"

"No," came the sound of Ellie's mother. "I can't stand cigarettes."

The heels again—it must have been Eric's mother—*click, clack,* down the porch and towards us. We could feel our collective heartbeat as it accelerated, amplified, sent us into a sort of shock. I couldn't break Angie's stare, and she seemed unable to break mine. We didn't breathe, not for what felt like a million years but was actually five seconds. We heard Eric's mother get down on her knees and then—

"Jennifer, we can see up your—"

"They're down *here*, Jeff. The kids are down here."

16.

Emily clutched my arm and inched closer to me, peering beneath the banister for a better view. Our parents' voices floated up to us, muffled and dispersed in the dim light of the house.

"They're exaggerating, honey. It's the media. They like to get us riled up."

"Stop calling me honey. Please."

"But you're so sweet."

"Please. Stop. I want us to start going to synagogue on Saturdays again."

"Okay."

"Okay?"

"Okay. If it will make you happy, I'll go to synagogue with you."

"And the kids."

"The kids, too. Synagogue on Saturdays. That'll stop them from partying on Friday nights."

We inched back up the stairs. We avoided the creaky floorboard at the top, and the one in front of my door. We crept to Emily's room. The light from downstairs showed us the way but we might as well have been closing our eyes. This was the fifth night of argument, the kind that didn't seem to be about anything, the kind that was too loud to sleep through. Emily stopped, the door held slightly ajar in her tiny hand.

"I don't want to sleep," she whispered.

"You have to. It's a school night."

"I don't want to," she said again.

I shrugged and turned towards my room. I felt a tugging at the bottom of my shirt.

"Can I sleep in your room?"

I looked at my watch. School in six hours. "Fine," I said. "But you have to sleep on the floor. You're too old to sleep in my bed."

"I don't wanna sleep on the floor."

"Then go to bed in your own fucking room."

Angela slept next to me. Her breath smelled like broccoli from dinner. Over her head, I kept a steady eye on the laser-red lettering of the clock. Thirty-eight minutes until her parent's projected arrival. That meant I had eighteen minutes of safety with Angie. Eighteen minutes to feel her body fold into mine, eighteen minutes of synchronized breathing. Eighteen minutes of hoping my arousal wasn't awkward or embarrassing for her. I didn't want to go home. I didn't want to write my research paper about *Romeo and Juliet,* due in two days. I kissed Angela's head the way I imagined one would in a movie, and I felt that I *was* Romeo, that Angela was forbidden and that we were destined for some cataclysmic end. The clock ticked forward another minute.

"Angie?"

"Yeah?"

Heat filled the space between us. I felt my oily, uncomfortable body, the pimples that sprinkled my chest and shoulders and threatened to overtake my self-esteem. I wanted to pick at them, no matter how many times Angie had run her hand across my torso and told me that she loved how young we were, how our bodies told the story of so many beginnings and so few endings. I thought that she should write my paper on *Romeo and Juliet.* She was the poet. I fumbled with my tongue, trying to say what I felt.

"I, um, I love you, Angie."

"Okay," she said, snuggling deeper into the blankets.

I pulled my pants up over my briefs. I tried not to make too much sound as my feet hit the floor. I peered out the window over the flowerbeds, the blue of the streetlights, the paved and twisting roads. The suburb slept through the ringing in my ears. It felt too cinematic, too poetic for my tiny, Jewish frame, my unkempt hair, my plain brown eyes…too vivid for a boy who would wake up in eight hours and eat two fried eggs, hop on a school bus, and sit at a desk for six hours.

"Where are you going?" said Angela, but she didn't mean it, not really. Shadows swathed the hazel of her eyes.

"I don't want my parents to kill me," I said. "Or yours."

"Good night," she said.

17.

My grandmother, my *bubbe*, couldn't remember mom's name. It struck me how my mother and Emily looked the same when they tried not to cry. Atlanta seeped through the window of the nursing home, sticky and sweet mingling in our nostrils and settling at the bottoms of our esophagi. I tried to pay attention to my grandmother as she spoke but the television took me over, as it always did, and I only half listened to Bubbe as the TV told me stories of rabid violence.

"…two dead in the last four days in what appears to be the rise of an unregulated synthetic drug…"

Something about my great uncle's wedding, in Czechoslovakia. Something about my grandfather carrying a motorcycle through a river. Something about the Russian occupation. I tried to absorb it. My brain ached from the heat. I felt swollen and claustrophobic.

"The question is, why are we making these chemicals available to the public…"

"And the meals," she said, "we would be lucky to have a little piece of pota-to." She motioned with one of her hands to indicate the size. "The rest of it was sawdust. But your great uncle, he knew that…that he was a strong one and didn't need as much as the others, so he would cut his potato in half and give it to the person next to him."

"Mom," said my mother, "you weren't in camp with uncle Bernie."

Bubbe looked hurt. "I was, we were in Auschwitz when, when—"

My mother sighed and told her that no, he was in Birkenau when she was in Auschwitz, and maybe she shouldn't think about this right now, maybe we should all get lunch at the nice vegetarian restaurant down the street.

"This marks the fifth outbreak of drug-induced violence in the month. If we continue to let unregulated substances…"

Mom grabbed the remote and shut the television off. I thought of Dad and Emily and my baseball team and Angela and my dumb homework assignments that I would have to finish before the plane ride home. I wondered if the time was actually passing more slowly or if I was going crazy. When I looked up, my grand-mother had pulled herself off of the couch and now hunched over the TV set, mumbling something about the cheap-o electrician. My mother held the remote and tried to explain that she'd shut the news off, that it wasn't broken. She even turned the TV back on to show Bubbe that everything was a-okay. The story about drugs had ended. A middle-aged man now filled the screen, asking us if *we* were prepared to spend taxpayer money on illegal immigrants. Mom turned the TV off again. Bubbe returned to her anxieties, hands shaking, head shaking, legs shaking.

I hung upside-down from the jungle gym. "Face-eaters?"

Ellie, situated somewhere above me, laughed and took a drag from her cigarette. She tossed the butt into the sand and swung down to meet me. "It's in all the papers. People are eating each others' faces." She pressed her hand against my torso and pushed.

I managed to hang onto the bar with the backs of my knees. "Yeah, because they're on crack. It's not a zombie apocalypse."

"Zombie apocalypse has to start somewhere." Her breath smelled of cigarettes. We hung there for a second, suspended. "Anyway they weren't on crack. It was bath salts."

"Bath salts?" I said.

"Yeah. From a drug store. And if you smoke them they infect you with this fungus and then you go crazy."

I reached upwards to grip the bar, slid my legs down, and dropped into the sand. Angela and Eric bounced into view from behind the brick-red elementary school, Angela's hair blowing lightly in the wind, individual locks fluttering behind her like streamers. She was talking to Eric. Maybe about the zombie apocalypse. Maybe about her parents. Maybe about me. I heaved a full body wave at them, jumping up and down in the sand. It was summer, after all, and our parents were letting us out together even though the news stations told them not to.

Behind me, Ellie lit another cigarette. "I wonder where James is."

She forced her nonchalance, like she always did when she talked about James. The rest of us knew that they'd been having sex. We chose not to talk about it but the way Ellie moved, and the way she smoked, and the way she talked had all shifted one week. We felt the presence of lust trailing around behind her like ectoplasm, sucking us in. When Ellie walked past Angela and me I had a sudden urge to hold Angie closer, to feel her breasts against me. When Ellie hugged Angela, I imagined them both naked. When she flicked her cigarette butts to the ground I remembered that night under the porch and tried to recall the feeling that had settled in my navel as I took a long, slow drag on Angela's lipstick-stained cigarette. I didn't smoke anymore.

"Maybe he's eating someone's face," I said.

"Maybe someone's eating *his* face." I looked instinctively to Ellie but couldn't decode her gaze. I felt her fear, though, the same fear that squeezed me whenever Angie looked stormy, the fear of losing gravity and falling away from the entire world.

Nearby, a whippoorwill began to call.

But there he was, rounding the schoolhouse, pushing through the damp, warm air, barreling towards us. I saw, through the summer haze and the fading light, a dull redness surrounding his pupils. He choked on tears as he dropped down onto the sand, his face collapsing violently in on itself with an intensity that startled me and must have ruined Ellie. We surrounded him, speaking in harried sentences and concerned tones. James just sobbed. The sand below him turned to nickel-sized slabs of mud as his tears fell and we could do nothing but wait, standing around him like statues, paralyzed by the sight of his ragged, swollen face. High, foreign-sounding sobs bounced across the playscape, through the jungle gym, and through our skulls.

"James. James," said Eric, finally. "James, what's going on?"

"We're moving." He squeezed his eyes shut. When he returned to us, he looked around dully. His gaze traveled around the circle, lingering slackly on each of us. He averted his gaze. "We're moving," he mumbled again. "If you're smart, you'll move, too. That's what my dad says. This town is going to shit."

He stood up and looked at us and it was like something had been severed. He turned away and walked. Ellie dropped her cigarette in the sand.

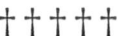

The growling entered my dream, first. Emily crying. *Dad?* she was asking, *Daddy, what's the animal? Why does the animal look like Mommy?* In my dream, the growling spilled out of a dark patch in the woods.

Mom. Mom, where are you? But I knew that she lingered in the empty space between the trees. And the growl had come from her. A hand emerged from the darkness, gangrenous and wilting. She growled again. I felt Emily pull at my legs, tripping me as I tried to turn around. *Daddy, daddy,* she was saying, and I looked around but couldn't find my father. *Daddy,* she cried again, and I looked down at her and then I looked down at myself and I saw that all of my clothing was too big, my shoes were too fancy, my neck itched beneath a tie. I tried to turn around but Emily held me tight, keeping me oriented towards Mom, my mother, the sallow, sickly, ravenous face in the dark.

My eyes opened into blackness: my pillow. Twisting free of my sheets I pulled myself up into a sitting position. I touched a spot of moisture on my forehead and felt alone. For a second it felt serene.

There was a slow scratching noise outside.

Somewhere at the bottom of my gut, I knew. We'd all been talking about it. We'd turned it into a big joke, even as the newspapers plastered our brains with a howling, tearing awareness of the disaster. On Friday nights, we no longer meandered through our suburban mess of a town. Instead we collapsed on Eric's couches, we smoked marijuana on his porch while his parents weren't looking. We ignored the newspapers and the news stations and for that matter all television. We escaped.

Scratch. I inched slowly towards the window.

Scratch.

I turned the light on, pulled out my phone and dialed Eric.

"Hello?"

"I hear something outside my window."

"Is it one of them?"

"I don't know." I glanced at the newspaper next to my bed, the one we'd passed around before class a couple of weeks ago. *Tests Confirm Risk Of Contagion From Drug-Born Fungus.* "I don't want to look."

"Is Angela at your house?"

"No," I said. *Scratch.* We'd boarded up the first floor windows, I reminded myself. I took a breath. Everything was okay.

Eric faltered on the phone. "Okay. Just go to bed. I'll see you in school to-morrow."

"Okay," I said. And then, "Eric?"

"Yeah?"

"I'm sorry for waking you up."

Mom and Dad on one couch, Emily and I on another. They clasped their hands in front of them. I bit my nails until they bled.

"Okay, so." Their faces tightened; they didn't know where to go from there. Okay, so. So your childhood is over. So the streets are no longer safe. So the world is ending. "We've decided, jointly, that it would be best for us all to move upstate."

"For a little while," added my dad.

"Just until some…things blow over," said my mom. She looked at my father.

"What things?" we asked.

"You might have heard us—"

"Is this about the zombie apocalypse?"

Emily began to cry.

My dad. "It's not the zombie apocalypse. It's not any apocalypse."

"We don't know what it is," said my mom.

"So it's the zombie apocalypse," I said.

Mom stared blankly at me.

"People are eating people's faces."

"Only the good-looking ones," said Dad. "So you're safe." He stood and left the room. Mom followed.

My whole torso felt empty.

18.

The new house was big and dilapidated. An old farmhouse. It felt safe and solemn.

Silence fell on us almost naturally. Our doors stayed locked. We left only when we had to. On Saturday mornings Mom sat alone with a shawl over her head and prayed. Afterwards she would come to lunch with us and shake her head as she played with Emily's hair. "I wish you would pray with me," she would mumble, and Emily would scowl at Dad across the table, and Dad would place carrots under his lips so that they looked like walrus tusks. Then he'd look at me and I'd see that he didn't really think it was funny anymore, that he was searching for the echo of a hazy Sunday that no longer existed. Tomorrow we would not wake up and make Orangutan's Rosy Bottoms, or if we did they wouldn't taste the same, because the stores up here didn't sell the orange juice that we liked, and Dad would not read the newspaper because he did not want us to see. Instead we'd eat cereal with milk from a local dairy farm and talk idly, and Dad wouldn't be there. He would disappear into his room and lock the door, and Mom would have to take a few deep breaths every time she looked over at the door. She'd recite the *shema* a few times, three fingers covering her eyes the way the holocaust survivors at synagogue used to do. *"Shema, yisrael. adonai, eloheinu, adonai echad."* Hear, o Israel: the lord our God, the lord is one.

The sounds of a news station slipped out from beneath Dad's door, and we waited.

19.

My head rang, all the way home. Part of me didn't believe it was over. In the afternoon light, the world outside of the car appeared foreign, small and crisp and ravaged. We drove past the trees and the fields and the farms and the silos and the cows with no more owners, into the swarms of broken houses and malls and office buildings, into empty and rusted playgrounds, into perfectly paved roads with bent and broken street signs. We turned right onto Milburn Avenue, and left onto Jackson Road, until I saw the one perfect house and knew I'd come home. We slowed to a halt.

We stared up at the house and its peeling paint. The boards we'd nailed over the windows were battered and rotting. The door behind the screen was still a ripe, out-of-place purple. I caught Emily's eye, and turned away. And then I walked—slowly at first, and then faster—towards Angela's house. I felt Emily and Dad and Mom and the house all watching me as I disappeared down the road, drawing the longest, sweetest breaths of my life. My muscles ached with atrophy but I kept running, all the way to the place where Angela's house pulled itself up in front of me, foreign and familiar. The sounds and smells of my hometown pressed against me without mercy. Thick wooden boards covered the windows. I knocked, unsure of why I had come or what I would say. I knocked again. I had barely taken my hand off the door when it pulled open.

Angela. I tried to speak and instead swallowed salt and fervor. I collapsed into her arms as she hugged me to her chest, the way I imagined one would in a movie, with all of the tenderness and awkwardness and adolescence that she could muster, with all of the confusion and all of the heartbreak she must have felt while I was gone, with all of the forgiveness she had for the boy who had gone away without a word.

A long, warm breeze pushed through my hair. I blinked at my tears.

I pulled myself from her and stood alone for a moment. I looked at Angela. She took my hand and didn't talk, the silence of her perfect house, and its dying lawn, and the history beneath it buzzing about us like an electric field. I stood.

We walked to the old elementary school, to the place where our lives used to start, through the untamed grass, through the hot air and the harsh feelings. We held onto each other and walked onto the playground, the sand kicking up into our shoes and filling our socks. We stood there and waited, for Ellie, for James, for Eric, for Emily, for my mother and father, for our families and our friends and our religions and our answers. The sun touched the horizon. Angela and I stood there, alone. The light evaporated, shrouding us in a fleeting dusk. We dug our feet deeper into the sand, searching for the earth beneath—the stuff that would not blow away.

by George Cotronis

We drove around for hours that night. The town was empty, sleeping. Dim lights disappearing in the fog as we passed them by. Like being lost in the expanse of space, there was complete darkness between each island of light created by a streetlight or a store's flickering neon sign.

The tape deck blared Black Sabbath songs. We found the tape under the passenger seat, the scrawling on the label no longer visible. When I showed it to the man in the back seat, he nodded. I pushed it in and the car filled with the chorus from "Paranoid." The man lay back and formed a half smile. He looked out the window, his breath fogging the glass. It started to rain.

"Where else can we take you, Brent?" Michael asked. He flicked his cigarette butt out the window.

The man in the back seat was quiet for a while and then mumbled, "Terrace View 34."

He coughed into his fist and then threw up blood all over the back seat.

Michael looked at me. "Oh, fuck," he whispered.

This car was fucked.

The Cadillac's spotlights tore the night as we headed up the hills. The man pointed when I needed to take a left or a right somewhere, usually with some hesitation.

"The town's changed a lot over the years," the croak came from behind my headrest. I wished he wouldn't place his head so near to my own, but there was no way to say anything without being rude. He smelled like the dead, desiccated flesh and the smell of wet earth.

He pointed at an empty lot. An old fridge had been abandoned in the mud.

"This used to be a coffee shop," he said.

We navigated the smaller streets until we found what we were looking for. The house was in ruins. Nothing specific, just abandonment and weather. And time.

Half of the roof had collapsed and that part of the house was covered with moss. The rest of the house looked just as bad.

The dead man in the back stuck his head to the window like a child, taking it all in. He sat there staring at the old house.

Michael fiddled with his bag. We didn't have too long till dawn now.

"Did you live here?" I asked.

The corpse shook his head *no*.

"Who then?"

He tried to speak, but he only let out a croak. He coughed again and said "My friend used to live here. When we were kids."

I nodded.

"What happened to him?"

He got out of the car and approached the house. I let him There was no one around anyway. This neighborhood was dead.

I got out and followed him. He wiped the dirt off the old mailbox that was laying on its side. He looked at the name there and showed it to me, but I couldn't tell what it said. I didn't understand what he was trying to tell me. I don't think he had the words to tell me what he was feeling.

He shook his head and let the mailbox slip out of his hands.

"Let's get out of here," he said.

We drove back, through the town and into the woods. We took one of the dirt roads deeper into the forest and parked in a little clearing we had picked out earlier.

Me and Michael got out. The grave was already dug. The dead man looked at the hole and fidgeted. I hoped he wouldn't run or jump us. I hate it when they do that.

"Hey, I'm sorry you didn't find your friend," I offered.

He looked at me and smiled, the mouth too wide, the teeth too many. The flesh was drawn back and his eyes had sunk into his skull.

"That's okay."

I nodded and Michael walked up with the rosary and read him the last rites.

"Do I have to go into the grave?" the corpse asked.

"No."

"Okay. I'm sorry."

"For what?" I asked. I hated this part. The man was dead, I shouldn't feel bad. But it was always hard.

"My friend died years ago. When we were kids. I made you drive around for no reason."

"That's okay. We liked driving around with you, man."

"Yeah," Michael added.

"I guess I forgot for a while. I thought he might still be alive. He never got to grow up, you know. He drowned when we were kids. He was my best friend," the man said.

"Yeah," I said. "Are you okay now? Are you ready?"

He nodded. "I just thought I'd say goodbye. I never talked about him when… when I was alive. I wasn't a good friend."

He looked around, at the trees and grass.

"I guess that's what I've been missing. Saying goodbye."

He closed his eyes then. I lifted my arm and aimed at his head.

"This is consecrated ground. You will rest here. Go, and be at peace," I said and pulled the trigger. He fell down into the grave and I shot him two more times in the head.

Michael picked up the shovel and started filling it in. That's the deal, one of us pulls the trigger, the other one digs the grave.

I sat in the car and listened to some Black Sabbath.

SNORING WAKES THEM

by Harri B. Cradoc

Lieutenant Bulger approached the bunk where the psychologist was sleeping and rattled the wooden frame with the butt of his rifle. "They'll be waking, soon, Dr. Pearson. It's time to psychoanalyze the dead again."

Pearson stuttered in mid-snore and sat bolt upright. "They're not here yet?"

"No. Would I be standing here making chit-chat with a narcoleptic shrink if there were zombies knocking at the door?"

The psychologist rubbed his matted hair, put on his glasses, and stood up. "If zombies had actually come out of the fort cemetery over there, I imagine you would be firing your weapon and making all sorts of racket. But you might also try talking them to death. You seem to talk a lot when you're tense. I'll bet bloody jaws chewing through that door frame would make you even more talkative."

Bulger spit on the dirt floor of the makeshift barracks. "Me talk to re-animated stiffs? That's a laugh. You know it might be that snoring of yours that wakes them. I never heard such complaining as comes out of your gullet when you can't get a breath down. Why you got to take a nap every two hours anyway?"

"I think better after resting. You should try it some time."

"Would that be the resting part or the thinking?"

Pearson laughed and went to the window that had three stiff boards nailed over it in crisscross fashion. He could barely make out a few white headstones poking up through the muddy pink glow that consisted mainly of bodies lying twisted face-down in mirrored pools of water.

The army had tried fire hoses first. It had worked for a while, until the fallen bodies clogged the intake hoses in the creek. They came until they were too close for mortars. Then it was all rifle shots and hand grenades. Pearson had never seen so many body parts laying disconnected, not in medical school, and not in that desert war where the enemy was trying to cut off arms and legs on purpose. He had put his time in over there, putting the mental pieces of a thousand soldiers back together. Some had come back to fight again. Pearson had tried to talk them out of it. Some wouldn't listen. Some fought harder after being knocked down.

"You know what I wish?" It was Bulger poking the rifle into the psychologist's back.

Pearson eyed him. This soldier was different. He would fight as long as he was winning. And he would fight hard to win. But Pearson didn't trust him to stay at his side till the last bullet was fired. Bulger would be long gone by then. He would be looking for higher ground, or whatever they call a strategic retreat these days.

"No, lieutenant. What do you wish? Another hour of daylight before the graveyard opens for business?"

The rifle end prodded Pearson again. "Hurts don't it? I wish you'd tell me what you're going to do when those crazies get here. Why not take a gun and get familiar with it? I could show you where the trigger is and how to point it about eye-high. I figure that's where you got to get them, in either the left eyeball or the right, if they still got either one. What do you figure?"

Pearson turned back to the crack in the window that was protecting the lieutenant and him from the outside world. They were the last two left, as far as they knew. No other chatter on the radio. Bulger had been efficient with ammunition so far. Pearson gave him that. But when it ran out, then what? Would they be drawing knives or climbing to the rooftops? The movies never show what happens after that. The building always goes up in flames and then the credits roll.

"I've seen this before. We keep firing at the creatures as they come over the creek bank that separates us from where they will be gathering. Their bodies fall down the embankment, disappearing into the water and being carried away by the current during the first wave. But then some of the bodies snag on the bottom and begin to build up a kind of dike across the water. Then a second wave scrambles over the dead bodies of the first, and then they cross and come for us."

Bulger played with the bolt action of his weapon, testing it, practicing some moves he might have to make in the very near future. He rubbed a day-old beard with some of the grease he found on the gun, and the black goo made streaks across his face. "What does that mean? You've seen it before? I don't get it. Nobody's ever seen zombies before, unless I'm crazy and this is all a dream. You still asleep, doc? You still on the couch over there? You want me to get you a nice glass of warm milk or something?"

Sarah was looking down at him. She knew she was supposed to wake him when he seemed agitated. He had suffered from nightmares ever since the war. She washed his forehead with her long brown hair and tried to get her husband to open his eyes. "What does that mean?" she asked him softly. "What have you seen before?"

Pearson sat up, his wet palms sticking to the soft cotton sheets. He had to shake his fingers to free them from folds in the covers. "Was I snoring again?"

"More like a nightmare," said Sarah, patting him around the shoulders and kissing him on the cheek. "You're wet all over. Must have been a bad one."

"I've seen it before. But it's worse now. It gets worse every night."

Sarah got up and let him see her in the naked moonlight. She could calm him just by turning one way with her body, and excite him by turning the other. She knew him better than any of his psychologist friends. Even better than the one he told his dreams to.

"Maybe it's the medication. You need time to find a new balance in your body. Tell that Doctor Smith or whoever you're seeing now. Or do you want me to call in the morning?"

Pearson admired the small round belly shadowed against the window. His wife was due to give birth soon, even though they had been married just short of nine months. They were surprised, but happy on the surface. Sarah had been planning to get pregnant all along, she said, but just hadn't thought to tell her husband right away. "We'll have ten altogether, if we like the first seven or so. We'll just see how it goes, okay?" That was how he knew she liked being pregnant. Pearson wondered why he hadn't figured that out earlier. She was always nurturing things like struggling plants and wounded animals. That should have been a clue.

"I'm seeing my own therapist today, just one doctor to another. We'll talk about the dreams and the pills, the sweating and the snoring."

"Well, here's to solving one of those." Then she kissed him full force on his open mouth just before he could frown. She always knew when he was in a bad mood, and smothered it with her love.

"I guess I'll get you that warm milk now."

The therapist's office was much like Pearson's own, with a lot of oiled paneling and potted plants and an LCD panel that advertised the benefits of a local health plan. Even the receptionist was familiar. Pearson thought he might have interviewed her once a long time ago, or fired her, or both, but she looked up at him with large green eyes and tightly curled red hair and smiled. She would have forgiven him by this time anyway, if he really had fired her. It could have been before the war, before his memory began playing tricks on him.

Jenkins was an old friend who had agreed to see Pearson as a favor. Professional courtesy he called it, up to a point. He charged for most visits, but not more than seemed usual and customary as the lingo permitted. When Pearson had a bad night, his old friend fit him in, and forgot to forward time spent to the billing department. Only Jenkins and the smiling redhead knew for sure.

"Why do I feel like a barber getting a haircut?"

"More like a priest confessing sins committed outside the church," said Jenkins. He rubbed his bald head and then waved a bony hand to the open seat across from his own. A large variegated schefflera bent from its floor pot as an overhead fan blew paw-like leaves around the chair legs and sent them clawing upward toward the men.

"The dreams are getting worse every night."

"It's a bit unusual, as I'm sure you know. Dreams are so short, so episodic, there is little room for development. They are like shots in the dark, roughly aimed at ill-formed ideas. They live for only a few seconds at a time before dropping and being washed away by the next brain wave that demands attention."

Pearson struggled to get comfortable. He had better chairs in his own office, plants that were better behaved, and a less cloying secretary. This must be how barbers felt when they have let their hair grow too long, or priests when they have finally figured out what has been bothering them.

"But I'm sure these creatures, whatever they are, will be closer tonight, and the next night. And they will get to where I am hiding or running and something bad will happen."

Jenkins looked up from his notepad. "You know zombies aren't real, right? And even if they were they couldn't kill you in your dreams. They're only manifestations of some other aspect of your life that your brain is trying to deal with. They're just stand-ins for the real bad guys, like Martians were used to symbolize Russian invaders in the 1950s, and giant ants were our own destructive tendencies as a society. We were making ourselves sick, and blasting ourselves with our own ray guns, not any from outer space."

"That's very comforting. I can blast myself all night long and not get hurt, is that it?"

"Basically, yes. You're just ruining the sheets with those over active glands. I gave you something for that. Are you taking it?"

"Sarah says I have to give it time. Let my body get used to it."

"So? What's the real problem? It can't be zombies. You admit they don't exist."

Pearson screwed his face up as much as if he was being gnawed on by one of the devils from his subconscious. "But what if I think they can hurt me? What if some part of me really believes they are coming for me? And then some night, they do?" He let out a little moan as if somewhere deep inside him a real pain was growing and clawing more insistently, with every denial of its possibility. "What happens if one night I choke to death on fear?"

Jenkins shook his head violently. "No, no. You're a doctor. You know better than that." Then he put his pen and paper down and stared at the potted plant that was brushing against his pant leg. He moved one rubbery branch aside with his hand and watched it recoil from his distaste.

On his way out, Pearson stopped to look at the receptionist again. She appeared even more familiar to him now that he had time to let her features sink in a bit. He was sure he had run into her before. She noticed him standing there and put her pencil down. "Coming back to you now?" she asked.

"How long ago was it?"

"About ten years now." She smiled as if she knew something he hadn't remembered yet.

Pearson studied her from a different angle. "Your hair was different then." It was just a guess. But he felt lucky.

"Longer. Much longer, as a matter of fact. It was getting in my way when I bent over all those forms in your office. I was too young to want to change anything about myself, and you were full of suggestions, which I didn't take too often. So we kind of parted ways one night at the end of a long work session, if you know what I mean."

"Of course, I can see you with the longer hair now. How are you doing?" Pearson bent a little closer to the desk, but prepared to pull back if she made him feel any more uncomfortable.

"Things are great now. I have a new hairdo, new glasses which I didn't need back then, and a boyfriend who makes very few suggestions that I don't like. So life is good again. I actually feel like I've come back from the dead." She flashed the big green eyes at him, and nodded toward the office door that Pearson had just closed behind him. "How you doing?"

Pearson wondered if she would think any less of him if he mentioned that he was afraid of people who had come back from the dead. Thinking better of that, he decided to admit one minor failing she might have heard before. "I've been having trouble sleeping, that's all. That might be due to a little extra tension. My practice is demanding. My wife's due to have a baby soon. Could be a combination of things, I guess."

She played with the red hair a bit, mulling over the details he had just shared with a near perfect stranger. Near being the operative word. "I don't know much about sleep disorders, but I've heard the doc in there say that it's possible to meet duplicate personalities in our dreams. We get to see ourselves as others see us. That can be pretty scary sometimes." She was twisting hair around a finger and making tight little loops that completely covered the skin with a ribbon of red from nail to bottom knuckle. When she got to the end of her wrapping, she began tugging which had the effect of budging her head slightly and forcing Pearson to refocus his attention.

"Yes, I've heard that."

"Which?" she asked with another jerk of her twisting finger. "You meet people like yourself, or you're scared of what you've become?"

"A little of both," said Pearson, edging for the door. "I'll let you know if I ever get it all worked out."

"You worry too much," she said, dropping her gaze back to her work. "I just hope you don't come to think of me as one of your bad dreams."

Pearson hurried through the outer office and went to hail one of the cabs that was stationed at the curb. The driver nodded and said, "Same as yesterday?" That shook Pearson a little as he tried to settle into his seat. The cab looked familiar and the driver's voice seemed like one he should know. Possibly it would come back to him as they drove on through traffic. Lately, he had to admit to himself, anything was possible.

The cab driver knew the route without asking. He even got the building number right and pulled up to Pearson's office door as if he did it every day. *Maybe he did*, thought the passenger as he got out and looked around. It was an ordinary day in the big city. Car horns and trucks gurgled like they were swallowing the cars in front of them. Overhead, the planes that approached the airport seemed indecisive as they circled and mumbled about the delay. Everyone had problems, not just overworked psychologists.

Pearson walked away from the curb with his shoulders swaying gently this way and that as if they were leading him by degrees. A little closer with one lurch, then forcing him to take a sidestep, and finally back on track. He would get to the office door eventually. Behind him the cab driver's voice sang out above the hubbub of the street. "That's okay, doc. I don't need any money today. I got plenty to last me till tomorrow."

Pearson stopped and wondered what the cabbie meant by shouting after him. Then he reached in his pocket and found the folded bills that he had intended to hand through the window. He turned and half opened his mouth, but no sound came out. The cab was speeding away and not waiting for him to wake from his distracted state. It could be true, he realized, that he had done the same thing before and just not remembered it.

The office door that opened next was so much like Jenkins' space that it sometimes caused Pearson to stop and make sure of where he was. The nameplate on the door was his, and so was the hat on the closet shelf in the vestibule where he had put his coat on an hour ago. The hat was still where he had left it, and it would be fine there for another few hours, until Sarah called and urged him to come home.

It was lunch time and the Pearson office secretary was reading a book. "Anything interesting?" the psychologist asked when he stopped to say hello.

"You should know. It's from your waiting room bookshelf. *Our Sleeping Selves*, by someone who works right here. At least it's got your name on the spine."

Pearson looked at the thin volume she held up for him. "Not me. You found my brother's book. He's the writer in the family. I have trouble putting words on paper.'

"That must be why you have a secretary," she said. "Did you know that we often meet ourselves in our dreams? That's what your brother says here."

"Does he say anything about talking to yourself and having a reasonable conversation?"

The secretary appeared to be searching for that part of the book. "No, he just says that all the characters in your dreams are really only one person, and that is the person who is doing the dreaming. There is no one else to talk to." She looked up at the psychologist and blinked. Pearson blinked back until she smiled and laughed. "Not meeting any interesting people in your dreams, Doctor?"

Pearson compared her to the receptionist who had been taunting him earlier. This woman was calmer and more settled. She had brown hair and brown eyes and a soothing voice, like the customer service representative who agrees to refund all service charges. Don't worry about a thing, her tone seemed to say. Nothing we can't handle today.

Pearson took that more encouraging attitude into his office and got to work. The time went by quickly and he hummed his way to five o'clock when the phone on his desk rang and it was Sarah's voice on the other end. She was feeling quite breezy this day and wanted to know if her husband would take her for a walk. They could talk about baby names and colors for the little room down the hall. It would be a pleasant evening, and then they could fall asleep in each other's arms. That sounded like something any man should want.

A loud noise woke him. He must have been snoring again. Funny how you never know when your breathing becomes so irregular, until the convulsions take over your entire body. "Was I disturbing you?" he asked when he rolled over.

Lieutenant Bolger gave out a sound from deep in his throat that may have been laughter, but there was a cigarette in his mouth and he was chewing on it. The white self-rolled paper bounced up and down as he twitched his lips. "I don't see how you can fall asleep so easy. You just had a nap a couple hours ago. It's dark now, which means time to be on your toes." He shoved the butt of a small hand gun into Pearson's palm. "Here, you dropped this about twenty minutes ago. When it didn't go off I decided not to kill you for being an idiot."

Pearson sat up and tried to focus on his surroundings. The room looked different, larger than before, with more locks on the door and more boards nailed across a bigger window. The boards were hanging at crazy angles, as if a blind man had put them there in a hurry, without caring if they were perfectly arranged or not.

"You might want to keep it pointed at that window over there."

Pearson looked down at the gun Bulger had given him. He must know how to use it, or the whole picture didn't make sense. He must be a decent marksman, or someone would have given him a shotgun. That's what they do to the guys with the shakes or bad eyesight, at least in the movies. Who knew what they would do in real life? Something that made sense, that's what. But what would that be at the moment?

"How long you figure?" asked Pearson. That sounded like something a cowboy like John Wayne would say when his back was to the wall.

"Any time now," said Bulger. "Try to stay awake." That sounded like what the other cowboy would say. But it also sounded like the most difficult thing to do.

Bulger pointed his rifle at the dirt floor. "I heard some rumbling from down below. Unless we suddenly slid into an earthquake zone, someone might be trying to undermine our position."

"You mean they're digging a tunnel?"

"What the hell you think I mean?" Bulger moved his cigarette out of the direct line of fire and spit tobacco stained juice on some straw at his feet. "I figure they come at us through a narrow opening right about here." He jabbed his rifle near where he had spit. "They start climbing out of this gaping hole here and we have to clobber them as soon as they come into sight, otherwise they're out in the open and all over us."

Pearson shuddered. "They'll just keep coming. Won't they?"

"Not if we jam this damn hole up with their lifeless bodies. They'll fall back down on the next bunch and maybe give us some more time."

"I get it, sure. Time for what?"

"I don't know," said Bulger. "Who do I look like, Jesse James? I never shot so many people in one day before. I lost count. Not that it matters. We only got so much ammo left, in case you didn't notice."

Pearson looked around him for the brown boxes with the yellow letters that had been full of spare ammunition the day before. He found them turned over on their side, their lids yawning like animals that had spilled their guts. "How long can we last?"

Bulger came over to him and gnawed at him with bloodshot eyes. "We last as long as you're willing to fight. Shoot 'em or cut their heads off with a knife, or beat their brains out with your bare hands. I don't care, as long as you don't go cowering in a corner or run screaming around the room. We'll make it."

Pearson twitched. "I never cut anything's head off before. I don't even like to clean fish after I catch them."

Bulger rapped him on the arm and made him jump. "It's always good to learn a new hobby."

Then the floor started shaking and some dirt fell into the darkness on the other side and Bulger's rifle began firing. Pearson heard a small cry that might have been his own voice trying to get out of his throat, and then he heard his own handgun blasting away at things that crawled up to him. One of the things grabbed him around the throat and Pearson shoved his gun into a throat that dripped a hot sticky blood over his hand. It was hard to keep his finger on the trigger to fire, but he repositioned his finger and prayed as he squeezed off another round. He heard the bullet go screaming into the ceiling and then he jumped sideways to get away from the falling body.

The floor seemed to grab at him as he slid away.

Pearson felt the hand rousing him, but didn't feel like moving. A siren went off somewhere in the night and then whimpered away as if wounded. He felt wet all over, especially his hands. He opened his eyes and saw red blotches where bloody fingers had gripped him and tried to turn him around.

"It's not your blood, it's mine."

"Why are you bleeding?"

"I think the baby's coming. I called to you but you didn't hear me. You were snoring so loudly." He felt her fingers gripping him so tightly that he wanted to get away from her, but he knew she needed him. He let her dig her nails into the bare skin of his arm and used the pain to pull himself back to reality. He turned to Sarah and saw that she had smeared her own face with tears. Those might have been from the pain she felt, or from the despair she felt when he hadn't answered her.

"I'm awake now. Did you call anyone?"

"Just a taxi. I didn't want to wake the neighborhood with an ambulance, just you. You can get me there, if I can get up, can't you?"

Pearson broke free and got up to get dressed. His skin was tingling as if bugs were crawling on it, as if he had died and had spawned some flesh-eating vermin. He shook off the feeling while pulling on his pants. He found a towel and wiped his forehead and hands, then his forearms. The towel was stained from where Sarah had left some of her blood on him. The birthing process had nightmarish qualities at times. It was normal to ruin a few towels.

The taxi was waiting when Pearson got his wife downstairs. "And look who it is," the driver said. "I might have known my day wouldn't be over till I saw you again." It was the same voice. "Have you found your wallet yet, Doc?"

"The hospital, as fast as you can."

Then there was nothing to remember. Streets went by without a glance at their names. Buildings rose out of the darkness and shrank back into it. Only Sarah's hand felt real. All else was ill-formed, like the notes of an orchestra tuning up behind a curtain. That thick curtain went all around the world and back again, smothering everything but his wife's gentle cries.

They let Pearson sit in the birthing room. He took to the couch against the wall and sank down in it as the nurses worked and doctors came in and left, all appearing on a kind of merry-go-round that had no music except the squeaking of crepe soled shoes on a polished floor, and the clattering of instruments on a metal tray.

"Are you all right?" asked one of the nurses. "Do you want to be near when the baby comes?"

"I'm right here," said Pearson.

"I meant, would you be willing to stand here, at your wife's side?"

"Why?"

The nurse looked up at the ceiling where sound deadening tiles were losing their battle against humming machinery and the scraping of rubber soles around the bed. She studied the watercolor prints on the wall and listened for the soft music that trickled out of hidden speakers. She nodded, as if concluding that the machinery of her world was all in order. The only thing she needed to add was a strong, reassuring presence, one capable of calming a woman who was about to do the most dangerous thing a woman can do. She turned to Pearson.

"In a perfect world, you wouldn't want to be sleeping on a couch right now."

"No," said Pearson, jumping up. "No sleeping."

A few minutes went by when the room emptied and then filled again. It filled and emptied like hope fills a heart, and fear drains it. The minutes jumped and lurched across the face of the clock, and the radio spewed random notes the way drunken men sing songs long after the band has stopped. Suddenly the room was empty of doctors and nurses. Only a man and a woman remained, clinging to each other because they were the only two left.

"We need the doctor now," said Sarah.

"The nurse went to get him."

"No, it's too late. You'll have to do it."

Pearson shuddered. "Do what?"

Sarah studied him gravely. "Catch the baby. Pretend the head is a baseball and you're the catcher. It's not a monster. It's a baby. Just play catch. Oh…oh."

Then Pearson saw the damp matted hair and felt water dripping on his outstretched hands. The water had an oily feel and smelled acrid like skin under an old bandage. The air tasted sweet as he breathed steadily and pulled his hands toward his own quivering belly. He would need to sit down soon.

The nurse came in and put her hand up to her mouth. "Untangle the cord!" she said through twitching fingers.

And so he did.

"You've been snoring," said the voice. "I thought you were dead except for the snoring."

Pearson looked around, wondering where he was. The room was nearly black and the window showed no light but stars squinting down. "I guess you're all right, after all."

Jenkins patted his patient on the arm, only to see the arm get jerked away. "It's okay. We kind of lost you for a while. You've been sleeping for two hours. They called me when you fainted."

"Fainted?"

"Don't worry. The baby's fine, and Sarah's doing well. The nurse caught the baby as you dropped to the floor. You were lucky though. I mean you could have hit your head on a heart monitor or something."

"Very funny."

"You know what else?"

"Tell me anything. I can take it."

Jenkins smiled. "Okay. My receptionist says you're flirting with her."

"We were flirting with each other, but that was eight years ago. Anything else?"

"Yeah, she also says you forgot to pick up the new medicine I left on her desk."

"Maybe I did. What was it supposed to do again? I forget."

Jenkins chuckled. "Not much, just improve your memory, that's all."

Pearson rolled around on his hospital bed. Someone had taken most of his clothes off and tucked him under a set of tightly rigged blankets. He struggled against them briefly, and then sighed. "I think I remember you telling me about some new pills. When should I be taking them?"

Jenkins held out a hand with two white candy-like beads in the center of his palm. In the other hand was a glass of water. "Any time in the next thirty seconds or so would be fine with me."

It was Pearson who laughed next. He kept laughing as the gurgling in his throat told him the pills were on the way to his stomach, and everything was under control. He went back to sleep as the figure of Jenkins faded out the door.

"All better now? Nice and rested?"

"Feel much better, thanks."

"Then maybe you wouldn't mind dragging this dead body off my broken leg and seeing how bad it is. You're a doctor, aren't you?"

Pearson shook off his drowsiness and looked Bulger in the eye. "How does it feel, the leg?"

"I'll tell you when you get the damned thing off of me."

Bulger gave a sharp cry when Pearson grabbed what was left of the demon and peeled its rotting carcass away from all that was still living. "I'm sorry. Did that hurt?"

The lieutenant smirked. "I'd say not half as much as when it got its brains blown out. It actually stopped squirmin' after you did that. I had given up, I tell you. Then they just stopped coming. You must have got the last one. Get him off me now, and we can all go home."

"You don't want me to cut the leg off, or anything. You know, like they do in the movies?"

The lieutenant rolled his eyes and spit violently. "No, it feels fine I tell you. It's just that some zombie has been chewing on it and wouldn't let go until somebody put a bullet through his brain. But it's all over now. We can sleep in our own beds tonight and I won't have to listen to your snoring." The soldier paused. "Thanks for being there, by the way. You caught that baby just in the nick of time."

Pearson grinned. "Yes, I did, didn't I?"

NOTHING ELSE MATTERS

by J. Rohr

"It does not take much to make life. Though it has often been the last rampart of those who wish to claim the ultimate supremacy of a higher power, there is little to prove life is a complicated construct. As with any mechanism eyed through ignorance, existence takes on a seemingly magical quality. Take for instance the automobile: a series of compartments funneling combustion to elicit the movement of parts which in turn propel one forward. This may seem like a simplified explanation; however, simplicity does not indicate inaccuracy. The point being that once something is understood it no longer possesses any mysterious qualities. How many people understand the principles that allow an airplane to fly? Yet few modern citizens find flight to be anything other than ordinary, practically mundane, an everyday occurrence. So I stick to my original point when I say that there is nothing mystical to the creation of life beyond our own ignorance."

- Professor Josiah Wilhelm's last known words, continuously circulated around the internet as an audio file since 2002 and disregarded by most of its recipients as spam.

Mark parted the curtain. The buzzing clouds paused as they circled the sky, tempted by the light slipping out the window. He shook his head and let the curtain fall back into place. He didn't turn an eye to the street, not wanting to bear witness.

"You been outside lately?"

"No."

"It's a fucking mess."

"Where did I put my bag?"

"People are getting twitchy."

"How's that?"

"How're they getting twitchy?"

"Yeah."

"I dunno. The usual ways. You know what I mean."

"No, I—ah! There it is. No, I don't, or I wouldn't've asked."

"You can see for yourself."

"I have more important things to do. Any sign of Henry?"

"Not since the last time I saw him and he told me, 'You tell Susie I'll be back in three weeks'."

"It's been three weeks."

"More like four."

"I hate it when he calls me Susie."

"I bet it'd be nice to hear it now."

The window rattled. A distinctive buzz saw hiss accompanied it. Mark felt sweat pepper his brow. He played with the flywheel on his lighter but didn't start a flame. Even the dimmest glow might be too much of an attraction.

Susan asked, "The window's locked?"

"Bolted and sealed. I put that canned plastic across it. You know, the one that sprays on and turns solid."

Flipping through her notebook, Susan nodded. She asked for a pen. Mark brought her one. He offered her a drink. She declined, muttering something about rationing. He took the tiniest swallow he could manage. They'd been locked in the apartment for two days, but it felt closer to six. Up from the street came a series of screams that the two understood all too well; the implications of certain sounds had become common knowledge in the last few years.

Mark said, "Sounded like two people."

"It's their own fault."

"Ice queen," Mark said, trying to joke.

Susan's sardonic expression came with her response, "They should know better."

"They're getting desperate."

"Them or us?"

"Both, I'd like to think, but it seems it's just us."

Susan scratched a few notes, dug a handful of newspaper clippings from her bag, and scanned for correlations.

Mark went into the kitchen to check on his cell phones. He'd rounded up a small collection of phones and power strips before the two sealed themselves in Susan's apartment. As long there was still power he kept the batteries charged on all the phones. The smaller ones, the Swarms, still instinctually went towards bright lights. At night he could toss a glowing phone to draw the Swarm's attention. It might give them a chance to get away if and when he and Susan had to run. Susan didn't think it would work, but she kept her opinion to herself. Mark needed to think he had a means to manage the current situation. However false it might have been, she let him have that feeling.

Henry held his breath. He could feel the stink permeating his skin. Up above, through the concrete, shambling down the streets, he heard the steady rumble of searching hordes. There were so many names for them, and yet no one knew what to truly call them, if they even had a name. Religious zealots, crowding the streets, oddly glad to see the end of times, dubbed them Locusts. Government officials, desperate to show they had control, titled them Entities-X (which made some people wonder what Entities pertained to the preceding parts of the alphabet). The everyday citizen simply called them Bugs. The commonsensical nature of the label made it popular. The simple word alone implied more than any fanciful term or too clever title.

A rat squeezed out of a narrow crack in the sewer wall. It and Henry shared a glance at one another that said, 'Don't blow my hideaway.' The rat darted out, chomped off a mouthful from a corpse, and ducked back in its crack. Henry heard a scuttling from a nearby manhole. Dark shapes, the silhouettes clearly not human, descended rapidly down the hole. He heard groaning. The two Bugs chattered at one another. Their clack-clattering voices shifted sharply into rattle-hisses. Not daring to move lest he disturb his makeshift cover of half eaten bodies, Henry let the noise tell what happened: the pick-axe stomp as the Bugs made jerky advances at one another; the groaning shift to a wail and heavy breaths akin to gasps of pain; the hard plastic crack of carapaces smacking against one another, fighting over the last scraps of the kill; a scream cut off as a gurgle; wet splashes; pick-axes clomping their way farther into the sewers. Henry knew what it all meant though he kept the implications out of mind, glad only to hear the two Bugs moving off, away from him.

Eleven Years Ago.

Gabriel Pruitt planned to be a decent kind of famous. Not the flashy look-at-me-with-my-swarm-of-paparazzi-pretending-to-hate-the-glamour kind of celeb. No, he'd put some style in the presentation, keep himself known but anonymous. People would know the name *Gabriel Pruitt*, though the face would remain a mystery. And like his brother told him, mystery is always sexy.

Gabriel figured on being a musician who always appeared in masks. He knew the kind of songs he wanted to hear but never had. Second step, according to his plan: get in a band. Bands are always looking for singers, and Mama loved his voice.

"Jesus will guide you proper," she always said. She knew. God knew. One day, Gabriel Pruitt would be history. But until then he needed a job, a starting point like all great men. So he got a job pushing a broom. It didn't pay much, but the cash was set to come later. He knew fame and fortune were only a matter of time. Although sometimes it seemed like his wallet never had any green. Girls like the green, his brother always said. So when Gabriel saw the flyer—VOLUNTEERS NEEDED. \$CASH\$—he wrote the phone number down, and called that night.

"What is all that?"

"Are you eating again?"

"I'm hungry."

"So am I."

"You want some."

"No."

Mark looked at the apple, half gone though he thought he'd only taken a few slender nibbles. Shaking it at Susan he said, "Don't let it go to waste."

"You finish it."

"I can't."

Looking up from her papers, Susan sighed. Her stomach rumbled. She took the apple and wolfed down the stem, core, and seeds. Mark half grinned as he chuckled. Susan couldn't help laughing either. Her pragmatic side said they might come to regret it, but she didn't care. It felt good to eat.

"You should take a break," Mark said. He sat down on the floor, cross legged.

Susan bobbed her head from side to side. "I know. I just worry." Her eyes turned to the drawn curtains. "The moment I stop looking at this, I'll want to look out that."

"Would it be so bad?"

Rubbing her eyes, sensing the blood cracks etching the white, Susan shook her head. "I don't know."

"What is all that?"

"Henry left it. He said it might be worthwhile."

"Is it?"

"So far? No. But knowing Henry..." Susan grimaced. "He might have left it to distract me."

Mark picked up a stray piece from the edge of the coffee table. His eyes didn't even absorb the headline. The same grim speculations from two years ago that everyone learned to get anxious at but ignore, like tabloid headlines that had some-how made their way into respected papers. The whole history of a decade reduced to a few scraps on a coffee table. Tossing the clipping back on the pile he snorted at the notion years can be condensed into a few paragraphs, giving all that time as much weight; the reduction not only being retroactive but potentially proactive: the future as reducible and meaningless.

Susan pushed back from the pile. "The only thing I can tell is that there's no mention of him."

Eleven Years Ago.

Tuesday afternoon. Rick Pena cut out early, claiming he had a date Gabriel doubted the retard ever did. "Unless it's another hooker the poor bastard thinks is his girlfriend." Gabriel tried not to laugh, like Mama taught him. He slapped himself twice. Jingling keys, he wondered if any college girls would be at the bar tonight. He didn't care if they had names, just perky tits. He hadn't scored with any of them yet, but it was only a matter of time. *Girls like guys who pound shots with them, especially when the guys pay.* He remembered his brother's advice to the letter.

He scratched at his arm. The doctor told him it might itch. For sixty bucks he didn't mind getting a little itchy. It reminded him of a mosquito bite. He expected that sixty would go a long way towards getting laid. He scratched again. Something felt weird. Rolling up his sleeve, he hoped the needle bite wouldn't look too… purple?

Gabriel leaned on his broom for a minute, trying to think. It looked like the little bump was wriggling, something squirming inside. It popped open, and a little fly came buzzing out.

Henry made his way back to the surface slowly. Daylight was breaking. The larger Bugs always stuck to the shadows after sunrise, though the Swarms still remained. He covered himself with more scent gland, harvested from a Bug he watched two larger ones cannibalize. Something in its stomach seemed valuable to the other two. They made off with it, leaving the ruined carcass behind.

The black clouds, pinpoints gathered in the sky, buzzed high over head. Dripping with stink, Henry turned west and headed back to—he hoped—Susan. He wasn't sure how long he'd been gone. Too long.

He tried not to think pragmatically because his mind kept telling him, 'This is a waste of time. She's either dead or gone. Go on alone.' Would it really be easier just to abandon her and her brother? Perhaps. It made more sense to travel alone. However, he needed her insight. There was information only she could make sense of if they were to get at a solution.

Josiah Wilhelm. Henry remembered arguing, years back that seemed like centuries past, "He proposed a radical new concept in gene manipulation, years ahead of its time, so far advanced there was no way to prove it and only three people understood what he was implying. I still have no idea what he was talking about, but I remember one of his articles. It blew my mind." He pointed at Susan's screen.

"The way this sequence is laid out is exactly like the, the, the LATTICE! The lattice he proposed. And there's a weakness there. We just have to exploit it."

Susan believed him. No one who had any authority did. And that was the end of it. Bugs soon spread all over the city. Reports started coming in from all over the state, and not long after…Henry sat in his apartment, drinking an eighty dollar bottle of cognac.

There hadn't been anyone in the liquor store. He took a bottle of cheap bourbon. For a moment, he thought about leaving cash by a register, then laughed and grabbed a more expensive booze. He snagged a carton of cigarettes, planning to smoke his first in four years. Sipping the fine amber, he watched live news reports. He did his best not to chuckle, but couldn't help himself.

Cackling drunkenly, he said to the screen, "I told them what to do. I warned them." Sometimes tears fell.

Looking out the balcony door he watched the Swarms, clouds of young Bugs hissing like buzz saws. They swooped down on the streets and tore into people, sometimes whole groups. Like flying piranhas the Swarms stripped off every centimeter of flesh in second, and from time to time ate even the bones.

"That's it for this hemisphere," Henry said to himself, "Unless they like the water." He shrugged. The Bugs might make it across the oceans. There was no way to tell, and he felt less reason to care. What did it matter at the end?

Certainly not that he'd found none of the Bugs reproduced, yet their numbers kept increasing. While he could still care, Henry did his best to track the epidemiology. Swarms, the Bugs' youngest developmental stage, always first appeared in a centralized part of the city, spreading out from there; and the swarms only came from this city.

But no one cared about the Bugs' origin, just their extermination. Then survival.

Eleven Years Ago.

"Doc, I'm on fire, man. I'm fuckin' on fire."

Josiah did his best to hush Gabriel, shushing him gently, "It's all part of the process."

"It was a bug, man. A fuckin' bug."

"The injection must have gotten infected somehow."

"I didn't…"

"Of course, it's not your fault, but you will need a round of antibiotics."

"Are they expensive?"

"Not at all. I can administer them, if you'll allow me."

"You're the doctor."

Mark licked the inside of a candy wrapper. He found it at the bottom of his backpack. It tasted like a chocolate-dipped ashtray, which was better than the bread in the fridge. The lights flickered for the second time in the last hour. He disconnected the phones and turned them off to save the batteries. Packing them in his backpack, he glanced at Susan.

She stood at the window, the curtains a hair's breadth apart, one eye to the sliver watching the outside. She sighed. That's all she seemed to do anymore. The newspaper clippings no longer kept her distracted. She spent hours at the window, many sitting with her back against it listening to the sounds outside.

He knew she wouldn't want to hear, but Mark brought it up anyhow. "We're…"

"It's time to go."

"We're leaving?"

"It's been too long." She turned her head, tightened her grip to close the curtain, hold back the tears. "He's not coming back."

"I…"

"There's nothing to say. Even if he's on his way it doesn't matter. We don't have water, the foods rotten, and they're starting to probe the building."

Mark nodded, his face grim. Last night he and Susan woke up to the sound of pick-axes stomping through the halls. Fortunately, they'd been in pursuit of someone. It sounded like a man when he screamed. Mark didn't even know there were other people in the building. But once the Bugs got suspicious, it was only a matter of time before…Mark offered to pack up the few essentials they could still use. Susan went about collecting her notes. They gave themselves fifteen minutes.

Henry needed to take the risk. Removing a flare from his backpack, he sucked in a quick series of breaths. Flare in hand he felt his whole body going taut. One last deep lungful. Hold it. Feeling his nerve cracking, Henry struck the flare. The hissing flame barely sizzled to life before attracting attention. Whipping it down the street the farthest he could fling it, Henry took off, pumping his legs to their limit. Sixty feet to go. He heard the buzz saw whine of the Swarm coming closer. His lungs burned and a sharp desperate gasp told him he'd been holding his breath as he ran. Out of the corner of his eye he saw the Swarm circling low over the flare. Five more feet. Sucking ragged gasps at the air, for a moment the distance to the door seemed to extend and then he was through, telling himself to breathe calmly, relax, the adrenaline making his hands shake.

But he didn't listen to himself.

Instead, Henry charged through the lobby, shouldering open the first stairway door he saw. He took the steps two at a time. She would still be there, waiting. He knew it because he wanted it to be true. And he had the answer, though he needed Susan to make it useful.

One source. The Bugs all came from one source. He'd been right all along, and now…about halfway up Henry's stamina started waning. His legs just wouldn't move any farther. He sat down on the steps, practically hyperventilating. It would be good just to be back. There was work to be done, but it didn't seem so impossible now. The last two weeks he'd been overwhelmed by the sense of knowing a solution yet being powerless to enact it. The only upside had been knowing there was somewhere to go: back to Susan. She'd know how to concoct the necessary poison.

A sound slipped up the stairwell, freezing Henry to the core. Peering over the railing he saw nothing but darkness below. He heard chattering, a clicking language he knew without understanding a word. Slowly, Henry got to his feet. Keeping to the wall, he made his way as quietly and quickly as possible. Every footstep sounded louder in his head than his ear. He fought the urge to run. The right floor at last, he put his hand on the bar to push open the door. CACHUNK—the door popped open, echoing down the stairwell.

Henry didn't wait for the sound of pursuit. Shouldering the door open, he hurried down the hall, door numbers whipping past in a blur. He found Susan's. He ducked through the open door and closed it, careful not to slam. 'Maybe this isn't the right room,' he thought. Susan would never leave the door open. She knew better. It didn't matter at the moment. He decided to stay here till it seemed safe to search for the proper one. It had to be the wrong room. There was no one here.

Stepping away from the entrance, Henry wondered if he could scavenge anything from the apartment. No sense wasting his stay. This looked like Susie's place, down to the Art Deco print. The realization she'd left hit him. Henry knew he'd told her not to wait, but somehow he expected her to. Seeing a slip of paper on the coffee table, Henry picked it up and read.

Henry,
We can't wait any longer. Mark and I are heading west to Minneapolis. He thinks it'll be safer there. We grew up there. I guess it always feels safer at home. If you can, come find us.
Love always,
Susan

Henry knew he shouldn't have expected her to stay. He'd told her to leave. It had taken too long. He wished she was here now and yet felt glad she was gone. Pick-axes tearing at the door.

† † † † †

Eleven Years Ago.

Josiah peered into the microscope. Yes, the size had been increasing. The little critters were growing, developing on their own, evolving. He licked his lips.

"MMMRraaawww…"

"Not this again." Stepping away from the microscope, Josiah rubbed his eyes. Every hour the damn thing needed food. Ever since he'd sealed the room the tiny gnats it disgorged hadn't been able to steal supplies for it. Yes, he'd caught them pilfering food, collecting portions of fruits from his kitchen, carrying them back to feed the growing hive. The living hive. Josiah would feed it himself, but lately—he looked at his hand, covered in dozens of red pockmarks, holes eaten into him. The little swarms attacked him whenever he entered the room.

Sometimes he saw what still passed for the boy's head, staring at him. Glaring? Looking through the peephole he'd put in the door, Josiah eyed the amorphous heap steadily filling the room. It didn't look human, more like a blob growing amongst volcanic rocks; Sections of what used to be Gabriel Pruitt were either spongy charcoal grey or stygian carapace almost concrete hard. Josiah hadn't anticipated this, which made him angry with himself.

The initial resemblance to a beehive, grown in the subject's upper arm, charcoal gray rimmed in black, had been close to his suspected outcome. The injections transformed parts of the subject into a living hive, one capable of producing the small flies that Josiah had designed. However, the transformation had not been insolated. The mutation Josiah induced caused sections of the subject to swell, painfully at first, gradually less agonizing over time, but they never burst. Instead the swelling spread throughout the subject, increasing its size and the amount of hives producing flies. And the flies themselves were now growing, changing.

"MMMMrraawwww…"

"Yes, yes." Josiah went to the kitchen to gather food. He kept it on a strict diet: high protein, plenty of carbohydrates, some sugar but not much. The problem was getting the food into the room. He'd installed a slot at the bottom of the door, like a sliding dog door. He could jerk it open and toss in the food. The swarms would feed the hive. The thing cried out again, louder.

From above, a stomping foot rattled the ceiling. "Shut the fuck up down there."

Josiah took a deep breath, let it out slow to calm his nerves. It would all be worth it. He'd been right all along. Life designed by human hands. The only problem had been designing it too close to the human template. Animals couldn't be used to incubate the first generation. And he couldn't be expected to experiment on himself. No, no, that made no sense at all. Who could understand the data other than himself? If he'd had more time, more money, hadn't been laughed out of…he let the past be the past, inalterable, unlike the future. He who laughs last and all that. Yes, yes.

Sliding the panel back, he tossed food into the room. He heard the swarm before he saw the cloud, a choking buzzing swathing black static. He felt their teeth rip into him and knew without seeing they were carrying pieces of him away to feed the living hive. Swatting at the cloud, killing dozens in the sweep of his arm, but doing nothing to stop the hundreds billowing out of the room, Josiah tried to shout for help only to have his mouth filled, his tongue and gums ravaged in seconds. He reached for the door slot. His hand burned the deeper it reached into the gnawing cloud. Turning to run, he tripped over his own feet. Choking, gagging, he opened his eyes and the Swarm consumed them.

Vacant cars choked the highway. Mark and Susan threaded their way through the mess. Some cars looked peeled open. Scraps of people littered the road: pieces of clothes, badly nicked jewelry, artificial joints, broken glasses, the occasional bone.

"How long do you think this'll take?"

"I don't know."

"Well, should we at least take a car?"

"You know how to hotwire a car?"

"No."

"End of discussion."

"But if we find one with keys, I mean, then…"

"Mark."

"Yeah?"

Susan sighed. Her little brother may have been 25, but sometimes he seemed nine years old. She tried to smile, "Fine. If one has keys, we'll take it."

"I'll keep my eyes open."

"Okay. You let me know."

"It's a long road, but we'll make it."

'Make it where?' Susan thought, but she kept it to herself. Mark needed to know whether their parents were alive or not. She assumed they were dead, but if nothing else it gave the two something to focus on. Although, she did her best not to believe herself. She didn't want their parents to be dead.

She said, "Can you imagine Mom hiding out like we did?"

Mark laughed. "It'd be like that camping trip we took."

"Remember how she told Dad to turn up the fire?"

"And he said we don't have more wood."

"So she said,"—they both quoted their mother—"'What's that got to do with it?'"

Mark shook his head. "Good times."

Susan smiled, genuinely. "Good times."

There was always a chance their parents might be alive, and Susan felt if that were true then maybe Henry was, too.

Henry had never stood on the ledge of a building. He didn't anticipate the wind trying to blow him off. Still, he pressed against the wall with every fiber of his body. He tried not to think about a random Swarm happening past.

He could hear the Bug tearing the apartment apart. The thing seemed to be going through everything to find him. Its clicking sounded angry, then distant.

Henry risked a glance inside. Seeing nothing, he cautiously climbed back into the apartment. Empty.

There was little the Bug hadn't ripped to shreds. Henry picked up the broken armrest from a chair. Susan bought it at an antique store on the Southside. She loved that chair. One less reason to think there'd be a semblance of the past at the end of all this, a chance to get closer to normal some day.

He tossed the scrap of wood aside. One less thing to hope for, but that didn't mean the end. Henry knew about the source.

Desperate weeks clawing through the ruins, wading waist deep in Bug filth and corpses. He once slept between two people who took the peaceful way out—a bottle of sleeping pills and red wine—hiding out among the dead to get a little rest. He saw things he could never erase from memory. The screaming child carried into the sky, devoured in seconds. But it would all be worth it because Henry saw the source: a squalid tenement house on the west end of the city overflowing with the charcoal hive pulsating with life, and spewing clouds of new Bugs. The sound of it haunted him. Not just the clack-clatter of dozens of Bugs, or the cacophonous buzzing of Swarms a thousand thick, but underneath all that, he heard what almost sounded like singing as if the hive itself uttered a soft lullaby to its children.

Wearing the carapace of a dead Bug, Henry snuck up to the hive and collected a sample. Susan would know what to do with it. She had the better mind. When he had pointed out Josiah Wilhem's Lattice in the Bugs' DNA, she saw a way to pull at a thread, unravel the whole tapestry. But she needed a sample from the source. Getting rid of the Bugs permanently depended on it.

Henry shook off the worry this was all just something he thought to keep moving, a fictional reason to stay alive. No, there was hope. He just needed to get back to Susan. So he set off for Minneapolis.

RUN FOR THE ROSES

by Gerri Leen

Zombie Horses can't be beat, doo dah, doo dah
Just be careful what they eat, all in the doo dah day.
—21st Century Folk Song

"They just got so fragile, those old-time race horses. One, two, maybe three races and boom, a condylar fracture, or a sesamoid break. Out for months, maybe for good. Retired to stud, to breed more of the same. It's why we don't use them anymore." Ramon patted Zero Tolerance on the neck carefully as the reporter watched. The horse bared his teeth and eyed the hand that fed him with something very different than affection. "You just do not want to fall off these horses."

"I saw the footage from Gulfstream Park."

"Maybe they shouldn't have called that filly Man Eater?" Ramon laughed. "These babies will run for days if you have the right bait."

Squalling infants would have been the best lure, but the public would never have gone for that. Instead, thrillseekers signed up to ride the pace truck. They got to skip bathing for three days so the "still alive" smell was ever so clear to the horses—horses that were run with muzzles but no whips. Whips were useless on them, didn't make them go—no pain, no gain. But brains…oh yeah, horses would run all day and into the night for some brains.

Fresh, though. Cadavers were of no appeal. Dummies rubbed with raw meat didn't fool them, either. Horses weren't the brightest of animals, but they were bright enough.

"Ramon, what do you have to say to the public outcry that racing should be stopped?"

"Because one jockey got eaten?"

"With a lot of people watching between the simulcast and ESPN coverage."

Ramon shrugged. "Real Thoroughbreds can't cut it. And people don't like to watch Quarter Horses the way they do Thoroughbreds. Personally, I'd rather watch a mule race but they make these babies look like pushovers when it comes to being trainable." He patted Zero Tolerance on the cheek and nearly lost his fingers.

The reporter was studying the horse. "Why do you work with him?"

"Why do lion tamers do that they do? Why do fighter pilots?" He laughed. "It's fun."

"It's idiotic. That horse would eat you in a minute if he got loose."

"Yep, he sure would." Ramon sighed. "Lady, you have no idea what it was like before the zombie horses. I was a rider before I became a trainer. I nearly was killed when Cyber Warfare broke his leg in the stretch of the Belmont. There's never been a zombie horse broke down that way. Never."

"I accept that. But the old time horses didn't eat people. Did you hear that this morning at Zia Park, a zombie horse veered off the track during morning works and ran into the group of clockers."

"Seriously?"

She nodded. "He bit three of them."

"Yikes." He shook his head. "They're off to Zombie Nirvana then. Damn shame. People willing to rise in the dark just to clock horses are few and far between."

"Your empathy is touching."

"The owners don't pay me for empathy. They pay me to get their horses to the finish line first."

"And you're the most successful trainer to do that. I mean look at Zero Tolerance—the favorite for today's race, right?"

Ramon tried not to preen.

"What's your secret?"

He smiled. "Creative feeding."

She took a step back.

"Not humans. You think I could get away with that in this day and age? Everyone is tracked." He smiled. "But there are other warm blooded creatures."

"I don't want to know." She seemed to shudder. "You realize I'm going to use this in the story."

He shrugged.

"You want me to use it, don't you?"

He laughed. "People think my horse here has recent experience with live meat, they may get a little spooked on the track. And this race is big. We both know that."

She nodded. "The biggest." She turned to the cameraman. "We've got what we need. Go get this filed."

The cameraman packed up and left, seemed to be happy to get clear of Zero Tolerance.

"You're not going to edit it?"

"Why bother? You orchestrated this from the beginning to say exactly what you want." She moved closer to Zero Tolerance. "I don't think you feed him live meat."

"No?" He touched her hair. "I could feed you to him."

"You could. If you want to spend the rest of your life in prison." She turned to look at him. "Or Zombie Nirvana if they decide to make the punishment fit the crime."

He dropped his hand. "Just joking around."

"I'm not." She smiled in a way that was distinctly creepy, then moved to the stall door, closing it—closing them in with Zero Tolerance.

"What are you doing?"

"The job I was hired to do."

He realized Zero Tolerance was making no move for her.

"*Eau de Corpse*. It's what David Marsh uses when he works with Captivate."

"Marsh?" Marsh had gone on record saying he was going to win today. That Captivate would take the race by a huge margin.

"He may have paid me to do this." Again the creepy smile. "There'll be an inquiry. The horse will be quarantined until the issue is resolved. The race"—she reached over and unhooked Zero Tolerance's tie-down—"will be long over by the time this boy races again. Do you think his owners will send him to Marsh once you're dead?"

The horse sniffed her briefly, then turned to Ramon, blocking his way to the exit.

"Why?"

"I get five percent of the winnings. That's not chump change. Also—just like you said. It's...fun." She laughed softly as she leaned against the wall and crossed her arms across her chest. "Bon Appetit, horse."

Zero Tolerance's big white blaze was the last thing Ramon saw before the pain began.

ONLY THE LONELY

by Conor Powers-Smith

[Applause]

"Thank you. Thank you, and welcome back. For those of you just joining us at home...*shame* on you."

[Laughter, perfunctory]

"Thank you. But seriously. Tonight we're joined by Dr. Ian Watt Johnson-Simpson, respected public affairs analyst and former Department of Defense Liaison to the Department of Health and Human Services. Thanks again for being here, Dr. Johnson-Simpson."

"A pleasure, Jack. And Ian's fine."

"Just Ian?"

"Dr. Ian."

"Of course. Now, Dr. Ian, before the break we were discussing the unusual circumstances surrounding the outbreak. Now, it's your feeling that this wasn't a failure of policy, so much as—"

"Absolutely not."

"So much as a breakdown at one specific facility."

"That's right. One localized incident, which seems to have arisen as the result of a sort of perfect storm of circumstances. You had the beginning of the flu season—"

"The flu! Then the movies were right, it *is* a virus!"

[Laughter, derogatory]

"Just kidding, of course. But I hadn't heard this about the flu."

"Well, Jack, it's simply this: on the night of the incident, three of the facility's employees, fully a third of its regular staff, were out sick, including the director. Of those present, there's reason to believe that at least two were suffering some symptoms of the flu."

"Not thinking straight."

"Well, we'll never know for sure. But certainly possibly functioning with diminished capacities."

"Sure."

"Then you have the nature of the crash itself, and its location. Usually these sorts of serious disasters leave the staff some measure of preparation time. But this one, as we know, occurred barely three blocks from the hospital."

"And the understaffed morgue."

"Yes. Therefore the standard procedures, which are spelled out very clearly in the official policy, had to be accelerated. There simply wasn't enough time to do things properly, and it appears that some items on the checklist may've been rushed, or even bypassed entirely."

"For example?"

"Well, both machine guns, and all but one rifle, were found with no or very little ammunition, and there weren't nearly enough expended shells at the scene to account for that. We're forced to assume, therefore, that they were never loaded in the first place. And the flamethrowers weren't even touched."

"Because there wasn't time?"

"Yes, and because of course they're rarely needed in the normal course of events. Usually the standard procedure works perfectly well."

"If you don't mind, Dr. Ian, I'd like to hear a little more about that procedure. You must remember, up until three weeks ago, none of us had ever dreamed such a thing might be necessary. Well, maybe the boys in the band. Right, Allen?"

[Laughter, knowing]

"You know what I mean, Doctor. Write their own prescriptions?"

[Laughter, one 'Woo']

"Yes, well. The standard procedure in such a case would call for the bodies to be burned immediately, or, if there were some doubt as to their states of attachment, they'd be isolated until that was resolved."

"Until someone came to claim them."

"Yes, or until it became obvious that no one would."

"How would you know that?"

"Well, Jack, you'd know that when they reanimated."

[Laughter, uncomfortable]

"Oh, yes. Of course."

"But that shouldn't have been an issue here. We don't know who made the decision, but apparently the bodies were placed in quarantine cells on arrival, rather than being sent directly to the crematorium."

"And that was the wrong call?"

"Very much so. It may have been intended as a temporary measure, while the furnaces were brought up to proper temperature. Again, there was very little lead-time."

"So they could've just…come back too quickly?"

"That's possible. The exact timing of a reanimation event varies widely be-tween individuals. There are links to age, body size, metabolism, a whole spectrum of factors, but the process is inherently unpredictable. Some theories say the exact degree of IAD may be a determinant, but that's difficult to quantify."

"And, IAD?"

"Interpersonal Attachment Deprivation."

"Oh, right. Loneliness."

"Well, in layman's terms. According to policy, every subject in this case, except perhaps the driver of the bus, should've been assumed to carry an unacceptably high risk of IAD, and of consequent reanimation. If the furnaces couldn't be brought up to temperature in time, backup protocols should've gone into effect."

"Exactly what—"

"Two rifle rounds to each subject's head."

"Right. Right. And the whole group—"

"Of course. The policy is unambiguous. They're on the list."

"They? Oh, you mean—"

"Jack, this was a busload of retirement home residents. They're not just on the list, they're near the top."

"Right below our audience."

[Laughter, self-deprecating]

"Like most facilities of its size, the Mercy General morgue had six quarantine cells, each designed to accommodate up to four subjects. On the night of the crash, three cells were already at maximum capacity, and two others were occupied by one or two potential reanimates."

"And these would be…?"

"Vagrants. Runaways. Anyone whose occupation or lifestyle was on the list. Anyone whose family or friends couldn't be contacted immediately, or demon-strated a below-average NER when informed."

"And—"

"Negative Emotional Response."

"Sadness."

"If you must. This is an important consideration, because of course it's pos-sible, even common, to be surrounded by associates, and yet still suffer from high levels of IAD."

"Alone in a crowded room, right?"

"That's one way to put it. In any case, the Mercy General facility was already at above-average capacity, and the bus was carrying 47 passengers, in addition to the driver. Quarantine should never have been considered. With the new influx, each cell was forced to house 10 or 11 subjects, and they were never designed to accommodate half that. While one reanimate, or even a small group, is far weaker than a comparable number of living human beings, their combined strength and weight, when focused on a single point—"

"Like say the door of a cell."

"Yes, exactly. Their combined weight can be quite overwhelming."

"And, as you said, they weren't ready for that."

"Not ready at all. From the positions of the remains, the staff appears to have been spread throughout the facility, apparently surprised in the act of going about their normal business."

"And the hospital as a whole?"

"No alert of any kind seems to have been given. The communicating doors weren't locked, in some cases not even closed."

"Doctors, nurses, orderlies. Patients."

"Yes."

"But doesn't that raise another question?"

"How do you mean?"

"Well, considering the abundance of...God, I don't want to say *food...*"

[Laughter, nervous, forced]

"Yes, I take your meaning."

"Well, considering...that. Why would they've left the hospital at all?"

"That's a question born of ignorance, Jack."

"Oh."

"The movies you seem so fond of may assume the prime motivator to be hunger, but that's a misconception. While cannibalistic behavior is certainly one of the more noticeable aspects of the phenomenon, it's actually a byproduct, a symptom you might say, of the larger urge."

"And that is?"

"That is, the urge to seek human contact. You must remember, IAD is at the root of the syndrome. What the subject was unable to establish or maintain in life, he or she seeks in his or her new state. The death of the OIA—Object of Intended Attachment, or victim, if you like—is a necessary but unintended consequence of the urge to consume him or her, which is in turn the result of well-understood psychological processes in the irrational, decaying, yet still human brain of the subject."

"And those processes?"

"The fear and trauma of a lonely death lead to the desperate need for reassuring human contact, which in turn leads to IAD of enormous strength and persistence. Impulse control, awareness of societal norms, and simple sanity are at extremely low or nonexistent levels. What in life would manifest as, say, an impulse to hug or caress, instead becomes a compulsion to devour, and thus to ensure that the contact is maintained indefinitely."

"I see."

"So subjects can be expected to seek out those places where human contact was strongest in life. Anyone in their path is, of course, liable to be pressed into service as a makeshift OIA, but rest assured, the subjects have more definite objectives in mind. Some will head for churches or other religious centers, which they associate with bonds of community. Others will move toward former homes or places of work."

"And in this case, Dr. Ian?"

"In this case we saw most of the usual patterns. Two churches and one syn-agogue in the area proved attractive to a few of the subjects. Of course, all three were closed at noon on a Wednesday."

"Thank God."

"Mmm. Investigators are still collating former addresses, but it appears a siz-able contingent were headed for the residential area several miles west of the hos-pital when authorities intercepted them. A few turned around and went straight back to the shopping center the group had just left, apparently having congregated there in days of greater interpersonal attachment."

"Now that *is* like the movies."

"If you say so."

"And then there was Apple Tree. Was that just on the way to somewhere else, or—"

"That was an objective in itself. The objective, in fact, of more than half of the subjects from the bus. It appears the nursing home had been conducting a program wherein residents visited the preschool several times a week to read to and play with the children. This was designed to both lighten the load on under-staffed teachers, and provide residents with just the sort of interpersonal contact so lacking in their day-to-day lives. On that score, it seems to have been extremely successful."

"But, then, why would they've come back at all? I mean, reanimated? We've established that only the—"

"That program was halted approximately 18 months ago, apparently for lia-bility reasons."

"Oh."

"Naturally, authorities had no way of knowing this was the subjects' destina-tion. The area around the preschool is wooded, as is much of the terrain between it and the hospital, so the sorts of random encounters generated by the other groups were lacking. Authorities didn't arrive on the scene until some minutes after the 911 call placed by one of the teachers there, and by then it was too late to do anything but eliminate the subjects."

"God. How tragic. Ah, my producer's telling me we've got to go to break very shortly here, Dr. Ian, but before we do, is there anything you, as an expert, would recommend to guard against these outbreaks in the future?"

"Well, we could treat each other with a modicum of humanity."

[Laughter, loud, long]

"Ha. That's very good, Doctor."

"Thank you, yes. Ha. No, actually, I'd recommend more flamethrowers."

"OK, very good. We'll take a break, but stay tuned for author—"
"Very high risk."
"How's that, Doctor?"
"Very high risk level, writers."
"OK, very good. Author Sue Dokes, when we return."
[Applause]

INSTINCT

by John Dodd

I grab the rucksack from the kitchen and take the gun from the side, checking that it's still got rounds in it. I take the list of things we're out of from the fridge door and make my way out into the staircase.

It's quiet here, they don't come to the stairs. Most of them don't understand how stairs work, so they end up collapsing against them, then getting up, then falling over them again.

You'd think they'd learn...

But of course they won't, that's what keeps me safe. It's been some months since the bomb dropped but the legacy of it is all around. Those that were left afterwards had to cope with a world filled with people hungry for blood but possessed only of instinct. They'll chase a person for miles if they think they're going to get a meal, but if you give them something that their brain recognizes, the instinct will kick in and distract them long enough for you to make a break for it. I check the batteries on the latest phone and start down the street.

Sunday mid-morning, best time to get supplies.

It's quiet out, most of them are sleeping in; the dead don't need sleep, but their instinct is to close their eyes and stay still for eight hours a day in bed. As long as you don't go waking them up and disrupting their pattern, they'll stay there and not get up. I stay on the side of the road furthest from the park. It's just past 0600.

Don't want to disrupt the morning runs.

It's a half mile down to the center of Times Square, a five minute walk normally, ten minutes when you're avoiding the looks from hungry cabbies in their solar cars looking for fares.

If we'd still had petrol, that problem would have gone away some time ago.

The candy bars in the store are reaching their expiry date, before long I'll have to travel further afield to find anything resembling sustenance. I hear the shuffling in the back and the shop assistant shambles around the corner. His face is gaunt with the skin loose around the atrophied jawline, mouth working up and down and eyes vacant as he locks on to me. I take a box off the shelf and hold it out to him as he gets closer.

"I want it wrapped," I say.

He takes the box and goes to the till as I put another box in my bag and walk out.

Got to love Draconian customer service training.

I leave the store before it realizes it can't wrap things and head back up the road. One of them looks at me from over the road. It's dressed in a very expensive suit and shoes that cost more than my car did. It looks me up and down and licks its lips.

Note to self, don't wear short skirts near the banking district.

I run as the well-dressed zombie closes in on me. I take the phone out and hit the green button, the phone beeps and then starts ringing as I throw it backwards. The well-dressed zombie stops and flails in the air to catch the phone, pressing it to its ear as I run onwards. There's a growl as a zombie with a brush sees me run across its patch and it starts lumbering after me. I run down the hill and stop with a sudden thrill of terror as I see the green all around me.

I'm in the park...

There's the sound of pounding feet and ten Lycra-clad dead people come jogging over the hill and see me in the middle of their lane. I run away from them and up towards the east side of the park. It's not that far to the apartment and all its security doors, but joggers are one of the few who know how to use steps, and they don't get tired like I do.

I sprint now, leaving them behind with their measured pace. They'll get me over distance but as long as I can keep in front, I'll be fine. I run through the east gate and up on the high side of the park, my lungs now feeling like they're bursting. I slow to a fast walk and continue up towards the church as the dead behind me emerge from the park and jog towards me. My watch beeps and I curse as the dead file out of the open church doors.

End of morning service.

The dead walk towards me, the joggers catching up with churchgoers as the whole mob continues towards me. I reach my building and fumble the keys, dropping them on the floor as the mob gets closer and closer. I put the keys in and hear the dead within metres of me.

If I just go in, they'll batter the door down.

I turn back and sit down on the stairs as the dead close in, joggers, churchgoers, bankers, now just hungry dead. Seconds before I get turned into burger...

That's an idea...

I cross my legs and cup my hands in front of me.

"Spare some change?" I call out.

Instantly the dead all look straight ahead, their eyeline passing above me as they immediately go about their daily business. I wait for a half minute and then go inside.

Got to love New York…

PRESERVATION

by Rebecca Boyle

"Have you been drinking today, Ma'am?"

Linnet scratched her tongue around the inside of her mouth.

"No," she croaked.

"Would you breathe into this, please?" The police officer held the instrument just outside the car window. Rain pattered gently on his hand. She leaned out and placed her lips around the mouthpiece.

"I need you to breathe into this in a long, steady breath," he instructed.

She stayed still. The rain fell softly in her hair, and she began to shake.

"Are you brea…" he shook his head. "Ma'am," he said sternly.

She removed her lips, then reached out and grabbed his hand. His brief surprise allowed her to draw it into the car and press his index and middle fingers to her throat. His eyes grew wide. He dug his fingers deeper.

Linnet swept his arm out of the car, turned the keys in the ignition and blazed off down the road. He faded into the distance, too stunned to follow.

"Yes?" the man said. A breeze wafted past her and into his nostrils, which wrinkled. He looked her over guardedly.

"Mister Jeremy Foreman?" she asked.

"Yes?" He had opened his main door, but a screen still separated them. Looking at her, he swung the door just a little further shut.

"You're a roboticist?"

"Yes…" he said suspiciously. "Can I help you?"

"I have a job for you." Linnet lifted the suitcase to face him and clicked it open. It only took him a moment to register what was in it. He opened the door.

"You'd better come in." He led her down a bare corridor into a cream-walled living room. There was a large television on one wall, a few beer cans in the bin. The chairs were black leather, and obviously new. Linnet hesitated before sitting in one. Once she sank back into it, she surrendered control over her body.

"What's the job?" he asked, sitting across from her. If he believed, as she thought he must, that she was approaching him for assistance with a crime, he was unperturbed by the thought.

"I…" she trailed off. One lost chance, one wrong word, and he'd throw her out. "Feel my pulse," she ordered.

He raised his eyebrow, glanced again at the contents of the case, and shrugged. He got up. Taking her hand, he rested his fingers against her wrist.

And stiffened.

He pressed his fingers in harder, then pulled away. The skin on her wrist had held the impressions he had made. Sniffing, he breathed in the scent that had flirted with him at the door.

"Is this some kind of joke?" he demanded.

Linnet pulled a compact mirror out of her handbag and offered it to him. He hesitated, confused. Linnet held the mirror to her open mouth. Understanding, he took it off her and repeated her action. Checked the mirror. No condensation had formed on the surface.

"Is there any particular reason we're going through this rigmarole?" he asked wryly. His ironic expression flickered like a dying light bulb. He glanced at the mirror again and the corner of his eye twitched, but he composed himself and gave it back to her. Linnet noticed the beads of sweat forming in his hairline.

They exchanged a long, potent look. Without warning, Linnet whipped a Swiss Army knife out of her bag and stabbed herself in the arm. Jeremy yelped and jumped back.

"What…the…hell?" he yelled. He stumbled back across the room. "I'm calling the police." He searched his pockets for his phone without success.

Pain echoed through Linnet dully. She was losing her senses slowly, but not slowly enough. A little blood oozed out of the wound, thick and clotted. She'd have thrown up if she could.

She waved the arm at Jeremy, the knife still buried to the handle. Look at me, she demanded of him silently. Look at me!

He did.

Jeremy fell back into his chair, eyeing the knife, clutching a pillow to his belly between two large hands.

Speak, she told herself. "I'm…" A wave of panic drowned her. She couldn't say it. "I'm…d…." She clawed at her hair with a hand, then snatched it back quickly. Scanned it for blood, skin, hair. God, she might pull herself apart. No, it was fine. She had to keep talking. "I don't know what will happen to me when I… dis…disinte…" Keep going. Just keep going. "I'm already slower. My…this body is getting harder to move. I think my vision, my hearing…are going to go as well."

There was no moisture in her mouth to gulp, but she made the movement. "What will happen to me when…when they do go? I'll be…" Trapped. In darkness.

She sped on, desperately. "You could build me a body. Enclose my skeleton in a…a replica of me. It won't need any electricity or power. I'd be the power. I mean…I can still move this." She raised an arm vaguely. "Maybe…you could give me cameras to see through for eyes, and recorders so I could hear…" She trailed off.

Jeremy was paralysed, his attention fixed on the floor. He was murmuring, "I must be dreaming, I must be dreaming, I must be dreaming," like a mantra.

He had to help her. By the time she found someone else like him, she'd be too far gone to act the supplicant. If only she could cry! Make this man feel for her, as a young woman. An attractive one. A rich one. Trapped.

She stood shakily and forced her legs towards him. He curled himself more tightly into the chair. She grabbed his hand. He was too frightened to pull away. He could have—she didn't have the strength to resist him.

His eyes swiveled towards her, glistening with fear.

"I'm not going to hurt you." She held his hand tighter. "My name," she said, "is Linnet. The money is yours. And however much more you need. As much as you want." What more could she say to convince him? "Isn't this a challenge?" she added hopefully.

His attention shifted to her hand. She released her hold. Jeremy lifted his own hand out in front of him like someone else's soiled tissue. His eyes fell shut heavily. His breathing slowed and deepened and after five minutes, when he opened his eyes, he met her gaze.

"I'll do it."

At her demand, he photographed her. That evening. Before she deteriorated any further.

So he'd taken his camera and aimed it at her from across the room, his fingers clicking only when she prompted him, as though the movement was only an involuntary nervous reaction to her voice. When she was no longer capable of directing the operations of this man, what then? Would he just leave her? Run?

A small part of her cried out that if it was her she'd have run already.

She watched from behind as he downloaded the photos onto his computer. They were appalling. Intimate and embarrassing. Linnet had orchestrated them, had known their importance, but to see them…

"They look like porn," she said softly. Jeremy jumped in his seat and whirled around. "Sorry," she said. He shuddered and swung himself back around to face the computer.

Involuntarily she began to chew her lip. Tasted stale, metallic blood. Stifled a yelp.

"Don't enjoy those photos too much," she said to him bitterly.

"Do I look like I'm turned on by dead women?" he spat.

"I…" Dizziness overcame her and she tottered backwards into a chair, burying her face in her hands. Jerked them away when she caught their scent. A little sob escaped from her.

Jeremy winced as she slumped in the chair. "Look," he said, softly, with difficulty, "I don't want to offend you, or anything, but…would it be possible for you to stay in the bathroom? The furniture is new, and the bathroom is easier to cl…" he stopped.

Linnet rose. "Which way is the bathroom?"

"Um…I'll show you." He led the way down a corridor, practically walking sideways to keep her in view. He flung open a door and let her shuffle in. "I… uh…need to go to work tomorrow, but maybe we can start tomorrow evening, huh?"

Linnet nodded. Jeremy nodded back awkwardly, and closed the door.

Jeremy took his laptop and wallet and dashed out of the house. Dazed and frantic, he drove to a pub down the road, then sat in the carpark, dithering.

He had a dead body in his house. And it was…walking. Talking. It had given him money and told him to take photographs of itself. Grisly photos. *Horrible* photos. It had sat on his chairs and covered them with…

Maybe he'd killed his girlfriend and his guilt complex was making her walk and talk. Sure. He didn't remember a girl named Linnet, though. And he didn't think he was the kind who'd kill his girlfriend. But maybe he had. The thought was almost comforting. Of course. It was his girlfriend. Maybe it was just an elaborate joke, she wasn't even dead. If only he could remember…He dialed a number on his mobile, fingers missing every second key.

"Duncan? It's Jeremy."

"Hey, man."

"Look…um…do I have a girlfriend called Linnet?" he crossed his fingers.

"What? You don't even have a girlfriend, mate."

"Do I know anyone named Linnet? Who might want to play a joke on me?"

"I don't think so."

"Are you sure?"

"Yes," Duncan paused. "Look, you okay? You sound like you're in trouble?"

"No, I'm fine. Are you…are you sure? Maybe not even Linnet, right, but someone…look, a woman, about yay high." He realised the stupidity of indicating the height with his hands. "Uh. No. Um…I don't know, average height? And with kind of auburny hair, uh…" Cold, pale skin. Deathly skin.

"I don't know, mate," said Duncan, exasperated.

"Okay…um…thanks, Dunk."

He had a corpse in his house. He'd taken photos of it. Felt its pulse. No, he didn't. He hadn't.

Decisive, he drove back to his house. He crept up the corridor to the bathroom in bare feet chill against the tiles. Opened the door a crack.

It was there. A corpse. Lying in his bathtub. The knife was still sticking out of its arm.

He slammed the door and ran straight back out to his car. There was another car there. Not his neighbours'. Hers? What if they were looking for her? Found the car and found the body? He'd have to get rid of it. They'd think he'd killed her. For the money. The money on his table. He should get rid of that, too.

Well…if he got rid of the car that should be enough.

But then what to do with her? Bury her? Throw her in a river?

No. It talked. And moved. It'd scream or struggle. He'd have to let it rot. In his…in his bathtub?

He wouldn't come back. Or he'd wait till she was helpless and then he'd bury her. And she wouldn't be able to do anything. She'd be in complete darkness. She'd go mad. Maybe that would be best. Go mad. Forget.

Linnet viewed the bathroom blearily. Cleanish, white tiled. A toilet with the seat up. A little row of aftershaves and deodorants before a slightly splattered mirror.

The mirror. She could just see it from the bathtub. She raised an arm cautiously, and watched the reflection rise. Then she steeled herself, and looked at it for real. She let out a yell.

Mold. She was growing…mold.

For the first time she noticed the thin coating of water around the edges of the bath. Daring herself, she lifted her arm to her nose and inhaled. She shrieked.

Wrenching the knife from its sheath in her arm she began hacking at herself. Skin and flesh parted from the bone in ragged hunks, falling in bloody shreds. For a short while, she was consumed. All she saw was the mold. The rot.

It passed. In some spots the bone lay bare—in other places, red muscle oozed. She threw the knife away, shaking.

She wouldn't last. She couldn't last. Even if he did come back, how long would it take him? And how long could she stay…herself…without her senses?

She heaved herself out of the bath and ruffled through her handbag. Finding a pen, she manipulated it awkwardly to write a few lines on a roll of toilet paper. In case he did come back. Oh, please, may he come back.

Her vision blurred. Her legs began to buckle beneath her. Tottering back to the bathtub, she collapsed into the malicious, seeping, water. With a hand she idly picked at the exposed flesh on her arm. Her mind wandered away.

Then he was back. She felt it. He was back. And he'd bury her alive. Alive? Yes, alive!

He couldn't do that to her. He couldn't.

She clawed her way upright and tried to walk. She could barely see. Raising her arms before her she felt her way across the room. Crashed into a wall. Turned. Kept walking. The door, the door! She had to find the door. He'd kill her. He'd kill her.

Jeremy reeled back and gagged. Holding his breath, he dived into the bathroom again. It was walking. Walking, arms outstretched, like in every B-grade film he'd ever seen. Its arm looked like someone had been slashing at it. A wet patch on the wall held the mark of a body that had careered into it. Even as he watched, it walked into another wall with a crunch, and left some of itself there. It turned. Began to walk towards him.

Jeremy screamed.

It tottered and fell. It crashed down on its knees and then collapsed on the floor. From its depths came heavy, grating sobs that wracked its body.

He had pressed himself against the wall. For a moment, he watched it shake.

Then he rushed over to it and with strong arms beneath its armpits heaved it to its feet. Half carrying it, half supporting its leaden attempts at motion, he guided it back to the bathtub and dropped it there.

Turning his palms up he examined them, then his clothes. He threw up.

Her vision faded out completely as he looked down at her. Her hearing caught a murmur then died. She flapped an arm. Kept flapping it. She was here. She couldn't let him forget it.

She didn't stop.

Jeremy addressed it knowing it was beyond responding. Perhaps even beyond hearing. Its arm flapped desperately at him. A plea.

"I'm going to have to get the flesh off you." His stomach roiled. "I can't take it." He moved off and as though she sensed it, the arm-flapping grew wilder. "I'm coming back," he snapped.

He made his decision suddenly, and it surprised him. It had sobbed. It had begged. There was a person, or the remnant of one, in that monster. If he died, and became something like that…He allowed the thought to penetrate for just long enough to give weight to his decision, then blocked it. He couldn't afford to think about the implications. The thing was just an it. This was just an experiment. There was no person in there.

He fetched a knife. Then he masked his face and put on three pairs of rubber gloves. He didn't bother to cover his already ruined clothes.

He carved what meat he could off the bones. Slithers and hunks of it accumulated in the bathtub. Concentric rings of pale red formed around its edges. He tried not to think about it. Just focused on the task, as he cleaned off each bone. Just like cutting a roast, or something. He could believe that.

The face was hard. It took him an hour of dithering, of indecision, to strip off that face.

Once he'd done what he could, he got out a large saucepan and boiled the rest off the bones. He couldn't stay in the same room. He would duck in to check the progress, gag a little and run out again. As each bone was done, he dried it on a paper towel. He went through a lot of paper towels. Then he took the bones down to his workshop. In twos, in threes.

Part of him—no, all of him—hoped the disassembly had destroyed her. It would be so much easier that way.

But when he took the last bones down to the workshop…the skeleton—the thing—had reassembled itself on the table. It waved a hand limply.

He flipped. With a screech he ran out of the room and into his bedroom. Slammed the door shut, and shivered beneath an armload of blankets. He didn't know how long he stayed there, and afterwards, couldn't remember what he'd been thinking. Maybe it was better he didn't.

Gradually, he became aware of a rattling and thumping down in the workshop.

The skeleton was walking itself into the walls again. Desperately pacing back and forth, all over the room. Falling down, hoisting itself back up. Crawling.

He guided it back to the table like he'd guide a blind man across a highway. Picked up the bones he'd left on the floor and put them next to it on the table. Told it softly, "I'm here. I'll be back." It seemed to know, and calmed down.

The bathroom. Going back to survey the carnage, he threw up what little was left in his stomach. He girded himself and fetched out cleaning materials. Scooping the meat out of the bath, he triple wrapped it in garbage bags and buried it beneath a cairn of stones in the backyard. Just as well his neighbours weren't nosy. When he went back inside he started the painstaking job of scrubbing and disinfecting. Haltingly. He couldn't stick to it for too long at a time.

The toilet roll had blood on it. Grimacing, he took it off. There was a scrawl in black writing across the sheets: "Give me ears first. Talk to me. Or I'll go insane."

He shivered and threw the toilet roll in the rubbish.

Jeremy cleaned the bathroom three times, using three bottles of disinfectant. Even when he was done he swore to himself he'd never wash in there again.

So he took himself to the laundry, where he used an entire cake of soap to scrub himself raw. And he still couldn't shake the feeling that he hadn't completely gotten rid of the traces.

He made it ears, but conveniently forgot why he was doing it. Just a whim. There had been no plea. No woman called Linnet. Just an experiment. But at night, when he closed his eyes, he dreamt he could never open them again, that he could never feel or hear or talk again. It was the only reason why, each morning, he kept working on it. Even though he made a good attempt to suppress his knowledge of his own motives. For his own sake.

He put the 'ears', or the basis for them, straight into the skull. The arm, constantly waving, halted halfway through its trajectory.

"Um...Linnet?" he said cautiously. "Uh...can you hear me? If you can, raise your other arm."

The arm was raised. He shivered.

"How's it going? Uh...I don't know what to say to you." What could he say? The skeleton looked impassive, just lying there on the table. Neither arm moved. He didn't want to speak to it, but if he didn't...left it alone, in the darkness...

"I'll just tell you what I'm doing in the workshop as I do it. How about that? Um...alright, when I ask a question, one wave means 'yes' or 'good' and two waves means 'no' or 'bad'. Okay?" One wave. "Okay."

She'd had to wait a week for her ears. In the meantime, her whole world had been dark and silent. She had periods where she couldn't remember anything she'd been thinking about, where it was all just blankness, or the rush of raw emotion. She tried to banish the blankness by thinking of her friends, her family. It didn't help. What were they doing? Were they looking for her? It only drove her deeper into the dark. She sang to herself instead, talked to herself about movies and books. Dismissed her family from her thoughts. She wouldn't be able to go back to them anyway. Well, maybe. For a little while. Until they started expecting her to grow old. But what excuses could she give for her absence?

Her first realization, after she'd lost all of her senses, was that she could feel Jeremy's presence. Just vaguely. So for a week she worried when he was in the room, waving to make sure he remembered her, yet panicking about what he was doing. What sick fantasies he might be enacting. Whether he intended just to keep her as a novelty.

But when he was out of the room, she had nothing.

Then she could hear again. And Jeremy talked to her. He wasn't a bright conversationalist. When he was measuring and building he'd explain what he was doing, what his plans were. He'd tell her when he left the room, and when he was going to bed so not to expect him for a few hours. But time meant nothing to her. She felt the same terror whether he left for five minutes or five hours…and it always felt like days. He told her he was working on her in the morning and the evening. Between work and sleep. So she was alone most of the time.

Jeremy's one-sided talks gave her something to focus on, but not enough. It was like reading a technical book on how to fix a computer. He never tried to involve her, though he could have, if he tried, devised a way for them to communicate. She didn't know Morse code so she couldn't force him to communicate with her that way. Part of her resented it. Didn't he realise what she was going through? But then, she'd rather not talk. She had nothing to say. Not to him. Better to stay silent.

When he discovered Linnet's name in the newspapers, about five weeks after he began, he wasn't sure whether to mention it. For one thing, it would force him to relate this—creature—to that woman. But the plaintive "I'll go insane", in that shaking writing, haunted him. But maybe she…no, it…would go less mad if it knew what was happening. It must be wondering. He decided to ask. If it wanted, he'd read it the articles. But that was all. That was the limit of what he'd do. He would not communicate with her actively, not unless he had to. He didn't want to get to know her…It! That was dangerous.

"Linnet?" he asked it. "There's a newspaper article here about you. Do you want me to read it?"

One wave.

It took a year. A year in which all Linnet heard was Jeremy's technical step-by-step, and the articles about her 'disappearance' in the paper. Quotes from her sister, her father, her friends. How they missed her. Had she been kidnapped? Murdered? All her loved ones questioned as though they had done something wrong, police suspicion flitting capriciously from person to person. All the people she cared about.

When Jeremy had asked her, she knew she should have said no. But she had said yes. And didn't regret it.

It was better to know. It gave her a sense of conclusion. That is where my association with them ends, she told herself forcefully. And the despair that washed over her then carried her off, far from reality. It was getting harder and harder to stay connected. Why not just lie here forever, mind drifting further and further away? Eventually, she might even die.

But she didn't have to keep losing herself. All this time, she might not have been slipping away if he had done something more. He could have prevented it. And he didn't do anything. He'd put the ears in within a week, why not the eyes? A voice? What the hell was he doing, leaving her in the dark, without any way of communicating, any way of holding on to her humanity? She'd rage about it for a while, then forget it all again.

Towards the end, he started reading her other things as well. She didn't know why he suddenly broke his rigid rule, but he did. He started reading her the football results. It was ludicrous. But it gave her a slightly firmer grip on the world. She felt grateful for it, then got angry at him that it was the best he could do.

And then one day he'd started leaving the radio on for her, which moved her despite herself. He left it on for her all the time while he was away. Sometimes while he was there. That way he didn't have to talk. But she had something.

The radio had been a spur of the moment thing. One night—late, late at night—he'd finished working for the day. After working on her so long, after having read yet another article to her on her own disappearance, he had been feeling sympathetic. He had those swings constantly: swings from a heartless, cold outlook, the mechanic's outlook, where he didn't have to try too hard to sever the connection between himself and his subject; and abrupt changes to pity. He normally left the room for the latter—he couldn't work if he started thinking of it as…real. But he'd stuck the radio on as he went out. The next morning, he'd determined he would turn it off. What a stupid idea. And walked in on her tapping along to a pop song with her skeletal fingers.

After nearly nine months of planning, and assembling what he could away from her, he coated the bones in steel for strength and started building her. Sometimes he felt guilty he hadn't given her the means to speak, to smell, to feel, before that time. He could have.

But it would have meant acknowledging her. Already he felt like a sadistic voyeur, one of those creatures that got their kicks feeling up corpses in a morgue. Particularly as she laid there, semi-complete, artificial skin covering the curves of her well-replicated body. Every time he touched her he felt like a rapist.

So he didn't put in the eyes, the pressure sensors, the voicebox…none of the sensory 'organs', until the very last moment, three months later.

And she could speak.

"Jeremy?" she said tentatively, then laughed. She heard a thump like someone jumping backwards in fright. The voice...it sounded like her. Who knew how, but it did.

"I'm here," came the voice. Gruff. Reluctant.

"Are you nearly finished?" she asked eagerly.

A long pause. "Just the eyes to go." Cough. "There are pressure sensors in your fingers. If you press them against the tabletop..."

She pressed, and the table felt heavy and solid. Her hand was lifted up and then she heard, "Now try again."

It was less dense, and she felt herself pressing it down. Couldn't feel the texture, but could feel it compress beneath her fingers. "Something like a sponge?" she asked cautiously.

"Close enough. A wad of cotton wool." He kept each word clipped, business-like. No connection.

"I didn't put the sensors everywhere. Feet, hands, lips, butt, a few other places. If you want any more, I'll add them in later." The voice suggested he'd rather not.

"Now, just...be quiet until I've got the eyes in, okay?" There was a blur, and Jeremy's face came into focus. A barely remembered face.

"Hold up some fingers," she said to him. He held them up. "Three."

"Which ones?"

"Right index and middle, left pinky."

A closed, but satisfied smile looked down on her. He was pleased. She knew he didn't want to be pleased, but he was. She laughed.

"You can turn off that radio now."

She raised herself slowly. He'd dressed her in a pair of jeans and a blue t-shirt. The body looked good. Better...it looked like her.

It was surprisingly easy to walk, once Jeremy helped her to stand. He led her down a corridor and into the bathroom.

She hesitated before the door. It was cleaner than it had been. The aftershaves and deodorants were gone, and the mirror was no longer splattered. The mirror.

She took a good, long look at herself. Wait! She held her breath and lifted up her arm, where she'd seen the green shadow. No...it was just an illusion.

The face. Yes, that was hers. Probably. Her eyes, weren't they a little cloudy? No, that was just the light. A fold of cloth at her side, just for an instant, looked like peeling skin.

"It's..." she hesitated. Wriggled the metal and plastic fingers. A fantastic feat of engineering. He could have won a prize for something like this. But he never would. "It's brilliant," she told Jeremy's reflection. And it was. It would just take a while to get used to. She'd manage. Better this than...than what she'd had to live with for the past year. She could live again.

He had not entered the bathroom for the past year, but he'd led her there anyway. It was the only place where he had a large enough mirror.

It smelt. He sniffed again. No, it didn't. But there, on the tile in the corner, was that a stain? He edged over to the bathtub, expecting to see her lying in it, bleeding. But she was over by the mirror. Occasionally she made a startled movement and clutched at some part of herself as though she'd been bitten by a spider.

But he'd done well. She looked good.

What was she going to do now? No, he didn't want to know. He did, but he wasn't going to ask. The whole experience had been poisonous enough. His responsibility for her…no, not her. It's an it. It has always been an it. His responsibility for it—it, it, it!—was over. But what could he do, throw it out of the house straight away? Could he throw it out at all? It was probably half mad. Could he let something like that loose? Look at the way it was examining itself, as if it was still…

Ugh. No. Don't think about it. Here his responsibility ended.

It turned to face him. She…damn! *It* was quite attractive.

Goddamit, he'd helped it enough.

"May I stay a week longer, just while I get used to this?" It asked.

No, it couldn't. Tell it to get out!

"Sure," he said.

She was getting more stable. Since getting her new body she had lapsed only once or twice: clawing at her impregnable skin in fright, sure it would rot away.

Jeremy stayed distant. He avoided her, and she avoided him. She owed him everything, but she didn't like him. Couldn't like him. Not after what he'd seen and done. After all he *hadn't* done.

At nights she still had to listen to the radio to keep herself from becoming hysterical with fear of the darkness, and sometimes she became the radio and forgot who she was.

But she was strong. She'd gotten this far. She'd make it.

It left with a short, quiet thank you at the door. Jeremy answered it with a curt nod. As it had gone down the path, he'd almost considered calling it back. Why? To savour the culmination of his skills a little longer? To save the world from that monstrous thing he'd given a form? It might live forever, now.

He still hadn't asked it what it'd do. Told himself he didn't want to know. He *would* cut this link, he *would* forget all of this. His hands shook by his sides as he watched its receding back. Saw, briefly, the bloodied corpse stumbling across his bathroom, the waving hand, begging him…the bubbling stew of bones, and his vomit on the bathroom floor. He didn't know whether to yell out, apologise for not doing more to help it…or force her—It! God damn It!—to the ground and take it apart again, throw its bones into a creek and let it go mad where it couldn't do any harm.

And waste all his work, all his sacrifices?

So he just stood there, and watched it walk away, not once turning to look back at him.

All around him the tombstones stretched away, plots covered in brown grass and dusty soil. An aging eucalypt bowed low over the tombs, casting a dappled, moldy light. He stayed by Duncan's open grave long after the rest of the crowd dispersed. Trying to convince himself that he wasn't betraying Dunk by leaving. But Dunk was dead. Really dead. That car had torn him apart, how could he not be?

It was fine. He could go. Move on. Relief coursed through him, and he began to walk away, almost happy.

And heard the scratching. He froze. There was a sob. A muffled cry.

No. No.

More sobbing. More scratching, quick and desperate. A stifled groan, a dry hand beating against an unyielding surface. Linnet, beating herself against the bathroom walls, leaving wet pink blotches on the white tiles.

"I can't see!" a voice screeched.

Jeremy ran. He had to get out of here. He couldn't do it again. The screech echoed in his ears though he knew he was already too far away to hear it.

Tears flowed down his cheeks. Half of him wanted to race back, to start digging…And start again the days of rot and the smell of blood and of cooking flesh and the fear and the pain and the darkness. What if it was him, down in the deep and the dark without hope or sight? He stopped still.

No. He couldn't afford to think that way. Could never afford to think that way.

He gritted his teeth. With leaden steps he walked out of the cemetery. Not looking back. Willing himself to leave Duncan…It…behind.

CARRION LUGGAGE

by Shane Simmons

The ticket said he was on a connecting flight out of Haiti to New York. There was a lineup of passengers for flight 207 to LaGuardia, and they all needed to be on board in the next ten minutes. The baggage checkers had to keep the pace brisk if they were going to stay on schedule. Still, they had to stop and look. He only had one bag with him and that would be easy enough to pass. There was just enough time to spare him a good lingering stare.

Florida's Panhandle International saw more than its fair share of oddballs and weirdos. Half the time they were also boarding a flight for New York.

This one was dressed like an undertaker, though not any undertaker of contemporary times. His clothes were black. Only the dress shirt under his vest and tie was a different color: white. He had on an old top hat, dignified, but scuffed and worn by time.

His skin was almost as dark as his clothes, deeply colored to the point where it nearly obscured the lines of his face in the poor lighting of the terminal. When his lips parted, the brilliance of his teeth drew the eye away from any less prominent feature. He smiled broadly. Too broadly. The smile didn't literally reach from ear to ear, but it came close, stretching right back to the hinge of his jaw as if his skin were too loose and his muscles too tight.

Margaret stood at her post next to the metal detector and waited for the man to approach. He looked down at her with yellow eyes magnified many times by the little circular glasses perched on the tip of his nose. The lenses were almost as thick as they were wide with dozens of tiny air bubbles trapped inside the glass.

"Just the one bag?" Margaret asked.

"Only the one. Yes," he said, barely moving his lips and never breaking his unsettling smile.

Margaret broke his gaze and placed the bag on the conveyor belt. She watched it disappear through the flaps of the X-ray machine and then pointed the man towards the metal detector.

"This way please," she said, gesturing at the open doorway when he failed to proceed. He was still carefully watching the machine his bag had just disappeared into.

Attracting his attention with a broad wave of her arm, Margaret ushered the man through the empty frame of the metal detector. He had to duck to clear the top bar. He repeated the motion after tripping the alarm with a plain steel cigarette case the first time. It was the only metal item on his person, and he was cleared on the second pass.

Sally, the youngest member of the baggage-check crew, watched the X-ray monitor. She gasped loudly as the man came through to her side. It wasn't a reaction to him, although he might well have elicited a similar response had she been looking his way. She was staring at the monochrome outline of the contents of his bag.

"What the heck are those things?" said Sally, although she'd already taken an accurate guess.

Rob, her supervisor, looked up from the handbag of toiletries he was picking through. He was as surprised as Sally, but didn't let on.

"Looks like bones," he said matter-of-factly.

Everyone at the baggage check exchanged glances. Sally was still staring blankly at the screen, which was now exposing the more conventional contents of someone else's luggage. Rob caught the tall man's bag as it came through the second set of flaps and dragged it onto the counter. Everyone did their best to look over his shoulder from where they were already standing as he pulled it open. No-one saw much, until Rob took out a darkened femur from the bowels of the bag for everyone to have a look at. The tall man watched the search carefully, but said nothing.

"That's a human bone, isn't it?" said Margaret.

"It can't be," Sally insisted.

Rob replaced it in the bag. When he withdrew his hand a second time, he had a human skull held carefully but firmly in his palm. Several gold fillings were clearly visible in the nearly complete row of teeth that hung down long and crooked. So was a wide fracture that spread across two of the skull plates in a jagged curve.

"My uncle," said the tall man in a tone that suggested he thought that would explain everything.

Everyone knew the flight was going to be delayed for sure now. The crew continued checking bags anyway as Rob telephoned security.

Eventually they had to let the flight go, forty-five minutes late, with one seat empty.

The tall man sat in the airport security offices. He'd calmed down only after he was assured he'd be reimbursed for his ticket and put on another flight if everything was cleared in the next couple of hours. Since then, he'd been sitting perfectly still on a stiff wooden chair, with his hat in his lap. He'd offered no words or explanations since he'd handed over his passport. He just waited, politely.

Andrew Isaki returned to the desk where the tall man, identified as René Shanda on his passport, sat alone with only the video-surveyed door offering a way out. Andrew placed the passport on the desk and sat down on a couch across from Mr. Shanda. Shanda made no move to retrieve his documents. He sat expressionless, following Andrew with his eyes. There were answers to be had, and Andrew wasn't going to have an easy time of it.

It was Andrew's job to politely grill people detained from getting on a flight, usually until the appropriate officials arrived. He spent most of his time entertaining drug smugglers who were too stupid to know what kind of trouble they were in. Sometimes he was called on to testify in court, but not often enough to make the job interesting. Today's guest was an uncommon one. The police weren't on the way to take him off his hands. Not yet at least. Calls were still being made looking into the origin of what had turned out to be a complete adult male skeleton, cleaned of flesh, stuffed into one medium-sized travel bag.

"Mr. Shanda," Andrew smiled. Shanda didn't return his smile or greeting. Andrew tried again.

"I'm Andrew Isaki from airport security. I'd like to ask you a few questions about the contents of your bag."

Nothing.

"You said the bones in your bag were your uncle's."

"My uncle," confirmed Shanda.

"And what was his name?"

"Auguste Shanda."

"So," said Andrew, briefly considering how he could ask the next question casually. "What were you doing with his bones in your bag?"

"I was to take them to New York with me."

"Why's that?"

"Because that is where I am going."

"I see. Do you have any family there?"

Shanda hesitated a moment. "None living."

"You realize that it's generally considered…inappropriate for passengers to be carrying somebody's mortal remains on a flight, don't you? Airlines are happy to transport a body provided it's in a proper coffin in the baggage compartment. They do that all the time."

Shanda tipped his head slightly forward and looked at Andrew over his glasses like he was a fool.

"The bones are to stay with me always."

"I can understand your reluctance to entrust them to baggage handlers, but still…"

Andrew trailed off. He could see Shanda's point. A body touching down in Hawaii on the same day it's to be put to rest in Iowa is an embarrassment to all involved and just adds to a family's grief. Extra care is usually taken to make sure coffins go where they're meant to, but mistakes still happen. The Hawaii/Iowa rerouting had stirred up a fuss only three weeks earlier.

Andrew switched tracks. "Were you very close to your uncle?"

"Where are the bones now?"

"We have them securely stored. Don't worry."

"Securely stored" meant "sitting under the desk of a secretary who was off sick." The airport staff lockers were big enough for most personal valuables, but couldn't quite fit Shanda's bag. Andrew didn't want to try to stuff it in. He didn't know how brittle the bones were.

"Are you planning to bury your uncle's remains in the United States?"

Shanda said nothing.

"Are you relocating his body? How long has he been deceased, if you don't mind me asking?"

"He has been dead these past eleven days."

"Eleven days?"

Shanda fell silent again.

"That's a pretty advanced stage of decomposition for eleven days."

Shanda furrowed his brow, questioningly.

Andrew explained, "Why is he…why has he been reduced to bones already?"

"I boiled the flesh from them only yesterday."

He'd said it much as he might have explained that pants are put on one leg at a time.

"Why would you do that?"

"Easier to carry."

"Excuse me a moment, would you?" said Andrew as he got up. "Sure I can't get you anything?"

Shanda offered no suggestions, so Andrew left without another word.

"I don't know, Bill," Andrew was saying five minutes later when he'd found Bill Mayer, his boss. "I don't know what local customs we could be dealing with here, but this sounds like some sort of weird serial killer racking up frequent-flier miles."

"Just give me the name, Andrew."

"He said it was Auguste. Auguste Shanda. Same last name."

"All right. I'll check with the Haitian authorities. See what they say. You just watch him.”

"Come on, Bill, do I have to? He's not exactly a sparkling conversationalist."

"Think of it as a cultural gap. Bridge it."

"I prefer the Haitian weed smugglers. They're chatty."

"Bring him a soda and give him a sugar rush. That might do the trick."

"It's creepy, Bill."

"It's probably nothing. Don't worry about it. Remember last time this sort of thing happened and freaked out everybody?"

"Yeah, but that was an anthropologist sneaking out of Argentina with twenty-thousand-year-old fossils. It's not the same. At least we were pretty sure he didn't axe murder his cargo in the dead of night."

"This one's probably not a murderer either."

"Tell that to the guy with the cleaved skull."

Andrew returned to his office to keep Shanda company until more calls could be made. He brought a diet soda for his guest and placed it on the desk, next to where Shanda was sitting. Shanda neither looked at the can nor acknowledged it being offered. Andrew took it in stride and sipped the foam off the top of his own opened can. He was getting used to the uncommunicative atmosphere in the room that day. When he sat down on the couch again, he drank quietly, neither looking at Shanda nor saying a word to him. When he finished his own drink, Andrew crumpled the can and accurately threw it across the room into the tin garbage can, where it clattered noisily. Only then did he look at Shanda once more. Shanda was staring back at him again, his attention drawn.

"How did your uncle die?" said Andrew casually once he'd regained eye contact.

Auguste Shanda had been the most feared houngan in all the villages that lined the shores of the Artibonite River in central Haiti. A high priest of a houmfor temple buried in the woods a mile back from the nearest road, he had been associated through rumour and hearsay with all the darkest dealings of voodoo lore. Presiding over traditional Saturday night ceremonies presented a legitimate front, but word spread through the towns and villages that on every other day of the week he was a boko, a sorcerer for hire, with no qualms about placing curses on friend or family for the right price.

The effectiveness of his doll curses was legendary, and it was well known he could cause anyone no end of misery with a wax-and-feather sculpture and as few as three of the intended victim's hairs—or a single toenail clipping. Folklore told of one occasion in Auguste's youth when he crossed paths with one of Duvalier's tonton macoutes, a policeman and thug who dared challenge the Shanda family's authority in their own village. The number of physical ailments the officer endured thereafter was limited only to the number of needles in Auguste's mother's sewing kit. Within a month, the policeman ended his own suffering with a spectacular self-immolation by gasoline and Zippo in the middle of the town square. The method of suicide, few denied, may well have been connected to the fact that Auguste chose to dispose of the man's figurine likeness in a smouldering barbecue pit.

Auguste was also implicated in several high- and low-profile disappearances. His penchant for poisons was apparent, considering the number of his enemies who died in their sleep for no good reason. But the missing persons, insisted the townspeople in whispered tones, had likely been recruited as zombies. Auguste was an obvious suspect, considering the formula for the fabled zombie drug relied almost entirely on a poison thought to be understood by only a handful of boko—most of them now deceased, most of them by Auguste's hand.

The recipe for the poison included an elaborate mix of natural toxins and irritants that promoted swelling and severe itching. The intended victim would speed his own demise by scratching madly at an infected area until the skin broke. The poison, initially applied by sprinkling it on an arm or a leg while the marked man slept, would then infiltrate the bloodstream. A catatonic and highly suggestible state of mind would result within a few days, and the victim would become a zombie ripe for the picking, submitting himself to slavery at the hands of the first person who tried to command him.

Regular doses of the poison, administered by cut or pinprick, could keep a healthy adult in such a state for years. A boko of Auguste Shanda's skill was said to be able to extend a zombie slave's existence past any form of natural life, creating a living death of tireless, endless manual labour. The extra precaution of a doll curse might ensure the additional fear and loyalty needed to maintain control over a slave forever.

Such cruelty was not thought to be beyond Auguste Shanda. Put quite simply, nothing was considered beyond him. This belief in the scope and malice of his reach kept a dozen villages in a grip of fear so intense, it started to work against him. After so many miserable years under his thumb, people began to believe Auguste's reign of terror had to end some way. Any way.

René Shanda told Andrew none of this.

"Andrew."

The call came from the door. Bill was looking in, waving him over. Andrew got up from his seat and walked over to Bill, who leaned in to whisper.

"Is he giving you any trouble?"

"He's not too cooperative," said Andrew, "but he's behaving himself."

"Think you can handle him on your own?"

"Sure, why?"

"I just got off the horn with Port-au-Prince police. Your friend Shanda there is wanted for murder. Guess who he killed."

"Oh boy."

"Yeah. A car's on the way from downtown, but the highway's packed with rush hour traffic. We've got him for another good half-hour."

"Okay."

"Packing?"

"Always."

"Good. I'll check in when the blue boys show up."

Bill dipped back out of the office, closing the door behind him. Andrew turned and saw Shanda staring intently. Andrew gave him a few moments of silence after he sat down again, then he spoke bluntly.

"Tell me why you killed your uncle."

Shanda answered immediately, calmly, like the question wasn't unexpected.

"You would not understand."

Andrew had convinced past guests to explain to him why they had tried to carry a gym bag full of hashish onto an international flight. Some had confided their reasoning for pulling a gun and shooting at state police who had them surrounded. He once even had a nineteen-year-old woman describe how she was coerced into carrying six latex condoms full of heroin in her stomach shortly before she died of an overdose when one of the condoms ruptured. The smuggling stories wore thin after a while. He never had anyone explain why they'd caved somebody's head in with a bladed weapon, though. He was hoping Shanda would level with him. Shanda didn't say much, but what he had said so far sounded true. If the tall man indulged him, Andrew was sure he would have a good story to repeat at this year's office party.

"Try me," said Andrew.

Auguste Shanda's time on this Earth ended when he was quite old, but still strong of body and spirit. Despite the threat of an uprising from his fearful and superstitious flock, his finish came suddenly and unexpectedly when an anonymous road worker took a break from laying fresh gravel long enough to march into the foliage and cleave Auguste's skull wide open with his shovel. The worker thought he'd seen the high priest giving him the evil eye from the path that led down to his secluded temple and had panicked, daring a direct assault upon the voodoo sorcerer rather than risk the suffering of a prolonged curse. The irony was that Auguste had only come out of the woods to investigate the source of the noise caused by the idling city-works truck parked next to the series of potholes that needed filling. He hadn't given the worker any sort of eye, for good or ill— had never even seen him, in fact, right up to the moment of his murder.

The worker had returned to his home without saying a word to anyone. He didn't dare tempt fate by talking about his crime, even though he would have been hailed as a hero for it. It was up to René Shanda to discover the body of his uncle days later, when he first started to emerge from his poison-induced haze.

René, like so many members of the Shanda family, had served as a guinea pig for Auguste's potions as he evaluated dosages and adjusted his ingredients accordingly. They were considered expendable. Whether they died outright or became mindless zombie minions didn't really matter to Auguste as long as they helped him find the correct dose for paying clients.

René had proven to be a particularly successful zombie. Strong and agile, he'd been a real workhorse for the temple, clearing the jungle undergrowth as it encroached on the compound with each new rainfall. But he had also been an unusually willful zombie. A wax figurine of him had to be pricked and tortured routinely to keep him from wandering off or disobeying. Combined with the poison, it had kept René in check for years.

However, once there was no-one to manipulate the doll or replenish the poison in his system, René began to wake up. He literally stumbled over Auguste's body as he walked through the woods, shaking off the last of his stupor. Another day went by before his head cleared enough for him to know what needed to be done.

René had been the only member of his family Auguste had bothered to keep at home. The rest—the ones who hadn't died outright from the poison—had been sold into bondage. There was a profitable demand for zombie labour among the Haitian-Red sects of Harlem. There were at least three restaurants operating in the north end of Manhattan that didn't need to pay their kitchen staff any wages. René had found out that a few of his closest relations numbered among the zombie dishwashers and floor-moppers. But before he could do anything about it, Auguste had made him his next victim.

Not that René had a plan back then.

He didn't know how the solution came to him. Perhaps in the years his conscious mind had been hidden away deep down inside, it still held enough of a spark to work on the puzzle. Ultimately, the answer was simple. René would make an antidote to bring to his enslaved family.

René knew just enough about Auguste and his perversion of voodoo rites to understand some of the principles behind his alchemy. He was sure, after dealing with poisons for so many years, Auguste must have built up a high tolerance to his own toxins. This immunity was in his blood, in his body, in his bones. The flesh was useless now—dead and rotting. But the bones could be recovered, the marrow dried and ground into a powder.

And the powder could be fed to his family.

That was the reasoning behind René's rapid departure from Haiti. He still had a passport, old and expired, but it could get him into America with enough tampering. A plane ticket was hastily purchased by selling off all of Auguste's possessions. By the time René was done pillaging his uncle's home, the only thing left of any value was an old cigarette case. René brought that along as his only personal luggage, ready to pawn it for cab fare once he arrived in New York.

The only thing left to pack was Auguste's boiled bones. Only now did René realize he should have waited until they were dried and ground to dust before trying to transport them abroad. It was the one miscalculation he had made in his haste. That and leaving the rubbery stripped flesh of his uncle behind where police might find and identify it.

"No," replied Shanda to Andrew's simple request.

"Why not?"

"I have said. You would not understand. You are not from the islands."

And that was the last thing Shanda had to say. Andrew tried to get something, anything, out of him for a few more minutes, but his guest had fallen into a meditative silence he couldn't cut through. He eventually gave up and resigned himself to the silent watch until the police came. He passed the time reading an airline magazine that was seven months out-of-date.

It only took twenty minutes for the police to arrive in the end. When they came, there were just two of them, neither detectives. They were there to transport Shanda to the feds in the city—glorified couriers, nothing more. Bill showed them in and the two uniformed cops cautiously set themselves at either side of Shanda. One of them had cuffs at the ready. The other had his hand on his holstered gun.

"Mr. René Shanda?"

Shanda didn't so much as look up.

"We're here to escort you downtown. We're placing you under arrest for the murder of Auguste Shanda, pending extradition to Haitian authorities."

Shanda didn't break the vacant stare he'd held since long before the police arrived. The only indication that he'd heard the officers at all was him holding his arms out in front of him, wrists together. The first officer snapped the handcuffs in place as the second recited Shanda's rights under American law. When the legal speech was done, Shanda stood, holding his hat in his cuffed hands, and let the officers lead him out, one on each arm.

No one could say how he spotted the bag on the floor when he was staring straight ahead the whole time. But suddenly, as they passed between the rows of office desks, heading for the exit to the terminal, Shanda pulled back sharply and broke the loose grip the cops had on his arms. The officers were slow to react, surprised by the sudden bolting of their formerly complacent suspect. Before they could turn, Shanda leapfrogged over the desk and landed on all fours next to his flight bag, which stuck out slightly from under the desk. The police had their guns drawn by the time he popped up from behind the desk again, his luggage in hand. They wasted a moment trying to tell him to freeze, but they probably wouldn't have been able to keep Shanda in place even if they'd fired at that moment or tried to jump him. He was moving fast, almost inhumanly so. He swung the bag wide, slapping both aimed guns out of his way with a sharp rattling of bones. In the same move, he stepped up on the table in front of him and was off, hopping from desk to desk as fast as a normal man might run across open land.

Shanda was out the door by the time the cops could get their guns pointed in his general direction. Neither of them fired. He was gone already, but they made chase.

Andrew and Bill followed the cops out. The police officers were waving people out of the way with their guns as they ran through the crowded terminal, leaving a clear path in their wake for the two airport security men. They knew there was no real danger, openly brandished guns or not. Shanda was unarmed, so there was no chance of a full-scale shootout. But he was giving them the best chase the airport had seen since three teenaged smugglers bolted from officers in three different directions a decade earlier. None of them had gotten as far as Shanda already had, dexterously bounding through business travellers, baggage carts, and sluggish tourists. The number of obstacles he had to detour around slowed him enough for the police, parting the crowd more easily with the sight of their guns and uniforms, to make up the distance.

Shanda might still have evaded his pursuers long enough to get outside and lose himself in the parking lot, if only he hadn't glanced back to check how much of a lead he had. In the second it took him to look over his shoulder, a baggage trolley stacked high with luggage headed home after a two-week Florida vacation appeared in front of him. He ran right into it and pulled the whole works down as he stumbled over the top. Suitcases popped open, sending cheap souvenirs and sandy bathing suits flying. Shanda's bag opened up and spilled its contents, too. No one had zipped it up since the search.

Half a dozen people were tripped up by the bones as they slid across the finely polished terminal floor. The skull landed right at the feet of a middle-aged woman fresh off the beach with a peeling sunburn and a Mickey Mouse hat to show for her travels. It took her a full second to realize what she was standing over, and another one to start screaming.

Screaming can disconcert a cop as easily as the next person and, after hearing the shrill panicked cries of the woman, one of them fired before thinking. As Shanda sat up suddenly, appearing behind the scattered pile of checked luggage, the lone bullet hit him mid-chest, slightly off-center, and sent him lying back down again just as sharply. Both cops were still covering him from a distance when Andrew and Bill boldly stepped over the refuse.

Shanda was sprawled out, looking quite relaxed. His eyes were shut, and his glasses were tipped up across his hairline. He looked like someone's grandfather who had fallen into a light sleep on the couch between sorting through the sports page and the world news.

Bill opened his vest, looking for the gunshot wound. Not finding one, he immediately checked the inside breast pocket and pulled out what he suspected was there. The bullet had pushed through the first half of Shanda's sturdy cigarette case, but had flattened out on the second layer of steel. Loose tobacco from the destroyed stale cigarettes trickled out as Bill opened it to see the slug embedded inside.

"Lucky bastard. He'd be dead if…"

"He is dead," corrected Andrew who'd already taken Shanda's pulse twice, once at the wrist and once at the neck, and had come up with nothing both times.

"Can't be," said Bill.

"His heart's stopped."

"Call an ambulance!" ordered Bill. For the first time ever, he started using the CPR training he'd learned many years earlier

He'd only pumped at Shanda's chest a few times before he stopped abruptly and felt the dead man's cheek.

"He's awfully cold for a guy who just sprinted halfway across the airport," said Bill.

"I know," agreed Andrew. "He feels like he's been dead an hour or so already. His fingers are getting stiff."

The crowd who'd disappeared into the woodwork at the first suggestion of a shooting were gathering around again to see what sort of grisly results the gunplay had delivered. The ones who weren't busy discussing whether the bones where real people bones or not saw the next thing that was pulled out of Shanda's inside breast pocket. It was a doll, like a plaything, but uglier than anything anyone would ever give to a child. It was crude and barely recognizable as a human icon, made more grotesque by the ragged hole in its torso where the policeman's bullet had torn through on its way to striking the cigarette case.

"I don't think he bought that at the souvenir shop," said Bill.

Andrew wasn't listening. He studied the face of René Shanda, who had died only moments ago and now looked like a corpse exhumed after a month in the ground. He was wondering how best to word a report to the FAA that wouldn't get him fired.

by KJ Hannah Greenberg

"That *Dr.* Pepperdine to you," she articulated as she placed the sole of her foot against his windpipe. That robust woman had little patience for individuals who were uppity just because they were rich, were well-positioned socially, or were otherwise able to enhance the lives of their subordinates, especially if such persons had already been to the grave and back. Just two short blocks from the university, where Marcy Pepperdine taught about dipole-dipole bonds, she had come face to face with a ghoul that not only wanted her pocket money, but that also insisted on occupying her piece of the sidewalk.

It was sufficient that Marcy's funding on magnetic molecules was being cut by NASA. Having to contend, as well, with a smelly example of the undead was more than any mama could tolerate. Besides, Junior was going to be late for his viola lessons if she didn't get immediately home. Marcy had no discretionary time with which to wrangle with a monster that wanted to pick her brains both figuratively and literally.

More to the point, Charles was likely at fault for her fiduciary predicament. His preliminary work on strontium ions had failed to prove her theory that all elements in the periodic table's second column were useful for quantum tunneling of magnetization. Rather, her junior associate merely reified that a silvery metal, upon which her decades of scholarship had been focused, possessed radioactive isotopes and that such an element offered advantages to doctors interested in the issue of cellular growth.

Moaning unpleasantly, the supernaturally animated fellow that Marcy had felled waved a freshly broken leg at her. He didn't need to breathe, so his loss of trachea was of small deterrence to his mission. He was stymied, however, by Dr. Pepperdine's shattering of his *umerus* and of his *femur*. It would now be both more difficult and more imperative for him to follow her to her lab to obtain strontium ranelate. After the science matron waddled past, that zombie soughed some more.

Elsewhere, Junior was chin deep in peanut butter and marshmallow fluff. Ever since he had turned twelve and one half, that child had insisted not only on preparing his own provisions, but also on being able to eat to his stomach's content. That he grew, on average, three inches per year meant that his mother had become a famous patron of the local grocers. What's more, although Junior was only fifteen, he was already over six feet tall.

"Saw a monster on the way home today, Kiddo."

"Mamflestump."

"I told you the chewy nut butter was harder to swallow than the creamy."

"Mifledoodlestck"

"Whatever. Have your fiddle and backpack ready in ten. I'm going to change."

Marcy smiled as she looked out of her bedroom window. Her university had wanted to relocate her and her son away from the rambling patch, which, albeit proffered just a small bungalow in which they could live, also was situated an enviable two blocks from campus. Junior, what's more, had wanted no part of leaving their trees and herb gardens behind and Marcy couldn't imagine having to dwell somewhere devoid of subterranean, rodent-infested passages, to which she alone was privy. In brief, neither of them had wanted to move.

Bravely, Marcy had dated a member of her school's board of governors in the hope that such a dalliance would benefit her by helping her retain her housing. She had deduced well; eventually, the head of her university's Department of Real Estate Operations had elected to relocate to a job in a big city hundreds of miles away. Immediately, her school's Department of Real Estate Operations had ceased its harassing phone calls and emails. Marcy, similarly, ceased her casual romance with the trustee.

Dr. Pepperdine shuddered when remembering having to fondle that man's toupee. She had not been arm candy, but ego stimulation, given her combination of plain looks and National Science Foundation awards. Besides, that span of trading kisses for secured accommodations had occurred years before her colleague, Henry Glick, had announced, at an international meeting of physical chemists, that research on magnetic molecules might provide a conduit for bringing back the unresponsive.

Whereas the government had to be coerced into sending monies to fund such research, many dwellers from beyond the divide had shown up frequently and unrelenting to compete for the rare places in Marcy's pilot studies. Already inert, such test subjects had little to lose. Concurrently and covertly, a certain large drug manufacturer skipped monies into an account on which Marcy's lab drew. The corporation's only stipulation was that it be the pubic source for a new, expensive, exclusive ointment for treating third degree burns.

"Boy Child, local transport is leaving in two point five minutes. If you're not aboard, you miss your lessons."

"Coming, Mom."

Notwithstanding the livings' and the departeds' conflicting agendas for applying Dr. Pepperdine's research, the two groups were in concord about the dangers such work presented to healthy beings. It seemed that unstable strontium atoms emitted sufficient ionizing particles to cripple even an elephant or at least to give a beast of that size a painful form of metastasized cancer. It followed that the rapidly increasing population of reanimated corpses pressed for further representation in magnetic molecule research, while living politicians tried to close Marcy's lab down. Given her most recent budget cuts, the latter seemed to be winning.

As Marcy and Junior drove to the part of town where a string instrument teacher ran a small music school, Marcy reflected on how the world could be different if only she were able to synthesize a stable icosahedron. If she could, somehow, bring to a standstill strontium's tendency to decay, she could generate the kind of ambulatory sentient that gene splicing research and software full of fancy algorithms had failed to achieve.

Magnetic molecules, built from substances such as strontium parent nuclides, showed all of the signs not only of being able to mend decaying muscle and skin, but also of being able to generate neurotransmitters, i.e. test tube synapses. As a result, Dr. Pepperdine's "solution chemistry," might provide its users with synthetic control over the remnants of their corpses. She had proven that polynuclear coordination compounds could bridge organic ligands. If Marcy could achieve such ends, Junior would be able to study at a conservatory after high school and Marcy would not have to depend on the pharmaceutical company for funding.

While Junior bowed under the tutelage of his great teacher, Marcy slung back colas at a local diner. She had brought along both her laptop and some paper notes. It had not escaped her attention, however, that touching the eatery's window was a small mob of late lamented humans. The establishment's purple-haired waitress had also noticed the new arrivals. That woman had dropped the ketchup bottle she was refilling and had run first into the cake display and then into the diner's kitchen.

Noticing the commotion outside, Marcy extracted a vial containing some fine particles she had yet to analyze, which had been given to her by the ethnobotanist with whom she paired during faculty tennis tournaments. Sighing, she powered down her portable computer. Theoretically, the vessel she held contained elements of a pharmacology designed to control shambling corpses.

Weapon unsheathed, the middle-aged mama exhaled noisily as she recalled her Finnish peer's report on synthesized magnetic molecules. The man had gotten as far as creating a compound consisting mainly of calcium and of iron before a pack of living dead had eaten away his face and both of his hands. It appeared that the other worlders, who had commandeered his office, had been too impatient with the Finn's work on vesicle fusion and too devoid of organs of intelligence to grasp that devouring that scientist meant devouring their best chance at regrowing missing corporal bits and pieces.

A formerly entombed fist punched through the restaurant's plate-glass. Suddenly, a drowsy police officer, her cigarette spat out on the formica counter, two teens who had been trying to surreptitiously finger each other's zippers, and an elderly couple who had been making much ado about sharing a single hamburger, were reborn as world class sprinters, all of whom were vying for the same kitchen door through which the lone service provider had escaped earlier.

A shoulder, a head, and the rest of a compromised torso broke through the storefront where the glass had been shattered. A dozen or so dead compatriots followed. Marcy sprinkled the green and yellow powder from her vial in a line in front of her section of the dining room. Assessing that her row of plant ash was her lone fortification versus resurrected pursuers, she grabbed her laptop and ran for the swinging kitchen door.

Marcy's tennis partner had hypothesized that bitter oleander, perhaps, or maybe even synthetic digoxin, had been used to reenergize the lifeless. Whereas such toxins could kill a living being quickly by stopping their heart, it was believed, in hushed biochemistry circles populated mostly by traditional herbalists, that those poisons had an opposite effect on the mobility of banshees. Hence, magnetic molecule-seeking specters had been raised and had, apparently successfully, woken more of their kind.

Flooring her car, Dr. Pepperdine raced to the musical school. Junior, who was popping a roll of sour candies into his mouth, one by one, except for the cherry-flavored bits, which he spat on the sidewalk, noted, through the windshield of the sedan bearing down on him, that his mother's face was manic. Either she was being chased, again, by monsters, or she had surfaced for enough minutes from her research-induced mind melt to discover that she had been obliged to hand in midterm grades a week ago. Either way, her driving telegraphed that Junior's night would be filled with drive-thru fish filet sandwiches and prerecorded network programs.

Shortly thereafter, Junior made a basket with one of his balled-up fast food wrappers. He flicked the television's control pad once more. Junior was tired of the nature channel, disinterested in cooking competitions, and really was only awake to spend "quality time" with his mom.

Mom, nevertheless, was busy IMing a friend in London, a neurologist whose specialty was natural toxins. Beneath her feet lay an emptied French fry carton and the remnants of her diet cola. Her London peer had isolated and synthesized the vital components of a traditional peach/licorice root extract and had successfully applied his toxin-binding, anti-inflammatory mix, at least at the level of human beta trials, to the Lyme disease patients. This colleague was noted, as well, for having fashioned a butter from cod liver oil, bifidus, and powdered cilantro that leeched most of the internal damages caused by juvenile lead poisoning. That substance, which was just emerging from final FDA approval, promised to make him rich.

Marcy reasoned that he might be savvy as to why her local ethnobotanist's powder had deterred zombies in the diner. If only she could buy a little time for completing her investigation of nanomagnetism in lithium and in aluminum, Dr. Pepperdine might be able to get her NSF monies renewed. Until then, while her international peers debated the external validity of her findings on lanthan series elements, Marcy had both to gird herself with cheaper sources of magnetic spin and to find a way to keep the undead away from her and from her work.

Junior stared at his progenitor, her face lit by her computer screen. Shrugging, he shut the TV, collected his mother's discards from around her feet and shuffled off to bed. First, however, he turned on the electric fence surrounding their property. Residents of the grave were not keen on transformer juice.

Later that week, Junior competed for a second chair slot in a nearby city's youth orchestra. While she waited for the judges' verdict, Marcy reviewed her Chemistry 101 notes. It seemed well within her pedagogical latitude to insist that her freshmen learn about the chemical characteristics of single-crystal growth magnetic molecules. She did not need those young thinkers to function like her graduate students, but she did want them to be able to disregard scientific tosh.

No fewer than two hundred freshmen were on the waiting list for Dr. Pepperdine's recitation sections of Freshman Chemistry. She assumed it was her gift of integrating enthymemes into her lectures that made her talks so popular. Dr. Pepperdine never considered that her reputation for fighting man-sized creepy crawlies combined with the random appearance, in her classes, of fascinating, if not fetid, creatures were the real draws.

Some time later, Junior, who had won his audition and who was preoccupied memorizing the second movement of Handel's "D Minor Sonata," distractedly answered his mother's phone. A dude yapping in German, who identified himself as a principle investigator at Der Fakultät für Physik, Universität Bielefeld, was on the other end. Junior greeted him by "Sie," not "du," but otherwise ignored the man's blathering. After spewing for nearly five minutes, the scientist cleared his throat and began, anew, in English. Junior's mom, apparently, had published her findings about the low-temperature thermodynamic parameter characterization of sodium just days before that irate fellow had gotten his own conclusions to press.

As that European continued to harangue his unwilling listener, idly, Junior made an origami cat and an origami crane out of some of his mother's notes. He failed to see the flesh-free arm that reached for his face. In fact, thereafter, Junior saw nothing more.

Dr. Pepperdine reviewed, as she walked home, the remarks made by her division's tenure and promotions committee. She served on that board since it was the least noxious form of departmental labor available to her. In that job, she did not have to be judge and jury for erring students or listen to want-to-bes state their cases for getting hired. Instead, twice a year, all Marcy had to do was to vote on whether or not to keep younger co-workers. If it had been up to her, she would have waved her hands at all of them and given the entire lot seats on the local academic chemistry bench. The committee, on the other hand, was rounded out by four other scientists, none of whom shared her view.

One fellow, a libertine who enjoyed the company and likely the companionship of pretty coeds, made a point, during each promotion trial, to question any perspective that advocated tolerance as a solution to intellectual prejudice. Accordingly, Marcy's sector lost a first rate metal specialist to an Ivy League school.

Another committee member, a fellow who was three years short of full retirement benefits, slept through most proceedings, opening his eyes and mind only to object to instructors who dared to conduct their classes in a dialectical, rather than in a rhetorical manner. The department lost many NIS scholars that way.

A third committee member, a gal who specialized in biochemistry, eschewed any faculty member who demonstrated, at international conferences or in international journals, a preference for integrating scientific literacy, general knowledge, and social accountability. Even though the woman, herself, had once been a cutting edge intellect, having bridged the study of life forms to the study of the nature of matter, long before such synthesis was popular or understood, these days, that woman disdained associates who wanted to expand the discipline.

The last member on the committee, Harold Callowin, had matriculated through graduate school with Marcy. Although he was intrigued with the attention she received from individuals missing vast catalogs of bodily parts, he remained uninspired to offer her any sympathy concerning the pending financial suffocation of her lab. In his mental economics, it was unfair that she was so successful while he, an expert in the nobel series, had to be concerned not with blue ribbons but with safeguarding his helpers. At least, in the history of his lab fires only two undergraduates had ever been burned beyond recognition.

Regardless, the junior professor, who had been up for peer review, had proven useful when collaborating on neutron scattering projects focused on static magnetic properties. In spite of his sufficient publications, glowing student evaluations, and admirable community service (a local news station had been enamored enough of the young scientist to have videotaped him), the committee had refused to grant him tenure. Thus, Marcy walked all of the way home, fell asleep in her home office, and rubbed the sand out of her eyes, at birdcall, before grasping that Junior was missing.

The undead are too dull to think of kidnapping and too desperate to think of prisoner exchanges. Hence, one had broken Junior's neck, while a second sucked had out significant portions of Junior's grey matter. Other oddments of his body, too, had been consumed; Junior was newly hampered by a missing lung, compromised vocal chords, and a chewed off tongue. Given the boy's additional, sudden lack of tendons in the limb with which he had driven off the hungriest zombies, he was reduced to howling in lieu of fiddling.

Junior presented his predicament to his mother when she opened their back door to assess whether or not she needed a sweater. The woman whose leg he tried to bite off was still wearing her previous day's work clothes and was muttering something about the stupidity of the tenure process. In answer, Junior muttered phonemes that sounded like "mamflestump" and "mifledoodlestck" despite the fact that his face was speckled with viscera, not peanut butter. As well, a large chunk of his top lip, philtrum, and left cheek were missing.

Marcy slammed the door on her son, thus propelling him backwards. Swiftly, she reached for the force field switch. Ever the good mother, Marcy moaned upon hearing the consequent sound of corrupt flesh sizzling.

In no time, though, using his still viable hand, Junior punched through the windowpane of the back door and then unlatched that barrier. The boy had retained, somehow, his sagacity. Dr. Pepperdine smiled at her child's intelligence before reacting to the danger he presented.

On their kitchen table sat a can of soda likely left behind by Junior. He had enjoyed quaffing copious amounts of carbonated beverages when he was whole, As undead, such liquids were lethal to him since those beverages contained crystals, more specifically polyoxotungstate clusters, which could provide diamagnetic scaffolding for promethium cations. Such cations were guaranteed to deter him long enough for Dr. Pepperdine to escape through her building's basement-level catacombs.

After splashing the fizzling substance on her former child and resisting, mightily, the urge to puke at the sight of his eyeballs swinging from their optic nerve anchors, Marcy grabbed her laptop and ran down her basement stairs. It was a pity that her soda-as-a-weapon was not going to be tested under sterile, replicable conditions.

That same disheveled woman deplaned at München Franz Josef Strauss Airport's Terminal Two. She was sorry that she had not responded in a more timely fashion to her junior cohort's request for collegial support. Charles was smart, earnest, randomly meticulous, and perhaps the lone individual who understood how to get the European nanomolecule team to cooperate with American chemists interested in magnetic molecules.

Some weeks after Dr. Pepperdine's arrival in München, her university's grounds crew tidied the yard of her former home. Her cottage was being given to the Brazilian researcher replacing Charles. That chemist specialized in botanical monomers and had been recommended to the department's search committee by Marcy's former ethnobotany tennis partner.

As for the good scholar, she had missed the end of the semester entirely. No trace of her child had emerged, either. Gossips inferred that she and Charles had run off to engage in escapades more flammable than the ones Dr. Callowin initiated in his lab. Other chemists, especially those at Hokkaido University and at the University of Florence, speculated that Dr. Pepperdine had given academia the finger and was homeschooling Junior somewhere where the sea was green and where mangos grew wild.

The latter group's thesis was closer to verity. Dr. Pepperdine had neither managed to outrun or to heal the automatons. Europe was more plagued with undead than was North America and somehow the residents of the graveyards near her former home had telegraphed to their German counterparts that Marcy Pepperdine was *en route*. Marcy suspected Junior has been involved in that conspiracy.

Junior had certainly remained in her sphere. Two miles beneath the surface of Waldfriedhof Cemetery, Marcy Pepperdine taught other fiends about networked inorganic magnetic molecules. Even though her students could no more hear or record her lectures than they could enjoy peanut butter, they seemed to appreciate that the creature that waved her arms and moved her mouth before them, by benefit of something only she understood as metal-oxo clusters and polynuclear coordination complexes, was keeping them from falling farther apart and was, concurrently, replenishing their food supply.

Glancing at Junior out of her own singularly good eye, Marcy shed no tears. She was still waiting for the outcome of the neutron scattering and magnetic resonance measurements of her polyoxomolybdates and reduced polyoxovanadates, hoping all along that a new magnetic molecular synthesis would enable her to keep her own fragile corpse and her even more delicate mind intact. Trouble was that her lab assistants continued, literally, to fall to pieces.

by Peter Andrews

I hesitated at the entrance to the gym. A tall zombie lurched through the door. He banged into me so hard that it turned me around. Katie was right. If you stayed clean, you were a nobody. So I hunched my shoulders and ambled in.

The girl at the desk had lesions across her scalp. She was well into decomp, but she still had enough human courtesy left to greet me.

"Welcome to the Decay Authority. How may I help you?" she asked.

"I'd like the, uh, value package?"

She looked me over. I felt like I was on the slab, being examined by the coroner. "We should be able to help you. The first step is an analysis. Would you like to start now?"

I wanted to say "no." But I figured that if I didn't get started right away, I'd never have the guts. So within minutes, I was standing in front of my advisor.

She was at least six inches shorter than I am, but I figured she'd been taller before she began to rot. I'm not naturally attracted to older zombies, but I have to say, with the missing eye and the jaw just slightly askew, there was a pleasing asymmetry to her face.

We went through the routine stuff: weight, height, time of death. I told her exactly which preservatives I was on, and I arranged for her to get my medical records. She asked about allergies, and I told her I had none. She seemed pleased. She explained allergies can wreak havoc with the standard treatments.

The routine of questions and answers calmed me. The equipment, which I initially took for instruments of torture, seemed less threatening. The howls and groans of the clientele took on a rhythm that was almost musical. I could do this. I really could.

But my trepidation returned when we began the tour. A short, stout zombie came waddling out of the acid bathroom. Her skin had a pleasant greenish tone, but the fresh, oozing abscesses turned my stomach.

The next stop was the excise room. Here, at the direction of the advisers, very specific pounds of flesh were removed. The overall effects weren't bad. I can appreciate the beauty of a gaping hole as well as the next person. But I had imagined the process itself was clean and neat. To discover that the wounds were created by blindfolded freaks with rusty farm implements disillusioned me.

Since I only was buying the starter package, I had just one more stop on the tour. Infections. Since my passing over had been precipitated by blood poisoning, this was the part I dreaded most. In fact, I might've made my way to the gym on my own, with no prodding from Katie, except for my aversion to pus.

Underneath it all, I guess I still had a certain pride in being well preserved—pretty eccentric for a zombie. Maybe if I'd never taken care of myself, if I'd carried extra weight or been a slob, it might have been different. But microorganisms did bad things to a body. Besides, they had taken away my life, and it was hard for me to choose them as part of my future.

I mean, if you want carbuncles or blisters or even tumors, I'm happy to let you make that choice. When Katie took out a loan for dental surgery—and turned her mouth into a wreck of broken bicuspids, impacted incisors and moldy molars—did I stop kissing her? No. I loved her all the more. She was expressing the inner Katie.

But I balked at infections for myself. And here, in front of me, was a potpourri of offerings: staphylococcus, salmonella, tetanus, bubonic plague and even society's current favorite, leprosy. I didn't find any of them appealing.

My advisor grew insistent. "You'll never be the zombie you were meant to be unless you have the courage to face your anxieties," she said.

Frankly, that was exactly the sort of statement I didn't want to hear. I don't know whether I was more angry or frightened, but I started heading toward the door. And then I saw it.

I don't know how often you think about fungus in general, or ringworm in particular. I suppose we've all seen the advertisements in the fashion magazines, but it's rarely the choice of those you know personally. I'd never seen it in the flesh. And there it was, raised, raw and beautiful. There's a subtle interaction just at the border between the healthy flesh and the infection that is remarkable. I'm not a sensitive man, but, honestly, I could write sonnets just to the beauty of that border.

Of course, ringworm isn't for everyone. If your skin is too pale or there's scarring in the general area, it's a disaster, aesthetically. Since I began to raise my own crop of fungi, some friends have followed suit. Truly, it doesn't do a thing for them.

But for me, ringworm has been a ticket to the center of the fashion world. It has changed my undeath. I'm all the rage. I get invited to all the best parties, and soon I'll be launching my own line of designer boils. You only decompose once, my friends. Don't settle. Find the route to putrefaction that was meant for you. You won't be sorry.

THE RISEN

by Steven Axelrod

Alice Tremayne walked down the long dark corridor that led to the office in her Manhattan townhouse, the zombie shambling behind her. It was the kind of moment when you told yourself not to look back, because something unspeakable was looming behind you, and it was catching up fast.

She was alone in the house that night, and unarmed, not that a weapon would have helped her against the rotting teeth and the inhuman strength of the undead. She stopped and listened to the heavy shuffle of the monster's feet against the polished wood floor. Thump, scrape, thump scrape. Soon the icy hand would clasp her shoulder, and turn her around to face the dead eyes and the gaping mouth, the foul breath and the unslakable hunger of the grave.

Or that's how it would have been, in a different lifetime.

In her lifetime: the good old days, when she'd actually been alive.

She spun around angrily. "Margo, what are you doing up at this hour? You scared me half to death. As it were. Funny, the phrases we still use, don't you think?"

The zombie made a guttural snort that Alice took for an agreement. No one really knew how much these long-timers even understood. They had to grasp a few key words, of course—enough to follow simple commands. And they responded to tone of voice, like dogs. Too bad about dogs. Alice thought. She missed them, along with so much else.

Well, get used to it, she scolded herself silently. *Eternal life is no game for sissies.* Her grandmother used to say that, talking about old age. Alice had often thought of trying to find her grandmother—she would have to be one of the saddest of the long-timers, half-rotted, shambling through the ghettos, eating Chewlean out of those bright green poptop cans and praying for another chance at death. Granny had been dead for almost ten years at the time of the Rising. Those creatures had their own religion, apparently. This world was Purgatory according to that gospel.

Maybe they were right.

Margo kept staring at her, waiting. The sluggish moronic inertia of the woman made her want to scream. So she did. "Go downstairs and clean the basement! Polish the silver! The whole second floor needs to be vacuumed! Find a job to do or I'll find one for you. Go on! Scat!"

The zombie nodded and shuffled away. No doubt she'd forget to change the vacuum bag and just go through the motions, leaving the carpets as dirty as when she started.

It was impossible to get decent help these days.

The long-timers couldn't do the work and the short-timers thought they were too good for it.

Alice walked into her office, turned on the light and opened her laptop. She had no new e-mails, no word on her ex-husband. He hadn't turned up in any of the cattle drives, he wasn't listed in any of the ranches, and no patrols had come across him. If he had been dragged into one of the 'crackhouses' where pulsers were dismembered a bit at a time for the desperate short-timers with black market dollars, she'd never see him again.

She had a detective checking the chopshops as some people called them, but those abattoirs were strictly forbidden and tough to find. They kept the pulsers sealed in the sub-basements where the stink wouldn't give them away.

Alice sat back with a sigh. The search was getting expensive. She'd have to give it up soon. POTUS disapproved—her obsession distracted her from her job and POTUS liked having your undivided attention. That much hadn't changed. Still, she needed to see David one last time, even with this crazy uncrossable gulf between them. They had unfinished business and, dead or alive, Alice Tremayne liked closure. "It's not over until it's over, David," she muttered, closing the computer and preparing to wait for dawn. There was no point in lying down, or closing her eyes. The drift into unconsciousness, the rush of dreams—that was for the living only.

She missed sleeping most of all.

David Tremayne jammed himself into the corner of the basement wall, listening to the footsteps. The creature was coming back again, the "Formie" as the others called him. The formaldehyde the funeral home had used made him look almost alive, yet hideously false at the same time, like a wax museum exhibit, or a teenager smearing pancake makeup over his acne. The other zombies seemed to despise the Formies. Their class system was rigid and brutal. Only the lowest of the low worked the chophouses.

David squeezed his eyes closed, but couldn't shut his ears and he could still hear the others moaning and whimpering. He could still smell the sweet roast chicken smell of burned flesh and the raw acidic tang of scorched hair. One of the men had no fingers left. Two were blinded—apparently the eyes were a special delicacy. The fat one had been castrated less than an hour ago, the gaping wound cauterized with blow torches. Somehow that was what David dreaded most—not the cut, not being crippled and dismembered, but the burn, the blue flame roasting his skin.

The footsteps sounded louder. Yes, they were coming back again, so soon. It must have been a busy day upstairs: payday. All the zombies who otherwise had to subsist on processed human lunch meat (He'd seen the ad on a street hoarding while he was on the run: **CHEWLEAN—It Makes Death Worth Living**) getting their bits and pieces of the real thing.

He tried to make himself smaller. His wrists were taped together behind his back, his mouth gagged. The door opened. Were they coming for him this time? He felt his bladder release. What did the small of urine do to them? He was shaking like a man with a fever, his teeth chattering. He held his mouth open and let his jaws vibrate in silence, chanting to himself "not me, not me, not me."

And he got his wish. The Formies had knives this time. They carved out one of the blind men's calf muscles. The guy screamed and the screams turned into rasping shrieks of agony, scarcely even human, a dog caught in a bear trap, when the torches came out. Finally the man fainted, the door slammed and the steps receded.

David worked his wrists against the tape, but it was no use. How long until it was his turn? His or the woman next to him? She looked a little bit like Sarah, the same high cheekbones and wide-spaced blue eyes. He swiveled himself away from her, put his nose to the cold, dripping wall. He didn't want to see the woman's terrified face, or think about his sister.

He had let them take her, he could never forgive himself for that. He deserved whatever happened to him now. Yet what could he have done? What was he supposed to do? The zombies who caught them had looked like remnants, and they were so relieved they'd been fooled for one crucial second. But they had never seen any of the aristos in the flesh before.

Whatever the appalling government experiment gone wrong that had brought the dead out of their graves all at once fourteen months ago, that moment, the Rising as they called it, re-animated everyone whether they'd been dead for decades or an hour…or even less. The President, as he styled himself, with his fat spoiled face and his grotesque comb-over, had died of a heart attack *ten seconds* before the event. Of course, he looked normal.

His body hadn't even had time to cool.

The ones where rigor mortis had set in, who walked a little stiffly, and the ones with post-mortem lividity, livor mortis Sarah had told him, where the blood had settled at the lowest point and whose skin was permanently discolored like a massive bruise, they were a step below the ones like POTUS, who seemed untouched.

Apparently zombies could tell by looking at each other how long they'd been dead and every degree of decomposition took one further down on the social scale. God help the ones who looked like real zombies, the oozing decomposed ones that had been the subject of all those movies in the Time Before. They were pathetic creatures, slaves and victims. All they wanted to do was die, really die and stay dead.

Ranisha had told him once, it was like African American culture when she was growing up—every degree of skin color signified your status and desirability. She was fairly light-complexioned herself, and had looked down on darker women. This was no different, and in fact it made more sense. You actually were superior if you hadn't been dead as long. The new "one percent" actually deserved their status, though they came by it at random—a homeless drunk was as likely to be a new aristo as a Morgan Stanley hedge-fund manager.

His ex-wife was one of the lucky ones. David had been on the phone the day of the Rising, getting the news of her demise from his son while he watched TV. The local station reporting the apocalypse was overrun with zombies in the middle of the broadcast. That pretty anchor woman was half devoured on live television before the screen finally went dark.

And on the phone, while the world died, David's son Joe (long gone now, victim of the first feeding frenzy) was telling him that Alice was dead, passed out drunk and drowned in her own bathtub.

Such a stupid, ugly way to die. But well-timed. She owned the world now, what was left of it.

Her and her kind.

Alice had always possessed a knack for timing: selling the house just before the bubble burst, investing in Apple just before Steve Jobs came back, dumping David before the label downsized and the recording engineers lost their jobs… but just after his father's will cleared probate. She would have taken him for everything he owned if he hadn't hired that detective.

She thought David was a fool, but she miscalculated there. David knew she was fucking someone else, she had to be, that was Alice. She had to be fucking somebody. She had stopped fucking David just before his own girlfriend gave him Chlamydia.

Perfect timing, again. The woman made it into an art form, and turned it into a way of life. Or death. Because she was dead now, she was on the other side, and in this new upside-down psychotic world they all lived in, she was his last best hope.

Sarah Tremayne walked through the vast obstetrics ward of the Santa Monica Ranch (or breeding station, as the zombies called it), checking the newborns, occasionally touching the spot where a cross had dangled from her neck in the old days, before the Rising, before she lost the last of her faith, thinking, "Happy Easter, everyone."

It was the perfect holiday for zombies.

She slipped a pacifier back into a baby's mouth, stroked another one's forehead. She marked the chart on her clipboard: a slight fever, signs of colic.

These children would never have an Easter egg hunt, never open Christmas presents or celebrate a birthday with a cake, never go to their high school proms, never get married, never really live. Some would be sent to the restaurants and the food packaging facilities. The healthiest ones would be fed and housed until they could be put out to stud or used as brood mares when they hit puberty.

Her job was keeping them alive until then.

She had told the zombies who captured them she was a doctor. That had saved her life. Of course it had put her life in jeopardy in the first place, since she and David and the others had only emerged from their Rustic Canyon hide-out to scavenge for non-expired drugs. Sarah was the one essential team member: she could sort through the stores of remaining antibiotics on the stock room shelves, pick and choose with the stopwatch ticking—in and out fast before the legions of the undead sensed their presence.

It had been a suicide mission, and most of them had died. Not all of them, though. Maybe David made it back to the canyon. That was the hope she lived on.

She had last seen her brother running for his life with a paper bag full of Cipro. He was a good runner—a high school track star who finished half marathons in front of the pack. Plus he was smart. And cunning. And reckless—you needed to be reckless to survive in enemy territory. Caution brought out the zombies faster than an open wound.

She checked her watch and headed upstairs to the breeding dorms. She had good news for one of her favorites, a Hispanic boy named Tavio who had been condemned to the restaurant system for low sperm count. It was just an infection and the course of amoxicillin—what Tavio called 'bubble gum medicine'—had cleared it up handily.

Tavio's sperm count was normal again, and he could look forward to a decade of impregnating as many girls as the zombie administrators could throw at him. It wasn't the most romantic way to lose your virginity, but it definitely beat the alternative.

Sarah smiled ruefully, thinking of that term, 'zombie administrator'. Maybe things hadn't changed that much after all. She'd dealt with more than her share of zombie administrators in the old world, and from what she could tell, the post office, for instance, seemed to work much better with real zombies behind the counter.

"How are you feeling?" she asked Tavio when she found him in the video game room. He'd been released from the infirmary the day before.

"Great, Dr. T! I feel great. I'm ready to do my thing."

"It may be a while. They like to wait until you turn fifteen."

"That's six months from now!"

"It goes fast. And you'll get a nice present when the time comes."

"Do I get to…you know…see the girl who…the person I'm going to…you know…"

The sexes were strictly segregated in the dormitories.

She pressed a hand to his arm. "I'll try to find someone nice for you. Someone a little older, who's had some experience."

"Thanks, Dr. T. For everything. You saved my ass in here, and I don't forget that shit."

"I was happy to do it."

"Listen."

He stepped closer, beckoned with a curling finger for her to lean down so she could hear him whisper. "I'm gonna tell you something. It's like—a secret weapon with these dead-ass putas. When it happened—the Rising, all right? My big brother Estevan was on a date. The zombies ate his girl friend right in front of him, like them crazy paranna fish in the Amazon, you know? Just tore her apart. But they dint do shit to Estevan. It was like he wasn't even there. It took him a long time to figure out why, but now we know."

Sarah looked around quickly but the room was empty except for two kids working the Pac-Man machines. The zombies loved those Pac-Man machines.

"Tell me," she said.

"English Leather cologne—can you believe that shit? I always hated that stuff but it must make you smell like a zombie or I don't know what, because you invisible when you wearing it. He took the last of what we had and took a run down to San Pete—figured he could jump a boat and get outta here. Never heard from him since so I'm hoping he made it. I got caught when I went looking for more. All I grabbed was this sample bottle." He pulled it out of his pocket so she could see, and slipped it back in quickly. "I thought they'd take it away but they didn't think nothing about it. So if you need it someday, like you gonna make a run for it, or whatever? Just let me know. It'll give you a chance."

"Tavio—"

"You deserve a chance, Dr, T. You *ser buena genta*, you know? A good person."

"Thank you." She kissed his cheek and continued on her rounds. She couldn't help resenting him though. He had given her a flash of hope and hope was the most dangerous emotion in the world.

Time was running out but David had a plan: pull off the duct-tape gag and drop his ex-wife's name. It wasn't much but it was all he could come up with. Alice had real power now.

She could be his shield.

He didn't even need to get his hands free, if he could move them from behind his back. His fingers could still grip the tape.

The others were dead. Only he and the woman remained in the cellar. One more customer upstairs and the torture would begin. What would they take first? The tongue was a special favorite. And the sinuses—why not? They came with their own delicious mucus sauce. He'd watched them slash open a little boy's nose and pull the sinuses out like a tangle of red spaghetti. The pain must have been unendurable. Just listening to the throat shredding shrieks and squeals...

Stop thinking. Move.

He forced his hands under his ass, pulled himself into a tight ball, his ankles tucked hard against his thighs. Somehow he had to scrape his wrists past his feet, jamming his heels back through the gap between his arms. His back spasmed with the effort. He couldn't do this. He was going to be cut apart and eaten alive because he couldn't get a fucking gag off his mouth.

A door slammed somewhere down the corridor. The Zombie with the knife and the blowtorch was coming back.

David's time was up.

He thrust again, his knees digging into his throat. The duct-tape chafed against the arches of his feet. Thank God they'd taken his shoes! This would impossible with those clod-hoppers on. It was almost impossible anyway. The tramp of those heavy boots was getting louder. Another fraction of an inch, he was at the balls of his feet now. One more lunge as the door swung open.

Done! His legs jabbed out spasmodically, every muscle cramping as he tore at the silver tape. It seemed to take half his stubble with it when it finally ripped free.

"Alice Tremayne!" he screamed at them as they closed in. "Take me to Alice Tremayne! You'll get a reward! She'll pay you! Alice Tremayne! In the President's compound! She knows me! Take me there."

And that was how he came to be standing, filthy and barefoot, in the plush executive office on the second floor of POTUS' Bel Air mansion, staring across the wide empty desk at his dead wife.

It was uncanny. She looked as alive as he did—maybe more so, with the make-up and the elegant clothes.

He launched into his prepared speech. "We lived together for twelve years, Alice. We had two children together. It ended badly but now we can begin again, We can make things right. We're in a unique position. We can bridge the gap between the living and the dead, use the love we felt to bring the world together, to stop the conflict—"

"There's no conflict, David," Alice said quietly. "Farmers aren't at war with their crops. Ranchers aren't at war with their livestock."

"But—"

"I don't want to talk about the world and the food supply and the status of the remnant population. I want to talk about us."

"Us?"

"Do you remember what you said to me before we walked into the divorce hearing? You had found the drugs and the…tapes I made with Raoul. You were planning to show the judge the more…explicit sections. You had my diaries and the police reports I thought I'd gotten expunged. You had witnesses lined up to testify against me. People from the S&M club. Drug dealers who had been given immunity. God knows who else."

"Alice, that was a long time ago. That was a different world—"

"Do you remember what you said to me? The exact words? Because I do."

"No, come on, listen to me…Wait a second…how am I supposed to—"

"You said 'I'm going to eat you alive.' Well, David…now it's my turn."

She leapt across the desk—he had time to think, *zombies are supposed to be slow—* and then she knocked him off his feet with one battering side-arm blow. She was upon him, her teeth tearing through his shirt and into his shoulder. She snarled like a dog as she bit into him. He tried to push her away but she overpowered him easily.

He was going to die here. The despair was as big as the terror. He had no strength to fight her. Another jab of her head, he felt teeth ripping flesh, warm blood spouting. He met her eyes for a second. It was like looking into the eyes of a seagull, blank and feral. Another bite, shearing off his left nipple.

"STOP!"

The sandpaper voice of Brad Morton exploded like a gunshot. One syllable was all it took. This was the President of the new United States. The smarmy real estate tycoon who had driven five casinos into bankruptcy before the Rising. The grotesque star of the reality TV show *Beg for Your Job* and author of its charming catch phrase "Get out of my sight!" Talk about born on third and thinking you hit a triple! This guy died on home base and thought he hit a grand slam home run.

"I'm dining at The Salt of the Earth tonight," he informed the drooling creature that had once been David's wife, as she pulled herself together and stood up. "I expect to see this delectable specimen in the viewing tank." He extended an icy hand, and pulled David to his feet. "We'll be meeting again very soon," he said, with a vacant hungry smile. "I'm looking forward to picking your brains! And I mean that literally."

Ranisha Davis crouched against a tree near the fence line, pressing her baby's mouth to her breast to silence him. The charge on the wires created some sort of electronic field disruption that confused the zombies, that was what Jack said. Good thing—the voltage wouldn't be enough to physically stop them, even if the power was on full force, and it hadn't been on full force for more than a month. Jack had told them—lectured them—about the dam on the stream that ran through Rustic Canyon. Members of the Nazi Bund had built it in the previous century, just before World War II, to make their little community self-sufficient.

Somehow Jack had gotten it working again. They had power and they stayed off the grid, just like those Nazis. Jack said Nazi ghosts haunted the place. Ranisha told him she didn't believe in ghosts. My, how he had laughed at that!

"You live in a world overrun with zombies, but you don't believe in ghosts. You're very particular."

Ranisha remembered David Tremayne trying to help Jack with the transformers. He made some kind of mistake and gave himself a solid shock. Jack had pushed him down, disgusted.

"You're useless. Get out of here. I'll finish it myself."

That was Jack—an impatient, coffee-addicted know-it-all. But he was the kind of person who could do things, build things, make things work, the kind of person you'd seek out if the world ever came to an end.

And it had.

So they were lucky to have found him. But the fact remained, she just wanted to slap him silly sometimes. And even Jack Brady couldn't make rain in a Los Angeles summer. The stream had dried to a trickle, and taken their steady power supply with it.

She heard the noises again, and held her breath. Footsteps in the underbrush. Shuffling, uncertain steps. Zombie steps. She wasn't protected by her pregnancy any more—for some reason the zombies ignored pregnant women ("Don't choke the golden goose," that was what Jack said). And the baby was a liability, she knew that.

And yet…she couldn't stop thinking about the day before the others found her, thinking about the miracle.

When the zombies burst into her little apartment on San Miguel in Lynwood, she had emptied the gun Darryl gave her, and clutched DeShawn's head to her chest, covering his ears as she pulled the trigger, over and over, knocking the zombies down but not stopping them. Finally the baby began to cry and everything went dark.

The next thing she knew, David Tremayne had her draped over his shoulder in a fireman's carry and his sister Sarah was running ahead with the baby.

But no one could explain the miracle, not Sarah the doctor, not even the great Jack Brady. No one understood why the zombies in her bedroom died while she and her baby survived. Finally the explanation didn't matter.

Miracle was good enough for her.

Ranisha's thoughts crashed to a halt as the figure lurched out of the bushes. This must be one of the aristos she had heard about. He looked human. But they never sent aristos on the search parties. She stared as he came closer—just a boy, a little Mexican boy, stinking of English leather cologne.

"Don't be afraid," he said. "My name is Tavio. I come from Sarah Tremayne. She figured how to kill the zombies, but they—they found out and they took her away, they put her into the restaurants. You have to save her before it's too late."

"I wanted to speak to you for a moment, before they disposed of you," The President said. David's shoulder was throbbing but he couldn't seem to feel his arm. His chest was on fire. His hand was a glove of blood. He felt dizzy. He could barely stand.

"What?" he managed.

"You interest me. This moment between you and Alice interests me. Apparently the only emotion that carries over into our altered state of being is hate. Hate and the lust for revenge. Not love or compassion. Not the aesthetic impulse, not pity or pride. Not curiosity or irony or shame. Only hate. How strange that it took the virtual extinction of the human race as we knew it to teach us our first rudimentary lesson about human nature."

David managed a harsh croak: "That's why I'm better than you. I feel more than hate."

"What you feel or do not feel no longer matters. You are food."

"I'm a human being! You're nothing! You're—an abomination. A zombie—"

"We frown on that term. We prefer to be called 'The Risen'. The word zombie stigmatizes us as the undead."

David laughed out loud, and felt another flat wave of pain shear through him. "You've gotta be kidding. You're dead! You eat living people. That makes you a zombie, pal. No way to spin it."

The President's voice was cold. "I told you not to use that word."

"You don't like it? Tough!" he put his thumbs to his ears and wiggled his fingers like a fourth grade school yard bully. "Zombie, zombie, zombie! Zombie, zombie, zombie!"

The president reached out and clamped a hand over David's mouth, silencing him. "Here's what I want you to tell me, Mr. Tremayne. Where does your group hide from us? We've traced individuals as far as Casale Road in Pacific Palisades. But we lose them after that. It's frustrating, like—ripe fruit in the top branches. But you're going to help us shake the tree."

"Never."

He turned to Alice. "Find me an acetylene torch."

She scurried out of the room and the President turned back to David

"They say torture doesn't work. But I think on you it will.'

The hand lifted off his mouth. David said, "I always thought you were a sadist. Even watching you on *Beg for Your Job.* "

"Well, this will be something else. 'Beg for your life'? Or perhaps just 'Beg for quick death'. But you'll have to be very quick indeed. Because I'm going to burn your tongue down to the root, first. Then you'll have to use sign language. Until we shear off your fingers."

David didn't break when they secured his head to the high-backed restraining chair, he didn't break when the metal clamps forced his mouth open But the first touch of flame on the tip of his tongue shattered him.

He told the President everything. He gave directions. He drew a map. And then the President had him dragged away to be eaten later at the zombie leader's favorite restaurant, dismissing the broken blubbering human traitor with his favorite catch-phrase from the Time Before.

"Get out of my sight!"

"It's a place called The Salt of the Earth," Tavio told the assembled survivors.

They were standing and sitting among the ruins of what had been the community theatre, during the days when Rustic Canyon served as an artist's colony. The low walls, still scorched from the terrible fire in the 1970s that had convinced the state to take the land by eminent domain, were over-grown with bougainvillea, remote, perhaps haunted as Jack believed. But the ghosts felt benign to Ranisha.

Tavio had passed the key test: they had made him tell a joke. The sense of humor never crossed the mortality line. "How many zombies does it take to change a light bulb?" Tavio had improvised. "Five—four to trash the room and one to eat the electrician."

Not great; but good enough. Even Jack cracked a smile.

Now the fourteen-year-old boy was giving them their marching orders.

Nothing too difficult: just walk into a crowded zombie restaurant in the middle of a zombie occupied city and walk out with Sarah, somehow not getting captured, killed and eaten themselves in the process.

They had two advantages. Three, counting the element of surprise. The first was the new stock of English Leather cologne that Tavio had scored on his dangerous trek across the city.

The second one: DeShawn Davis, all of seven months old.

"That's what Sarah figured out," Tavio told them. "That's what blows away these fucking zombies. It's like—the opposite of us. The sound that gets us out of bed at two in the morning, wide awake—that's the same thing that shuts down these fucking *pinche gueys*. You get it? The baby crying, *pandejos*. That's all it takes. That's why none of these fucking zombies ever came into the nurseries. Sarah, she saw something go down, something bad, and she figured it out. That's why they took her away. To the lobster tank restaurant, that's what they call it. All the people are behind the glass wall and the zombies get to choose which one—who they're going to…you know. And they wear bibs…with pictures of people on them."

"Do they have an early bird special?"

It was Ragland Bennet Campbell—'Rags', everyone called him—a stringy old geezer with a nasty sense of humor. But he'd fought with the Delta Force in Viet Nam and he'd been a mercenary all over the world since then. People said he could kill you six ways without even touching you. Maybe his bitter jibes were among those techniques. Ranisha looked down, clutched her baby to her chest.

She knew what was coming.

The assembly was silent for a moment or two. They could hear the wind moving in the sycamore trees and the faint gurgle of the stream. Somewhere high above them, near them old fire road, a deer crashed through the underbrush. A bird called out, sharp and plangent. Another one answered—sounds from another world.

Finally Jack Brady spoke to the group.

"Here's what's going to happen."

It worked the way Jack said it would, until it didn't.

Stealing the cars went smoothly. Both Jack and Rags knew how to hotwire a car; the drive to the restaurant proved uneventful. Zombies still drove—they even had carpool lanes on the freeway. That sped things up a little. On the way, Jack and Rags checked the weapons, big automatic rifles with giant packs of bullets stuck into them. Ranisha hated guns. They didn't really hurt the zombies anyway, just kind of stunned them—and disfigured them. A bullet hole in the face was a social disaster for a zombie, or so they had heard; kind of like a fever blister or a mole. You burn zombies, but you had to burn them all the way to the bone or they kept coming and there wasn't enough gasoline in the world to do that job right.

She was the real weapon, she and her baby.

Jack's plan came straight out of the Delta Force playbook: a pincer attack with an overwhelming show of force. The machine guns would work about as well as tasers against the undead "But don't underestimate a taser," Rags told them. "Tasers are sweet."

"Decisive action in a field of confusion," was how Jack described it. "Rags and Billy and Tavio go in the back. I go in the front with Ranisha and Luther."

Billy and Luther were best friends from the Time Before—Billy was a skinny mean-spirited meth dealer who'd killed at least three people in the course of doing business and dreaded running into them as zombies. Luther was a body builder who'd worked as a bouncer until he got rich writing what he called 'chick porn' under the name of Lucretia Lovardo. He had copies and they had been duly passed around the Rustic Canyon compound.

Sarah Tremayne enjoyed them guiltily; Ranisha thought they were dumb.

But Luther was strong and fearless and spoiling for a fight. That was all Jack cared about. He could put a zombie down for five minutes with one good punch to the head.

They split up, Rags' car heading down the alley behind The Salt of the Earth, Jack parking a few blocks away. Jack and Luther were hiding the machine guns under their coats—the first shots would be the signal for Rags to attack from the rear.

Ranisha had DeShawn bundled out of sight under her raincoat. "He's a good boy. He don't hardly ever cry."

Jack stared her down. "He might not have a choice."

They walked along the sidewalk, stinking of English Leather, staying near the dark store fronts. Ranisha's heart was pounding in her throat. Pulsers, that's what zombies call living people. Supposedly they could hear your heart like a bass drum, taste the bulge of blood in your veins, the way you could taste sugar in the air at a carnival. She held her baby tighter and hurried to keep up.

Suddenly Jack shoved them into the entry alcove of what had once been a plumbing supply show room.

"Shit," he hissed softly.

"What?" Luther said.

"There's Secret Service outside. Two of them. The president must be eating there. There's gonna be a couple more inside, too. Aim for them, Luther, as many head shots as you can squeeze off. And feel free to blow that asshole Brad Morton away. I want him looking like fucking swiss cheese when we're finished. If there's propane in the kitchen set the prick on fire. This might be a good opportunity for us. You know what they say—*cut off the head*—all that shit. I'll shoot out the viewing tank. Rags should be coming in from behind. He'll grab Sarah. Do not let those motherfuckers use their radios. Once the alarm gets out, we'll have the whole army and the police force down on us. Every zombie who can put on a uniform and a couple of thousand who can't. And Ranisha? Get ready to hurt that little boy. We may need him screaming."

To Ranisha, the attack on the restaurant was one long explosion of sound.

The men opened fire on the Secret Service agents, bowling them over and charging inside, guns blazing. Maybe DeShawn was crying—it was too loud to hear anything but the thud of gunfire, the smashing glass and the screams of the zombies. The restaurant itself was something out her worst nightmares. Living men and women, and even one child, were clamped paralyzed (by some drug?) to the tables where zombies in those hideous bibs were devouring them.

Blood spurted everywhere. The place was a slaughterhouse. It must have taken hours every night just to drain off the plasma and clean up the gore.

Two waiters were bringing Sarah to a table, preparing the injection. So they did use drugs! She was crying for help, and Luther leapt forward, straight punching one zombie, and emptying the magazine of his Kalashnikov into the other one's face.

"David!" Sarah screamed.

Jack stopped for a second. David was gone, everyone knew that.

Two hideous monsters lurched at Ranisha. A lash of bullets swept them off their feet. Rags emerged from the kitchen, splashing propane from a can. The place would go up like a torch. Then Ranisha saw David Tremayne, splayed out on the Presidents' table.

"It's him," she shouted over the artillery roar of the automatic weapons. "It's David!"

Luther spun and saw David, pulled the trigger and held it against the bucking rifle. The zombie with the syringe was whipped backward, hosed by hot lead.

Jack leapt to the table, cut the leather straps and slammed an elbow into the President's face, splintering the creature's nose and tipping over his chair.

"We're out of time," Jack shouted, cleaning out his last magazine and then using the gun as a bat. Someone must have gotten the alarm out. Ranisha could hear the shriek of sirens closing in from every direction.

They fled the restaurant. Rags was just behind them. He threw a match and dove out the door split seconds ahead of the fireball. The explosion flattened everyone, smacked them to the sidewalk in a rain of glass and mortar. Ranisha twisted to fall on her back. She landed on her elbow and her ribs, her head bounced against the pavement.

Lurther helped her up and little Billy jabbed two knives into the eyes of two zombies staggering up the street toward them. The creatures reared back so hard they pulled the knives from Billy's hands.

The sirens grew louder.

They pulled themselves to their feet, dazed and bleeding, everyone looking at Jack. For once, the big man was silent, stumped, beaten. They were surrounded, unarmed, far from home base.

David spoke up. His voice was choppy, indistinct—something had happened to his tongue. "Thay's a 'ecording stuio fie blocks away. We haf to et there. I an record the baby, jack the vaume up."

"Set your speakers on the window sill," Rags grinned, understanding instantly. "Blast the Quad. Just like at college."

"Yeah, man," Billy said. "Rock out."

There was no time to backtrack to the cars.

"Run," Jack commanded them.

And they did.

They ran for their lives, David Tremayne leading the way, dodging into the alley behind the buildings, staying out of sight. The breath rasped in and out of Ranisha's lungs. The baby seemed to weigh fifty pounds. She knew she couldn't last much longer.

Then the guttural roar of a hundred charging zombies made her forget everything else. They were cascading out from between the buildings like turgid flood water, like a ruptured sewer line. Two of them grabbed Billy and took him down. His screams were muffled by the press of bodies.

"I have a few more shots left," Rags panted. "I can hold them off."

No one had the breath to argue. Ranisha heard gun shots, not bursts, but one carefully aimed pull of the trigger after another. She risked a glance back. Rags had knocked down enough of them so that they were tripping on each other's fallen bodies, tipping over into piles, blocking the alley.

His work was done, the path ahead was clear. Rags sprinted to catch up, but Ranisha saw a blur above him, a zombie jumping from a low roof. It landed on Rags' back and tore his head off his shoulders with one swipe, like a leopard taking down an antelope on some Wild Kingdom video. A thick fountain of arterial blood shot up ten feet and collapsed as Rags's feet ran out from under him and the pack began to feed.

The whole world was a Wild Kingdom video now, Ranisha thought, gasping for breath. And we're the antelopes.

The trick was: don't be the slowest one.

By the time she got to the recording studio door, Jack had kicked it open and the others were already inside. Hands grabbed her, dragged her into the darkness. She could still hear growls and shouts and sirens from the street outside. The zombies knew where they were hiding.

Jack and Tavio were piling furniture and filing cabinets against the doors. David and Sarah found the electric box and threw the breakers. The place lit up and Ranisha saw them pounding for the control rooms. She followed more slowly, giving DeShawn her breast and suffering the sharp pain in her elbow, breathing shallowly against her cracked ribs. The place smelled like fried electrical connections and old trash. Framed record jackets lines the walls: The Shins, Vampire Weekend, Mountain Goats. No hip hop, no rap, no black people. Just white teen-agers. Well, they were all probably dead by now anyway, like Rags and Billy and all the others. She might be the last living black woman on earth. And her baby might be the last living black boy and if what Tavio said was true, her little DeShawn could wind up saving the world.

It was too much to understand.

This is how it happened.

Jack and Luther found hammers and nails and two-by-fours from some interrupted renovation and secured the doors while David got the recorders and amplifiers and microphones up and running, working the control board like they were going to cut a hit single.

Then they were all together, barricaded into the big room with God knew how many zombies surging against the building, trying to break in—a thousand? Ten thousand?

Ranisha heard a crash and she knew it was the filing cabinets going down.

The zombies were inside the building.

"Make him cry," Jack told her.

"For God's sake, just do it," Sarah said.

She shook DeShawn half-heatedly, but the little boy just grinned. What was she supposed to do? Hit him? She couldn't hit her child. She couldn't, she wouldn't. It was all crazy talk anyway.

"ere's ano-er way in," David blurted.

Jack turned on him. "What?"

"The ontrol room. You nail uh ome boars afer me."

Sarah said "David—?"

"I'll buy us ome time, lea them away."

"No."

Jack held up a hand to silence her. "He's got something to make right, don't you, soldier?"

A tremendous crash jolted them. The barricaded double doors bowed inward but held.

Jack ignored them. "You sold us out, didn't you? They put the torch to your tongue and you told them everything."

David looked down.

Jack pressed a big, scarred hand to David's shoulder. "Don't kick yourself, son. Everybody's got a breaking point. Bridges fall down eventually. Even metal gets fatigued. Go on. Go do what you have to do." He turned away from David's grateful tears, and pointed at Luther. "Get the last boards, move it. Before it's too late."

The two men gathered up the supplies and sprinted for the control room.

Jack faced Ranisha. "It's up to you now, honey. Make him cry."

Another shuddering impact on the big double doors; and a massed howl of frustration. Another surge. They were pulling the nails out of the wall. How long until the doors flew open and the avalanche of the undead thundered into the room, mouths open, teeth bared?

A minute? Less than that?

Jack's voice was raw. "Do it!"

Ranisha was sobbing. "I can't. I can't."

They heard a rumble of footsteps, moving away from the doors.

"They're chasing David," Sarah whispered.

"Use the time he bought us," Jack snarled. "Pinch the fucking baby. Yell at it. Something! Anything."

Ranisha was sobbing. "No, please…he's my little boy."

Another rumble of surging footfalls. The zombies were coming back. They'd taken David and ripped him to pieces. And all for nothing. David was just the appetizer. The main course was inside those double doors.

"Fuck this," Jack said.

He grabbed the baby and punched the baby's mother hard in the mouth. She tumbled over backward and he kicked her fractured ribs. She bleated in pain and the baby knew his mother was hurting and finally he started to cry—huge terrified high pitched keening sobs that seemed to come all the way up from the balls of his feet.

The doors exploded inward and the swarm of zombies charged them.

In the control room, Luther red-lined the volume, just like David had told him. The blast of sound filled the room. It howling like a thousand babies, a hurricane of tears.

And it mowed the zombies down: a thresher in a hay field.

They kept coming and they kept falling, wave after wave. Finally the doors were blocked by inert bodies and there was no movement outside the big studio. Luther cut the sound. Jack helped Ranisha up, handed her back her baby.

The silence was epic, impossible, deafening.

"I'm sorry," he said.

She managed a smile. "Any time."

"What now?" Sarah asked. "We can't go back to Rustic Canyon. The zombies will be there."

"What we gonna do, man?" Tavio said.

"Yeah," said Luther coming back into the room. "What's the plan, cap?"

Jack smiled. "The plan is—we rig us a sound truck and we take us a drive."

They drove around the city for two days, reaping the zombies. Once the amplifiers broke down and a massive crowd of hideous decomposing monsters surrounded the truck. Luther thought it was the end.

Jack knew better.

"Just wait," he said.

One of the zombies, it seemed like he was the leader, shuffled forward.

"Please," he choked out through his rotten palate and his dissolving tongue. "Please."

"They want us to fix it," Jack said. "They want to die."

And it was true. Jack jury-rigged the repairs and Ranisha could see a kind of bliss on their ruined features as the shrill squawks of the sobbing baby took them down.

Gradually they gathered up other pockets of surviving humans and set to work burying the dead. Everyone seemed to move around in a joyful trance. The weather was mild, life was beginning again. At a stroke the war was over.

Or so it seemed.

But in the moments before the sound truck had cruised down San Miguel Street in the Lynwood section of South Central Los Angeles, one of the zombies lying on the floor of what had once been Ranisha Davis' apartment rolled over and woke up.

A few minutes later, as the others began to stir, the sound truck passed by. The noise bothered him for a few seconds—like an asthma attack when he was a child. Then it was gone. He had nothing to fear from a crying baby.

He smiled, showing bloody teeth. The old phrase floated into his mind from the Time Before: what doesn't kill us makes us stronger. And hungrier, he thought, the smell of flesh and blood strong in his nose, making his stomach growl.

Much hungrier.

EXPEDIENCY

by Paul Lorello

I should report the bite to the Ministry of the Undead, but I don't want them to go after my family. They'd do it, too. I know. I work for the Ministry.

Just at the moment of breakthrough as well. The Cargsguile plates needed to be *negatively* charged in order for the thing to work. Thanks to our research, we know that cell death occurs at a constant rate, given a specific decrease of brain wave frequency. And how, pray tell, is one supposed to record such a thing with *positively* charged plates? An unbridled ass I am!

I reached in to remove the plates not more than five minutes ago, and Arthur—otherwise known as specimen 325-G, the rotter we procured for experimentation—took a healthy chaw at my wrist.

I now have one hour and fourteen minutes before liquefactive necrosis occurs. I can already detect the aroma of living guts from passersby on the street below.

In an hour and fourteen minutes, if I've not devoured my apprentice (Jenkins, the poor sod, is on errand at the moment), I will be handed over to the Biomech Department and fitted with a vest and breech of alloyed copper, and half my useless brain will be replaced by the Department's latest patent: Fenton's Automation Engine, or FATE. If I'm lucky, I'll wind up as a swab on some *ballon-guerre*. If not, it's the mines for certain.

An hour and fourteen minutes to register the patent on my prognosis device. It's a rather poetic dilemma. But if I don't get the patent, that means no subsidies for my family. And by virtue of the New Revised Poor Law they'll be herded into some d—ned parish corral before they're even finished mourning. I can't go with that on my mind. Clara will forgive me for not spending my last hour with her.

I scribble a hasty note to Jenkins on a mercury slate, and I tack the thing where he'll find it. I marvel at my ability to sum up the whole story in three incomplete sentences and a postscript: *Bitten. Prognosis device a success. Off to obtain patent and die. P.S. Don't get too close to Arthur.*

As I leave the lab, I'm assaulted by a barrage of sights and sounds and smells, and everything is screaming. I hear a voice like some long lost friend calling me from the depths of memory awash in the din.

A vendor is roasting cobnuts outside the Patent Office. I'm going to miss the smell of cobnuts, as I'm going to miss the summer airship rides over Lily Field, and the sweetness of the flowers in that purified air.

There's a small line in the office. There's always a small line. The ceiling is low and the room is cramped and because the day is dim the gaslights are turned up, and these are sucking all the atmosphere out of the place. The man in front of me is holding plans for what looks like a perpetual motion machine. I can smell the alcohol in his liver.

It's finally my turn. As I make my way to the window, a clerk with a tallow-coloured face pushes a stack of sheets across the counter.

"Fill these out, won't you please? The time is three-seventeen p.m., third of June. When you're through, hand in forms C-24 through 29, then you'll need to go to the Patent Data Logging and Docketing Agency in St. Giles to apply for your Ministry waiver and to pick up a voucher and punch card. They'll assign you a docket number. Bring the voucher and the punch card and the docket number back here and submit the rest of the forms at that time. Thank you. Next on line, please!"

"St. Giles? That's on the other side of town! And besides, I don't require a waiver. I can pay the application fee here and now."

"You work for the Ministry, do you not?"

"I do."

"Right, sir, I could tell that by the pin on your lapel. All those who work for the Ministry are required to wear that little pin on their lapel. It's a lovely pin, sir. A lot of prestige in that. Although I did hear of a man what pricked himself with it while tacking it on and suffered a miserable death of tetanus eleven days later."

"Yes, that's very interesting, but please—"

"Ministry employees are required by law to waive their application fee, sir."

"Very well, but how long will it take?"

"Only a few minutes to waive the fee, sir. A stamp and a smile, as we like to say."

"No, I mean how long will it take once I bring back the waiver or voucher or whatever? How long before the patent goes through?"

"That all depends, sir. If you can get back here by four o'clock we can have your paperwork submitted by end of day."

"Fine then, I'll go—hold on…what do you mean *submitted?*"

"Submitted for review. Next on line, please!"

"Now see here! Submitted for review? How long does it take until it's reviewed?"

"It's possible it can be reviewed within the hour, sir."

"Good."

"Or it's possible, if it's late in the day as it is, and we get a lot of applications, that it could take as long as three days, by which time you'll be notified by wire to report to the review office in order to sign the required sheets, list your successor or successors, and receive your certificate and punch card which you'll bring both back here to be filed duly."

"That won't do!"

"Well, you could send them by post, sir, though I wouldn't recommend it."

"No, I meant—"

At this point I catch a glimpse of a copper-breasted rotter retrieving a stack of folders from off the desk behind the clerk. The face has been applied with salts in the usual manner to retard spoilage. Like all the others, it's a shriveled, peeling, loathsome mass of broken skin and sparse, sticky hair. And at the front of its scalp, the FATE retrofit, glistening sickly in the gaslight glow.

"Next on line, please!"

A throat clears behind me. The larynx smells of game. I turn to the gentleman and beg his pardon and patience. Then it's back to the clerk.

"Is there any way the whole process can be...expedited?"

"Expedited, sir?"

"Yes. You see, I need this patent granted by four o'clock; no later than four-fourteen."

The clerk looks as though I'd asked him to tell me the nature of man's existence. "Oh ,dear," he says, and licks the corner of his mouth. "You best be on your way to St. Giles, sir. Get back here as soon as possible. What more I can tell you beyond that, I don't know. Next on line, please!"

I glance at my timepiece. Exactly forty-five minutes left. By now the bite on my wrist is beginning to bleed through my bandage. I feel it sticking to the inside of my cuff.

In disgust, I hail a hansom. In disgust, I arrive at St. Giles Circus twenty minutes later. I'm in St. Giles Circus because the driver doesn't know where the Patent Data Logging and Docketing Agency is located. In disgust, I beg the pardon of a man in business attire who is snorting a great deal of snuff from a wide expanse of webbing between his thumb and forefinger. At my approach, he claps the box shut and stiffens like a soldier.

"The habit's an old and haughty one, squire," he says. "You'll not find a sharper wit for investing than yours truly despite it, look high and low, you won't."

"I'm not interested in your habit or your abilities. I need to know where I might find the Patent Data Logging and Docketing Agency."

"Well then," he says, brightening, "you might find it along the dusty Kampoli road in Ceylon, where the rubber trees line up like sentries, eventually bowing down in solemn reverence to the Temple of the Tooth in the Kandyan jungle. Along same road you'll find that famous monk who it is told walks the entire length of the path backwards from start to finish and over again all day long without cease, and who's been at it for well on fifty-seven years now. Or you might find it at the height of an opiate revelation in the wee hours of an August morning, squire, with the scent of tombs on you from the depths of the den. Either way, you might find it, although either way you'd be terribly wrong. You will most definitely find it, however, up on Dorset, in the alleyway between the milliner's and the thread shop."

I'm suddenly seized with the desire to bite into his cheek, with relish, and with rage. "Thank you," I say instead, and head off.

He's screaming after me. "I'll be d—ned if I'll fully recognize the Kandyan Convention of '15, squire! D—ned if I didn't lose a fortune in ink investments due to the capitulation of the weak-kneed liberals responsible for negotiating that abomination!"

I stop and I turn and the world blurs around me. I shake my head once, and at that moment realize that my jaw is distended, and the man is now cowering in terror below me. My hands are rigid and clamped onto his shoulders. My spittle has glazed the expanse of his chin.

"I didn't mean anything by it, squire! It was an overall good thing to have occurred, the Convention! Long live the governor! I'm heartily grateful for it! No need for violence!"

I let go of him and amble away without any further discussion of the matter. My head is, as they say, spinning.

The Patent Data Logging and Docketing Agency is a dismal little cell which makes a palace of its parent on the other side of town. As I enter, a rotter with a crackling FATE module is pushing a line of dirt across the room. It looks at me. It used to be a woman. It leans in, apparently trying to smell me. The smell sense is obliterated in the retrofit, but memories are not, and a rotter that has a hearty appetite before the modification retains its lust for meat afterward, and needs to be monitored carefully. There's a kill switch on its breast plate that delivers an electrical shock when thrown. I give it a flick, and the thing that once possibly loved a man with the frailty of a lamb convulses with a hideous series of grunts, and a yellow ichor issues from the corner of the salted lips. Something like tears come into its dead eyes. But there's nothing in that blank slate of a face to indicate a recognition of betrayal; nothing recalls to the tattered husk of its mind the dimmest memory of a broken promise or unjust injury. I wonder where my memories will be in less than twenty-five minutes now.

"Your waiver, sir," says the Patent Data Logging and Docketing Agency office clerk, a squinting, blinking, twittering little bee in a frock and collar, sporting an autostylus prosthetic which has the nasty habit of wheezing between strokes. "Note the date and time on the voucher. You'll want to get that back to the Patent Office promptly."

"And my punch card and docket number?"

"Sir?"

"They said I'm supposed to receive a punch card and docket number."

"Yes sir, they'll be administered once we enter your information."

"When will that be?"

"Sir?"

"*When*, you infernal baboon?"

"No need for epithets, sir. Ministry employees ain't exempt from civility."

"I'm sorry. Now please, for the love of the Maker Himself, please tell me the soonest I may expect to receive my punch card."

"And your docket number."

"And my docket number."

"That would be anywhere between one and three days, sir. You'll be notified by wire."

"That won't do!"

"They could send it to you by post, sir, but I wouldn't recomm—"

"No! You don't understand!" I glance at my timepiece. "Fifteen minutes. My G-d, I have fifteen minutes. I can feel the disease eating my brain away. Don't you see? I'll bite into your chest! I'll eat your wife! I'll make fruit of your daughter's head! *I'll eat her guts*. I need this patent today! Now! Before I turn. G-d! *I can feel it*." I clutch at my temples and feel a sinking, sickening depressurization, an implosion. Lethargy is beginning to weigh at my limbs. I'm not sure I know the next words I need to use.

"Bitten," I say. I think I'm crying. "I've been bitten. Do you understand?"

"Ah, I was going to ask you, sir, for I noticed all that blood seeping through your cuff. Hold on, there's a wire here what just came in. Where is it? Ah, yes. Here we are. Says here, yes, it says here folks who been bit who are inquiring into patent registry must report to the Office of the Patent Fast Track Division. You'll go right through, sir. You really should have said something in the first place."

"Where is it?" I think I say.

"Two doors down, sir. There's a temporary office on the other side of the millinery."

Upon entering the Temporary Office of the Patent Fast Track Division, I'm greeted by the amiable countenance of Jenkins, my apprentice, seated at a plain table heaped with paper in the middle of the almost empty room.

"Well, now," he says in his usual jovial manner. "Never too late, I guess. I called you outside the lab but you just kept walking. I went in and that's when I read your note."

He gently takes my wrist and lifts the cuff. "Oh, dear. Ol' Arthur really got in a good one, eh?" There's something of a chuckle in his voice. "The Ministry is looking for you. I'll notify them that you're here. In the meantime, sign this form." He slaps a single sheet before me, and pushes dip and ink across the table. "We'll have a patent by six o'clock tomorrow evening. Under 'successors,'" he points to a line, "I took the liberty of listing the names of your wife and children. I take it your will's in order?"

I nod my head. I think. I think I nod.

"Very well. I also took the liberty of summoning them. Your family. They're having tea in the back. You don't have much time I take it?"

I think a tear is falling from my eye. I'm not too sure.

Jenkins slides his spectacles to the tip of his nose. "I learned expediency from you, sir. Now that we know the exact time until reanimation, a fast track to patents for inflicted inventors is a necessity, as it will save the government a fortune in solicitor expenses. The Patent Office is now an official subsidiary of the Ministry of the Undead, once the papers all come into order. Not to worry. It's a matter of high priority for them, in light of recent scientific developments." He puts a finger to his nose. Winks.

He seems to want me to say something. But I don't know the words.

He reaches over and puts a soft hand on my shoulder. "Expediency is expediency, sir, the officials understand this."

I make my mark upon the sheet, as the smell of guts becomes nearly too much to bear. And then I go to my family…

There's darkness where I am…

Dahh darhheher werrr aaaerrnnngg

by Thomas Logan

5

JANE: "Then there were five."

"Once upon a time not long, long ago, there were others aboard the mighty seafaring vessel the *Endeavor*. But not anymore. And where the captain and crew and other Janes went, our final five Conduits did not know. They could not even find their friends the Twins. They didn't talk about that, though. Thoughts like that were too dark and dastardly."

I had to ask Asian-American Jane how to spell "dastardly" because Smart Jane was busy arguing with African-American Jane about Rambo or something but then "Perfect" Jane, she really calls herself that, our "fearless" leader, she was listening. Get this, video diary, she said, "What, you writing a book or something, Young Jane?" I said yes, because I was, you know, and she leapt up from her bunk and looked like she was going to hurt me.

That's why I keep my stories to myself. I just write in this little spiral notepad, see? Look, every page has its own story. I even drew what I think a zombie looks like. That stuff's supposed to be blood. Let me see if I can focus you in on that. Hey, listen, want to hear something really good I wrote? It's on the next page.

"The dead walked the earth. Their multitudes were so vast they spilled out into the sea. One was on board! A new kind of moan could be heard on the *Endeavor*. The moan of the living dead. It's just the wind, a Jane would say, but you knew better. If you placed your ear against the floorboard, you could hear it move softly, almost invisible. None dare venture outside the cabin. Pro— Prov-i-zi—" It means *food*. "... were brought by Janitor. Armed with his self-made mop-spear, the Captain's sword, and the boat's only gun, he protected the Ship's treasure. They just had to wait; that's all. But they each were waiting to be next. One at a time, or two for the Twins, like silent musical chairs. It was safest in here, but how long would they have to wait? How long could they?

"Once upon a time, there were thirty-two of the most beautiful women in all the world personally selected by R. Drew to live fairy tale lives as Janes aboard a Metagnosis luxury ship called the *Endeavor*. But a zombie or zombies had come aboard that ship, and now there were only five true Conduits remaining in all the Earth whose female powers—

JANE: —paid bills. You hear me? You ever been to Fire Island? You know what has two thumbs and has? Me. Yeah, me. I'm being real with you. You ever eaten fugu, the poisonous Japanese blowfish? I have. Makes your tongue tingle like coke. I ate a 24-carat gold dessert after. I've been to Tokyo, Berlin, and Paris. I've done it all. These tits, this face, there's no way they're real. You know Tim Fuse, the famous actor, right? Likes his Conduits dressed up like schoolgirls, does it from behind. This behind. I know. From experience. As a Jane.

And that's how we're going to stay: loyal Janes. That's why I'm perfect: loyalty. And I've got all the ideas. Like documenting our loyalty while we're all locked up in this room—my idea. Something to take the mind off, you know. That's it; just a waiting game. Just gotta have confidence, make life whatever, you hear me? Contestant Number One: me, Perfect Jane. Yeah. That's why I'm leader. I got my shit in perspective. And I do as I'm told. Got me to where I am today, a mega-yacht.

We lived the dream, still living the dream, yo. You know what I'm saying. Superstars. If those horsehumper hicks back home could see me now…

But that ain't gonna happen. They're infected and all dead and up walking around again. Losers. Sucks to be you, bitches. Your whole shit hole trailer park, your whole town gone zombie. Oh, well. You made your choice; remember when you laughed at me? So a billion less shit heads, boohoo. Big fucking loss. If there's one good thing about the end of the world: gets rid of lots of trash. Just look at the other Conduits and you'll see why I'm leader and how their—

JANE: —mental capacity appears acutely insufficient to ascertain the magnitude of the calamity at-hand. *Entre nous*, fellow transparent Metagnostic and future viewer of events recorded by this antiquated Sony VHS camcorder, as to my fellow Janes—those who left and the seven, now five, who remained and remain—the male of the species has its needs, and it is not for tight, moist brains.

It is error to believe this hour's apocalypse is our first. The destruction that exiled to Earth our sentient life force we, in human tongue, call Eth was far greater still. Those who fear simply nonderstand the true evolution of the species as revealed to R. Drew etched upon the ancient Metagnostic gold tablets. The True History foretells these final days. The beginning of the end shall put to an end our beginnings. And so grows our crystal of humanity in the crucible of catastrophe.

As Janes, distaff Metagnostic Conduits, female carriers of great Eth, it is our sacred duty to remain strong. As R. Drew distilled in words utterly Transparent:

"Survival is the sole goal of humanity."

Praise R. Drew. His prescience in establishing the Metagnosis fleet, including this ship of intimate pleasures, will ensure the continuance of The Doctrine and its spread to a new generation, a new Earth cleansed of the religistitious occlusions of Judeo-Christian populism. His Greatness forestalled ascension multiple times so that he may witness this day. It has come. And for the video record, not a day elapses that I do not thank the Powers for releasing the plague. Amen.

As to this, *faute de mieux*, "zombie," let me make explicit this certainty: There is no zombie aboard the *Endeavor*. A Transparent vessel cannot become infected. It is a physical impossibility. His or her biological cells have been made pure. No disease may we suffer, not even cancer or occluded bowels. Any suggestion otherwise is—

JANE: —kinda pathetic. At the first sign of, the Spiritual Masters split. R. Drew's brief return wasn't a homecoming; it was an airlift. They ran back to their families, their real lives. All the whispered sweet nothings were, well, nothings. We Janes weren't special. Jesus, that's the truth. And now, now it's been nearly a month of just us, the Janitor and the Janes. Sounds a little like a 50s surf band.

But the band's been breaking up.

The other Janes, they were supposed to radio us they made it off the boat. That didn't happen. The seven of us locked in this four-bed cabin stood around the walkie-talkie listening, waiting to hear word that they'd made it to the submarine and were off to somewhere, somewhere I suppose safer than a ship at high seas. All we heard was static. Now the Twins have been missing for two days.

Insert spooky, repetitive 70s slasher-movie synthesizer score over this "Real World" confessional. Because we're trapped. Here. In this room, on this yacht. The world's ending and the best we can do is complain on VHS. And enjoy our time together.

Here, take a look at what my bunkmates titled their tapes: "Jane's End of the World Video Diary," hearts, butterflies, smiley faces, exclamation marks; "You Hear Me? True Confessions of Perfect Jane, a Celebrity Conduit, Part One"; "Metagnosis: One Account of a Magnificent Mind." This one's crossed out but looks like "Transparent Like Me" with a new title squeezed over the swirls "Endangered Species, or My Observation as a African Goddess Aboard—" then runs out of space.

No one will ever see these tapes. No one.

So if you're watching, oops, my bad, you proved me wrong—

JANE: —about how, if you're the only Black person in attendance, look out for yourself, sister. Then he went off to college and got hurt and lost his scholarship, and I don't know where he is in all this madness.

I mean, just listen here for a moment: This. Is. Serious. We stay, we could starve, die of dehydration. Cannibalism. How long we got? I could be the last sister alive on the whole planet, the last Black woman on Earth. Just think on that.

So maybe it's a zombie. They're afraid? Of a zombie? You ever seen one of them walk? Look like my second cousin Jimmy Mac from that branch of the family tree that could use a little trimming, if you get what I mean. He got hit crossing a street by some bus, which is what it took for him to come off the pipe. Now, because his brain's all contused, well, he still shakes like he used to but can barely walk now too, his whole body shaking, vibrating, but like he's underwater because he moves so slow. That's what they look like, someone having a seizure underwater. At least from what I seen on *Endeavor*'s satellite TV.

Maybe it's zombies. Okay. Maybe not all the Masters left with R. Drew after he came back; he did just touch down and go. A pirate maybe. A stalker. "There are only converts and perverts," R. Drew said, but I'd say there can be overlap. Maybe another Jane went crazy. Maybe mass spontaneous combustion. Don't matter what happened to them. I'm getting off this boat.

The Twins got the right idea. Just got to man up. Do this. Go.

Look, this is our ship; if there is something out there, let's face it instead of hiding. Someone's gotta go through that Door #1 and do something, make a stand. Look around, it's got to be me.

Janitor works quietly. Before R. Drew's return, he cannot remember having ever spoken. To fill the air with words is not his nature. He would rather listen than speak, look than listen. He is silent and alone but never lonely or entirely mute for his actions speak for him. They transmit his loyalty across the ocean to those whom he loves who placed him—him!—in charge. His work speaks louder than words. It is proof positive of his devotion. It is the conclusion of his decades of service aboard the Endeavor. *And again his actions speak as he weeps with happiness.*

4

JANE: "Four, the perfect number, even pairs, number of corners on a square. These four brave flesh goddesses would survive being out on a dark and stormy sea, shipwrecked upon this metal island in an ocean of undead afloat in a world turned upside-down, topsy-turvy, and mean. Their divine purpose: to bring pleasure to the planet where physical bodies house our interplanetary Eth. They were so lucky to be born women and be blessed with pleasing appearances. In this form, they could serve their Spiritual Masters. And prized they were, highly prized. Only a Conduit, transparent of any occluding transgressions or nonderstandings, was strong enough to accept the brute power of a Transparent male.

"But in the end, despite all the protections of the world, nothing could stop the return of the dead."

Well, I guess, really, they're not really the dead-dead, but "return of the dead" sounded cooler than—Not that zombies are cool. I mean—Oh, say, she was so pretty. What happened to her was wrong. Wrong.

Zombies are so mean.

"On a dark and stormy night at sea, such an evil badness came aboard the Endeavor, a holy place, where the faithful came to forget their worldly woes. Here, true Metagnosticians were shielded from the sickness and violence of the terrestrial world. Or so they thought.

"Now, the door shut and locked again, the lottery of death continues with each girl asking: Will I be next? When will R. Drew return? When will—

JANE: —you ever shut up?

And she was like, "Make me," written all over her face. So I hit the bitch, yo.

I'm not a violent woman. No, wait, I am. I've hit a lot of princesses in my time, you hear me? Just saying. I'll punch anyone. And when that little whiny-ass bitch Young Jane all innocent and young—I don't care how young—who, whatever, okay, it doesn't matter because I have sophistication and experience, but she did try to get in and replace me with R. Drew like last year's model. Me. Yeah, me. Fucking her. Fuck her. I'm forever. Like a diamond. I hope she's hearing this. Oh, it felt good to knock her tweenie, skank, skinny, no-titty, little no-ass ass stinky cunt around. I hope she gets a black eye or one of them things in her head that kills you. Sounds like anal-jism. You know, what gives you a stroke.

Anyway, now four of us: the Chink, Crybaby, Einstein, and me. Oh, and Janitor who still brings us food and whatnot and chops off heads. Whatever, and I ain't saying zombie, but whatever killed Black Jane wanted a better look at her insides. Her uterus was all stretched out and looking like a wrinkled pink legwarmer shoved into some corned beef. Her body all ripped to hell, chest open wide and stuff drooping like a snot rocket of blood and lungs. Never seen nothing like it, and I've seen some shit. How the fuck she got from wherever outside back to the cabin with all her insides on her outsides, I don't know. Fucking enigma, yo.

But so I'm standing there—door's still open, Janitor's walking off with Black Jane's body over his shoulder, her chopped-off head in hand—trying to make sense of all this shit, and Youngster's all keeping on talking, right, I mean, about diseases, asking if we should follow Janitor, find out what happened to the Twins, asking where'd the others go and are you sure and who's next and are we ever getting rescued. Not okay. Talking, talking, always fucking talking, and she's too young to see she's spooking people for real, yo, you hear me? So I hit her. And again. Then a few more, right, really whaling on the bitch before the other two Janes broke us up.

Stupid ass people piss me right the fuck off. Who said violence never solved anything? Wasn't R. Drew. Now there was a leader who knew how to—

JANE: —maintain our superior wherewithal and be led by knowledge, not brawn. The milieu of our present juncture offers no opportunity for democratic assembly. I am a Gamma Level 7, Step III. If need be, I will assume leadership—at least until the Masters return and can tell us what to do.

Surely unity is of the utmost importance in this dire interim. This oceanic vessel is a sanctuary, a place of sexual worship. We are Conduits. As the stronger of the paired sexes, we must not give into any base impulses, including the bodily assault of one another. Despite the persistent and escalating temptation.

Young Jane's observation, prior to being pummeled, bears consideration: The Twins, driven by claustrophobia and anxiety, must have absconded to somewhere after they egressed. True, she errs in believing the absence of any Jane is evidence of a zombie's, or plural zombies', presence. A pure may not be infected, and contradictions do not exist. Contradictions indicate a lack of receptivity and/or moral strength and/or volition toward ascertainment. Ascertain. Retain. Maintain. A.R.M. yourself. In the clarity of R. Drew whose hand welded the pen that wrote:

"Those among the population who think they understand but lack Transparency can never understand their nonderstanding but nonderstand their understanding as inevitably revealed to others through Transparency."

Amen. *QED*, no zombie is aboard. Period. Definitive end stop. There is simply nowhere for the virus to obtain. Besides, would Dark Complected Jane's final words not have been to warn us of such a threat instead of expending her final breath letting the revered name of R. Drew pass her lips? And if a zombie, could not Janitor, so apt at *coup de grâce* decapitating as we've all now seen, dispense such a threat forthwith?

So let us explore alternate suspects and scenarios that do not test credulity's elasticity. While highly unlikely that an infected person may have boarded a ship that has not docked in four years, this does not eliminate an intruder. Let's presume, then, that the wayward Janes made it to the submarine. Could they not, and here let us grant our Judases an "inadvertently," have led raiders back to our ship? Yes, this a solution elegant in its simplicity. And per Occam's razor—

JANE: Zombie: onboard. World: ending. Accept, kiddies, because it's only going to get worse.

There was a time dimly remembered when Janitor had a name, a time when people who didn't know this name would say, "Hey, you, kid," and acknowledge his presence among their own. It was a time he'd all but forgotten until a shadowy semblance was resurrected recently when the Endeavor's *Captain, speaking with a Spiritual Master in heated whispers near the pool, noticed Janitor cleaning nearby. They quit their whispering, afraid Janitor might be listening in on what he had overheard. Then, hours later, this same sensation of self resurged when, addressing him directly, the Captain gave Janitor three terse orders. That moment Janitor was the happiest he'd been since that time dimly recalled when people knew him by a name, since age fourteen when he was castrated and enlisted.*

3

JANE: Yeah, well, whatever. My fucking stepmom'd help me masturbate with pillows, yo. We'd lie with a pillow between us and—

What? It's just fucking; happens a billion times every day. Maybe more. Well, not anymore, but—Whatever. Look, you can't be afraid of sex; you can't live in fear. That's the first thing R. Drew teaches. It's the first thing I learned when I was personally selected for my Conduity, the second Jane ever to come—yeah, like that, too—aboard. It's my whatchamacallit now that I'm leader. M.O. Motto. Mission statement. Whatever. You know what I'm saying.

So that snot-nosed Tweenie Jane scribbling in her notebooks is gone? Boohoo. Me, afraid? Nah. One less, you hear me. That's why you've gotta, like me, be smart, treat this shit like a competition. "Survivor" for real.

Some people say television's fake, but they don't know what they're saying. Actors are real. I've touched them, and they've touched me. All over. Word. Just saying, I've fucked more than my share. Tim Fuse, like I said before and I'll say it again, nice cock. Uncircumcised. No lie, yo. Whatever. Young Jane, she's gone; I'm here. I'm being real with you: I'm in it to win it. Cougar trumps kitten for the win.

Who will survive? Who knows? Not Young Jane. It's like the universe was saying to the little youngster: Doesn't fucking matter how young you are, how well you worked, whatever, how beautiful, dead is dead. And sorry, missy, you can't be fifteen forever. It gets you to thinking—

JANE: —intelligence is a loop. You start at Point A, which is autistic un-responsiveness, and travel nearly full circle, three-hundred-and-fifty-nine degrees and fifty-nine seconds, to arrive at autistic brilliance. All the difference rests in a single second. And so, too, by such a sliver does brilliance from revolutionary madness hang. Teetering, and all that is required to turn the wheel is a single drop of truth.

So how do you ascertain whether your mind has ruptured and sunken into the murky depths of madness? Truly? Is it the asking of an inordinate number of questions? Because I have been doing so. Because they left us. Because this ship is not a sanctuary and these women are not my sistren and the men who visited did not worship us as Conduits. They screwed us. Verily.

I thought I understood Metagnosis. I thought I understood life. I don't know anything anymore. I don't feel smart. I feel foolish.

Because this isn't real. No one will be watching. Not R. Drew, not any of the Spiritual Masters. Because no one cares about us. They never did. I—

I don't believe I am expressing this clearly.

You cannot escape yourself. You can scream and scream and scream, and it's really you, in hysterics, screaming while the planet and all hope has eclipsed and your fellow Conduits, still half-believing the circumlocutions that kept you all aboard the ship, watch you as if you've truly gone insane, which perhaps you have. And I am better now. I understand. There are no zombies, no pirates. I know who. It would appear you've got to—

JANE: —do as you're told.

Where else are you going to go? Who are you going to tell? You're stuck on a boat in international waters. You've been shanghaied.

She was a small, mousy girl, all of fifteen years old. We were always too busy being jealous of R. Drew's favorite to consider her youth, that this would be her teenage years, her life. That it was ours.

May Young Jane rest in peace. No. May Young Jane be forgotten.

Her name was Joanna Dakota.

Look, I don't really know how I'm supposed to take this. I think Smart Jane had engaged in sexual fantasies of her own, those of motherhood. I found a noose. I was putting Smart Jane in bed and trying to get her to quit laughing and crying. And—

What do you do when you know someone's going to commit suicide? What do you when it looks like it's the best thing for them? I found this. See how she's lovingly taped it back together using what looks like a single strip of invisible tape divided sparingly into a hundred economic, tiny bits and strips? You probably can't read it, but on the back of this full-page photo is an article about Young Jane, her up-and-coming rise to stardom as a tweeny singing and acting sensation. Except here she has a name. Joanna Dakota. I don't think any of us believed this was where our lives would lead, would end.

Janitor knows the peace that acceptance brings. After a few months at sea, Janitor would forget the face of the boy next door, then his name would fade coeval with the guilt. Eventually, all memories of his childhood prior to the Endeavor *would dissipate as well. For the greater portion of his life, over two decades now, he has embraced his present, a duration without future or past, his concerns never wandering far from what is needed of him—fresh towels, sheets washed, pool cleaned—while remaining a nonpresence aboard the pleasure yacht. He never questioned his life. Until recently. Until Jane. Pressing his ear against the wall separating his quarters from the closet they had made into a confessional, Janitor pretends the words they record are meant for him. He has heard her say how mistakes can decide a life. He understands. Her words are as beautiful as she.*

2

JANE: Well, well, well, guess who's still in the game, yo? Yup, yup, yup, that's right: Me. Next up: Asian Jane—miss "my pussy's some kind of waxed golden Chinese treasure cookie," like we couldn't have gotten a Bangkok piece for hella more cheap. A real Asian'd be glad just to have it so good, you hear me? But I guess they don't speak-ee the English so good. She's prolly an extinct species now. But, whatever. I'm special, too. More special. I have a destiny. As long as you tell yourself that—

No. Scratch that.

As long as you *know* you're special, you will be. Negative thoughts, not okay. Yeah, sure, it sucks that, what, like, most or like ninety-nine-point-nine-nine-nine-nine percent of the world's dead now. But make fucking lemonade, right? I mean, look what we lost. Like flushing a toilet, yo. Just saying. I'm being real with you. Survival of the fittest, that's what Metagnosis is all about.

Look, something will work out. It always does for the shamelessly beautiful. The Masters will be back any minute now. Any second. Because, believe it, if men are still around, they need it. You hear what I'm saying? And, shit, we got it. And we got it good. Besides, after all, after all those years, all that work it took to look—

JANE: —death in the face. The moans are still there, distant. I can make them out over the cabin creaks, the hollow sounds of the waves hitting the hull. It's only a matter of time.

My thoughts are mostly empty. Sullen, I suppose. Quiet. I think I understand Janitor. Metagnosis took his balls. It took our lives.

I try playing solitaire. I sit and turn over another card, and I'll try to drown out Jane masturbating and pray she will be next. Not because I don't want to die; I've made my peace. The world's ending. But it always was. Once, we had that onboard. The illusion. That we were living. Champagne parties and shore leave—even if we had to wear electronic anklets to make sure we returned. We forget about death, but that doesn't keep it from forgetting about us.

I realize I'm next. I can't wait in here any longer. I realized it earlier today when, playing solitaire, I saw—reflected in the metal hasp of Young Jane's journal—Perfect Jane, All-American supersized breasts getting in the way of her arms, alternate between humping her hand and rubbing herself, crying out, even after all this, to R. Drew.

Keeper of the Ship. Janitor did not feel honored when the title was bestowed upon him; he does not feel honored now—though these absences are not felt the same. The first absence lacked any emotive response. The persisting lack of late, though, feels the very opposite of feeling honored; it's a meager sensation nearing shame and inducing much mental confusion. Janitor looks upon the bodies he has collected, orderly column and row of nearly thirty naked Janes, and a thought he has recently fought returns: This present is nearly over. When, after so many years at sea, he eases the valve to his imagination to envision his future, instead of seeing out into the world, the planet pours into him and he chokes.

1
JANE: It was her idea, these tapes. Seems only right I finish this out. Maybe one day others will watch these. There could be others. We survived. We weren't anything special. Lucky, that's all we were. Maybe. We'll have to see. But we will. We'll live to tell the tale if any remain to listen.

Around an hour ago I awoke and saw the door open, him just standing there.

He beckoned.

I followed. My feet and body were numb standing beside Janitor in the freezer. There, laid in orderly lines, were my sisters, my namesakes. I'm not sure how I felt about some of them alive; I could barely bear to see them dead like that. Those we had cursed aloud for leaving, hoped secretly had escaped on the sub, their faces were blue, frozen with asphyxiation's panic. Bulging eyeballs. So blue. He took my hand, led me away.

We went to the Captain's quarters. Perfect Jane's corpse was laid nude on its back on the Captain's desk. Our all-holy leader was there. Kinda. Not really. R. Drew's clothes were still in fair condition except for the broken fly of his slacks. His balls were gangrened. His left ear hung on by threads. He was rotting. And that rotting son of a bitch was having his way with Jane's dead body as he chewed on her corpse.

Or going through the motions of sex. As I watched, unable to turn away, thinking how he brought the infection with him, maybe even hoped of being buried at sea like a maritime pharaoh with his harem of slaves, his teeth worked through her breast bag, and he got a mouth full of saline.

Zombie R. Drew wasn't interested in us, but I couldn't take my eyes off of him. So I didn't see when Janitor drew his pistol and made his final kill.

Janitor has done as he was told. He has. He kept the Janes from fleeing. He fed R. Drew. He told no one. These were his three orders; now Janitor cleans up his last mess. He will do his duty; keeping to R. Drew's original deathbed request, he will leave no Jane on board the En-deavor alive. The warm gun in his hand has trouble finding its holster; Janitor is overwhelmed by emotions and very nervous. He has studied the maps, has selected an island, and has supplied the submarine. Yet fear coils his intestines and saturates the room in intense white when he turns to look in her eyes. He did not love Jane from the moment he saw her, but her words have worked a magic. He croaks and tries again. He says he's sorry. She hugs him until his chest finishes heaving and his eyes dry. He asks her to call him Bruce. She says her name's Angela, but people call her Angie. They don't live happily ever after, but who can? It's the end of the world. They live happily enough for a while.

0

by E. Manning-Pogé

Squatting in the ruins of the FDR Drive, beyond the safety of the night lights, amongst the skeletal frames of countless automobiles, abandoned and gutted by flame, I feel the snowflakes land on my face.

From out the night sky they fall, unbidden.

Unwelcome to the heatless, uncaring for the prayerful, they mark the start of another long winter, here, outside the light.

Across the East River stands Brooklyn. A wasteland. A nightmare.

Countless blackened windows, staring, like eyes.

It isn't the windows which watch me, though; it's what lurks within. In the shadows. In the darkness.

The lost merry hatters.

Some nights, I can hear them howling and screaming from the rooftops over the black water. Tonight, they are quiet.

To the south, I can see the glow of Staten Island. They have their own power plant there. I've heard stories about what they fuel it with. Some say people.

Here, on Manhattan Island, only the wealthy have power, only the chosen have light.

I live among the ungifted, the unneeded, the unable to offer anything to a society that, itself, has nothing left to give. We huddle together in packs—some forged of convenience, others born of years of shared experience—in the warmth of trashcan fires and burning sedans, on the banks of the turbulent waterways that ring the city, doing what we can to survive.

My pack numbers eight this night. I know all of them. I like most of them.

Gloria A-Street is our leader. She's petite, but she's fierce. Unlike most people who find themselves in charge of others, she is also fair.

Like everyone else alive, we've got our buzz on. Little Eileen, as usual, has hit it too hard, gone over early. Full metal megilla. Some Johns like that.

We joke between tricks and pass flasks and glass pipes, wrapping ourselves in smoke and lies and heavy clothing against the cold.

We're dressed for the weather: fur leg warmers and mittens; thick cardigans over topless corsets; mukluks over fishnets.

We're selling sight unseen.

I'm not worried. They always like what's under my fur: the curves and muscles, the ink and piercings. Mostly, though, they go for my face. Unscarred. Unblemished. Underage; just.

Twist. Hit. Shiver. Recap.

The snow catches fire over Brooklyn, like it does. Something about chemicals in the ice crystals. Gloria tried to explain it once, but I'm not real smart when it comes to science.

The flakes burn out long before they reach the ground, illuminating the night clouds with waves of color, never reaching the haunted tenements below.

The falling snow burns green to red and some of the girls go, "Ah!"

I've seen it before. Boring as fireworks. People like to say, "Ah."

"Meat wagon," chirps Sarah, the new girl from uptown, north of Central Farm.

There's a rickshaw coming. Not public. This is money.

Showing no indication of slowing, without passenger, it approaches through the snow: white lacquer with brass trim and running lamps; a black, cloth canopy with full sides and gold tassels brushing massive, spoked wheels banded in iron; an athletic, well dressed pilot, complete with bow tie and bowler, peddling toward us at a healthy clip.

A few of the girls take refuge behind an auto carcass.

I light a cigarette.

The rickshaw draws to a halt and Gloria steps up as the pilot quietly removes himself from the apparatus.

He takes a step forward and trips on a crack in the asphalt, stumbling.

Some of the girls laugh.

Composing himself, the man reaches into a coat pocket, removes a small leather bag, dumps an object into a gloved palm.

It's a podicle.

Taking it between the fingers of his right hand, he places it over his right eye and presses the button on its side. Once the podicle whirs to life, he begins to walk among us.

We know the drill. He's filling an order.

Some of the girls begin to remove their scarves and balaclavas in preparation of the scan. It's too cold out. I wait until he gets to me.

I take my hat off, push my hair back. I stare into the eye of the podicle.

From the color of the lens—ghosted grey; a dead fish—it's obvious he is using some sort of graphic overlay, probably a photograph. He's looking for someone.

I don't sweat it. I'm no one.

He begins to move on, then returns to me. He studies my face from the front, the side. He looks me up and down, as though taking measurements.

After a minute or so, he removes the device from his eye, drops it in his pocket, and addresses me.

"Permit me to introduce myself. My name is Templeton Poole. I am personal assistant to, and messenger for, Master Addison James. He wishes you to join him at his residence this evening."

"Master of what?" Gloria asks.

"Of me, for one," he answers, not taking his eyes from mine.

"How come me?" I ask him.

"Based on the physical specifications given me by Master James, you quite fit the criteria for his…date."

I'm looking at the rickshaw. Upscale doesn't shop down here very often. I can soak him. I'm trying to adjust in my head. Math.

I look at Gloria. She knows what I'm thinking. She has her hand pressed to her hip, three fingers pointed down.

Thirty stamps. It feels like a push. No one would pay thirty for me.

"I am prepared," the man says, "to offer you eighty stamps for your time."

"Eighty!" someone gasps.

It's more than any one of us makes on a good week, even Gloria. Never for one trick. Never.

"I'll go," jumps in Rachel Crash, trampling gutter etiquette.

Gloria elbows her into silence.

Finishing my cigarette, I put my hat back on.

"Let's do it," I tell him.

"Stack it up, sugar!" someone roots.

As I settle into the passenger seat of the rickshaw, Gloria calls to me.

"Kitty Cat, you safe?" She holds up her canteen.

"To the top," I tell her, patting my own, clipped to my belt.

Poole quickly climbs onto the machine, turns it about, and hurries us back the way he came.

It takes him a few minutes of clumsy maneuvering around rusted wreckage and snow-dusted garbage, but he manages to find his pace and we are soon sailing along briskly, his legs pumping the pedals, snowflakes pelting my face.

I yell at his back. "Eighty stamps is a lot of scratch."

"Is it?" he responds, over his shoulder.

"What did I sign on for?" I ask. "Sadists? Satanists? Religs trawling for converts?"

Without breaking stride, he answers, "I can assure you, Master James is none of those dreadful things."

I light a cigarette. We encounter a group of street children playing, testing their courage, running circles around a deranged man, poking at him with sticks. Poole navigates the mayhem with ease.

"Why is he your master?" I ask.

"Who, do you suggest, should be?"

I don't know what to say. I'm not good with those kinds of questions.

I sit back in the seat, keep quiet, watch the city go by. We pass the gas lamps that mark the beginning of the area of law enforcement. The police are corporate. The laws change daily.

My buzz is strong, but I don't know if I'll have access to my hooch when we get where we're going. I take the canteen off my utility belt.

My canteen is a good one, military issue. I found it dumpster diving. It doesn't rust and it's hard to dent and it makes a fair weapon in a pinch. Tonight, it's full.

Some people are particular about their hooch, worry themselves over where it comes from. I try not to give it too much thought.

If the tapster tells me it's apple hooch, then apple hooch it is, even if it does taste of oily cogs and rancid cardboard.

Twist. Hit. Shiver. Recap.

The shiver. Up the back of my neck. That's how I know it's real. Whatever else it might be, it's alcohol, and that's good enough.

We reach the gang gate at 12th and 1st. It is strung with paper lanterns. Half a dozen men on guard, shotguns, leather jackets sporting Third-Eye Army colors.

Poole rolls us up to the gate and pronounces, loudly, "Forever, House Wren!"

The men snap to attention and echo his cry. "Forever, House Wren!"

The call is taken up, briefly, throughout the surrounding tenements.

"Forever, House Wren!"

House Wren is one of twenty-six corporate houses that run the city. They also run the street gangs.

Successful turf-hopping is purely a matter of knowing what gang belongs to what corporate house at what time.

I know all of the passwords. I don't know what any of the corporations do.

The gate is opened and we continue our journey.

The streets become brighter as we head inward, gas lamps giving way to electric torches, the snow shifting from orange to white.

I can already hear gunfire from the west side, over the Hudson River. Assault weapons on full auto. Hoboken Ferry, New Jersey. Gateway to the west.

With the bridges blown and the tunnels flooded, the ferry is the only way on or off Manhattan Island. The fighting never stops on the mainland side, with an endless horde of hatters from the heartland trying to get at the soldiers stationed there.

Some people argue that, for the few refugees who find their way to Hoboken Ferry each month, a number which grows smaller with time, it isn't worth the cost in manpower or ammunition to keep the ferry running. Others see it as a statement; the last known outpost of humanity east of the Hudson.

I don't know about any of that, but I would like to have one of those guns.

The deeper we go into population, the more unease I feel. I've travelled the whole of the city, but on the outer rim. The interior is largely unknown to me.

I've heard the stories. Corporate slaves. Mad scientists.

Suddenly, there are rickshaws and bicycles all around us; people crowding the sidewalks, haggling at market stalls over clothing and food items; loudspeakers everywhere, voicing instruction, so many that I can't tell what any one of them is saying.

Twist. Hit. Shiver. Recap.

"Are we almost there?" I ask Poole.

"Indeed," he answers, hanging a sharp left.

Another turn puts us on a side street lined with tired brownstones. We stop halfway down, on the right.

Poole climbs off his seat, stands on the sidewalk beside the rickshaw, and holds out his hand.

I look at it. "I'm supposed to tip you?"

He rolls his eyes. He doesn't even try to hide it.

"Your hand, madam," he says.

"Oh." I laugh.

He helps me out of the rickshaw and offers me his arm.

"You are such a gentleman," I tell him, looping my arm through his as I clip the canteen onto my belt and flick my cigarette butt into the street.

"Quite," he says, escorting me up the stone steps and through a grand wooden doorway, into the building.

The first thing that hits me when the massive door closes behind us is the warmth. Real warmth. The kind of warmth that lives in a place. The kind that takes the pain out of your bones.

The scents follow. The air is rich with them. With wool. With cinnamon. With things I can scarcely imagine. It is heavy with comfort and safety and sleep without dreams.

Finally, there is the silence.

It is absolute.

More silence than I have ever heard before.

Poole shifts behind me, the rasp of his trouser legs a curse in my ears.

"This way," he says, stepping around me, "if you would."

I follow him through lighted rooms crammed with books and statues and paintings and…furniture. Such marvelous furniture. Cushions and pillows and couches and chairs and things I don't even have names for. I want to sit on every one of them.

We arrive at a pair of wooden doors, floor to ceiling, which Poole opens. He ushers me through with a wave of his hand.

I enter a room of dark wood and red material; of ornate rugs and embroidered couches; of strange plants, towers of books, and shelves piled high with all manner of gadget and treasure. There are pictures on the walls, framed photographs, more than I would know how to count. There is a fireplace, burning noisily, throwing light and heat everywhere.

Beside the fireplace stands a middle-aged man. Handsome, he is wearing a tuxedo. He is smiling.

Poole says, from behind me, "Your host for the evening, Master Addison James."

"Hi," I say, moving further into the room.

The man approaches me, but says nothing. He walks around me. Twice. Three times. He stops in front of me. He studies my face for a long while.

I'm watching his eyes. They go someplace else.

"Templeton," the man whispers, "you are a genius."

"Thank you, sir. She was exactly where…"

He's back.

"That will be all, Templeton."

"Yes, sir."

Poole leaves without another word, closing the doors behind him.

Master James stands, staring. He looks at me like he knows me.

I don't like it.

Looking down at his clothes, he laughs and says, "I apologize if I am overdressed. I don't do much entertaining."

"Are you the one that's going to pay me?" I ask.

"Of course," he says, taking a stamp book from inside his jacket. "Yes, of course. Forgive me. Here, as promised, are your eighty stamps."

He tears out two pages, hands them to me.

I take them, quickly.

"Plus," he says, "a further twenty, for the lateness of the hour."

I stare at the blue sheets in my hand.

"There are one hundred stamps there," he tells me.

I look up at him.

"What do you want to do to me?" I ask.

I hope it isn't going to hurt too much. I want the stamps.

"Please," he says, "allow me to finish."

He opens the stamp book again, goes to the back. He tears out another page, this one gold.

"There are four stamps on this page," he tells me, "each worth fifty stamps."

I look at the gold paper. It is shiny.

"Do you know how much fifty times four equals?"

I try it in my head.

Fifty and four is…no. Fifty fours equal fifty-four…no. Five…

"These four stamps," he tells me, "are equivalent to two-hundred stamps. Twice as many as you now hold in your hand."

My head starts to hurt. I fold up the blue pages, tuck them deep into my coat pocket.

Behind Master James stands a small table with two chairs. Laying his own stamps upon the polished wood, he comes over to me.

"You have a choice," he says, his voice soft. "You are free to take the hundred you now have and leave, if you wish."

"You're just going to give them to me?"

"You have already earned them, merely by coming."

It feels like a setup. He will probably call the police.

I look at the gold stamps on the table. They reflect light onto the wall.

"What is my choice?" I ask.

He smiles.

"Should you agree to spend the night, help me with an important project, I will give you all of the stamps. That is a monetary total of three hundred stamps."

Three hundred.

I feel light-headed. I stare at the fire, sweating in my furs.

"Can I take my outsides off?"

"Yes, of course. Where are my manners? Please, make yourself comfortable. Would you like a drink?"

"I have my own, thanks." I pat my canteen.

"Yes," he says. "Well, you settle in and I will get myself some sherry."

He hurries out of the room.

I undo my buckles and snaps, my pins and straps, pealing off layers of fur and leather, dropping them into a pile on the floor. My hat and utility belt, my jacket and vest, my bracers, my chaps. The last, I slip off over my boots. The boots come off for no one.

Master James comes back. He's carrying a bottle. It's green. Real glass.

I stand before him in fishnets and garters, tattooed and topless, bodmods catching the firelight.

"Oh, my." His hand goes to his mouth.

"It's what you paid for," I tell him, grinning.

Hurriedly, almost clumsily, he places the bottle on the mantle and takes off his tuxedo jacket, holding it out to me. He looks at his shoes.

"Please, if you would," he says, "do put this on."

"They're your stamps," I say, taking it from him.

I slip into the garment. It is silk-lined. It feels like feathers and honey on my skin. I roll up the sleeves to free my hands. I don't button the jacket closed. I think his embarrassment is funny.

"Please," he says, taking my arm. "Please, come sit."

He leads me over to the table. I bring my canteen. He pulls a chair out for me.

"Please."

I sit.

He takes the seat across from me.

"I have invited you here tonight to help me finish a little experiment," he tells me.

"What kind of experiment?"

I button the jacket.

"Nothing dangerous," he says.

I look at the exit.

"It is purely cognitive."

I eyeball the stamps.

"What shall…"

"This better be worth it," I interrupt.

He looks confused. "Excuse me?"

"This." I look around the room. "Whatever it is you have planned here, it better be worth these stamps."

He sits up straight.

He takes a breath.

"What shall I call you?" he asks.

"Kitty," I tell him. "Kitty Cat."

"Okay."

"Kit, some people call me."

"Fine, yes…"

"Cat."

"That's fine. Kitty. May I call you Kitty?"

"I just said you could."

"Although I will be conducting a very important experiment here, Kitty, you are not going to be the subject. You will in no way be harmed or put in harm's way. You will merely be a mimic."

"A what?"

"A mirror."

"I'm going to be a mirror."

"Of a kind, yes."

"What does that mean?"

"Allow me to show you. Just do as I do."

He places his hands on the table.

I look at them.

"Go ahead," he says. "This isn't a trick."

I put my hands on the wood, palms down.

"Now, do what I do."

He lifts his right hand and touches his finger to his nose.

I lift my right hand, touch my finger to my nose.

"Very good," he says. "Now, mirror me. If I use my right hand, you use your left. You do know right from left?"

"Of course."

"Good, let us try it."

He touches his nose again, right hand. I do the same, with my left.

"Excellent," he says. "Now, rather than do it after I do, try doing it at the same time."

"How can I do that?" I ask. "I don't know when you are going to do it."

"Try it," he tells me.

I try. I fail. I try again.

We do it for a long time. I get it right. I get good at it.

We take breaks. He teaches me things.

"What do you know about the cure?" he asks me.

"It kills you," I say. "Turns you into a hatter."

"Did you know that it was once, in actuality, a real cure?"

"For what?"

Twist. Hit. Shiver. Recap.

"For everything," he tells me.

I listen.

"The cure had been discovered," he begins, "quite accidentally, by religious fundamentalist scientists trying to create a new bioweapon with which to bring about the Apocalypse. When they had realized what they had actually created—a cure to every disease and illness known to mankind—even they couldn't resist sharing it with the world.

"Within months, the global scientific community had embraced the vaccine, beginning a robust program of inoculation. Not only, they soon discovered, did it prevent diseases such as cancer, lupus and HIV—horrors which, thankfully, no longer exist—it actually reversed the course of these diseases in those already afflicted.

"Suddenly, everybody endorsed the cure. Everybody wanted it. The only problem, they soon learned, was one of logistics."

I fiddle with my canteen.

"Do you understand what I'm talking about?" he asks.

I don't get all of the big words, but I catch the meat of things.

"It was medicine," I say, "but there wasn't enough."

"Exactly," he tells me. "No matter how fast they worked, they could not produce and dispense the vaccine fast enough to satisfy the demand. Soon, worldwide riot broke out, along with accusations of top-down inoculation, with the wealthiest people and countries apparently getting treated first. War erupted between two-dozen countries. We had discovered a cure for the ills of man and the world was destroying itself in conflict over that very cure."

He points at my canteen.

"Why do you drink that?" he asks.

"So I don't get sick," I tell him.

"Sick from what?"

Now he is asking stupid questions.

"Sick from the cure."

"But do you know why?"

I don't.

He tells me.

"While the limits of the cure virus were being studied in a laboratory in Sweden, it was discovered that it thrived in fresh water, multiplying at an astronomical rate, and that it could be ingested, effectively, by humans.

"It wasn't long after that a decision was made to dispense the cure by seeding the drinking water. All of it. Every bit of fresh water on the planet. Within six months, there wasn't an illness left to man. Pandora's box had been closed."

"What box?" I ask.

He shakes his head. "It's not important."

We do more exercises.

I'm a mirror.

He moves faster.

I keep up.

"What do you call the undead?" he asks me.

"Lost merry hatters," I tell him, "like everyone else."

"Yes," he says, "lost merry hatters. Do you know where the name comes from?"

I don't. I shrug.

"It began in South America, the death," he says. "It started with the best and the brightest. Physicists, statesmen, scholars. One moment they were Nobel Prize winners, the next, homicidal maniacs without a hint of reason. They killed at random, without provocation, anything that moved. Anything, that is, but those likewise afflicted.

"The media referred to the infected as the angry dead. *Los muertos enojados*. It has since, through time and culture, been bastardized into lost merry hatters.

"Within weeks, it was global, the disease spreading like a pyramid, striking the intelligentsia first—the thinkers, the policy makers—before moving into the lower, more populated rungs of mental acuity.

"Mankind's brain trust was eradicated and, with it, our hope."

"How come you didn't get sick?" I ask him. "You're smart."

"Like many," he says, "I am more educated than I am intelligent. My IQ is scarcely higher than man Jack's."

"Who is Jack?"

He gets up from the table, walks to the wall, takes down a photograph.

Returning to his seat, he places the small frame on the table, picture-side down.

"She was the one who first realized it," he says. "My wife, Dr. Victoria James. She was the first to see the connection between the cure and the epidemic. It was she who realized what we had done; what we are, you and I."

He starts to lose me.

"What we *are?*"

"I'm going to show you something now," he says. "A photograph. I don't want you to be frightened."

"Frightened of what?"

He flips the frame over, places it before me. I stare at the picture.

It is me.

There is something different about the hair, something around the eyes, but it is a picture of me.

I have never seen a photograph of myself before.

"What is this?" I ask. "Why do you have this?"

"That, Kitty," he tells me, "is my wife, Victoria."

"This is me," I insist.

"Although I do agree, you do bear a remarkable resemblance to one another, I can assure you, that is a photograph of my wife. You were asked here tonight specifically for the resemblance."

"So, what is it you want?" I ask. "Role play?"

Shaking his head, he gets up from his seat, comes around behind me.

I wait for the hands on my body.

Pulling out my chair, he says, "Please, follow me."

I get up and follow. I bring my canteen.

At the far end of the room is a door I had not noticed before, hidden in bookshelves and shadows. He unlocks it with a key from his pocket and we step through. He leads me down a flight of spiral metal steps lit with electric light. There is another door at the bottom. He unlocks it and disappears. Gripping my canteen, I follow.

The room I enter is white, empty of decoration. Along one wall is a cot with white sheets, a pink dress laid out on it, a black wig. Beside the bed stands a white, cloth dressing screen. On the opposite wall is a desk of some sort, covered with buttons and small video screens. There is a small wooden stool in front of the desk. On the far side of the room is another door.

Picking up the dress, Master James hands it to me.

"Please," he says, "put this on. I will help you with the wig when you are ready."

I take it from him, go behind the screen.

I remove the tuxedo jacket, hang it on the corner of the screen, slip into the dress. It fits. It has long sleeves, a high collar. The collar is snug, but I can swallow.

I step out when I am done.

"These as well," he says, handing me a pair of black, leather gloves.

I take them from him and pull them on as he arranges the wig on my head.

"It worked, you know," he says. "The cure. It worked."

I keep silent and let him fuss.

"It killed everything. Every disease." He speaks around a mouthful of hair-pins. "What they didn't count on, what they couldn't know, was that *we* are a disease. Our humanity. That thing inside of us which compelled us to tame fire and invent the wheel and look to the stars. That thing which placed us, head and shoulders, above all other living things.

"That thing was never ours."

I try to keep up.

He steps back, nodding.

"Good," he says. "Good."

Turning, he walks to the next door and unlocks it.

"This way," he says.

He continues to talk as I follow him.

"It is a disease, this intelligence of ours, these minds. These people we think we are, by the very fact they can think at all, are not natural to these bodies. Humanity is a virus that found a ready host inside the brain of our homo sapiens ancestors.

"By curing the disease, we killed everything that we are."

The next room is a proper bedroom, with a bed and armchairs and a vanity with a mirror and chair. I walk over to the vanity, inspect the items on top. There is a hair brush—thick, black bristles and a sparkling white handle—and a statue of a girl with small wings.

"They realized it in England first," Master James says. "The only people who didn't seem to be infected by the outbreak were inebriates. It wasn't long after that the World Health Organization instituted the declaration that all citizens of all countries must drink alcohol, frequently. Regardless of age. Even unto their death. For reasons nobody understands, alcohol renders the cure dormant.

"And that, Miss Kitty, is why you carry that canteen."

I look into the mirror. It is black.

"What is this?" I ask him.

"Yes, good," he says. "This is the reason you are here. This is the crux of the experiment. Please, sit at the vanity."

I do as he asks.

"And don't worry," he tells me. "The glass is shatter proof. She can't hurt you."

"She who?"

"I will be right in the other room, watching and listening to everything."

"She who?" I start to get up.

He places a hand on my shoulder, stopping me.

"Please," he says. He suddenly looks very tired.

I settle down, stare at the black mirror.

"Who is she?" I ask.

A door closes. He has left the room.

"You will be able to hear me the whole time," says Master James' voice, through a speaker above me, "and I, you. She will not be able to hear either one of us. You will, however, be able to hear what is going on in her room. It should help with your mimicry."

Mimic. That means mirror.

I hear a buzzer. A light comes on. I can see the reflection of the bedroom in the mirror. The bed. The chairs. The statue of the winged girl.

I don't see me. There is someone on the bed.

I turn around.

The bed is empty.

I look back into the mirror and realize it is a window looking into a room exactly like the one I am in, but reversed.

The figure on the bed sits up. It is dark on that side of the room. The figure rises. I can't see details, but I can tell it is a woman. She moves slowly. She moves toward the vanity. She moves toward me.

I want my canteen.

"Her mirror will stay black until she sits," Master James tells me. "Once she does, however, remember your training. Mirror everything she does."

She reaches the chair.

"You only have to keep it up until the music stops," he tells me.

"What music?"

She sits.

A light comes on above, illuminating us both. She is looking straight at me. I want to scream.

It is Victoria. She is a beast.

Her hair in disarray, her dripping, yellow teeth exposed in a vicious snarl, she stares at me. Her eyes are black. Not human. Something far worse.

I can hear her growling.

"Remain calm," says Master James. "She has never seen herself as...she is. You are her face."

Her features are familiar, but twisted. Glimpses I have caught of myself in the scavenged car mirror I use when I wash. She is me, as a lost merry hatter.

"Four hundred stamps!" I want to shout, but I am too frightened to move my mouth.

She stares at me a moment longer, then looks down at her vanity top.

"Mirror!" snaps Master James.

I lower my head, as she has, but I don't take my eyes off of her.

She is dressed as I am: pink dress, black gloves. Slowly, she reaches a gloved hand toward the statue, as do I. We pick them up, in unison, turning them over to expose their undersides. Silver keys. Music boxes. We turn our keys together. We place the music boxes back where we found them. The winged girls begin to spin.

Mine makes no sound, but I can hear the music from hers. The song is light and cheerful. It reminds me of snowflakes. Not the ones that burn. The perfect ones. The beautiful ones.

"Tchaikovsky," says Master James, over the speaker. "The Dance of the Sugarplum Fairies. It has always been her favorite."

I don't know that the first word means, but I guess that is the name of the song.

I watch Victoria. She starts to move again. We pick up our brushes. Slowly, she begins to brush her hair; I, my wig.

"The religious would have us believe," says Master James, "that the cured have lost their souls. That is why they have regressed to such an animal state."

We draw the brushes downward, slowly. The music plays. Victoria has her eyes shut. Mine stay open, watching her.

"The philosophical would have us believe that the cured are dead by virtue of the fact they no longer retain anything inside of them which was human."

I look through the mirror, over Victoria's shoulder, and wonder what it would be like to live in her room. A place with no fighting, no cold, and no hunger. A place of care and protection, where the face in the mirror is always young and pretty.

I wonder if, in her way, she is happy.

"I believe that somewhere," continues Master James, "in the human brain, is a mechanism for learning, for understanding. For feeling joy. I believe that our loved ones, whose personalities may or may not have been initially introduced via contagion, are still there, imprinted on the brain itself. I believe that they can be drawn out, that they can relearn themselves, who they were. Who they *are*. It is my endeavor to prove this."

I try to keep up. He wants to prove something.

Victoria opens her eyes, looks into mine.

The music box stops. The mirror goes black.

I still hear the tune. Someone humming. Dry, raspy.

Victoria.

It stops.

I sit for a moment, waiting for Master James to come in. When he doesn't, I leave the room.

I find him at his console. He is weeping.

"Are we done?" I ask, quietly.

Without looking at me, he dismisses me with a wave of his hand.

I want to say something to him. I don't know what.

I find my way back up to my clothing, remove the outfit, get myself dressed. I take the gold stamps from the table. Templeton Poole is waiting for me by the front door. He escorts me out to the rickshaw and drives me back to where he found me.

I watch him ride away, tire tracks in the snow.

Twist. Hit. Shiver. Recap.

The sun is coming up over Brooklyn. The pack has gone back to the hunker.

On my way to the containers, I stop at the twenty-four and do some shopping. The girls know about the original eighty stamps. I buy them gifts. Pills, chicken foot kebabs, two gallons of pear hooch, the real deal. A payoff. Enough to keep from getting my throat slit in my sleep.

The rest of the stamps go into my boot.

I don't know if Master Addison James got what he wanted. He didn't seem very happy. Although, I'm not real smart when it comes to science.

AUTHOR BIOGRAPHIES

Peter Andrews (*Zombie Chic*) is a full-time, independent writer. He has hundreds of nonfiction articles and dozens of short stories (in *Reflection's Edge*, *On the Premises*, *Dreams & Nightmares*, *Sniplets*, and *Staffs & Starships*) in print. He has worked professionally in PR, and as a Web producer, speechwriter, and radio producer. He holds writing workshops online. He is the author of the popular How To Write Fast Blog, http://howtowritefast.blogspot.com/ and humorous memoir postings on http://blameitonthemuse.com.

Steven Axelrod (*The Risen*) holds an MFA in writing from Vermont College of the Fine Arts and remains a member of the Writers Guild of America (west), though he hasn't worked in Hollywood for several years. Poisoned Pen Press kicked off his Henry Kennis Nantucket mystery series in 2014 with *Nantucket Sawbuck*. The second installment, *Nantucket Five-Spot*, is scheduled for 2015. Also in 2015, he'll publish his dark noir thriller *Heat of the Moment* with Gutter Books. Two excerpts from that novel appeared in recent issues of *Big Pulp* and *PulpModern*. Steven has written for TheGoodmenProject and Salon.com, and he was recently elevated to the masthead at the internet arts journal *Numero Cinq*. A father of two, he lives on Nantucket Island where he writes novels and paints houses, often at the same time, much to the annoyance of his customers.

Noah Bogdonoff (*Dust*) hails from New London, CT. He recently completed his undergraduate degree in Environmental Studies and is currently attempting to make a living.

Rebecca Boyle (*Preservation*) has a degree in Film Production. She is currently working part time for a video streaming company while completing postgraduate studies. She lives and works in Brisbane, Australia. This is her first publication. You can visit her blog about writing and movie madness at www.rebeccamboyle.wordpress.com.

Cecelia Chapman (*Pool #4*) is an artist working in writing, video and mixed-media. Her work focuses on image, perception and the human condition. Visit her online at ceceliachapman.com.

J. Adrian Cook (*The Southron Wind*) is from the beautiful, windswept province of Saskatchewan, Canada. There, he spends the quiet life of a country gentleman:

writing, playing Celtic music with his band, The Residuals, and raising his excellent daughter to adulthood. He thought zombies were cool wa-a-a-y before you did.

George Cotronis (*Last Rites*) is the chief editor at Kraken Press and has published stories with Kazka Press and *Phobos Magazine*.

Harri B. Cradoc (*Snoring Wakes Them*) has written fiction and essays for over thirty years. He studied forensics in a U.S. Air Force program designed to train computer science instructors. After many years as a systems administrator, he now teaches computer programming and has developed his own course in cyber security. His home is in Port Dickinson, New York.

John Dodd (*Instinct*) is working on a project to write a million words of original work in 2014. Follow his progress—including his story in this publication—at http://www.millionwordman.blogspot.co.uk.

Douglas Ford (*The Staggering Boy*) lives on the west coast of Florida with his two kids and a significant other whose love and patience makes his work possible. His four cats merely tolerate him. His previous work has appeared in *Wicked Hollow*, *Spinning Whorl*, *Poe Little Thing*, along with other publications. His story, "Processed Meat," received a Stoker recommendation a few years ago.

Milo James Fowler (*Survival of the Fittest*) is a teacher by day and a speculative fictioneer by night. His work has appeared in *AE Science Fiction*, *Cosmos*, and *Shimmer*, and many of his stories are now available on Amazon for Kindle readers. When he's not grading papers, he's imagining what the world might be like in a few dozen alternate realities. www.milojamesfowler.com.

KJ Hannah Greenberg (*Mama Noodle*) flies the galaxy in search of gelatinous monsters and assistant bank managers. Some of the homes for her writing have included: *AlienSkin Magazine*, *AntipodeanSF*, *Morpheus Tales*, *Strange, Weird and Wonderful*, *Theaker's Quarterly Fiction*, *The New Absurdist*, and *Weirdyear*. Her two most recent collections of speculative fiction, both issued by Bards & Sages Publishing are: *The Immediacy of Emotional Kerfuffles* (2013) and *Don't Pet the Sweaty Things* (2012). What's more, Hannah's an Associate Editor at *Bewildering Stories* and at *Bound Off!*

Rich Hawkins (*Fathoms*) is a horror writer from Salisbury, England. He has several short stories published in various anthologies, and his debut novel *The Last Plague* will be released in summer 2014.

Christopher Keelty (*Graveyard Slot*) is the author of several short stories, two novels currently locked in a government warehouse in New Mexico, and thousands of ill-conceived tweets. As a non-profit fundraiser he has worked to defend equality and free artistic expression, advance strong science education, and improve access to healthy food. Chris likes food, ice hockey, and craft beer. He lives in Harlem with his girlfriend and cats, blogs at ChristopherKeelty.com, and tweets in varying states of sobriety as @keeltyc.

Gerri Leen (*Run for the Roses*) lives in Northern Virginia and originally hails from Seattle. She has a collection of short stories, *Life Without Crows*, out from Hadley Rille Books, and stories and poems published or accepted in such places as: *Escape Pod*, *Ares Magazine*, *Sword and Sorceress XXIII*, *Spinetinglers*, *She Nailed a Stake Through His Head: Tales of Biblical Terror*, and *Dia de los Muertos*. See more at http://www.gerrileen.com.

Thomas Logan (*The Chosen*) has had short stories, essays, and other works appear in various small journals and anthologies and currently serves as fiction editor for the Portland, OR literary journal *The Grove Review*. He's instructed students in writing in New Orleans, Southern California, and Indiana and is proud of his ongoing membership in the Buntho Speculative Fiction Critique Group, which grew from an Ursula Le Guin class at PSU.

Paul Lorello (*Expediency*) is a freelance writer from Ronkonkoma, New York. He recently finished his first novel and will one day write a second. His vitamin D is low. He likes science fiction and cats. He knows very little about everything.

E. Manning-Pogé (*Alice, in Decline*) lives in New York City with her wife, PJ (a half-elf gypsy expat), Razzle (an enchanted puggle), and a menagerie of crickets, mushrooms and succubae. They reside aboard the Manning family dirigible, The Cheshire Moon, which has stood anchored to the west pylon of the Verrazano-Narrows Bridge for generations, is fashioned entirely of saltwater taffy, and must be filled weekly with kitten sneezes to keep her aloft. The author has previously been published in various places—including **Big Pulp** (as E. A. Manning), *Blithe House Quarterly*, and *Word Riot*—and is currently working on her first novel, a supernatural noir thriller. When not writing, the author enjoys chemistry.

Conor Powers-Smith (*Only the Lonely*) an active member of the SFWA, and has had stories appear in *AE*, *Daily Science Fiction*, *Nature*, and other magazines.

J. Rohr (*Nothing Else Matters*) has been published numerous times in magazines such as *The Mad Scientist Journal*, *Fiction Vortex* (where his story "Time to Sell" won 2nd place in the editor's choice contest), and *Jupiter*. Currently, he runs the website www.honestyisnotcontagious.com.

Katherine Sanger (*Like the Jellyfish*) was a Jersey Girl before getting smart and moving to Texas. She's been published in various e-zines and print, including *Baen's Universe, Spacesports & Spidersilk, Black Petals, Star*Line, Anotherealm, Lost in the Dark, Bewildering Stories, Aphelion*, and *RevolutionSF*, and edited *From the Asylum*, an e-zine of fiction and poetry.

Shane Simmons (*Carrion Luggage*) is a Montreal screenwriter and the author/illustrator of the acclaimed *Longshot Comics* graphic novels that have seen multiple printings in multiple languages around the world. A devout curmudgeon, he is known for his bleak sense of humour, encyclopedic knowledge of film, and affinity for collecting things like classical antiquities, vintage pulp fiction, and insane cats. Much more of his work can be found at eyestrainproductions.com.

Cheryl Elaine Williams (*Ferals Like You*) resides in Pittsburgh, PA and has been published by tabloids *The Sun* and *The Weekly World News, Chicken Soup* anthologies, Hellfire Publishing, Dorchester media, and through Smashwords and Amazon online publishing. In September 2014, Desert Breeze Publishing will publish her 100K YA novel, an angel/paranormal story with strong romantic elements titled *Stairway to Heaven* or *Minx and the Dark Angel*, under the pen name of Sharlana Williams.

Lee Clark Zumpe (*Wild With Hunger*) has been writing and publishing horror, dark fantasy, and speculative fiction since the 1990s. His short stories and poetry have appeared in a variety of publications such as *Weird Tales, Space and Time*, and *Dark Wisdom*; and in anthologies such as *Horrors Beyond, Corpse Blossoms, Best New Zombie Tales Vol. 3, Cthulhu Unbound Vol. 1* and *Future Lovecraft*. His work has earned several honorable mentions in *The Year's Best Fantasy* and *Horror* collections. An entertainment columnist with Tampa Bay Newspapers, Lee has penned hundreds of film, theater and book reviews, as well as numerous interviews. His work for TBN has been recognized repeatedly by the Florida Press Association. Lee lives on the west coast of Florida with his wife and daughter. Visit www.leeclarkzumpe.com.

ARTIST BIOGRAPHY

Ken Knudtsen (*cover illustration*) is a writer, artist and loyal drinking buddy. He has been fortunate to have worked on projects ranging from David Geffen (*Inventing David Geffen* - PBS), *Wolverine* (Marvel Comics), and, of course, the adventures of a little girl and a crazy monkey (*My Monkey's Name is Jennifer* from SLG Publishing). It is never a bad idea to surprise Ken with a bacon snack.